THE FREEBOOTERS

NIGEL TRANTER was born in Glasgow on 23rd
November 1909 and educated at George Heriot's
School in Edinburgh. After leaving school he
trained as an accountant, but took up writing full-
time in 1936, a career only partly interrupted by
service in the army during the Second World War.
Almost his entire literary output is concerned with
Scotland's history. His non-fiction, from his first
book—*The Fortalices and Early Mansions of Southern
Scotland* (1935)—deals principally with his life-
long interest in Scottish architecture. He has also
written over eighty novels, many of them drawn
from his unparalleled knowledge of Scottish history.
Notable among these are *The Gilded Fleece* (1942),
The Queen's Grace (1953), *Balefire* (1958), *The Bruce
Trilogy* (1969-71) and *The Wallace* (1975). His
novel *The Stone* (1958) is concerned with the Stone
of Destiny, a subject of great interest to Tranter,
who was involved in negotiating the return of the
Stone after its theft from Westminster Abbey in
1950—a theft which he had foreseen in *The
Freebooters* (1950). Nigel Tranter lives near
Aberlady in East Lothian.

The Freebooters

NIGEL TRANTER

B&W PUBLISHING

British Library Cataloguing in Publication Data:
A catalogue record for this book is available from
the British Library

Cover illustration:
detail from *Iona Croft*
by F. C. B. Cadell (1883-1937)
Photograph: Portland Gallery
Courtesy of the Estate of F. C. B. Cadell

Cover Design *by* **Winfortune** *&* **Associates**

Printed by Werner Söderström

I

THE young man took off his soaking tweed jacket, shook it, and draped it over a projecting knob of stone. He flapped his arms crosswise against his sides, cabby-fashion, and stamped about the rock floor of the cave—not to warm his feet, which though wet enough were not cold, but in the interests of his general circulation, not to say morale. Also, taking a moment or two off from flapping, he pulled out an already damp handkerchief from his flannels' trouser pocket, to wipe away the water from his eyes. It was tears, not rain, for the wind out there was blowing great guns; he had met a few winds in his day, especially on the high tops, but he could not recollect another which had started so suddenly and continued to blow with such sheer bellowing bludgeoning intensity—the sort of wind one met with in the open cockpit of a fighter-plane. His eyes, his ears, even his nostrils and the corners of his mouth, ached with the flail of it, as though tugged at and stretched; between it and the chill driving rain that went with it, his whole face felt like a chiselled slab of extremely cold marble. Once, somebody—a romantically-inclined female, naturally—had told him that she adored his chiselled features; perhaps she had had something there, after all. For the last hour that cave had been a haven of comfort and security beckoning him on, as he had battled up the long heather slopes of Ben Ure.

Getting a pipe going with some difficulty—for his fingers were as though frozen, and his matches less than bone-dry—he very quickly felt better; and was sufficiently introspective to shake a head at himself for being so, merely out of reaction to a whiff of burning weed and a warm briar bowl in the cup of his hand. But such is man.

Moving to the low entrance of the cave, he knelt, and peered out, an involuntary and irrational gesture, for there could be little worth looking at, little to see different from

1

what he had seen only too much of before he came in—driving rain and soaking hillside. That is all he did see, beyond the brief foreground of glistening quartz-shot stone, black peat-hag, and brown heather—only the grey driving curtains of the rain, with somewhere behind it, perhaps, a hint of darker grey that might be the outline of some spur of Ben Lomond across the unseen valley. All that he could expect to have seen, undoubtedly—though one might have thought that, with such a wind behind it, the rain could hardly go on and on like this. Shrugging, the man turned back down the slight slope of the cave's floor, to a sort of recess heaped with old and dried heather, on which he sat himself, to puff at his pipe and consider the bleached and scraped toes of his sodden brown Army boots.

It would be unfair to say that he slept—though indubitably the fact that he had a good grip of his pipe both with fist and teeth helped to keep his head from sinking either forwards or back. But, as well as the almighty battering he had taken from that wind, he had walked and climbed a good fourteen miles already that day, and moreover his present altitude being in the neighbourhood of two thousand feet, the atmosphere might fairly enough be said to be slightly rarefied and therefore torpifying. But that isn't to say that he slept.

Nevertheless, it was with something of a jerk that he presently became aware that he was no longer entirely alone on that lofty hillside, or even in his hard-won haven; somebody, with rock-scraping iron-shod boots, was inserting his or her-self through the narrow opening of the cave-mouth—and, by the very nature of things, thereby blocking out the light.

" 'Afternoon," the seated man murmured, politely, just catching his now-cold pipe in time, but receiving no answer. He waited, interestedly.

From the sound of him, the passage-blocker had turned round, and was no doubt staring fruitlessly into the black interior of the Spree Cave—though that was pure conjecture, of course. He might not have heard the greeting, in all his puffing and scraping.

"Blowy," the first man said again, conversationally.

The newcomer, by the pause in his panting, obviously heard

that one, but apparently was not going to be rushed into any injudicious commentary. Evidently recognising the cause of the general obscurity, he edged round to one side, warily, as one does in a dark cave, thereby letting in a stream of pallid but blessed light from behind his back. In its admittedly greyish but welcome lumination, he perceived the sitter, and subjected him to a comprehensive stare.

"Aye," he said at length.

The other had been staring, too. "Good Lord," he gasped. "Rob Roy himself!" Perhaps he was still feeling the effects of the altitude.

"Eh . . . ?" The latest arrival frowned, and his frown was as impressive as the rest of him, and not to be taken lightly.

The first man recognised that, and hastened to prove that he did. "I beg your pardon. A slip of the tongue," he said. "Not very pleasant climbing weather, is it?"

"No." That was agreed and accepted, if briefly. The other shook himself like a dog, off-slung a haversack into a corner, ran a great hand once or twice through the gleaming wet curls of a thatch of riotous flaming-red hair, and moved over to the farther wall of the cave, where he leant a massive shoulder, and so stood, seemingly plunged into deepest meditation.

The man on the heather eyed him with unconcealed interest, as well he might. The newcomer was enormous, a young giant, even allowing for the effect of the cave's restricted space, burly, hulking almost, his features boyishly freckled but craggily-pugnacious, dressed in a stained and faded ex-Army kilt and a thin open shirt that, clinging wetly to his tremendous torso, moulded its challenging contours to perfection. He wore huge steel-studded boots, over which his grey stockings were rolled down, and on bare arms and legs and throat the red rash of hair lay plastered like soaked fur. Beside him, the other occupant of the cave felt puny, fragile, and insignificant.

He was bold enough, just the same, to further interrupt the big fellow's heavy silence. "Come far?" he wondered— which was a foolish question, indeed, since nobody could have reached that place without coming far, by pedestrian standards, by any standards.

The red-head turned to look at him, slowly, as though

3

considering the wider implications of that. "Far enough," he said at length, and spat judiciously, as though to prove it.

"M'mmm."

Quiet returned to that place—almost an uncanny quiet, considering the rage of the elements without. Wind does not seem to howl around a cave as it does round four walls, and even the heaviest rain makes little sound driving into long heather.

The smaller man—and he was no pigmy, being of a little above medium height, and adequately if slenderly built—was of a persistent mentality, obviously. He tried again: "I started from Aberfoyle, along by Loch Ard, up the Ledard Burn, did Ben Venue, came down by Lochan a Cheaird to the Chon valley, and on up here." He spoke with a nice modesty that satisfactorily underlined his feat. "That dam' wind caught me at Loch Chon, and I had it in my face all the way up."

"Oh, yeah!" his fellow-shelterer observed. Which seemed to be about as far as he was prepared to go on the subject. The other was regretfully deciding that it looked as though his further communings must be, as before, between his pipe, the toes of his boots, and himself, when the newcomer cleared his throat thunderously, seemed as if to spit again, but instead actually launched into speech. "Bluidy rain!" he cried, and with a sheer intensity of anger and ferocity, such as to charge the confined atmosphere of that cave as though with electricity.

Quite literally the man on the heather sat up, swallowing. "Yes, isn't it!" he managed with difficulty, and with an immediate and quite novel recognition of the fact that it was his turn to sound fatuous.

The giant did not seem to notice it—did not notice the remark even. Once launched, apparently, there was no stopping him. "Baistards!" he said.

"Er . . . undoubtedly."

"Och, tae hell!"

"Quite!"

There was a pause. The storm of eloquence looked as though it had blown itself out, though the thundery atmosphere continued. The older man—that is, the one in flannels and his shirt-sleeves, and all his twenty-nine years—was trying to think

4

up just where the conversation might go from there, when there was another rumble.

"Och, I've had it. They'll no' make it." Wrathfully the other hurled that at his involuntary companion. "They'll be feart for the bluidy rain, an' they'll no' make it. I'm tellin' you."

"The, er . . . buzzards?"

"Yeah. This ay happens. They've jist tae daunder up frae the damned bus at Drumbeg. I was to meet them here, at this Spree Cave, at three today. What's the time, you?" That was positively shot out.

The first-comer consulted his wristwatch. "Half-past three," he said. "And, h'm, my name is Hope—Adrian Hope!"

"Eh . . . ? Aye, then—I tell't you, didn't I? Baistards!" the big man reasserted, with entire conviction. "They're soft, like a' the rest o' them!"

"I see. *You* haven't just daundered up from the bus at Drumbeg, then, I take it?"

Scornfully the other looked at him, as though such a question required no answer. Then he shrugged. "I've been up Stobinian an' Ben More," he mentioned. "Last night I was in yon hostel at Crianlarich."

"Good Heavens!" His hearer stared. "That's twenty-five miles away. More!"

"Sure." That was shrugged away. "An' these guys canna' make it up frae the bus! Soft, they are, jist. They're a' soft. The whole country's soft."

Keenly the man Hope considered him, now. "I'm inclined to agree with you there," he said.

"You'd be blasted-well blind if you didna'!" he was told, scathingly. "I'm jist aboot browned-off. I'm gettin' oot o' it."

"You mean, out of the country? Emigrating?"

"Aye. Australia for me!"

"Isn't that a bit drastic? I mean—I've heard that they're not all just so tough there, as they used to be, either. Seems to me, Scotland needs all the husky chaps she's got, here and now—like she's seldom needed them before."

Swiftly askance, the big fellow looked at him, with all Lowland Scotland's chronic suspicion of sentiment and flag-wagging—save in its cups. "Damn that!" he said, but with his

5

first trace of unease. And then, more strongly, "Scotlan's done, anyway. It's had it, Mister—it's a' washed-up. I'm gettin' oot, like I said."

"A pity," Adrian Hope observed.

The silence returned, and now it seemed to be the new-comer's turn to feel it irksome. He lounged to the entrance, hunkered down on his great haunches, and peered out. So he remained for a space till, cursing disgustedly, he turned and came back.

"Fair stottin'!" he reported. "Och, they'll never make it. They'll be awa' hame in their stinkin' wee bus!"

"I'm sorry. I hope it won't spoil your holiday?"

"Holiday! Hell—it's no' a holiday. I'll be back at the yaird at eight the morn. It's jist a bit walk."

"Oh? A bit walk! And Crianlarich last night! On a weekend hike—since midday yesterday?"

"I hitched a lift tae Ardlui, climbed Vorlich, and doon."

"Still . . . ! And Ben Vorlich, too." Hope gave the merest shake of his head. "I think I'm beginning to sympathise with these others—your friends! They may not be quite so soft, after all!"

The other's snort was as eloquent as his words. "Aye, they're soft, a'right—they couldna' be anythin' else. We're a' soft, the whole country. I'm soft, mysel'."

"You . . . !"

"Aye, me. If I wasna', I'd have been awa' to Australia long ago—or seen if I could *dae* somethin' aboot it!"

"Do something?"

"Aye." That was heavily said.

His companion had cocked his head to one side. "Such as . . . ?" he demanded, and the sudden eagerness in his voice was not to be hidden.

Probably that was why the red-head stalled. "Och, I dinna' ken," he shrugged. "That's the hell o' it. What *can* you dae?"

The other, turning his pipe in his hands, only looked at him, and said nothing.

His silence seemed to work on the man opposite, for thrusting out his great jaw suddenly he roared, with abrupt violence, "What this country needs is a bluidy revolution!"

Save for a quick-drawn breath, his hearer still offered no comment.

The big man apparently interpreted the other's silence as incredulity, hostility. He took a step towards Hope, and his huge fists clenched, so that the knuckles showed whitely. "I'm tellin' you!" he cried, with that same quivering intensity of anger. "A revolution—that's what it needs!"

"I'm not denying it," the other assured, quietly. "I shouldn't wonder if you're not perfectly right. But it won't get it, just the same."

"Will it no'? Why not?"

"Because you, and such as you, prefer to go off to Australia!" he said, simply.

For a moment it looked as though the giant would complete that forward movement with feet and fists, and hurl himself upon the smaller man. Hope sat still, quite still, while the other glowered, and the quivering tension in that cave was a thing that almost could be seen.

With a quite visible effort, the kilted man controlled himself. "Clever guy, eh?" he managed to get out, hoarsely.

"No—just logical. Scotland can't go on losing her best, as she's been doing for generations, without paying for it—paying dearly. Especially at this stage."

"Scotlan's done, I tell't you."

"Nearly—but not quite, I think. And if she's done, she needs no revolution, surely?"

"Och, forget it!" the other pleaded—or commanded rather, for that one did not plead.

Adrian Hope inclined his head agreeably. "So you are a shipbuilder?" he mentioned, to change the subject.

"A shipbuilder! Jings—no' me. I'm jist a riveter."

"The same thing, isn't it, more or less? A good satisfying sort of job, I'd have thought?"

"Satisfyin' your granny! An' it isna' the same thing, either—d'you ca' hammerin' wee bits o' iron a' day in a bluidy shop, shipbuildin'?"

"As near to it—as near to doing a satisfying complete job, perhaps, as most of us get these days."

"Hud your wheesht, man—what d'you ken aboot it? Go

7

slow, ca' canny, dinna' dae this, dinna' dae that, see an' no' work too hard, dae as the Union tells you—an' a damned English Union, at that!—dae as the foreman tells you, dae as the shop-steward tells you! D'you ca' that satisfyin'? An', hell—oot o' the yaird, isna' it the same? You're to dae what you're tell't. You canna' dae this, an' you canna' dae that! You canna' get a decent dram, you canna' buy a packet o' fags! You maun ha'e a permit to wipe your . . . neb—the same blasted neb's you pay your taxes through! Och, tae hell—what's the use!"

At the sheer honest righteous wrath in the man's voice, Adrian Hope nodded agreement. "I know," he said, simply. "It's all there, I admit. So you come out here at the weekends, to try and walk it out of you? That it?" He looked up, almost speculatively. "How many more are there like you in Glasgow today, I wonder—in all Scotland?"

"Guid kens!" the other shrugged. "No' many, I'm thinkin'."

"I'm not so sure. This trouble, this frustration, that you've got so badly, isn't confined to you, you know. I've got it, we've all got it, a whole generation's got it—it's a national disease. The trouble is, there's not so many know that they've got it—and of them, fewer still would be prepared to do anything about it. Look here, I . . ." He stopped, and, turning his head, smiled. "Looks as though you've been traducing your friends. Here they come."

Hoarse breathless voices sounded at the cave's entrance. One, throaty, in particular. "Jings—if yon big gorilla Ginger's no' here, I'll ha'e the daylights off him!"

"Goad, will you!" The whole cave trembled to that.

Adrian Hope sat back.

For a while there was chaos, the true and original chaos of noise and darkness, as men crept inside, tripped over each other, stamped and slithered, bumped into unyielding rock, cursed, shook themselves, and shouted, shouted incessantly. When at length light and a semblance of order, if not quiet, returned, Hope, who had been prepared to count a dozen at least, found four more young men had joined them, young men, like the big fellow, coarse-voiced, strident, aggressive, mannerless, dressed in the surplus of Government stores, British and American. But there any resemblance ended. Here were no giants, in physique or in personality, no arresting dominating characters, no smouldering volcanoes—just the miscellaneous but very ordinary products of the streets of a great industrial city, undistinguished, uncouth, tending to be stunted, underdeveloped. The man on the heather, in quick critical assessment and comparison, could find little to admire in them—least of all, perhaps, in the utter pathetic lack of imagination that led them to call their outstanding colleague Ginger. Though they would, of course!

Out of the noise, shouting, abuse, and uninspired profanity —it could nowise be called conversation—the listener gathered that the party had been late in setting off; the misbegotten Jakey apparently had slept in. They hadn't left Waterloo Street till nearly noon, and so had missed the wee bus at Balloch. But they'd cadged lifts on various vehicles to Drumbeg—though they'd had to wait there for a while for the grossly immoral Alicky. But what a climb, what unquotable weather, what thrice-blasphemous wind and utterly print-melting rain! This was established in a chorus of competitive impiety. The man couched in the little recess was, needless to say, completely ignored.

The red-head listened to it all with a heavy lowering scowl that was saved from being merely bovine only by the intense liveness of his noticeably light-blue eyes. At length, he tossed an impatient head, and all the tangle of red curl lifted and settled again. "Shurrup, you!" he roared, and the gabble of sound was shattered. "Whae's got the grub? I'm hungry!" Two of them hurriedly unfastened their soaking packs.

"Here y'are, Ginger," one of them, the thin dark-faced youth called Jakey cried. "Plentys. Sangwidges an' baps. An' Sandy's got the beer. . . ."

"Aye—see's the beer!" the individual known as Alicky shouted. "To hell wi' your sangwidges—gi'e's a slug o' beer! Let's ha'e a bit spree. Jings—we'll ha'e a bluidy spree in Spree Cave!"

Uproariously they laughed, appreciating the delicious humour of that—all except the man Ginger, that is, who was fully occupied in filling the gaping cavern of his mouth with provender. If he had done what he said that he had done that day, he deserved all of it.

With the newcomers still discussing the finer implications of the spree joke, Adrian Hope spoke up. "The spree, in this case, means cattle," he said, more to introduce himself than anything else. "The place is called, in the Gaelic, *Uamh nan Spreidh*, or the Cave of the Cattle. Not that they'd get many cattle in here, I admit—but probably it had something to do with a cattle-raid, one of Rob Roy's escapades, no doubt. This Macgregor country's full of caves, and with a Rob Roy legend attached to each one!"

All of them were staring at him, now, the four latecomers in a mixture of astonishment, suspicion, and resentment, the big man with a sudden searching scrutiny.

"Say—a damned toff!" the youth Jakey complained.

"Jings, aye!"

"Hell—see what's gotten oot here, boys! Kelvinsaid!"

That was hardly fair. Adrian Hope's voice, though that of an educated Scot, was scarcely that of accepted toffishness, and still less that associated with the refined neighbourhood of Kelvinside.

"He kens a' the big words, tae, the . . ."

"Shurrup!" That was the big red-head again. "You," he said, and jabbed a fistful of buttered bap in Hope's direction, "what's a' this aboot Rob Roy? You were at it, before, were you no'?"

"Rob Roy? Good Heavens—don't tell me you don't know about Rob Roy Macgregor, the biggest freebooter and cateran this country has ever produced!"

"Look, Mister," the other jerked, dangerously. "Watch yoursel', see! *My* name's Macgregor!"

"Lord!" Hope said, eyes widening.

"Yeah? An' what's wrong with that, eh?" The menace was only too apparent, now. Obviously the four latest arrivals saw it, and waited in pleasurable anticipation. "What's wrong with Macgregor?"

"Nothing. Ye gods—nothing at all! It's just too good to be true! I mean . . . well, it's a matter for congratulation." As he saw the other's eyes narrow, he raised a hand, quickly. "But,

10

skip it. I thought you would know all about Rob Roy. . . .
After all, this is Rob Roy's country."

The big man said nothing.

"You have heard of him, surely?"

"I've heard the name," Macgregor acceded cautiously. "At
the school. Was he no' a guy in a play?"

"Unfortunately, yes. But . . ."

"There's a pub doon the Gallowgate, ca'ed the Rob Roy,"
somebody volunteered.

"Jings—you can take the tram to Robroyston. . . ."

"Och, there's a bit sang aboot it," the lanky Alicky declared.
"I ken it fine." And lifting up a quite excruciating voice, he
bawled,

"Ma name is Alexander Duncan John Rob Roy,
I dinna' like the school at a', I like Key-Hoy.
Ma faither says that he was jist the same when but a boy,
For his . . ."

"Shurrup!" came inevitably from the gigantic Macgregor,
to cut him short. "This guy—you sayin' he had somethin' to
dae with this cave?" he demanded.

"Well, I don't know, of course—but it seems likely. *Spreidh*
means cattle, and cattle-stealing was his speciality, you see.
And this is where he hailed from—he was uncrowned king of
this country, despite the Duke of Montrose. His father was
Macgregor of Glengyle, down at the head of Loch Lomond
there. But he was a natural-born rebel, and no respecter of
authority, so he slept more nights out of his bed than in it.
Caves like this were just up his street. He was a great lad, was
Rob Roy Macgregor!"

The man Ginger was regarding him in silence now, and the
others, wisely no doubt, took their cue from him. Suddenly,
he thrust a great hand into the paper-bag he held, and drawing
out another jam-spread bap, tossed it to Hope. "Here," he
said, briefly. "A rebel, was he? A guid guy, eh?"

The other nodded, in acknowledgement both of the question and of the offering. "He was, yes. He was a freebooter—
but he was more than that. He didn't like the way things were

11

in Scotland, then, and he set out to do something about it. He stole cattle from the rich, in a big way—but he often gave them to the poor. He cared less than nothing for the laws and rules and statutes that were oppressing the people, so he made his own. He blackmailed the southern Highlands, and a big slice of the Lowlands, too, into paying him protection-money, so as not to steal their cattle, and to prevent other folk from stealing them likewise. Single-handed, almost, he defied the authorities, and the authorities took it. He collected his enemies' rents at the point of the broadsword, and he ambushed and beat-up the Government troops sent to discipline him. But he endowed the minister and kirk of Balquhidder year after year, he never cheated, and his word was his bond. That was Rob Roy Macgregor!"

Nobody said anything. The four looked at the big fellow, and he continued to stare at Adrian Hope thoughtfully, chewing steadily. "Aye," he said at last. "But all this would be a while back—long ago?"

"A while, yes. Two hundred years and more."

"Aye."

"Sounds like the first oreeginal member o' the Pairty!" Jakey said—but not to Hope, of course.

"The Party . . . ?"

"The bloomin' Commynist Pairty," the man Sandy explained, jeeringly. "Jakey's a red-hot Commynist. Up the Ruskies!"

"An' what for no'?" the dark youth demanded, furiously. "What's wrang wi' the Commynists? They're the only folk'll *dae* anythin' mair than jist talk—the only folk'll get Scotlan' oot o' the clarty mess it's in, I'm tellin' you!"

"Heavens—another of them!" Hope murmured.

"Shut your face, you! Whae's talkin' tae you?" Jakey glared. "Say—whae *is* this guy, anyway?"

"Aye, then. . . ."

"He's a guy that says Scotlan'll no' get a revolution," the red-headed Macgregor mentioned, by way of introduction. And there was just a gleam of humour in those blue eyes, as he said it.

"Will it no', then!" Jakey yelped. "Why will it no'? The Pairty'll see it does, right enough—you bluidy reactionary!"

"Och, jings—the Pairty again!" Sandy groaned.

Hope shook his head, smiling a little ruefully, apparently unoffendable. "The first time I've ever been called a reactionary!" he assured. "But you're wrong, you know. Even the Communist Party won't arouse this country to revolution, the way things are today."

"Why will it no', smart guy?"

"Because there isn't the spirit there. The nation is soft, like our friend Macgregor says. . . ."

"The Pairty's no' soft!"

"Maybe not. But it isn't arousing the spirit of the country. Communism is an economic theory. You've got to appeal to the spirit before you'll make Scotland rise out of the mire it's in. Look"—he sat forward with a new eagerness, a real urgency in his pleasantly-modulated voice, as well as postulation—"a revolution, a revolt, any sort of national upheaval, happens when a people's blood boils over. Only then. I know." He looked grim for a moment. "I happen to have had a little experience in the matter. No would-be dictator, no national saviour, can do anything till the blood is there, simmering, for him to use. Right? But is that blood simmering in Scotland today? You've answered that already, yourselves. Not only is it not simmering—it's not *there*. Scotland today is suffering from anaemia! What she needs isn't a major operation, like a revolution—she couldn't take it. Not yet. She needs a blood transfusion!"

"How?" That was Macgregor, almost in a bark.

"That's the rub. How? I haven't got any ready-made solution, I'm afraid—only a few vague ideas. Some sort of a demonstration is what's needed, I think—not a revolution. A forceful, spectacular demonstration, of course—something to waken Scotland up to the fact that she can't stay down, grovelling, much longer without being out. That the count's running out, and the gong is going to ring before long. That London nationalisation will be the end of her. That lying down, to be trampled under the feet of an inept soulless bureaucracy, can only have one ending. Some sort of demonstration, some gesture, to awaken the country . . ."

"Hell—you'll need mair than any demonstration," the big man interrupted. "You'll need mair than that."

"You need a Joe Stalin!" Jakey cried.

"Better wi' a Tito. . . ."

"Jings—what aboot a Peron—Eva an' a'!"

"We need a Bruce or a Wallace!" Adrian Hope declared, soberly.

"Maybe, then," Macgregor conceded, and shrugged. "Here— gi'e's a drink!" He took a metal-capped bottle from the man Sandy, and in one and the same expert movement, smashed its neck against the cave wall, threw back his head, and raising its jagged mouth above his own, poured the amber contents down his throat, gulping rhythmically. The last drop done, he grimaced and snorted. "Bah!" he cried. "Blasted swill!" and tossed the empty bottle into the farthest corner, where it splintered into a thousand fragments.

Looking from the man to the broken glass, and back again, Adrian Hope rubbed his chin, but said nothing.

He had still said nothing when the gangling Alicky, from the cave-mouth, reported that the rain had stopped and the sun was nearly out.

"Then we're gettin' oot, tae!" the red-head announced. "Let's get the hell oot o' here. Get a move on."

"Och, jings, Ginger . . . !"

"Say—what the hell . . . ?"

"Ha'e a hert, Ginger man—we're no' that long in . . . !"

"Shurrup! Put a sock in it! We've wasted owermuch time in blethers, a'ready. We're climbin' Ben Lomond right now, see. Get crackin'!" And he reached for his haversack.

Grumbling and cursing, the four did likewise.

At the low entrance, Macgregor turned, before stooping, and looked backwards. Hope had risen to his feet. "Aye, then," he said. "Uh-huh. Bruce or Wallace or Joe Stalin—it'll take a bluidy revolution!"

"Perhaps," the other shrugged. "Who knows!"

"I do," the giant said, simply. "Even if I dinna' ken a' aboot Rob Roy!"

Hope smiled, at that. "Look," he said, "I have a book about Rob Roy—I'd like to lend it to you. I think you ought to read it—being a Macgregor yourself."

"Och, I'll dae fine wantin' it."

"Possibly, yes. But I'm sure you'd find it interesting—certain of it. Rob Roy and you have a lot in common, I imagine, besides your name. How could I get it to you?"

"Och, if you're a' that keen, I'm in digs at 17, Macharg Street . . . or you could hand it in at Mike Doolan's Bar, doon the Bridegate. I'm there maist nights."

"Doolan's Bar, Bridegate. Right-o—I'll remember. Would you be there on Tuesday evening, if I handed it in?"

"Maybe," Macgregor said, non-committally. "S'long, then."

"So-long, Gregorach!"

II

THE girl tossed her head in the most natural fashion in all the world—and not a single strand of her perfectly coiffured nut-brown hair was disarranged thereby. And the faintest suspicion of a pout was as spontaneous—even if it had the effect of emphasising just a little the warm red lips, delicately, provocatively, modelled.

"So you won't talk, huh?" she said. And if that was not entirely original and spontaneous either, its reproach was most charmingly articulated.

Her escort described cartwheels with the base of his near-empty tumbler on the black glass of the bar counter, and smiled. "I can't," he said. "I'm struck dumb."

"So I notice," she observed, raising quite perfect and entirely sceptical eyebrows.

"Your beauty, I mean, of course," he elaborated. "Quite breathtaking. You excel yourself tonight, Helen—if that is possible!"

"And yet you scarcely look at me!"

"My dear, I see you everywhere I look!" And that, perhaps, was literally true, for everywhere about them, walls, pillars, and fittings were so hung about and furnished with glass and tinsel and gleaming chromium and dazzling lights as to make of the place a very Hall of Mirrors. The Grand Metropole's famed Glass Slipper was well-enough named, Adrian Hope acknowledged—about as substantial, authentic, and fitting.

"Baloney!" the young woman returned, briefly. "Adrian—you're holding out on me!"

"Impossible," the man assured. "Especially in that frock. Stunning is the appropriate word, I believe?" His companion looked at him through narrowed eyes—and sacrificed little, so large and lustrous were they in the first place. "The same hardly applies to *you*, at any rate," she declared. "I'm not fussy about clothes, I hope—but tonight you seem to have dressed out of the rag-bag. Why, I'd like to know? Not in my honour, I take it?" Despite the narrowed eyes, there was no trace of nagging or carping noticeable in her voice—only interested enquiry.

Though she exaggerated, of course, her enquiry was perhaps not unreasonable. Adrian Hope, in stained and worn Harris tweed jacket, shapeless and creaseless flannels, and khaki shirt of faded but vaguely military aspect, was a little oddly clad for the Glass Slipper—especially taking into account the company that he was keeping, for Helen Burnet, without being overdressed, was extremely well-dressed, as was her habit.

"I didn't change," the man explained, patiently, "because I've got to make this call tonight. I imagine that these things— have I the nerve to call them my working-clothes?—would be more suitable for where I'm going."

"And that is, Adrian . . . ?"

"I told you, when you phoned—I've got to go down town for a little." He wiped an incipient frown off his too-expressive features with a quick smile. "Look, Helen—have another drink." And he tossed off what was left in his own glass. "Another of the same?"

"You're very thoughtful."

He raised a finger towards one of the Italianate elegants that lounged amongst the serried ranks of exotic bottles and coloured glassware. "A gin-and-lime, and a small whisky," he said.

"Sorree, sir—the wheesky ees feeneeshed."

"Confound it! All right—better make it two gins, then."

"Veree good, sir. Thees will be the last geen, sir."

"Good Lord!" Hope exclaimed, sourly. "What is this—a bar or a Rechabite Lodge?"

The willowy swarthy attendant spread his hands in silent eloquence, and the girl laughed.

"It's good for you, Adrian—good for your pocket, too."

He stared morosely into his replenished glass. "What a country!" he muttered.

"There's worse wrong with it, than a shortage of intoxicating liquors," his companion observed, lightly.

"And thus we come to the profundities!" he said, but less lightly.

Thoughtfully the young woman considered him. "You're not in a very good temper tonight, are you, Adrian? In fact, you haven't been for some time. Months, now. Inclined to be moody. I wish I knew what the matter was . . . ?"

"There's Ronnie Weir," he observed, "just come in. Fortunate. You'll be able to talk to him, while I'm away."

"I've seen the day when you damned Ronnie Weir heartily, whenever he hove in sight!"

"Unfair of me! I'll have to offer him my apologies. But it's doubly fortunate him turning up just now—he'll no doubt be able to afford to regale you with Chartreuse or Benedictine. They won't be out of those, surely!"

There was just a little pause, into which the music of the dance-orchestra sobbed its peculiar invitation, before Helen Burnet spoke quietly. "That won't be necessary, I think. I'm coming with you, Adrian . . . down town."

"Oh no you're not!" he said. That was very definite.

"Why not? What's all the mystery about?" She even managed to smile as she said that. "Where *are* you going, Adrian?"

"I told you. Down town—the Bridegate area, actually. I have an appointment. There's no mystery at all—only where I'm going, young ladies would hardly fit in."

"Indeed! This is most intriguing. I'm more determined to come than ever."

"Don't be silly, Helen," Hope said, almost sharply.

"Adrian!" There was just a suspicion of an edge even to her melodious voice, now. "Don't tell me you've actually fallen for some Bridegate tart!"

"Good Heavens, no!" His laugh was honest enough, jerked out of him. "Though it's an idea, perhaps! No, I'm afraid I'm only meeting a mere man in a pub. A fellow I met."

"I don't know that I believe you," she declared, coolly judicious. "What sort of a man?"

"Just a fellow I came across the other day. We had a chat. I said I'd see him tonight. That's all."

"And is that book you left at the hat-place, with your scarf, for him?"

"Lord—you're a sharp-eyed minx!" he cried. "Or should it

18

be lynx? You ought to have been a lady-cop, Helen, you ought indeed!"

At his change of tone, she drew a quick breath. "I'm sorry," she said. "I beg your pardon." Her voice went level, flat.

Hope shook his head. "No, no. No need. Forgive *me*!" He glanced at his watch. "Just time for a dance, before I go—if you care?"

"No, thank you."

"Very well. I'll just get along, then. I shouldn't be more than an hour, I think."

"Don't hurry, please. In fact, I wouldn't come back here, at all, if I were you. I shouldn't think I'll be here when you come."

"No? Not even with Ronnie Weir for company? I'll risk it, anyway. *Av revoir*."

She nodded, unspeaking, as he moved away. But she did not turn to follow the direction of his going. She did not need to. In a great mirror opposite, intently, unwinking, she watched his slender shabby figure in its progress to the vestibule, and out.

Frowning, the man pushed his way through the revolving doors of the Grand Metropole Hotel, into Buchanan Street.

It was just after eight-thirty, and the April evening had drawn to an early dark, under the grey pall of drizzling rain that had drifted up the river to cover the sprawling city. Winding his University scarf more tightly about his throat, and tucking the book inside his loose and already bulging jacket, Adrian Hope hurried, head down, along the greasy pavements, threading his way through the aimless throng that still drifted like the rain about the inhospitable streets, and peered wistfully in at such few lit-up windows as thought it worthwhile to display their nakedness and the gall and wormwood of goods for export only.

At Argyle Street, he boarded a red tram that took him rocking and clanging northwards to the Anderston area. At Cranston Street he alighted, and hurrying along that grim thoroughfare, he turned off into a huddle of narrow mean streets and alleys, ill-lighted, where salutations, hoarse guffaws, and skirling giggles followed him from the yawning caverns of

19

dark close-mouths and entries, and so into the comparatively brilliant if garish canyon of the Bridgate. Here, met as by a wall by the atmosphere of fish-and-chips, stale beer, and that curious indefinable smell that emanates from funfairs, amusement arcades and the like, he paused, to consider his further progress. His first enquiry, of a hunched individual supporting a street-lamp, elicited no response at all; his second, of a couple of passers-by, brought forth only a flood of gibberish and gesticulation that might have been Yiddish, Polish, or Double Dutch; but his third, from a large bowler-hatted man walking on his heels and singing *The Rose of Trelee* with pathos and feeling, produced not only the information that Mike Doolan's Bar was just a mite further up on the other side of the street, but the blessing of the Mother o' God on him, into the bargain. Gratefully, Adrian Hope detached himself, and proceeded across the road.

He stopped at the doors of three public houses before he actually reached it, all of which sounded so extremely quiet within, as he passed them, as to suggest to him that his late Irish friend must have been in the happy position of carrying his own supplies with him. At the Family Entrance to the third, he had the opportunity to decline, politely but firmly, a bored lady's offer of an exchange of hospitality. Then, beyond the belching mouth of a palace of light, music, and slot-machines, he came to Mike Doolan's Bar, thankfully.

Opening one half of the narrow swing-doors, he slipped inside. It was a long low-ceiled room, hazy with smoke and fumes, and not over-lit, with dark walls of glazed olive-green tiles, reminiscent of a public-convenience, many fly-blown advertisements, sawdust on the floor, and no seating accommodation. Strictly Business could well have been Mr. Doolan's motto. The place was fairly well filled, but with most of the customers congregated at the other end, away from the door. Hope's entrance went unnoticed, and standing quietly where he was, he scanned that company. But though the man for whom he searched ought to have been readily discernible, he saw no sign of a red head and vast shoulders towering above the ruck. The wall-clock, furnished with the letters YOUNGER'S ALES instead of figures, said five to nine. Time yet, no doubt.

20

Even as he stood watching, a chorus of groans, catcalls, and objurgation shook the low ceiling, as the shirt-sleeved barman self-consciously hung up a roughly-printed notice inscribed NO SPIRITS, to neighbour one already up, marked NO CIGARETTES. The noise came from all over the room, but most vehemently, without a doubt, from a group of young men at the far end of the bar, a compact group of about a dozen, that constituted fully two-thirds of the evening's patrons, dressed in the overalls and ubiquitous battledress-jerkins of factory and shipyard, the nipped and waisted one-time elegancies of the multiple-tailor, and the shiny blue double-breasted serge and thin pointed shoes of the corner-boy. Their verbal assault on the unfortunate barman was searching, blistering, and sustained. No item of his ancestry was overlooked, nor that of his employer's. The fact that the proprietor was not on the premises, appeared to be the crowning insult—for all the barman's assurances that Mike Doolan himself couldn't produce another drop out of bone-empty casks. Adrian Hope smiled grimly, appreciatively. But he did more than smile. He pushed through the press towards that vociferous group. However universal the singsong Glasgow accent might be in those hoarse voices, he recognised as loudest, or at least most penetrating amongst them, the high-pitched nasal whine of the dark Jakey, disciple of Lenin.

As he reached the counter, near them—it was noticeable that there was a tiny no-man's-land between this group and the scatter of the other customers—and ordered a small lager, there was a sort of progressive hush. Any speech such as his, of course, might have caused it, in that place. Then Jakey's vehement voice rose shrilly.

"Goad—look whae's here!" he cried. "The bluidy caveman frae Kelvinside, himsel'!"

"Jings, aye—get a load o' this!"

" 'Evening." Adrian nodded, equably, and raising his mug, said "Cheers" and took a sip. "I'm looking for your friend, Macgregor. Is he here, tonight?"

"No, he isna'," Jakey answered, glowering.

"Will he be coming?"

"Hoo should I ken?"

21

"I see. He hasn't been, and gone, by any chance?"

"No, he hasna'. Anythin' else, bonnie boy?"

"He's no' likely tae be, if he's no' here by this." That came from a different speaker, older than the others, a man of thirty perhaps, clad in dungarees.

"Oh. Thank you. A pity." Hope turned to the barman. "I have a book here for Mr. Macgregor. You'll know him—the tall red-headed fellow? Yes. He asked me to hand it in here. I wonder if you would give it to him, next time he's in?"

"Sure, Mister. I'll . . ."

"Here—see's the book here," Jakey interrupted. "*We'll* gi'e him the damned book." And he leant over, and thrust out his hand.

Just for a moment Adrian hesitated; then, shrugging slightly, he handed the volume over.

Jakey looked critically at the coloured dust-cover, with its picture of a Highlander in kilt and plaid and bonnet, red-bearded, with claymore raised on high. He turned it this way and that, at arm's length. "My, my. *Rob Roy Macgregor, The Scottish Freebooter,*" he said, in the mincing accents affected by the salt of the earth when confronted with the effete products of education. "*By Mark Campbell.* Now, isn't that nice!"

There was a howl of mirth.

Hope took a long drink at his lager.

"*Mister* Macgregor—Mister *Roderick* Macgregor—will enjoy this, won't he!" That was still in the same ingenious rendering of cultured tones. "Dearie me, he'll be up all night reading this!"

Further appreciative hilarity. Jakey managed to combine humour and Communism, most evidently.

Adrian spoke to the wary-eyed barman. "You'll mention to Macgregor that I left it, will you? Just in case our friend here gets so interested in it that he forgets to pass it on!"

"Sure, Mister. . . ."

"You bein' clever, eh?" That was jerked out with a swift transition from humour to suspicion.

"I wouldn't dream of it—not with all the jolly competition," Hope assured, dryly.

"Oh, yeah?" Jakey opened the book at page one. " 'Chapter One, The Proscribed Jolly Clan,' " he read out, falsetto. " 'Since the Clan Alpine, as the Macgregors jolly-well call their clan, in legendary descent from Kenneth Jolly MacAlpine . . .' "

Adrian Hope gulped down the last of his lager, and set his mug down with something of a clatter. "Good night," he said to the barman, shortly.

"Aye, well . . ."

" '. . . who was King of Jolly old Scotland in the century before . . .' "

Drawing a smoothing hand over his face, Hope turned, and threaded his way towards the door. Uproarious laughter ushered him out. Once again he met the cold thin drizzle thankfully, but with a frown. An empty matchbox on the pavement he kicked with sudden almost vicious intensity, as he turned down the Bridegate again.

He walked all the way back to the Grand Metropole, rain or none. He felt that way inclined. He would have walked further still, right back to his lodgings in Hillhead—only, in a sort of way, he had given his word, unfortunately. He had various stresses and strains to try and iron out within his mind, *en route*.

Whether or not the ironing-out process was entirely successful, when he arrived at The Glass Slipper he was perhaps unreasonably glad to find that Helen Burnet was still there. She was dancing with Ronnie Weir, certainly, but when the music stopped, they both came across to join him, whereafter, with commendable promptitude and tact, Weir withdrew himself on unspecified business—a gentleman, undoubtedly, despite all his father's wealth.

These circumstances may have had their effect on Adrian's state of mind, for indubitably he was rather more frank and forthcoming than when he had left. And if the girl asked no questions, her glance was speculative.

"I shouldn't think that there'll be anything left to drink but thin beer," he said. "Can you face that—after Ronnie's hospitality?"

"I could," she allowed, generously. "Though I'd be happier with iced lime. You have not been long."

"No," he admitted. "An iced lime and a small lager, please—if that isn't too much for the establishment! No. I didn't contact the fellow I was to meet, after all."

"No? You mean, he didn't turn up?"

He paused, and then shrugged, a trifle ruefully. "Yes, I suppose that is the position."

"Disappointing."

"It was," he agreed.

At the way that he said it, she looked at him, keenly. "I'm sorry, Adrian."

Her sympathy went unacknowledged.

She went on, "It meant something to you, didn't it, him not turning up—I mean, more than just a wasted hour?"

He frowned a little. "Oh, I don't know. Quite a trivial matter, really. And the hour wasn't wasted—I did deliver the book." And then, because he was a little sorry for himself, perhaps, and the obvious interest and concern of a good-looking young woman, however dangerous, however suspect, is apt to be a potent tongue-loosener, he went on, "But I suppose I *was* disappointed, a bit, really. I suppose I'd rather hoped for something from the fellow—foolishly, no doubt."

She said nothing, but her eyes were on him.

He could hardly leave it, there. "I had hoped that we might get together, somehow—that he might *do* something. He seemed the likeliest type I'd come across. . . ."

"Do something . . . ?" she repeated. "For you?"

"No . . . or, at least, yes—for us all, for the country, for Scotland!" He had leaned forward eagerly, but checked himself in time, and sipped his useful lager instead. "We need something done for us, you know," he ended, and smiled, but not mirthfully.

She did not miss any of all that. "You aren't very happy about the state of the country, are you?"

"Who is?"

"Yes. But I mean, you seem to have it rather on your mind. You seem to have been getting more and more dissatisfied with things ever since you came back from the Army—with yourself, too. Is it the country, or just yourself, that's at the bottom of it, Adrian?"

"Both," he returned, promptly. "Both, undoubtedly. But it's the first that's at the root of the second. That's a certainty. For me, as for others. You know, as well as I do, that it's a whole generation of us that's gone wrong."

"Perhaps. But it's worldwide, isn't it . . . ?"

"May be. But this is Scotland." There was no careful curb on his urgency, now. "Scotland's got it—and it may well be the end of her."

"Scotland's been in low water before, and survived to tell the tale."

"Yes—but never in such a fatal conjunction of circumstances. Never was she being completely taken over, body and soul, by a quite alien bureaucracy, and never before was she paralysed by such a complete spiritual collapse as to fail to do more than grumble about it!"

Subconsciously the girl was keeping time with the toe of her shoe to the syncopated rhythm of the orchestra. "You may be right," she admitted, with just the merest suggestion of a sigh. "I don't claim to be any sort of expert on the matter. And you think this friend of yours, who didn't show up, might have been able to do something about it all? Rather a tall order, surely?"

"Tall, yes." Hope nodded. "But, perhaps, not too tall—not to make a start, anyway." He gave just a glimmer of a smile. "He is on the tall side, himself, you see. I'd hoped that, in some way, we might between us be able to sort of touch off a spark. But no doubt I was quite wrong."

"A spark, Adrian? What sort of spark?" There was a hint of anxiety there.

He recognised it. "Oh, nothing very drastic. Actually, I haven't anything very clear in my own mind at all, as yet. Just an idea or two that might help to wake the country up a bit. I'm hoping, you see, that Scotland's much-vaunted spirit *is* only sleeping, and not entirely dead."

"Adrian! You wouldn't do anything foolish, would you? Anything to run yourself into trouble?"

"I'm afraid not, my dear," he said, almost grimly. "I very much doubt it. Indeed, it looks as though I won't have the chance!"

25

Helen Burnet shook her trim head. "I wish you wouldn't talk that way. I've been hearing too much of it for a while. No wonder you make Daddy see red."

"And yet it was Prof. Burnet, bless him, who showed me what was wrong with Scotland today—in his lecture on pernicious anaemia. It was your esteemed parent's eloquence on the corpuscles that did the trick!"

"So you say. But you won't pass your exams by reading politics into Daddy's lectures. Nor by rubbing him, and the rest of the staff, the wrong way. A fourth-year medical just hasn't time for politics—especially one of your years."

"My grey hairs rise up to condemn me, now!"

"I'm sorry, Adrian—you know I don't mean that. But your war service cost you a lot, in time. You've a lot of time to make up, if you're going to be a doctor while you're still young enough to, to . . ." She baulked at the completion of that.

The man knew what was in her mind, there, but he did not help her. "If . . . !" he said, significantly.

She drew a quivering breath. "What do you mean?" she asked.

"Oh, not what you're thinking, my dear Helen." That was a little weary. "Just if I'm going to be a doctor, at all. You know I'm not too happy about it. I've been wondering for some time whether it's worth going on with it. All this nationalisation of the medical services, this direction, this ordering and controlling of the profession by the confounded government, has taken the heart right out of it, as far as I'm concerned. I'm really thinking I'd be happier in a croft, somewhere up in the Highlands."

"Adrian—you wouldn't be such a fool!"

"I would, indeed. Anything, rather than be just another cog in the wheel, another number on the register, even the Medical Register."

"Indeed! Well, I can assure you, Adrian—I'd never care to become a crofter's wife!"

"No? I'm sorry about that, Helen."

The orchestra came into its own again, for fully a dozen bars. Then, controlling her voice, the young woman spoke again. "This is rather ridiculous, isn't it?"

"It is, and it isn't," the other returned, slowly, carefully. "My idea of maybe taking a croft, or some sort of farm anyway, for instance, isn't ridiculous—nor the fact that Scotland desperately needs wakening up."

"Well, we won't argue about it, Adrian." She smiled, brilliantly, and she had a heart-turning smile, that girl, as well as a very excellent control of herself. "Only, I warn you, m'lad, that if you either go wandering off to pioneer in the wilds of Wester Ross, or get into trouble with the police wakening up this long-suffering land, I disown you right away. Get it?"

"It's as well to be warned, isn't it," he answered her, soberly.

"Just what I thought, Doleful Desmond!" she agreed, and her laugh was silvery. "As well, too, I think, that you didn't meet your wild man from the Bridegate! But, cheer up—you can take me home, now, and be quit of me!"

"It's not so easy as that, I'm afraid," he said. And his smile was but a pallid imitation of hers. "But, come along."

III

ADRIAN HOPE was an obstinate man. If he had not been, he would never have been parachuted, six years before, into the wilder parts of Occupied Europe, and certainly never have got out again, especially with a Military Cross and a Croix de Guerre. Nor, probably, would he have gone back to school again, after the life he had been living, and applied himself to the three years of medical studies that he had already put in, amongst colleagues who looked on him as on the verge of senile decay. His obstinacy, then, is established. And it was sheer obstinacy, no doubt, that was responsible for his continued preoccupation with Roderick Macgregor—that, and possibly a certain unworthy and unsuitable pique in that Helen Burnet so definitely disapproved. Such was the man.

The following Sunday saw him in the Rob Roy country's hills once again, but if Ginger Macgregor and Company were thereabouts, he saw no signs of them. He waited for one more day, and then let his impatience have its head. A red-tabbed superior of his in Military Intelligence had once remarked that Hope was a glutton for punishment.

On the next Tuesday evening, then, he once more found his way by tram to the fairly central if less than salubrious district of Anderston. He had no idea where Macharg Street was, but imagined it was almost certain to be in this neighbourhood somewhere; also, he had forgotten the number, but had a notion that it was either Seventeen or Seventy-one. Anyway, in his haystack it was no needle that he was looking for.

He traced the whereabouts of Macharg Street, after some small confusion—it seemed that there was another of them, in a different area altogether—and set off through the maze of grimy chasms and defiles classified in Glasgow Postal Directory as C.10. He found Macharg Street, in the failing light, as no better and no worse than the rest—a featureless corridor of dark smoke-blackened stone, with one end blocked by neigh-

28

bouring tenements, and the other by the tall brick-walling of a factory of sorts. Into its shadows and smells and noises he plunged.

Any sign of numbers had long since gone from the entries, but a brief computation showed that, with only approximately twenty closes on either side, there was unlikely to be a Number Seventy-one. Enquiries from a selection of the rising generation producing nothing concrete, but finding one of the gaping entrances chalk-inscribed, amongst other designs and slogans, with the figure five, he counted his way up six more entries, assuming the result to be seventeen.

Pushing along the dark and noisome tunnel, he knocked at the first door he came to. It was presently opened to a blast of gramophonic sound and a fat lady, who, startled as she was by the apparition and its manner of approach, nevertheless divulged the information that Big Ginger Macgregor bided with Mistress Munro on the top flat, before she managed to get the door safely shut.

The stairs were dark, the treads worn into hollows, and the man climbed warily. But no darkness could hide the pairs of water-closets at half-floor levels, some of them even without doors. A rough calculation, based on the number of houses on each landing, seemed to indicate that these closets were provided at the rate of one per three establishments. Contemplating this, Adrian rapped on Mrs. Munro's door, four flights up.

But though she was less suspicious than the lady below, Mrs. Munro proved a disappointment. Yes, Roderick Macgregor stayed with her, right enough, she admitted, quietening the uproar of three children. But he was out. If the gentleman was that keen on finding him, he'd likely get him at Mike Doolan's Bar, in the Bridegate. With a sigh, Hope retraced his steps.

Obstinate and determined as he might be, it was with a certain reluctance that Adrian pushed open those swing-doors of Mike Doolan's, and ventured within. As he stood back against the tiled wall, for a minute or two thereafter, some craven part of him was almost hoping that there would be no sign of the outstanding figure for which he sought, this time either.

29

The scene was notably similar to that when last he had viewed it—even to the notices announcing the absence of spirits and cigarettes. The clock showed almost the same time, the place was similarly filled, and the clientele seemed identical. Only, above the compact group at the far end, a blazing head and mighty shoulders towered. With something like a sigh, Adrian moved forward.

He was quickly spied. A warning from the man Alicky, and a volley of shouts, whistles, and witticisms greeted him, a barrage of sound into which he pressed, still-faced. But shortly, as he reached the counter, it died away, and eyes were trained on the dark Jakey rather than on the newcomer. And Jakey, though he eyed the latter narrowly, kept an eye on the red-head also. Undoubtedly he was less inspired than formerly.

But he did not disappoint entirely, of course. Seeing the big man make no sign, he lifted up his voice. "Jings—here it's, again! Off wi' your caps, boys—d'you no' ken when you're in the presence o' the aristocracy!"

That brought forth only a titter. Definitely it was not up to previous standard.

Adrian ordered a pint of lager.

Jakey tried again. "He's brought us anither book, maybe. A great guy for the books, him. Hell—maybe it's the *Adventures o' Robin Hood*, this time—or the *Babes in the Bluidy Wood*!"

"Shurrup, Jakey!" Macgregor mentioned.

Adrian looked along, and raised his mug. " 'Evening," he said. "You got the book?"

"Aye," the other nodded.

"Good."

Into the pause, voices gathered and rose again—but not directed at the newcomer now. The big fellow seemed to have some quite substantial control over the company.

Adrian moved nearer. Alicky, muttering something, made way for him. "Still think it will take a revolution?" he asked, casually, smiling a little.

"Yeah."

"M'mmm."

"Jings, it will!" Jakey substantiated. "A revolution o' the proletariat."

"Och, can it, Jakey!" another said—the older man who, on Hope's previous visit here, had raised the only vaguely helpful voice. "Your damned proletariat! It's no' got a kick left in it—no' a blasted kick. Look at Glesgy—no' a kick in it. Glesgy's done. The Hielants are done. Bluidy Edinburry's done—never been anythin' else but done. An' if the Hielants an' Glesgy's done, Scotlan's done. . . ."

"Aye, Donal's richt," the man Sandy agreed. "Pair auld donnert Scotlan'."

"It's thae English. . . ."

"English, naethin'!" the individual called Donald declared. "The English are jist as hudden doon as we are. Nae guid blamin' the skitterin' English. It's oor ain fault. If Scots'd get thegither, stand thegither—if they'd dae any cursed thing thegither . . . !"

"If they'd jine the Pairty!" Jakey put in.

"Hell—your Pairty! An' be hudden doon wi' a shooer o' Coammissars, instead! We can dae wi'oot your Pairty. . . ."

"What aboot the National Pairty, then?"

"Jings—the Nationalists! Wee kilts an' beards an' soirées! Goad—you'll no' save Scotlan' wi' yon!"

"The I.L.P., then . . . ?"

"Deid! Deid as a doornail, them."

"The Clann Albainn Socie'y, then . . . ?"

"This Convention . . . ?"

"Hell—jine the Salvation Airmy, while you're at it . . . !"

"Quiet, you!" That was the red-haired giant, who, seemingly, did not argue. He did not say any more, either, as the uproar died away. Undoubtedly, he had a gift for silence, that man.

Adrian tried a change of subject. "Have you read any of the book?" he wondered.

"Aye."

"Much of it?"

"All o' it."

"Oh." Heedfully, he looked at the man. "Indeed. Er . . . what did you think of it?"

"No' bad," the other said. He seemed almost as though about to say something further, but restrained himself in time, and finished his beer instead.

31

Hope decided that he probably ought to feel encouraged. "I've been thinking about our conversation in the cave the other day," he said. "Thinking quite a lot. I've come to the conclusion that I was wrong when I suggested that what the country needed was a Wallace or a Bruce. I reckon it's not ready for either."

The big man made no comment, but his glance was keen.

"I've come to the conclusion that what it needs today is another Rob Roy Macgregor!"

"Goad save's a'—here he goes!" That was Jakey, of course.

"Jings—he's awa' again!"

"Up the Macgreegors!" somebody cried from the back.

Adrian ignored them all. "Captains and generals like Bruce and Wallace need armies to lead," he went on. "I doubt if they'd find so much as a battalion to follow them in Scotland today. It's the lack of blood I was talking about. I said we needed a blood-transfusion—the patient couldn't stand a major operation. And how d'you start a blood-transfusion? You start by giving the patient a jag with a needle. The jag's the first thing—the blood flows along later!" He grinned, suddenly. "I'm studying medicine, you see—so I know all about it! The needle's the first thing, then—not the knife or the saw. Rob Roy gave Scotland such a jag, one time. He was no great warrior or national hero—but he set the country by the ears, just the same. He was a showman, more than a general. That's what we need, just now—a showman, who'll play to the gallery, the gallery that's so damned fast asleep. You get me?"

It scarcely looked as though they did. Like a blank wall, the glances of that company met him, a blank wall on which suspicion and prejudice and raillery were scrawled, as in large-lettered chalk. But it was not at the company that he looked, only at the big man, who stared back at him, heavily, stolidly.

"Weel, what aboot it?" Macgregor said, at length.

"Just this," Hope declared, leaning forward. "If we had a modern Rob Roy, if there was such a man to be found in this country, today, a man of the people, strong, tough, none too scrupulous, not afraid of taking a chance—a lot of chances— fed to the teeth with things as they are, footloose, with some sort of leadership in him . . . and maybe a group of men that would follow him. If there *was* such a one . . ." Adrian paused, his easy voice abruptly changing to a quivering intensity. "If there was, by God, I believe he could do a lot to save Scotland, here and now!"

Roderick Macgregor, whose massive jaws had been working rhythmically for a little, stopped now, with his mouth just slightly open. For fully half a minute he looked at the other, unwinking, with only the sides of his nostrils flaring—to very peculiar effect in that otherwise still, almost expressionless face. "What?" he said, at last—and nobody else had thought to speak. "Dae what?"

"Plenty," he was assured. "Plenty. In time, he could set this country into a ferment such as it hasn't been in since the 'Forty-Five. But first, he'd have to set the heather on fire—like Rob Roy did. He wouldn't have to ambush troops, and levy blackmail, and set men to burning each other's houses. But he *would* have to defy authority, and what's worse, the cramping weary inertia of an over-governed, official-ridden, spirit-stifled people. He wouldn't have to protect peaceable folk's stock and homes from robbers and raiders, at a price—but he would have to deal with their modern counterparts. What's sapping away the spirit of the cities and the Lowlands, today? Restrictions, prohibitions, artificial shortages, lack of incentives, lack even of decent honest-to-goodness food. He could do something about that—especially the last two, the food and the incentives."

"How . . . ?" someone demanded.

"Scotland produces lashings of food—beef, mutton, and fish—more than we can use. But do we get it—*any* of it? How many of you have seen a piece of fresh beef, for years? It all goes South—and we get the frozen stuff, and precious little of that! The same with the whisky—your Number One incentive! Where does the whisky go? *We* don't get it. Time we thought about *taking* it, taking what's our own. Redistribution, if you prefer it that way. A start could be made on the redistribution of beef and whisky. As the gesture I was talking about—the jag to wake us up!"

"Noo you're talkin'," said Alicky.

"What's ruining the Highlands today—besides emigration?

Creeping bracken, unburned heather, flooding rivers spoiling the arable, shortage of labour in the brief harvest-season, herds of uncontrolled deer eating the crops, lack of drainage, tracks and bridges falling into disrepair. These things he could tackle, with his band—not on a big scale, of course, but as an example, as a demonstration. They could descend on a crofting area, cutting bracken, burning heather, repairing river-dykes and fences, rebuilding tracks and bridges, dealing with the deer, helping with the harvest and the ploughing."

Hope glanced around him, and did not need to plead for any hearing, now.

"What's holding back folk from going up there, and settling in the Highlands, and opening up *new* crofts?" he went on. "Your Clann Albainn people will tell you it is rules and regulations and red-tape—Crofter's Act clauses, restrictions on the use of land, no permits to build houses, no permits for timber or petrol, no permits for anything, no permission for development, no priorities for road-building, bridges, or piers. Confound it, the Highlands are being throttled. And, confound it again—couldn't a determined ruthless gang of men, caring not a damn for the flood of orders and restrictions that pour out of Whitehall and St. Andrews House—couldn't they make one hell of a difference? Couldn't they slice through coils of that red-tape? Couldn't they *do* what's shouting to be done, and to the devil with the dead hand of all the Boards and Departments! Couldn't they show the way to a muzzled and demoralised people? Couldn't they make a stab at waking Scotland up? Couldn't they, I say!"

There was a murmur, a rumble, that grew into a confused babel, as men, aroused by Hope's enthusiasm, broke into mingled support, questioning, and disagreement. Some of each, there was, undoubtedly, and none of it couched in whispers. For a few moments everyone was talking at once, and with increasing vigour. Everyone, that is, except Roderick Macgregor, who still stared directly in front of him, not so much at the student, as through him, his jaws working again, his expression rapt if abstracted.

Hope's eyes never left his face.

The man Donald it was who raised his voice sufficiently to

be heard above the hubbub. "I'm no' sayin' but what you're right, man, maybe," he declared. "But hoo's your gang goin' to live, whiles? Whae'll be payin' them? It'll no' be your crofters, I'm tellin' you. You'll no' tak the breeks off a Hielantman!"

"Sure. You've said it, Donal'!"

"Aye, man."

"You're right." Adrian Hope took him up swiftly, eagerly. "Not the crofters, for a fact—they couldn't. I'll tell you who'll be paying them. The Government!"

"Eh . . . ?"

"Och, jings . . . !"

Now he had them all staring at him as though he was mad—all save Macgregor that is, who still seemed to be preoccupied. "Listen," he urged them, unnecessarily. "You all know about the hydro-electric schemes and the Forestry Commission? The only two things the Government has any interest in, in the Highlands . . . because England's desperately anxious about the coal situation, and the one will produce power for the fuel-hungry Midlands and the other pit-props for their mines. Well, they're both crying out for labour, skilled and unskilled, seasonal labour, casual labour—any kind of labour. And they can't get it, because of the remoteness of the working-sites—and they can't get local men because there are none, any more. So now they're willing and anxious to pay good money, mighty good money, for casual labour—anything to get the men to go up there, Irish, Poles, Germans, D.P.s, anybody—to build the dams and plant the trees. I was travelling up in the train to Kyle of Lochalsh a week or two ago, and in my compartment were three fellows going back to the Loch Roig scheme—fellows from Glasgow here. And they hadn't just been home for the weekend, mind you, or the week, or the month even. They'd been taking a few months' holiday—four months, actually. And they could afford to. Getting paid so well, living in camps so far from anywhere, and with absolutely nothing to spend their money on up there, they save enough in four months to live on it in idleness for the next four. And there you are! If a certain proportion of the members of this hypothetical gang were always working at the power-schemes or

35

the forestry, taking it in turns, they would provide the funds for the others to live on and work on. And all at the Government's expense. Could anything be more suitable?"

His hearers looked at each other in something like awe. "Jings—can you beat that!" somebody asked, and received no adequate answer.

Roderick Macgregor seemed to have come out of his trance at last. He turned a penetrating, not to say challenging, glance at Hope. "Mister," he said, deliberately, "what for are you no' ha'ein' a breenge at this Rob Roy racket yoursel'?"

The other nodded. "That's easy," he said. "I'm willing and ready to take a part, of course, to help organise the thing. I could do that. I did the same sort of thing during the war, when I was dropped in the mountains of Dalmatia, to organise resistance amongst the Yugoslav partisans. But I wouldn't do for the leader, the big fellow, the showman I was talking about. I'm not the right type, you see—not colourful enough. I'm no Rob Roy. It would take the authentic Highland cateran touch . . . and I haven't got so much as a hint of Macgregor about me."

There was no escaping the significance with which he said that—nor the unanimity with which all eyes turned on the big man, in speculation. For the first time that evening, the noise of the traffic in the streets outside could be heard in Mike Doolan's Bar. Even the tick-tock of the Younger's wall-clock. Then a voice spoke up, with the uneven vehemence of embarrassment.

"Up the Macgreegors!" Though lacking in originality, perhaps, that individual at the back had an undeniable sense of timing, and used it, within his limits.

Adrian, keyed up as he was, and with the balance trembling, recognised the possibilities. "Exactly!" he cried. "I'd second that, in the way it should be seconded. I'd drink to it—only my glass is empty! I'd stand you a pint, all of you, to drink to it—only I can't afford it. I can't even afford another for myself . . . and that's Scotland today for you!" And his laugh sounded entirely frank and natural—though his gaze was fixed as firmly as ever on the big fellow.

And out of the hush, that man responded—responded as he was intended to respond. After all, if his name was Roderick

Macgregor, he had Highland blood in his veins, despite his Lowland voice; moreover, that colouring, those urgent eyes, the spectacular postures, those dramatic monosyllables and potent pauses, all told their own story. The man was a true Gael, and therefore a natural-born actor, with an eye for the telling gesture, an instinct for the flourish. So he responded.

"You can't, eh, my mannie! Weel, I can! You'll ha'e one on me. Aye, jings—the hale bunch o' yous'll ha'e one on me!" He drew himself up, thrust a great hand into his trouser-pocket, and brought out a miscellaneous collection of articles, from which he selected two very crumpled notes, and tossed them across the swimming counter, in the direction of the wide-eyed barman, with magnificent display. "You," he ordered, "gi'e the gent a pint o' your swill. Gi'e's a' a pint—aye an' yoursel'. Gi'e yoursel' a pint, man, tae!"

The quick-drawn breath that greeted that from all around, was good and sufficient verdict and reward, as every glance centred on the student.

That man bowed, gravely. "Spoken like the Gregorach!" he said. "You are very good. Thank you."

"Nae thanks required," the other snapped, almost snarled, indeed, suddenly embarrassed. He grabbed the second full mug, and thrust it ungraciously at Jakey. "Here—take it," he commanded. "An' you, tae, damn you." He fixed a baleful eye on the dark youth all the time that the other mugs were being replenished. But before the last had reached its recipient, he had his own tankard raised. "You'll drink to Rob Roy Macgregor, then!" he said. "The lot o' yous." And that was no suggestion.

No objection was raised. Only an amendment, and that from Adrian Hope, greatly daring. "Bracket that with *Roddie* Roy!" he proposed, strong-voiced. "Roddie Roy and Rob Roy Macgregor!"

"Roddie Roy, aye!"

"Whoopee!"

"Attaboy—gi'e it big licks!"

"Up the Macgreegors—the hale billin' o' them!"

"Shurrup!" the big man said, but almost conversationally. And he drank with the rest.

And Adrian, setting down his mug, found Macgregor's gaze on him, directly. For a long moment they stared at each other, eye to eye. It was the big riveter who spoke first.

"Weel," he said. "What aboot it?"

"Eh . . . ?"

"Hoo do we go aboot it?"

"You mean . . . ?"

"I mean, when do we bluidy well start, Mister!" he explained heavily patient.

"Well, I'm damned!" Adrian said, and he sounded entirely as though he meant it.

Out of the noise and confusion that followed, Hope at last made himself heard. "You mean that?" he demanded. "You'll do it?"

"Sure, I'll dae it. I'll ha'e a stab at it, anyway—if it's worth daein'. What d'you take me for? I'll gi'e them their jab!"

"It'll be a big thing, you know." Adrian, used to rather different mental processes, was a little startled by this abrupt and wholesale concurrence. "Maybe you'd better think it over, a bit . . . ?"

"Hell—what for?"

"Well, it means big risks . . . leaving jobs . . ."

"Jobs!" That was spat out. "What's any job worth, right now? Damn your job! You're jist a bluidy detail!"

"There speaks the disillusioned ex-Serviceman!"

"Aye. Third Seaforths."

"The I. Corps, myself," Adrian vouchsafed. "I should have guessed, brother. But these others? How about them? Will they come in—any of them?"

"Sure they will," Macgregor asserted, with, apparently, complete confidence.

Hope turned, and looked around that group. "Will you?" he asked them, doubt writ as large in his voice as on his face.

The murmur that rose in answer was just a little confused. The glances were on the red-head, not on the speaker.

"Are you prepared to give up your jobs, and take a chance?"

"Look, Mister." The big man's voice was ominous. "*I'm* sayin' they'll come in, okay. I'm *tellin'* you. See? They're no' a' in jobs, anyway. Alicky'll dae fine makin' his book any place . . . an' Fachy's no' a' that taken up wi' sellin' papers! They'll come in, a'right—maybe no' a' for the first breenge. You jist gi'e us a bit start."

"You think so . . . ?"

"I'm *tellin'* you. What aboot yoursel'?"

"I'm prepared to drop my classes at the University." He paused. "The whole thing will take a lot of organising."

"Aye, well. We'll organise it. What's the first job?"

"Hang it all—let's walk before we fly," Hope protested. "Give me time."

"Flyin's quickest," Macgregor observed, dispassionately. "An' we'll want a guid start."

"That's true, I agree. I have an idea that we ought to start the way Rob Roy did. Cattle."

"Eh . . . ?"

"Cattle," Adrian repeated, nodding. He looked about him. "But we can't go into details here, obviously. Another time, it will have to be. But there's one thing we could get fixed now. We haven't got a butcher in the house, have we? Or anyone connected with the trade?"

"A butcher . . . ? No. . . ."

"My brither's a butcher," somebody volunteered. "He's in the Co-op Fleshin'."

"Aye—Sandy Robb's brither, Jamie."

"Good. Can we get him in?"

"I dinna' ken. He's mairrit, wi' a shooer o' weans. But, och, he'll gi'e us a bit hand, right enough."

"Fine. Advice is all we'll need from him. Now, where can we meet—in private, somewhere—and get this thing organised? There needn't be a crowd, to start with—just one or two. Somewhere not too kenspeckle."

"You'd no' ca' my lodgin's kenspeckle?" Roderick Macgregor suggested.

"No. Right, that's grand. What about seven o'clock to-morrow?"

"Sure, Mister. Suits me. We want to get crackin'."

"We want to get organised," the other returned. "And the name is Hope, you know—Adrian Hope. I've been called Ian, for short."

39

"Sure, Mister."

"All right." He smiled. "Good night, Roddie Roy. Good night, all."

In silence they watched him go.

"Is yon guy nuts, or isn't he?" Jakey asked of all and sundry, as the swing-doors banged.

He got a variety of replies to that. And none from Roderick Macgregor.

IV

TO get cracking, or to get organised—that was the question,
the argument, the battle. A battle that arose out of more
than any mere divergence of opinion, and on the outcome of
which hinged far more than just the standard of success at-
tained on their first venture. The difference of attitude was
fundamental, springing out of the essential natures of the
protagonists, the difference between thought and action, between the planner and the exponent of spontaneous com-
bustion. On the result of this preliminary struggle, depended
not only the fashion in which the campaign was to be conducted, but Adrian Hope's entire position therein; whether he
was to be anything more than just a backroom-boy, a mere
projector of ideas. It was a dour ding-dong contest, with the
scales weighted, bulkily if not heavily, in favour of Macgregor.
Hope had but the one supporter for his attitude—Donald
Lamont; but he was the most substantial of the gang, as well
as the eldest, and Big Roddie respected his opinions, inferentially if not obviously. An ex-merchant-seaman, presently
working as a dock labourer, his backing was important.

Neither side won, in the outcome. If the organising took an
unconscionable time, to Macgregor and his impetuous friends,
it was not nearly completed to Adrian's satisfaction before his
hand was forced. They moved before he was satisfied that
they were ready, in the end—and quite a considerable time
after the last drop of the big fellow's patience had run out.
The underlying conflict, then, remained only partly resolved.

There was a great lot to be done, of course, so much to be
organised. That was evident to most of them; the question at
issue had been how much of it must be completed before they
actually started operations. And if Adrian was dissatisfied in
the result, at least he achieved much, in the month allowed
him.

Ginger's gang, if a gang it could be called—for by Glasgow

41

standards it was scarcely that, being only one of innumerable groups of young men that took their pleasures *en masse*, and based their fairly innocuous activities on some low-browed pub or other in a city of such—was a loosely-knit, fluctuatingly-numbered, and fairly easy-going company of kindred spirits, averaging around two dozen of regulars and hangers-on, of which more than half seldom appeared together on any one occasion. Roderick Macgregor was their undisputed leader, Cranstonhill and the Bridegate area their stamping-ground, and Mike Doolan's Bar their howff and headquarters. They were held together by the bond of their years, the curious tradition not of their city but of their stratum of that city—possibly the degenerate flowering of the clan spirit—a common discontent with the *status quo*, and not much else. There was little of discipline about them, and less of organisation. Also, they did not sport a single converted razor, broken bottle-end, or sock filled with nails, amongst them.

Out of such material, Adrian Hope's attempt to forge an instrument for the purpose he had in mind, was a task of some magnitude. About eighteen of them signified their willingness to take some part in activities, in a general way, but wholehearted out-and-out support was a different matter—and not unnaturally. Only eight pledged themselves there and then to throw up their jobs, or what passed as jobs. Others reckoned that they would, but did not actually commit themselves. Roddie Macgregor assured that they all would, once action was forthcoming. Action they must have. If only they would get *cracking*!

Four rather doubtful enthusiasts, with the eager co-operation of the Ministry of Labour and the Hydro-Electric Board, were despatched to an outlandish corner of Inverness-shire, to move mountains for £8 per week—of which, heroically, they promised to send south £5 each, promised and performed. Before the end of that month, Macgregor had cashed money-orders from them to the impressive total of £52 12s. 6d.—how this odd figure eventuated was never fully explained, though the incidence of a game known as pontoon amongst lonely hydro-electric workers might have had something to do with it. With such sinews of war at their disposal, it was the general opinion that almost anything could be done. It required all Hope's persistence, with Donald Lamont's support, to convince them that further organisation was necessary.

Adrian had a link or two with the Press—one, a wartime colleague, now one of the chief representatives of The Press Association in Glasgow, another an old school friend who was sub-editor of the *Glasgow Chronicle*. Both were men wide-awake to the country's state, as, being good journalists, they were bound to be—the first it was, indeed, who had given Hope certain of the ideas he now sought to put into practice; while the second, being half Irish, could be accepted as a well-wisher in any ranny-hannery. These two he contacted, found them sympathetic if sceptical, and primed them to be ready for eventualities. They offered him advice, which he did not take, promised to visit him in Barlinnie Gaol, and assured him, in the improbable event of any success, of the very fullest publicity that the story would carry. With that he had to be content.

He saw very little of Helen Burnet, that cold wet May. Nor did he shine in his examinations. He was not even particularly good company for anybody with whom he came in contact. Normally, he was not an irritable man. But his efforts were bearing some sort of fruit. A number of young Scots were prepared to *do* something for what they conceived to be the cause of Scotland. Some of them were prepared to back up their convictions to the extent of going to prison. They had certain funds at their disposal. The gang had acceded to a change of name—from The Ginger Boys to The Gregorach; they had even started calling Macgregor, Roddie Roy. Even, indeed, under duress and with ribaldry, they had listened to a sort of discourse on Rob Roy Macgregor himself. And Adrian Hope had actually achieved the improbable, and graduated beyond the title of Mister; his name, of course, being impossible, and any diminutive not to be considered for such as him, the casual mention once that in another life he had worn a crown on his shoulder, solved the problem in a trice. Thereafter, he was The Major, to Macgregor, and presently to them all—and twice the man that he had been. Perhaps this was his greatest achievement. He was accepted.

And then a crisis was precipitated. Donald warned them that a shunters' and goods-yard workers' strike was due to start in a few days. And, since it might go on for weeks, invalidating their plans, there was no time to be lost.

Operation Beef was fixed for two nights hence—Friday.

V

AS usual, it was wet, a dirty cold night, with drizzle out of the south-west, against which Adrian Hope turned up his jacket collar in ineffectual protest. But it was dark, which after all was the vital matter; though mid-May, and only ten o'clock, it was black as any winter's night. He stood at the corner of Veitch Street and Cranstonhill, waiting. And frequently, he glanced at his watch.

However, he had no cause for complaint. The lorry was no more than five minutes late. Jakey drew up with a screech of brakes—Jakey Reid, in an imperfectly organised world, was constrained to earn his daily bread as no more than a lorry-driver for a firm of private enterprise contractors. From out of the cab Roddie Macgregor's great hand thrust, thumb jerking backwards. Adrian moved obediently round to the rear, where willing hands from under the damp canvas hood reached down to help him up over the tailboard. The lorry jerked on again, as he fell amongst a tangle of limbs and bodies.

"Enter the Major, heid first!" somebody shouted.

"Aye man—watch your feet on the lobby gas!"

Loud laughter greeted the entire performance. Obviously the Gregorach were in good heart.

They rattled on along the Dumbarton Road at what seemed to at least one of the passengers, excessive speed. Adrian would have preferred to be in the cab, where he could exert rather more influence on events. No doubt Roddie Roy knew as much. This operation was going to be carried out according to *his* specification, most evidently.

Somewhere in the Dalmuir area, the sidelights of another vehicle came up behind them, and there clung, despite the pace. Eyeing them out of a gap in the canvas hood, Adrian was just a little anxious, till in the brief illumination as they lurched past a lit-up garage, he ascertained that it was a red van,

45

belonging to the Fleshing Department of the Braehead and District Co-operative Society. All was well.

Past the dreariness of night-bound Kilpatrick and Bowling, Jakey projected them. Dumbarton itself received them, and held them up a little amongst the bemused floods pouring from its emptying cinemas, Jakey blowing his horn with strident indignation. Then they were out on the Helensburgh road, Adrian sighing with relief, his colleagues singing lustily and being echoed from the van in the rear.

Presently, they swung off the main road into the dark side streets on the right, crossed a couple of railway bridges, and turning sharply, began to bump down a long lane between the blank walls of railway sheds. Then, at a locked white gate, they stopped, brakes protesting again, agonisingly.

"There y'are, Ging . . . Roddie Roy!" Jakey sang out. "It's a' yours."

Adrian jumped out. "Can't you be a bit quieter, Reid, for Heaven's sake!" he said, urgently.

"Och awa', you—or the coos'll get you!" Jakey scoffed, amidst mirth.

Roderick Macgregor had got down from the cab, and gone straight to the big padlocked white-painted gate, a hammer and a cold-chisel in his hand. A few metallic blows and a splintering of wood, and he was back.

"Shurrup!" he ordered. "You a' here? Fifteen, there should be. That's the gate. Jakey—get your lorry turned. You tae, Jamie. The rest o' yous—follow me. An' hud your tongues."

All that they did, obediently. In a long silent line, twelve men filed through the gate, and tailed along in the big man's wake. Hope brought up the rear.

They were in a great goods-yard, the marshalling-yard of Levenbank Goods Station, silent and deserted now, save for the puffing of a shunting engine somewhere away over to the left. Only a single light or two glimmered feebly over that vast acreage of rails and sleepers and trucks, around each of which the drizzle cast its faint halo.

Roddie Roy, crossing two or three sets of rails, led them briskly along another line. Ahead of them, from some distance off, came a moaning sound. The big man paused.

"Hell," he said. "Must have moved them. They're aye on this line."

"Sounds a good bit further over, further west," Adrian exclaimed. "What foul luck!"

"C'mon," Macgregor said.

Crossing diagonally over many more sets of rails, on which the thin rain gleamed dully, they pressed on. Frequently they had to dodge round or through lines of stationary trucks. Intermittently, the moaning sound in front guided them on. At length, Roddie stopped and turned, leaning one hand against the end of a tall wagon that had loomed up ahead, and from which came a puffing rustling sound, and a warm country-like smell.

"What's wrong wi' oor luck, noo?" he demanded. "Here's a bit platform. They've saved us half oor trouble, movin' the things."

"This must mean that they're bringing more in. First thing in the morning, I suppose . . . ?"

"Let them," the other said, grimly. "They'll need to!"

Climbing up on to the platform, a substantial if rough-and-ready affair constructed out of old sleepers, they moved along the line of dark trucks. Macgregor sent Alicky ahead to count them, while he himself tried one of the door-fastenings, and found it to open easily. Alicky came back with the word that there were sixteen of them—though a few were empty. At ten per truck, say, a hundred and twenty head.

"Aye." Roddie Roy was peering about him into the dark.

"We're a sight nearer the ither end, noo—the west entrance. Nae guid goin' awa' back to the lorries. Art—awa' back, an' tell Jakey to drive roond to this end. An' to see to the ither gate. . . ."

"That means we'll have to cross round by that back street," Adrian said. "What's its name—Balrose Street?"

"Aye." The red-head turned. "Weel, boys—this is it! You a' ken what to dae? Get crackin', then—an' let the dam' coos make the row!"

And they did. Two men to each truck, they ran to the doors, unfastened the hasps, and were in amongst the bullocks and stirks. For a little there was much grunting, puffing, mooing,

47

and muffled cursing—and little to show for it all. Then the first beasts, the smallish shaggy black and brown cattle of the Scottish uplands, came running out stiff-legged on to the platform, wide-nostrilled, heads tossing. Immediate confusion followed, as inexperienced herdsmen hustled their brutes hither and thither. Most set off at a spanking see-sawing high-tailed gallop westwards along the platform, but two or three went the wrong way, and managed to get down the ramp on to the rails. Men were going after them, when Macgregor stopped them.

"Nae time for that," he told them. "Let them awa'—we've plentys. Awa' up the top o' the platform, an' get thae brutes into a huddle. Jump tae it!"

The second series of trucks were now being opened up. It had all taken much less time than had been anticipated—mainly because of the platform; they had reckoned on having to improvise ramps out of unhinged doors to lead the brutes down on to the rails. While the last trucks were being emptied, Adrian Hope hurried along the line of wagons, and chalked on each one emptied, in large letters: RECEIVED FROM MINISTRY OF FOOD, 10 STIRKS ON ACCOUNT OF SCOTLAND'S MEAT RATION—ROD ROY MACGREGOR. He was decorating the eleventh truck thus, when the big man came up to him, panting.

"C'mon," he said. "That's the lot. They're a' fleein' awa' up there, like Auld Sawny was efter them."

Adrian snapped his chalk in half, and gave the other a piece. "You do that wagon," he said. "Put 'Received from Ministry of Food, Ten Stirks on . . .' "

"Damn a' that!" Roddie Roy roared, and dashed off his own legend. TO HELL WITH LONDON—UP SCOTLAND! "C'mon, you."

They found men and cattle waiting for them beside a range of railed-off pens. This Levenbank Goods Station was the official depot for truckloads of store cattle, collected by the Ministry from all over the West Highlands, to be assembled into trains and despatched to the South, three times a week. A wide gate in front of them, at which a couple of men were rattling ineffectually, held the herd up. There was no sign of Jakey or Jamie and their vehicles.

Roddie Roy strode forward. "Here—let's see this," he cried. "Oot o' the road." A quick inspection of the padlock and bolt, and he snorted and turned his attention to the spike-topped palings flanking the gate. Gripping one of these by the point, he tested it, tugged, and then with a sudden explosion of strength, wrenched violently. The thing came away in his hand, at the top, with a crack, and a single jerk loosed it at the foot. Grabbing one on either side with each hand, he repeated the process. Soon, he had a sizable gap cleared, sufficient to let a couple of bullocks through side-by-side. A kick and a twist demolished the supporting bars. "Get crackin', then," he commanded.

It was unnecessary, of course, for Jakey's lorry came up just as the first beasts were driven through; but the enthusiasm with which the feat was greeted by the rank-and-file forced Adrian to admit that it might not have been entirely wasted effort. Who was he to decry a gesture, anyway?

So far, they seemed to have aroused no sort of alarm. The shunting engine went on shunting, making its strangely lonely-sounding clanging and bumping of trucks. But otherwise the place seemed to be entirely deserted. The cattle were lowing rather more than previously, of course, but that might well pass unnoticed in that district. The drizzle had increased to real rain, now.

Adrian had been counting the bullocks as they passed through the gap in the palings. One hundred and twelve head. He hurried up the slope after them. Roddie Roy was leading the way, well in front, but having almost to run to keep there. The beasts, after the constriction of the cattle-trucks, were eager to stretch their legs. The goods-yard entrance, at this end, gave on to a one-sided street of tall tenement houses. Right-handed along this, Macgregor turned, and, after a little persuasion, four hundred and forty-eight hooves pattered after him. Behind and around the trotting herd, a dozen amateur drovers ran and whacked and swore—but this latter beneath their breaths. The lorry and the van brought up the rear.

It was after eleven-thirty now, and though there were still a few lights in the tenement windows, there was little life about Balrose Street. One man only they encountered, who hailed them convivially, threw an empty bottle at the nearest stirk, and then sat down heavily, singing *Ragtime Cowboy Joe*.

Soon their street entered at right-angles another wider thoroughfare, flanked on either side by small bungalows, and here all the lights seemed to be out—at least, to the front. Turning left along it, they were facing due north. Ahead stretched bungalow-dom, villa-dom, farmlands, and the empty hills. But it was a long, long road—or rather, a succession of roads, for they kept turning off up avenues and terraces and parkways, to avoid traffic, observation, and comment. You could march the Choirs of New Jerusalem through suburbia at midnight and attract no attention. And always they trended north by west, and always they tended to climb. Only one bullock they lost, that blundered over a low fence into a cluster of allotments, broke open a glass-frame, and thereafter started off on a private stampede of its own, in the direction of Helensburgh. Promptly they washed their hands of it. But if only one was lost, many erred and strayed. The temporary herdsmen raced and sweated and imprecated. If only they'd had a dog or two. This for a life!

But at length the houses thinned, the large gardens and grounds of the villas faded into the rough knobbly whin-dotted fields of small whitewashed farms. Here other cattle lowed to them out of the gloom, in greeting. They were on high ground, now, on the upper flanks of that hog's-back of land that reaches down between the valley of the River Leven, running out of Loch Lomond, on the east, and the long arm of Gare Loch, on the west. Away down on their right, the street lights of Alexandria twinkled.

They followed a narrow spinal road now, pointing north-west, that served the scattered farms and smallholdings. They were moving through the dripping darkness of a large wood of stunted trees, when Roddie called two or three of the men forward. With these he formed a barrier across the roadway. With a stone dyke restraining them on the right, the cattle were forced to turn left-handed, into an almost unseen entry amongst the trees. In there they were driven, the leaders, heads going down to nibble at the long grass, being jostled on by the press at the rear. But soon they could go no further forward, being confronted by solid rock. Milling round, the beasts found ferny rock on every side, save directly behind. Safely coralled in a disused quarry, they snorted and pushed and tried to forage.

Behind them, the lorry and the van drove in, blocking the entrance. Owing to a bend in the track, they would be unseen from the road. The vanman, in the rear, turned off his light altogether, but Jakey, switching on his headlamps for the first time since leaving Levenbank, flooded that rocky hollow with yellow radiance, turning it into a devil's beef-tub indeed, in which the whites of alarmed eyes gleamed, dark bodies stirred and eddied, and from which steam rose into the night.

"This is where we get *right* crackin'!" Rod Macgregor shouted. "Jamie—Jamie Robb! Come on, an' dae your stuff!"

If Roderick Macgregor seemed to enjoy what followed, it is to be doubted if all of his followers did, however hard they tried to make it seem so. Certainly Adrian Hope did not.

Jamie Robb, a stocky red-faced fellow, very unlike his brother, came out into the glare of the lights, very much the butcher in shirt-sleeves and blue-and-white striped overall. He said that things wouldn't do just as they were—they'd have the whole herd crazy with fright in no time. But he had noticed, as Jakey's headlights had swung round on coming in, that there was a much smaller working to the right, a sort of bay to the main quarry. They could try that. Roddie Roy, with an electric torch, clambered over rubble and through nettles and elderbushes, to survey it, and to announce that it seemed just the job. Jakey was ordered to manoeuvre his lorry so that its light shone into this lesser hollow, while Jamie Robb, selecting a bullock, proceeded thereto, in lordly fashion, followed by three herdsmen more or less propelling the unfortunate victim.

The elders and the bank of rubble screened them from the sight of the rest of the beasts. Without a word, Adrian handed Robb his Army Browning .45. The butcher examined it, twiddled the safety-catch with his thumb, nodded, placed the pistol behind the bullock's twitching ear, and pressed the trigger.

The bang of the report was not so loud as Adrian, at least,

had been prepared for. The brute grunted, shuddered, stood swaying for a moment, and then pitched heavily, all but knocking over one of its gaping drovers. And there it lay, jerking its legs, as the blood oozed out from nostrils and mouth.

Robb and Macgregor spared the sacrifice barely a glance. They hurried up through the elders, to peer over at the herd. The cattle did not seem to be much affected by the noise of the shot. The men guarding them assured that the report had sounded quite muffled in there. And any breeze there was, being from the south-west, would tend to blow the smell of blood in the other direction. Satisfied, they moved back into the smaller hollow.

"The damn brute's no' deid!" a fascinated drover declared, pointing. "See—it's movin'."

"It's deid, right enough," Robb asserted scornfully. "Yon's jist nerves. Awa' an' fetch us anither."

And so in the same casual fashion, another bullock met its fate. As it fell, Jamie handed the pistol to Macgregor. "Here— you cairry on," he said. "I'll bleed them."

Thus, while Robb bled the still-quivering carcases, and showed others how to do it, Adrian included, Roddie Roy went on with the slaughter. Eight more of those hundred and eleven bullocks, he killed, before the ammunition ran out. That was the entire stock that Hope had brought back with him from the War; he had tried to buy more, but had found it impossible without a Firearms Certificate—which, of course, his now-illicit Browning did not carry. Jamie Robb was elaborating on some bloodthirsty way of killing cattle with a knife, when Adrian cried a halt, pointing out that ten carcases was quite as much as they could handle, anyway—possibly overmuch. Almost reluctantly, Roddie Roy agreed that that was so.

Anyway, the cattle in the main quarry were becoming restive; probably the scent of blood was reaching them now. Time they were off; they had a long way to go. Roddie detailed Alicky and three others to the job. They had to drive them just as far as they could, before daylight, up into the hills, the real hills, and there wander them. It was only half-past one. They had four hours—they ought to be able to get them a fair distance, by then, seven or eight miles at least. That should take them up above Glen Fruin, around Ben Avich. Off with them, then—and see and not lose themselves in the hills, in the dark!

So twelve men and ten dead bullocks remained in that quarry, twelve busy men—or eleven, rather, for one was kept on guard over at the road, just in case somebody should come along the lonely highway, notice the reflection of Jakey's headlights on the trees, and decide to investigate; an unlikely event, there and then. Under Jamie Robb's expert guidance and blistering tongue, with the selection of instruments that had come in the Co-operative van, they skinned and flayed and cut and hacked and sawed. It was not an edifying performance, it was not a pleasurable one, it was not even an economic one, and the butcher's bullet head was frequently ashake over the spoiling of prime joints and the sad mangling of choice cuts and portions. There were a hundred and one things wrong, of course—the carcases were not thoroughly bled, they should have hung uncut for days, the meat should not have been cut hot, parts were anything but traditionally disjointed, and collops and cutlets of totally unrecognisable proportions were legion. But for all that, there was little real waste. The tongues were cut out of the heads, the tails were detached, unskinned, the liver and kidneys, even the sweetbreads, were salvaged from the steaming entrails.

For two solid hours they wrought grimly, by the light of the headlamps, in a welter and stench of blood and unpleasantness, before Adrian thrust his watch at Macgregor, and the big man gave the word to stop. Any further cutting-up must be done later. So all the variously sized and shaped haunches and joints and sides and lumps of meat were carried laboriously to the waiting vehicles—and an alarmingly great pile they made; infinitely more than had been visualised—the heads and hooves and hides rolled up in bundles and likewise stowed, a weighty item in themselves, and the enormous mass of entrails dumped in holes and excavations in the quarry, and rubble and soil scraped down over it. All this took over half an hour, for they were dealing literally with tons of slippery unhandy material. It was after four before they were finished, and they piled themselves on to the overburdened transport, crushing into the cabs and on the running-boards, in an evil-smelling, bloodstained huddle—for there was no room left for passengers elsewhere. Donald Lamont had the grace to thank Adrian and his Maker that they had stopped killing when they did.

Groaning with the weight, the two vehicles backed out of their sanctuary on to the road, and turning south-east again, headed back towards Dumbarton and the city.

Apart from a brief stop, early on, where a bridge crossed a small tributary of the Leven, for a superficial washing of gory hands and arms, they had a clear run in, through silent suburbs and empty rain-washed streets. If an odd heavy-eyed police-man, deliberately pacing or standing at a corner, turned to consider them reflectively, it was undoubtedly for want of anything better to look at. Nothing held them up, not even the foolishly-blinking traffic-lights.

Their first call was down a narrow lane at Dalmuir, where they stopped at the dark entrance-gateway of the Northern Tanneries Limited. Here, the bundled heads, hooves, and hides were dumped, in an unappetising heap at the principal office door, embellished with a scrap of paper on which was scrawled A PRESENT FROM ROD ROY. YOU TAN THEM—WE'LL TAN WESTMINSTER!

They lurched on.

Nearing their own neighbourhood of the Bridegate, Jakey, leading, turned off to the left, into the wilderness of side streets, eventually arriving at a road flanked by a long barrier of high corrugated-iron uprights, along which they drove slowly, to stop at a gateway, on which was painted boldly ST. BRIDES FOOTBALL CLUB. STAND ONLY.

Here, Art M'Vey climbed down, reaching for a key. Art was St. Bride's centre-half, a member of the Committee, and some-thing of a hero on occasion. Unlocking the side-door, he passed within, and soon had the wide double gates standing open. Jakey drove in, followed by the van, and the gates were shut.

"Five past five," Adrian reported. "We're late."

"We're daein' fine," Macgregor asserted. "C'mon."

The night was paling, now; had it not been for the rain, it

would have been almost light. "We'll have to be pretty smart, here, or the light will catch us," Hope warned.

The big fellow grinned. "Dinna' you fash your heid, Major—we'll be smert, a'right. Awa' hame if you're scare't!"

They drove to the back of the high corrugated-iron grandstand, where M'Vey, fumbling for another key that lay on a hidden ledge, opened a door into a dark storeroom, under the tiers of seats. "In here wi' it, boys," he said. "Plentys o' room. See an' no' fall ower yon gear."

And so, a shade wearily, the beef was transferred from the vehicles, into the dark interior of the grandstand. They made a great heap of it just inside the door, first, so that they could get the door shut, and dare switch on the light. Thereafter, it was all laid out in rows on the ladders, benches, poles, posts, and the like, with which the store was filled. But not quite all of it, of course; some small quantity of the choicest cuts remained in the lorry and the van.

By just turning half-past five, they were done. As they locked the door under the stand behind them, it was getting alarmingly light. Art, sent ahead to the main gates to scout, reported all-clear; fortunately only the brick walls of a brewery were opposite. They drove out into the street, with at least one heartfelt sigh of relief, and M'Vey jumped aboard.

"Attaboy!" he cried. "Chops for breakfast!"

"No' likely!" Roddie Roy scoffed. "Tough as an auld boot. Kidneys for me."

"Whoopee!"

Jamie Robb's van, with its passengers, swerved off and left them, two streets on. Jakey soon was dropping people at road-ends, each with his newspapered parcel of meat. As yet there were no walkers on the wet pavements, though here and there an early plume of smoke curled up from a chimney-stack.

With all the laden Gregorach deposited, except Roddie and Adrian, Jakey swung along Argyle Street, heading for the very centre of the city. Into Queen Street and George Square they turned, and halted. Hope pointed to a handsome building, with lights shining from its windows.

"That's it—with the lights," he said. "Sorry to push the dirty work on to you, Reid—but I might be recognised there,

55

and Roddie here would be an eyeful, anywhere. Just dump it inside the door. If there's anybody about the vestibule, just say it's for Mr. Duncanson. . . ."

"Fine ham an' haddy, that!" Jakey grumbled. "What aboot me?" But he got out just the same, taking the bulky brown-paper parcel with him. "Jings—whatna weight! You gi'ein' him a hale coo?"

"Get crackin'," Macgregor mentioned.

Thus adjured, Jakey slouched along with his load, turned in at the impressive portals of The Press Association's premises, deposited his burden, inscribed: *Archibald Duncanson Esq.*— HANG WELL, OR BE HANGED! on the marble-inlaid vestibule floor, and slouched out again, unchallenged.

"No' a cheep oot o' *them*!" he reported, scornfully climbing back into the cab. "A' asleep, if y'ask me." And, out of some obscure reasoning of his own, viciously: "Bluidy ca*pit*alists!"

"Sure," Roddie Roy agreed. "Get crackin'."

"*Glasgow Chronicle* Office, Hope Street," Adrian directed. "Then home."

"I'd hope so, tae!" Jakey cried. "Jings—d'you ken I've to be on the job in twa 'oors, wi' this bluidy lorry a' cleaned up?" And for once, the monotonous and inevitable adjective was accurately descriptive.

Outside the *Chronicle* offices, the same performance was enacted, only this time Jakey had Mr. Jack Findlay's parcel taken from him by a yawning porter, much as though it had been the laundry. All exceedingly humdrum and anticlimactic. His last task was to drop his two passengers at the sombre entrance to Macharg Street—Adrian was officially away for the weekend, as far as his own landlady was concerned, and Roddie's Mrs. Munro was easy-going and already knew him well.

"See you at the match," Macgregor called, to their departing driver.

Endeavouring to cover the nakedness of his unwieldy burden with a quite inadequate piece of sodden and torn newspaper, Hope yawned. "D'you think Mrs. Munro will ever be able to use all this meat?" he wondered, beginning wearily to climb the stairs.

56

"You jist watch her!" Roddie assured. "An' you an' me'll help her oot, b'Goad!"

"Not me," the other demurred. "I don't think I'll ever look a piece of beef in the face again!"

VI

THREE hours' sleep in an almost seatless armchair, and Adrian was awakened by Mrs. Munro with the breakfast of porridge and fried kidneys. The sight and smell of the latter all but put him off the former, but with an effort he got the porridge over. Rod Macgregor arrived almost simultaneously—he had been out buying a couple of morning newspapers. For the first time, the *Glasgow Chronicle* found its way into 17, Macharg Street, where the *Daily Record* and the *People's Journal* had hitherto reigned supreme. But their night's activities, of course, were too recent to have got into the morning papers, much to Roddie Roy's disgust. He scanned every column, while he wolfed enormous quantities of provender, but in vain. Hope was subjected to certain pithy observations on his friends of the Press.

Ferguson's yard was having to do without one of its riveters today, and by nine-thirty they were on the move again. Walking the Saturday morning streets, Adrian found himself wondering if Scotland was a hard taskmistress. The rain had stopped, but seemed as though it might start again at any moment. Glasgow looked very grey.

Crossing a network of side streets, where ash-buckets were being emptied, children played screamingly, and radios and gramophones competed from open windows, they came eventually to St. Bride's Football Ground. Avoiding this time that side wherein lay the main entrance, they moved round to the back, where it was bordered by the sad trees and beaten earth of Murray Road Park, suitably deserted at that hour. Counting along the corrugated-iron panels of the lofty palisade, Roddie reached seventeen, eighteen, and stopped. Then, glancing about him swiftly, to ensure that they were unobserved, he stooped, gripped the foot of the iron, and pulled it to one side. It swung loose from a central rivet, creating a sufficient gap, into which the big man dived with surprising agility, and disappeared. Adrian followed, and the panel was replaced. It was as good a way as any for getting into a football-ground without the drawback of paying for admission.

Keeping under cover of the inside of the fence, they skirted the empty expanse, and made their way round to the stand. They found the key in the door, and half a dozen or so members of the gang already there, including two or three who had not been present during the night's high jinks. Laurie Martin worked on the night-shift at a gasworks, and Frankie Sinclair was a member of a dance-band.

While the business of cutting and sawing up the meat into manageable proportions proceeded, and newcomers drifted in in ones and twos, Rod Macgregor gave them their instructions—or, rather, it might be more accurate to say, his version of Adrian's instructions. They were to go for the fish-queues, not the butchers. They were not to get involved in any arguments—say it was a present from the Hielands, and leave it at that. No talk, no answering questions, and any refusals to be accepted at once. And after the first basketful of supplies that they took with them, they weren't to come back here for more. There would be fruit-barrows at the corners of Bridegate and Templar Street, Cranstonhill and Veitch Street, and the end of the Yorkstoun Road, where they could refill their baskets—the owners had agreed to act as depots, at the price of a substantial haunch each. Don't go over the same district twice. No trying to make a bob on the side. And watch out for the police, for any favour!

Thereafter, the emissaries of good-will and prime beef slipped out one by one, mainly not with genuine baskets at all, but with much less conspicuous pasteboard cartons under their arms, as containers. Each carried a good stone of meat, wrapped in newspaper, some more. But they seemed to make precious little impression on the total pile, for all that.

Only Macgregor, Donald Lamont, and Adrian remained behind in the stand, cutting and slicing and hacking.

Art M'Vey turned up presently, to announce that Baldie O'Keefe and his billposter's van had arrived, out in the road. Were they ready? Would he let him in?

They weren't really ready, of course, but Roddie ordered

admittance. So the main gate was opened, the van beckoned down from a street corner, and driven in, and the gate shut. And while Baldie and his youthful assistant pasted up a vast and colourful poster on the flat back of the grandstand, to the effect that Argentino Beef-Extract would make a New Man of You, the others bundled large quantities of the raw material thereof into his van, amongst the paper and the paste-pails, for delivery to the fruit-barrows and the waiting distributors. Consistently enough, Baldie O'Keefe placed his poster where it would comfortably cover the Stick No Bills notice.

So that Saturday forenoon, in sundry favoured if no longer fashionable localities around the north-central area of Glasgow, surprised housewives in many a fish-shop queue, and elsewhere, had bloodstained newspaper parcels thrust upon them by embarrassed young men, who, assuring them that it was a present frae the Hielands—and devil the bit of horse about it—very promptly made off. Certain others, whole closes of them at a time, found rough packages of meat on their door-steps, to their equal astonishment and very natural suspicion. Great was the argument, the postulation, and the wagging of tongues. Extraordinary were the explanations propounded. No great proportion of that meat found its way into the pot, that day.

The noon editions of Saturday evening papers, in Glasgow as in other parts, tend to cater for a holiday-conscious clientele, largely bound for an afternoon's sport. News is a secondary consideration. This situation, taken in conjunction with the fact that, in the early hours of the previous morning, while butchery had been in progress above Alexandria, the current international conference of Foreign Ministers had actually reached agreement on one of the items of its agenda, must be held to account for the unanimous lack of interest on the part of the Scottish Press on what was going on at its very doorstep. At least, so Adrian Hope accounted for it, if with only moderate conviction.

At the foot of a column devoted to Next Week's Films, the *Evening Times*, under the heading CATTLE REMOVED, had allowed almost an inch of valuable space to report the unauthorised removal of a number of graded cattle, the property of the Ministry of Food, from Levenbank Goods Station. Investigation, it added, was proceeding. The *Evening Gazette* was rather less dramatically precipitate. It contented itself with announcing, under Dumbarton Brevities, the disappearance of certain bullocks from a goods-train at Levenbank the previous night. That was all, save for the ultimate and third line of type which, unaccountably at first, ended with a reference to the Old Kirk's forthcoming sale-of-work. A little research established the fact that this line had undoubtedly got detached from a paragraph two places above.

"Well, I'm damned an' coopered!" Rod Macgregor exploded. "The baistards! That your bluidy Press? Save us a'— let's get oot o' here."

That was where Adrian started to explain, as has been mentioned. It took him all the way back, from Mike Doolan's to St. Bride's F.C. ground, to do it.

That Saturday afternoon was a weariness. Indubitably the light seemed to have gone out of things, for most of them, if not all. The Press couldn't be blamed entirely. Unquestionably, the unending cutting-up of vast quantities of raw meat tends to pall on the uninitiated, in time. Also, the fact that the rest of Glasgow was enjoying itself in its own fashion—a large proportion of it, it seemed, directly above and around themselves—had its effect; the Ginger Boys, as a gang, were of course perfervid supporters of St. Bride's F.C., and the present situation a doubly galling one, with Yoker United requiring to be pulled down a peg. That they were tired, too, after a sleepless night, may have had something to do with it.

They were all there, under the grandstand—even Alicky Shand and his three colleagues, only recently returned by bus from Loch Lomondside, after an epic of droving that they could not, unfortunately, get any of the others to listen to. Art M'Vey was absent, of course, out on the field, but otherwise it was a full house. Even Jamie Robb, who as a family-man was not really a member of the gang at all, was there, with knife and steel. It was to be hoped that no official of the St. Bride's F.C. was likely to discover a crying need for any of the posts, planks, poles, and suchlike, deposited in that storeroom, in mid-game.

At half-time, with the bulk of the meat divided up, and wrapped into innumerable newspaper parcels, one or two of the company slipped out to check-up on the situation. They came back, gloomily, to report Yoker leading three-one, a record crowd, and the rain started again. Also, that there were a couple of policemen standing just in from the main gates.

At nearly full-time, the police were still there. The meat was practically all cut and bundled—except for the huge pile of bones, which were put into sacks, left, and were to be collected by Jakey at night, and dumped at the Duncrub Bone-meal factory. Consulting Adrian's watch, Roddie Roy ordered two of his henchmen to sally forth, pick a judiciously-placed quarrel with some of the Yoker supporters—always a simple matter— and draw off those policemen. They'd five minutes. See and get a good rammy started—and then, if they could, get out of it and come back for their beef. Undoubtedly the Macgregor would have liked to have gone, himself. Nothing loth, the two warriors went.

The men were all lined-up, twenty-one of them, and the moment the full-time whistle blew, they were ready, grasping their boxes of parcels under their arms. Out into the streaming crowds they hurried, mingled, and were promptly swallowed up. One minute there was a score of them, the next, none, engulfed entirely.

Fighting their way back against the tide was not so easy, even though their hands now were empty. Replenishing, with more packages, was only the work of a moment, and they were out again. It was dead easy. If one of the hurrying football-fans would not accept their offering, the next did. The great throng offered almost complete anonymity. No bother. And what's half a dozen policemen in a crowd of ten thousand? Long before the last triumphant Yokerite and the last resentfully-disputatious disciple of St. Bride had passed through the corrugated-iron gateways, the store beneath the grandstand was empty, of all but the sacks of bones. Apart from Jakey's nocturnal date with the said relics, Operation Beef was completed.

The coloured editions of the Press that night informed that Yoker United had beaten St. Bride's F.C. five-three, amongst other news of like import, but not a bullock, not so much as a cutlet of beef, was mentioned.

The Sunday papers were quite as disappointing as the Saturday ones—but then, of course, with two exceptions, they all emanated, spiritually if not materially, from south of the Border. One of the exceptions published a brief paragraph on the unauthorised removal of cattle from Levenbank, without comment other than the significant adjective "mysterious". As a Sunday paper, it owed its customers that, perhaps.

Adrian was on his rather depressed way to his classes the next morning, when the placard caught his eye—just chalk on a blackboard, but noteworthy enough under the highly orthodox auspices of the *Glasgow Herald*. AMAZING OUTBREAK OF CATTLE-STEALING—CATTLE TRAIN RAIDED. He hurried within, to get tuppence worth of the *Herald*.

But on the newsagent's counter, a veritable battery of outsize type assailed his startled eyes, in which ROB ROY, RAIDERS, REIVERS, CATERANS, and CATTLE stood out, from half a dozen substantial organs of public enlightenment. Swallowing hard, his *sang-froid* laid on heavily indeed, he collected a sample of everything in stock, and fled the scene.

The Press, after all, had spread itself, in its own time; headlines in most papers, prominence in all. It would be safe to say that not even the most casual reader of a morning newspaper could remain unaware that a great herd of cattle, variously numbered from two to five hundred head, had been spirited away by somebody calling himself Rod Roy Macgregor, that quite a substantial proportion of the population of Glasgow had received free dinners as a result, that certain tanneries and suchlike had been presented with the hides and bones, and that the police, at the request of the Ministry of Food, were investigating.

Adrian decided to skip first period's blood circulation, in the interests of current affairs, and repaired forthwith to the University Library.

Like the headlines, the reports varied greatly. While one paper stressed the actual stealing of the cattle, describing the station layout, the circumstances involved, and giving the personal accounts of sundry singularly uninformed railwaymen, another concentrated on the distribution of the meat, quoting housewives, football fans, and fishmongers as to their experiences. Comment ranged wide, from speculation as to the identity of the perpetrators, the numbers involved, and possible reasons for the astonishing performance, to hypothetical political implications, fat-stock prices, and historical notes on Rob Roy Macgregor. Some noted an anti-London bias in the scrawled statements, others descried the Anti-Partition campaign and the hidden hand of the I.R.A.

There were even one or two leaders, and leaderettes. The *Glasgow Courier* was severe, justly pointing out that, however bold and picturesque, this peculiar exploit was a serious criminal offence, and the culprits liable to very severe penalties. The *Scotsman* was dryly humorous and detached—as it could afford to be, at fifty miles distance—remarking that if this sort of thing continued, the name of Macgregor would probably have to be proscribed again. The *Sentinel* was practical, reminding its readers that new-killed beef is the tenderer of a few days' hanging, while the *Echo* suggested that this could not have happened under a Conservative administration, and that Mr. Macgregor should be elected an honorary Empire Crusader. Only the *Chronicle* went deeper, as was perhaps natural. Under the heading, DOWN TO THE BONE, it wrote:

> The astonishing news that a train-load of Scots cattle has been appropriated by somebody calling himself Rod Roy Macgregor, and thereafter distributed free-gratis in the form of cutlets and chops, should give food for thought to all Scots, even if the actual meat only went to the working-folk of Glasgow. The incident undoubtedly calls for digestion on the part of the Government, also. Leaving apart side issues, either romantic or legalistic, certain facts about this affair should be noted. First, the cattle taken were not the property of individuals, but of the Ministry of Food, which had bought them throughout the West Highland area, for transport south of the Border. These beef-shipments are a regular, not to say monotonous feature of the Ministry's activities, while Scotland, a cattle-producing country which could feed itself twice over

with fresh beef, is fed microscopically on frozen imported meat—even the cattle-growers themselves. Then, no wastage of the products appears to have occurred: the skins, hooves even, having been presented to a tannery, and the bones to a bone-meal factory. As far as is known, no payment has been exacted from any of the recipients of this largesse, which, taking into account the amount of organisation required to dispose of so large a booty, and the numbers of men necessarily involved, seems to indicate a very real concern with principles, and a disregard for any sordid gain. The distribution was inconspicuous enough not to attract any public fuss or outcry in the densely populated parts of the city; therefore, it must be assumed that the distributors were of the people themselves.

Taken in conjunction, these facts would seem to indicate something new in Scotland, the uprising of a new spirit—or perhaps, the resurgence of an old one, long dormant—which is prepared to act to bridge the yawning abyss of frustration and *ennui* in which the country finds itself today. Whether such demonstrations and activities are to be encouraged, is for the people of Scotland to say, not for us.

The verdict of the people will be awaited with interest. And possibly with more than interest, in Westminster.

Definitely, Jack Findlay had earned his haunch.

Adrian Hope found the thought of medical classes intolerable. For the first time in his life, he found himself assailed by an urge to write to the papers. Flinging out of the Library, he boarded a tram that would take him to Waterloo Street Bus Station. He would write to them on the heather above Loch Lomond.

VII

IT all made a notable nine-days' wonder. The problem was to ensure that it made something more than just that. Few of the Gregorach were optimistic enough to imagine that Scotland's deeply-sleeping spirit was likely to be awakened by anything so temporary by way of a jag.

It was to this intent that Adrian wrote his letter to the newspapers. Up there, on a birch and heather knoll high above the blue waters of the loch, he compiled it—or rather, them, for though the wording was the same in each, he penned many copies, one for each major publication. He wrote, eventually:

I, RODERICK ROY MACGREGOR, declare:

That I did not kill a few bullocks, thinking thereby to make any worthwhile contribution to the fresh-meat starvation of the Scots people. I made only a gesture. I shall make others.

That there are a host of worse evils, with which Scotland is bedevilled today. If the country is not to be strangled by them, she must strangle *them*. Fight.

That Scotland has forgotten how to fight. If I have to, I will show her how, again.

That we make no mistake, our fight is not against the English. It is against a system of government, a soul-destroying, smothering bureaucracy, a Thou Shalt Not administration, that is utterly foreign to us, damning and damnable.

That I do not hate the English. I love the English. They are as ill-used and misgoverned as we are. Let them rise also, and smite the horde of third-rate busybodies that holds them down—them and us.

E'en Do, And Spare Nocht, is the Macgregor motto. I offer it to you all.

LOCH LOMONDSIDE,
20TH MAY.

That was by no means his first attempt, of course. Indeed, he bit a lot of pen and crumpled a lot of notepaper, before he satisfied himself that this was the sort of letter that his Rod Roy Macgregor, his conception of the character that he was forging, would write—in the unlikely assumption of his writing to the papers at all. His first effort was an infinitely more scholarly and long-winded exposition of aims and objects, that in its meticulous, moderate, and reasoned phraseology had about as much relation to the spirit of Rob Roy about it, as a Government White Paper to The Declaration of Independence. It was all very difficult.

He wandered back towards Balloch by way of the lower reaches of Glen Fruin, but saw no signs of any of their surplus cattle thereabouts. Back in Glasgow, he posted his batch of letters at Buchanan Street Post Office.

That evening, in the private room of Mike Doolan's Bar, the Press reports were conned, dissected, and debated, by an excited and on the whole approving company. There were complaints, of course. Jakey Reid considered that insufficient comment had been made on the feats of transport involved; Alicky Shand reckoned that newspapermen must be unable to count, or they would have realised that the great majority of the bullocks remained to be accounted for, and that the droving and hiding-away of such might well have been considered to be the most impressive part of the whole performance; Sandy Robb, with commendable family loyalty, claimed that the very expert butchery was really the kingpin of the thing, and the sooner it was recognised, the better. But, generally, the Gregorach were considerably impressed. Roddie Roy and Donald Lamont alone had noted the significance of the *Chronicle* leader, the latter with satisfaction, the former with his innate restless questioning and sense of challenge.

"Uh-huh. Aye, well. Fine," he declared, "but what noo? Where do we go frae here? We've got to get crackin' on this— nae guid pattin' oorselves on the back. I'm a riveter—you've got to hammer in a rivet when it's red-hot. We've got to keep goin' with this."

"Right," Adrian agreed. "But give us a chance. Give us time." He showed him his letter to the papers. "This ought to clear up some misconceptions," he said.

The big man, though he scanned the draft of the letter in silence, was far from silent when he got to the end of it.

"Hell!" he roared, with one of his sudden quivering gusts of anger, banging down his vast fist on the table and setting the beer slopping. "So Roderick Roy Macgregor says a' this, does he? Hoo d'you ken that? Whae tell't *you* to write my letters for me?"

Hope looked upset. "I'm sorry. I'd no idea . . . it never occurred to me that you'd feel that way about it. I wasn't writing personally at all—just in the name of us all, the whole gang. . . ."

"Look," the other said, "there's jist the one Roderick Macgregor, an' that's me, see. Naebody else. An' I'll write my ain letters. You got that, Mister?"

Adrian noted that Mister, again. "Very well. I'll remember. But you approve of the contents of the letter, I hope? Something of the sort was needed."

"I'm no' so sure that I dae. Whae tell't you I loved the English!"

Hope smiled. "That is something of a figure of speech. We've got to avoid any suggestion that we've any bias against the English. It's the London Government we're up against, not the people of England, who have almost as much to put up with as we have—that, and the stultifying influence of our own St. Andrews House! That's true, isn't it?"

"Och, aye—maybe. But you needna' ha'e said anythin' aboot lovin' them!" the offended giant returned. Undoubtedly, that was his major complaint.

"I apologise," Adrian assured gravely. "I'll see that it doesn't occur again."

"Aye. You better no'." Roddie Roy nodded. "Noo—what aboot this whisky ploy . . . ?"

"M'mmm. Well, I thought we might work it this way. . . ."

Helen Burnet was waiting for Adrian as he came away from his last class, the following evening. She was dressed in something fresh, summery, and very feminine, and made a quite delightful picture to come upon in a dull place after extremely dull studies. All the same, the man greeted her with only moderate fervour as they approached, his smile somewhat diffident.

Not so the girl. She was almost as gay as her appearance.

"Stranger!" she cried. "Fancy meeting you here! This is a surprise, isn't it?"

"Is it, Helen?" he wondered, cautiously.

"Well, isn't it? I mean, the chances of finding you round about the University, these days, are getting remote, aren't they! One must grasp such opportunities as turn up, with both hands, especially if you are a humdrum stay-at-home sort of creature, like me. I'm sure you agree, Adrian? You know, I've almost been tempted to set out on a tour of the Bridegate." She paused. "Or even of the Dumbarton area!"

Swiftly he glanced at her. "Indeed!" he said.

"Yes." She tucked a hand within his arm. "How about taking me somewhere and giving me a cup of tea?" she suggested. "My turn to pay, actually."

"M'mmm. I'm afraid I've got an engagement this evening, Helen. . . ."

On a quick breath she seemed about to say something, but changed her mind, and nodded, instead. "I see," she said. "Well, what about having just a short stroll in the park? You can spare me that, can you?" There was no reproach there, just hopeful enquiry.

Uncomfortably, the man turned to her. "Of course. Delighted." If he sometimes had a desire to hurt this girl, he very quickly suffered remorse. "You are looking very charming, Helen." He added, as a slightly strained afterthought. "But you are always that, of course."

"How nice of you to notice," she acknowledged, all sunshine. "Now—tell me all about it, Adrian."

"All about what, m'dear?"

"What you've been doing. You've been very busy, haven't you?"

"Have I?"

"Adrian, my pet," she chided, "don't prevaricate. Even women read the papers, you know. And I can make two and two into four."

"I see," was all that he found to say to her, he who was by no means ineloquent.

"That book," she went on, "the one you had with you that night, about a month ago—the night I was so 'lynx-eyed'. I saw it was about Rob Roy Macgregor!"

"Ah," he said.

"Yes. And you told me, remember—perhaps in an unguarded moment—that you had hoped to do something to waken up Scotland . . . to touch off a spark, I think you said. Am I to assume that all this Rob Roy business in the papers, so soon after, is just a pure coincidence?"

"No," he said, shaking his head, slowly. "I'm not suggesting that you assume that."

"Then you confess that you are mixed up in all this affair?"

"Confess is hardly the word that I would use, perhaps," the man protested, mildly.

Her hand, resting on his sleeve, gripped his arm. "Adrian," she said, urgently. "You've got to stop this. You've got to get out of this, this crazy stunt, at once. Before it's too late. You must!"

"You disapprove, do you?"

"Disapprove! Good Heavens—it's not a matter of approval or disapproval. If you go on with it, this folly will be the ruination of you. Don't you see that? Oh, Adrian—don't you see it?"

"Shall we say that I remain to be convinced?" he answered her, gently.

She shook her nut-brown head. "Listen to me," she pleaded. "What you are attempting is absolutely impossible. You won't—you *can't*, get away with it. It's crazy, and it's wrong. The *Herald* said it was criminal, and so it is. And that means, if you're caught, you'll go to prison!"

"If . . . ! And prison isn't so bad. I've been in prison before, remember—and I imagine our prisons will be much more comfortable!"

"Oh, don't be stupid, Adrian! Please be serious. Being a prisoner of war, and a—a convict, are mighty different things. And you come out of the one something of a hero—out of the other an outcast, a ruined man."

"I could still take that croft," the man mentioned, lightly. "And they haven't caught me yet, you know."

"But they *will*! They're bound to. If I can find out, others can, surely. The police can."

"But you were in rather a privileged position, weren't you?" Adrian pointed out. "I mean, it isn't everybody in whom I confide—nor everybody who knows about that book."

"But some others do."

"For instance . . . ?"

"There's the hat-check man, at the Grand Metropole. And the people at that pub where you left it. And my father knows about it, too."

"Damnation—your father! How on earth . . . ? Lord—I never thought *you* would go talking. . . ."

"And I didn't!" she cried, her self-control less in evidence than formerly. "But after that night, I wanted to see what was in that book, that you were so keen on. So I asked Daddy to get it for me, out of the 'Varsity Library. When he asked me why, I told him that you seemed to be very interested in it. . . . I wasn't to know, then . . . how could I have any idea . . . ?"

"And you think he linked it up, when the news broke?"

"Well . . . yes. He mentioned you, at any rate. And you were absent from the visit to the Infirmary on Saturday morning, he said, and from his class on Monday. John Caird, in the Library, was asking, too, he said . . ."

"Great Heavens! Caird, too! That gossiping old fool! Even your father might have had more sense than to go talking it over with him!"

"I should say, if anyone should have had more sense it was you, Adrian! Anything more senseless than your whole performance would be hard to imagine. And if you don't bring it to a stop pretty quickly . . ."

"*You* will, eh?" That was snapped out. "In fact, it looks as though you might have started the process of stopping me, already, you and your father between you!"

"Adrian, are you suggesting . . . ?"

"Only that in future, you won't find quite so much discussion of my private affairs necessary!"

"I see. Believe me, *no* discussion of your affairs will be necessary, after this, as far as I'm concerned! I'm sorry it's come to this, Adrian—but you leave me no alternative. And I warned you, you'll remember. Goodbye!"

Gravely, almost pensively, he looked at her, some part of his mind noting even then that the flush of anger on her face, so unusual with that young woman, only enhanced her loveliness. "I think *au revoir*, again, might meet the case," he suggested.

"I think not," she assured, briefly. "Goodbye."

"I will see you on to a tram. . . ."

"I would infinitely prefer that you didn't."

"Very well, Helen." He watched her go, set-faced.

The next morning's Press was something of a shock to Adrian Hope. Having bought a selection of papers, to see if they had printed his letter, he found the correspondence columns full of letters from Rod Roy Macgregors, Rodericks, Rob Roys, even Wee Macgreegors. It was amazing. Adrian's first thought was that all the gang had been writing on their own, but a brief perusal of the contents disposed of that theory. All the wags, cranks, opportunists, and axe-grinders in the country seemed to have seized their pens and dashed into print under the glorious pseudonym of Rod Roy Macgregor. Their styles and themes were legion, and their motives varied. While the majority, probably, were concerned with humour and the refined art of leg-pulling, many were more seriously intended, ranging from special pleading for a variety of objects and organisations, to forecasts of terrible things to come, challenges, and even threats. One Roderick Roy urged an immediate removal of the Stone of Destiny from where it was to somewhere else, a second asserted that the Highlands were about to declare themselves an independent state with Oban as the Capital, while a third temporary member of Clan Alpine informed that he proposed to blow up Edinburgh's St. Andrew's House forthwith. In all this flood of correspondence, Adrian's own letter had tended to get submerged. In only two papers had it managed to gain a toe-hold—not including, strangely enough, the *Glasgow Chronicle*. However, that pillar of journalism appended a footnote to its Letters to the Editor column, to the effect that, owing to the unprecedented number of letters it was receiving on the subject, indicative of wide-spread public reaction and feeling, it intended to devote an entire page on the morrow and the day following, to their publication. It added that correspondents could co-operate by keeping their letters brief, and that offerings of humane-killers, fiery crosses, high-explosives, etc., should not be sent to the *Chronicle* offices.

In his survey, Adrian came across certain other letters, differently subscribed, having some bearing on their activities, in one or two of the papers. Some were from animal-lovers, protesting at the wanton slaughter of dumb creatures, and invoking the S.P.C.A., or propounding the benefits of vege-tarianism; others from egalitarians, demanding to know why their districts of Glasgow had been overlooked and slighted in the distribution of free beef. One, only, struck Hope as being significant. It was from somebody signing himself Highland Farmer, and giving no address, requesting advice as to what he ought to do with a certain black bullock that had suddenly and unaccountably made its appearance in his herd. Oddly enough, he added, by way of postscript, two or three of his neighbours happened to find themselves in the same position.

The spirit of Scotland might not yet be wakened, Adrian decided, but it certainly seemed to be talking in its sleep.

At Mike Doolan's, that evening, a certain amount of ques-tioning revealed, from Alicky Shand and his three colleagues, that they had indeed improved on their Friday night instruc-tions to wander the surplus cattle somewhere in the hills west of Loch Lomond—hadn't they been trying to tell them the story of it, half a dozen times? They had, with praiseworthy energy and initiative, dropped one or two of the beasts off at every farm and smallholding and establishment they had passed, disposing thereby of more than half their herd. To Adrian's complaint that this was not what had been planned, and that now they'd have to write-off the whole lot as a dead loss, Alicky protested that weren't they supposed to be acting like Rob Roy, hadn't he given them a lecture on Rob Roy describing how he'd taken cattle from the rich and given them to the poor—and weren't the Government rich enough, and these crofters and bits of farmers poor enough? Well, then! And who wanted any more of that beef-cutting-up business, anyway? All with appropriate adjectival embellishment.

It was while Adrian was attempting to counter, not without difficulty, these cogent arguments, that Roddie Roy arrived, late. He took the centre of the stage promptly, as by right, and without any shilly-shallying. With the door of the private room slammed behind him, he nodded curtly to their greetings, and spoke forcefully.

"Look," he said. "We got to get crackin'."

Despite his interrupted argument, Adrian had to laugh. "What? Again?" he wondered.

Macgregor ignored him. "We got to get crackin', an' we got to get oot o' this, damned quick! The polis are efter us."

"The polis . . . ?"

"Jings—the polis!"

"Aye. The polis. They've been at my digs the day, speirin'."

"Hell, Roddie . . . !"

"You saw them? They questioned you?" Adrian demanded.

"No. It was this afternoon. I was oot at the yaird. They jist seen Maggie Munro. But they askit her plenty."

"And she told them . . . ?"

"Och, Maggie's no' sae blate. She seems tae ha'e kept a hud on her tongue. They tell't her they were checkin' up on a' the Roderick Macgregors. They askit her a' aboot me, what like I was aboot politics, what time I was in my bed on Friday night, whether I was at my work on Saturday. They said did she get any o' the bluidy beef? They were speirin' if any o' my claes had bluid on them."

"Whe-e-ew," Adrian whistled. "And you think she was able to stall them, at all?"

"I dinna' ken. She said she tell't them she never kens when I come in—I ha'e my ain key. She's aye in her bed, early. She says she tell't them naethin' they didna' ken, a'ready. There was twa o' them—a sairgeant an' a plain-claes guy. She says they wrote doon a' she tell't them in their wee books."

"But, at least, they didn't wait for you!"

"No. They left efter aboot half an 'oor. But they can aye

come back!" He paused. "Aye—an' anither thing. They askit if I was a supporter o' St. Bride's!"

"Damn!" Adrian swore. "That's the worst, yet. If they've got a line on that . . ." He glanced around him. "Where's M'Vey?"

Art M'Vey was not present. But Fachy Macrae mentioned that he'd seen him in the afternoon, and Art had told him that he likely wouldn't manage to come along in the evening, as there was a special meeting of St. Bride's F.C. Committee called for that night.

"A special meeting!" Hope's and Macgregor's eyes met. "I'm beginning to think that maybe you're right about getting cracking," the former said.

"Aye. It's the hills for us."

"I'm afraid so. I got a hint, myself, yesterday, that I'm not above suspicion in certain quarters. It looks as though it would be only a question of time. . . ."

"Aye, time. But hoo much time? If . . ."

The door opened, and Art M'Vey came in. It did not demand a great deal of perspicacity to see that he was perturbed. "I came's quick as I could," he announced. "There was a special meetin' o' the Committee. It wasna' sae guid! They're gey near on to us, boys."

"The polis, you mean?"

"Aye. They're at the back o' it, anyway. They've been on to the Secretary, an' he ca'ed the meetin'. They reckon the cattle-racket was worked frae the ground, there. An' only the Committee has keys. Eight guys—an' the maist o' them wi' alibis!"

For a moment, there was silence.

"You weren't actually accused?" Adrian asked.

"No. But they a' sorta looked at me. They ken aboot the Ginger Boys, mind. I reckon we'll ha'e to make tracks."

"I'm afraid so. We were saying that, when you came in. We'll have to take to the hills—some of us, anyway."

"Aye. But when . . . ?"

"Right awa'," Roddie declared.

"But that'll take a bit of organising, too," Hope pointed out.

"Weel, you'll jist ha'e to organise it frae there, then. Or frae the jail!"

"And what about the whisky job?"

"We'll dae the whisky ploy first. Right awa'. We'll dae it on Friday night. An' then, off wi' us."

"Friday . . . ?"

"Aye, Friday. I'm no' sleepin' in Maggie Munro's hoose again. Tomorrow's late enough. Och, it's no' that big a job. You hear, boys? Friday night."

"Aye, then."

"Sure, Rod."

"Weel, here's the dope, me an' the Major's fixed up. . . ."

VIII

SO, on the Friday night, they tackled the whisky job. Compared to Operation Beef, it was a simple affair. No great number of men was required—could be fitted in, in fact; six, all told, would have been ample for the task, but Jakey Reid insisted that they take along his crony, Fachy Macrae. Jakey's invaluable lorry was, of course, an essential feature of the night's activities.

Picked up at various street-corners around eleven o'clock, Jakey drove them north-eastwards this time, by the Garscube and Maryhill districts, and through Lambhill. At Cadder they were out of the built-up area, and they rattled on through the urbanised country, bypassing Kirkintilloch. By midnight, they were only a few miles west of Kilsyth. Turning south off the main highway, they followed dark narrow roads across the night-bound vale of the Kelvin, in the general direction of Croy. Crossing the railway, they climbed rather sharply up a short hill, and then, with another arching bridge lifting in front of them, swung off to the left, along a rutted track, and so proceeded slowly, lights dimmed. They were following the bank of the Forth and Clyde Canal.

Presently, at a touch from Macgregor, Jakey drew up, and the big man got down, and disappeared into the darkness ahead. There was no singing this time; Roddie had stopped that a mile or two back. It was a quiet night, not raining, and the air was heavy with the oily rankish smell of the canal water.

Roddie Roy was not back for about quarter of an hour, by which time Adrian at least was getting a little restive. Then he materialised out of the gloom, moving silently for so big a man.

"Okay," he reported. "Everythin' quiet, but there's a light in one o' the top windys o' the pub. You can drive the lorry on anither fower hundred yairds maybe, an' then we'll ha'e to manhandle her. But keep her quiet, Jakey, b'Goad!"

77

So, with the engine just ticking over in bottom gear, they crept forward along the old towpath. After quarter of a mile perhaps, they halted again, where the canal passed through a strip of woodland, and Macgregor went forward once more. He returned to say that he thought they could risk another hundred yards, where there was another strip of this wood. Also, the light had gone out, in the pub.

They ground forward a short distance further, to the edge of a thin plantation of larches, and stopped. Getting down, they gathered in a knot, and peered on into the darkness.

Visibility was better than on the night of their previous escapade. Ahead of them, with the canal swinging off towards their right in a wide arc, a building loomed up blackly about three hundred yards off. But their glances did not linger long at the house. Down to the right, to the canal bank, they stared —and saw only darkness. A faint stirring in the treetops above them, was the only hint of life and movement in the scene.

"Right. In you get, Jakey. We'll gi'e it a bit shove," Roddie Roy whispered. "Noo, the meenit I say stop, you stop, see. We canna' risk a noise. C'mon, then."

So, with Jakey at the wheel, they put their backs into it, and pushed. It was a heavy lorry, and took a lot of moving, but there were six of them to do it, and Roderick Macgregor's strength was phenomenal. Gradually, the thing moved, and, the initial inertia overcome, they kept it going without great difficulty. Beyond a crunching of the wheels, and an occasional faint rattle and creak from the superstructure, the men's panting and grunting were all the disturbance to the night.

After about one hundred and fifty yards, the track forked, the towpath following along the waterside, the other branching off towards the dark building. Macgregor stopped them.

"Bide you here, the noo," he directed. "Donal'—you comin'?"

"I'll come, too," Adrian put in.

"Twa's plenty," the red-head said, briefly. "See's that rope, Jakey. C'mon, Donal'."

The others grumbled, but stayed where they were.

"I hope Roddie won't be unnecessarily rough," Adrian mentioned, but obtained no answering assurances—no answers, indeed. They waited, in silence.

In some five minutes, Donald Lamont was back. "It was easy," he announced. "Once we found the right one. Nae bother. Baith asleep an' snorin'. They hardly gi'en a kick. Noo—we've got to get this lorry movin', again. It's no' far—aboot the same as to the pub."

It was harder to get the truck going, without Roddie's help, but eventually their efforts prevailed. Slowly they steered it along the towpath.

Presently, the outline of a large barge beside the canal bank materialised, black against the wan glimmer of the water. "No' yon one," Donald whispered. "Yon's empty. So's the next—there's three o' them. It's the end one."

Past the first barge they pushed. The second was close beside it. Both were dark, lifeless. The third was a little distance further on—fully seventy yards. But, for all the extra pushing entailed, they could have wished it further still.

Alongside it, they silently parked their lorry. Seeing a shadowy figure moving above him, Adrian climbed up on to the barge.

"Here," Rod Macgregor's voice whispered hoarsely, "gi'e's a hand to get mair o' this tarpaulin off. There's blasted acres o' it. This corner."

A dozen hands hastened to do his bidding, with not a word spoken. In a couple of minutes they had half the great canvas cover of the barge's hold loosened and laid back. Underneath, were neatly stacked dozens and dozens of wooden boxes. Peering close, it was just possible to make out that each was marked—*John MacClure & Co. Ltd., Glenlogie, Scotland. Dew of Glenlogie Pure Scotch Whisky. One Dozen Bottles. For Export Only.*

"Aye, weel—up wi' them, an' doon wi' them," Roddie Roy directed. "Twa to a box. An' no' a sound oot o' yous! You've plenty time—but be *quiet*, for any favour!"

Quiet they were, quiet enough even for Adrian Hope. Most of them were wearing rubber shoes, and the boxes, being well-packed for shipboard, did not rattle. Yet, working in sets of two, a pair on the boat, handing down, a pair on the bank to receive, and a pair on the lorry to stow, they laboured swiftly as well as silently. In quarter of an hour, they had forty boxes transferred, which they reckoned to be sufficient. They replaced the big canvas cover.

"Fine. Back to the lorry, boys," Macgregor whispered. "I'll be with you, in a wee."

With the big man, Adrian made his way aft, to the half-deck-house, half-cabin, at the rear. These were big self-propelled barges, with bunks for two men. A flotilla of half a dozen of them plied between the Board of Trade bottling-store at Camelon, served by the distilleries of Glenlogie, Glenochil, Carsebridge, Rosebank, and Cambus, and the Clyde estuary at Old Kilpatrick, where the whisky was loaded on to the waiting ships on its way to more favoured lands. It took the barges two days to negotiate the forty-odd-mile canal, and every night one of them full and another empty, tied up outside the little inn and lock-keeper's house at Dunsheil, approximate half-way house between east and west.

In the tiny cabin, the Macgregor switched on his shaded torch carefully, to reveal two angry-eyed but trussed and gagged recumbent figures on the bunks.

"Look, boys," Roddie said, reasonably. "I'm right sorry aboot you twa gettin' the thick end o' this. But we need your whisky, see. Let's see the ropes. Och, you'll be fine an' comfortable there—your mates in the ither barge'll put you right, the morn. We canna' jist risk freein' you, the noo. But here's somethin'll maybe gi'e you a better night's sleep," and he thrust a hand into his pocket and fetched out a bundle of bank-notes. "Five quid—jist a bit present frae Rod Roy Macgregor," and he pushed the notes under one of the men's belts.

"And here's a receipt for forty cases of a dozen bottles each," Adrian added, laying a paper down on a bunk. "That ought to keep you right with your employers. I don't see that there should be any trouble in this for you, apart from present discomforts—they can hardly blame you two. In fact, you ought to get a bonus after this, as danger-money!"

"Uh-huh. Fine, that," Macgregor concluded, backing his great bulk out of the cabin. "Weel, s'long, boys. Keep smilin'—it's a' in the cause o' Bonnie Scotlan', mind!"

They recommenced the lorry-pushing process. Fortunately, they did not need to attempt the herculean task of turning the thing on the narrow towpath. After just a little backing, they were able to wheel it round in a wide circle in front of the inn, and so back to where the tracks joined again, puffing hard in the doing of it. As they passed the front of the dark building a dog began to bark, somewhere at the back. It went on barking, in a desultory fashion, but produced no apparent reaction, other than muttered profanity from the straining pushers. Jakey kept a hand on the self-starter, ready.

However, its use was not necessary. On reaching, breathlessly, the first strip of trees, they looked back. No light was showing, nor any trace of alarm.

"Right," Roddie Roy said. "In you get, boys. Jakey—get crackin'."

The starter whirred, the engine broke into life, and slowly, in bottom gear, they moved off.

"Jammy!" Fachy Macrae declared. "Money for auld rope! Whit for did I ever *buy* the stuff!"

Once off the towpath, Jakey let himself go, and they hurtled back towards Glasgow in more typical fashion. In the back of the lorry, for all the jolting and flinging hither and thither, they were extremely busy with cold chisels, hammers, and pliers, opening up those well-packed cases. Roddie was travelling in the back this time; perhaps he felt that his orders, that there was to be no sampling, called for a little personal enforcement.

They waited till they were well into the city before they started their deliveries, partly on account of natural sympathies, partly because they felt more secure amongst familiar haunts, but mainly for the reason that the large number of licensed premises made their task immeasurably more simple. To Adrian, the prevalence of pubs was quite remarkable.

So, at approximately one-forty-five in the Maryhill district, they commenced the second part of the night's activities. Choosing side streets, they drove slowly up or down, and at every public-house they came to—and it was indeed surprising how many corners were thus enhanced—they stopped, and unloaded either a case or half a case of Dew of Glenlogie.

Where possible, they deposited the boxes at back or side entrances, but in a great many cases this was impracticable, and the offering had to be left lying within the front doorway. Where the door was flush with the street, and the box would have to actually lie out on the pavement, they left none—such would only have drawn the attention of undesirables, including the police. This entire distribution was unsatisfactory, crude, and probably wasteful, but they saw no alternative, in the time at their disposal. A certain amount might be lifted by local residents and passers-by—but then, the stuff was for them, ultimately, anyway. A brief note was tucked into each case. GOVERNMENT BOUGHT SPIRITS. SCOTLAND'S SPIRITS ARE SO LOW, WE CAN'T AFFORD TO EXPORT ALL OF THEM. A PRESENT TO THE CUSTOMERS—SEE THEY GET IT, OR . . . ROD ROY MACGREGOR. Fifty of these, Adrian had laboriously scribbled that afternoon.

With ample manpower for the job, they were able to drop a scout at the top and bottom of every street or block, and so were never disturbed by patrolling police. Not that Glasgow's sensible constabulary make a point of patrolling the side streets of such areas at two o'clock of a morning. Once or twice untimely and unidentified pedestrians caused them to move on hurriedly, and on one occasion an individual issuing from a close-mouth just as they were offloading a box, wanted to know what it was all about. He was handed a bottle of whisky, told to ask no questions, and to scram—which he very promptly did. So did the lorrymen.

But such interruptions were very minor affairs, and the work of delivery proceeded with satisfactory rapidity. By three-fifteen they were in the Kelvinhaugh area, and their last box disposed of. They still had about seventy loose bottles in the back of the lorry, extracted from the half-cases. These could not be left about in corners, on the ground. But Mike Doolan deserved a little consideration. They were glad enough to turn their vehicle round, and make for the Bridegate.

Back in their own bailiwick, they knew their way around. Two or three judicious right-angled turns off the Bridegate, and their lorry was crawling in low gear down a narrow dark alley between dismal broken-down warehouse property and derelict back-yards. At a gap in a tumbling brick wall, only theoretically blocked by a reeling wooden gate, they stopped, the bottles were unloaded with loving care, and Jakey was told to get his lorry to blazes out of it. Roddie dealt with the gate in a knowledgeable fashion, the bottles were passed inside, and the gap closed again. Then, each carrying three or four in their arms, they followed their leader across rubble-littered yards, around gable-ends, through cat-smelling passages, till a solid line of dark building held them up. But Roddie—indeed, all of them save Adrian Hope—knew just where they were, and their jaunt ended at a blank-seeming window. It was iron-barred, but that did not worry any of them. The central bar was apparently halved, the top portion lifted up further into the lintel, and by pulling outwards and down, could be taken out altogether, allowing its bottom half to be drawn up and out likewise. The window within was not snibbed, to raise the lower sash was the work of a moment, and in a couple more Macgregor had squeezed through and was inside, and his colleagues were handing the bottles through to him. While the other four went back for more whisky, Adrian climbed within also. Mike Doolan's Bar had more to commend it than appeared at first sight.

With all the bottles stowed—or nearly all, anyway—and a note left for the proprietor, Roddie and Adrian climbed out again, and the bars were replaced.

"Noo, scram—the lot o' yous," the big man directed. "Make yoursel's scarce. Me an' the Major's got some things to dae. Make your ain way, in your ain time, to yon Spree Cave up on Ben Ure. You a' ken the place, an' what you've to bring wi' you. We're a' goin' hikin'—but no' in a bunch, see? There's nae hurry—but let's see you a' there by tomorrow night. Got it?"

"Aye, man."

"Sure."

"Spree Cave, then. . . ."

"Right. An' look. Whaeivver drinks any o' this whisky, it's no' to be us, see! A guy that's drunk, talks. An' any guy that talks has to settle wi' me! You got that, tae?"

There was a silence.

"I say, ha'e you *got* that?" The red-head's voice quivered, ominously.

There followed a hurried chorus of assent.

"Aye, well. Then that's the lot, boys. C'mon, will you. . . ."

Adrian just beat him to it. "Let's get crackin'!" he suggested.

IX

THE sun, setting in an extravaganza of flame and colour behind Ben Vorlich and Ben Lui, was soaking all the brown hills in its orange radiance, filling every fold and hollow and corrie with purple shadow, and etching each outcrop and boulder in sheerest jet. But only the merest reflection of all that brilliance reached the narrow mouth of the *Uamh nan Spreidh* high on the south-east face of Ben Ure, and the group of men that sat and sprawled and lay in the entrance thereto, were in deepest shade. But they added their own quota of colour to the scene, nevertheless, by their variegated shirts and vests, their shorts or up-rolled trousers of corduroy or khaki drill, even the kilt or two that they sported.

They were all there, as directed; not only the eight zealots who yesterday had drawn their last pay-packet, and whose employment-cards were forthwith going to become a headache to the Ministry of Labour, but all the more or less active Gregorach—save of course the four faithful fund-raisers in the North—nineteen of them in all, footloose or still city-bound. They had arrived, in ones and twos, throughout that broiling afternoon and evening, via Balmaha and Drymen, and even Aberfoyle. All were there—except Roderick Macgregor.

Adrian Hope assured them that he would be back soon. He had been gone since early afternoon—the two of them had arrived at the rendezvous before midday, having travelled all through the early morning. Apparently, even up here, Rod Roy was preoccupied with the necessity of getting cracking.

This information had been met by a chorus of groans. There was a certain amount of grumbling. Roddie was okay of course, but he was ower keen. What was all the hurry about? And this whisky ploy; what sense was there in handing out liquor to all the bloated publicans, and not to have so much as a drink themselves? What way was that to carry on? He was just about as bad as the man Cripps—Austerity Roddie!

They'd be damned well coopered if they'd carry on this way! Adrian Hope, obliquely, as instigator of it all, and a convenient target into the bargain, garnered his fair share of the opprobrium. He accepted it without undue alarm.

The argument had reached the stage of mooting very tentative and unspecified reprisals, when a shout from somebody drew attention to a figure approaching round the flank of the hill. Even at that range there was no mistaking the identity of the climber, and a magnificent picture he made as, bathed in the glory of the sunset, clad only in a kilt and great boots, he strode hugely, his red-furred torso and flaming head like a torch in the level flooding refulgence. And over his massive shoulder he carried a half-filled sack, slung like the merest trifle.

"So that's you, is it—seventeen, eighteen, nineteen o' yous," he greeted. "The hale bang-jing. Fine. Here's your supper. Oatmeal. You can ha'e it as it is, mixed wi' watter frae the burn, you can ha'e it as parritch, or you can bake bluidy cakes oot o' it. Please yoursel's."

"Jings, Roddie—oatmeal!"

"Och, tae hell—parritch!"

"Aye, parritch. They tell me Rob Roy used tae live on oatmeal, jist. An' there's plenty tea. You'll no' come tae any harm wantin' meat for a wee—you must be fair stuffed wi' it. Any o' yous seen a paper?"

None of them had, all having left Glasgow too early for the afternoon editions. The morning Press, of course, would have been printed before any word of their night's activities could have leaked out.

"Gi'e them time, Roddie," Jakey Reid said. "You'll get your heed-lines a'right. There's nae hurry. . . ."

"There's plenty hurry," the big man contradicted, emphatically. "We want a guid story oot o' the whisky ploy, afore we slap anither on tap o' it. See?"

"Aw, jings, Roddie . . . anither?"

"Sure. But this time, it's goin' to be a wee thing different. I've been takin' a bit look round, an' ha'ein' a crack wi' some o' the folk doon the glen, there. There's plenty needin' put right, aroond here. But this time it's no' jist a bit ploy, see. This time, we'll ha'e to work. Real work."

There was a pregnant, an ominous silence, as the company took that in. Then the bold Jakey spoke up. "*Work*, did you say, Roddie?"

"Aye, then. Work. Hard bluidy work. The stuff naebody likes, any mair. I've got it a' fixed. See—get crackin' wi' that fire. . . . An', Alicky, get the watter for the supper—the burn's jist doon the brae a wee. Noo, I'll tell you. . . ."

As Roderick Macgregor said, there was a lot needing to be put right in that ancient district of Buchanan, as elsewhere in Highland Scotland. But it was not the typical Highland problems of lack of access and transport, depopulation, and the neglect due to remoteness, that was the trouble here; this area, Highland in topography but only partly so in economy and general living conditions, situated on Glasgow's very doorstep, did not suffer from lack of roads or so-called amenities. But it had its own problems—other than the universal ones that sprang from restrictions, state interference, and the like. The overriding claims of the Glasgow Water Works was one, and the Forestry Commission's widespread activities another. Both of these had their advantages for the local people, but also their drawbacks—the drawbacks inseparable from the vast impersonal monopolistic occupancy of land, where the interests of the small tenants were inevitably subordinated to those of the great organisations. There was not a great deal that could be done about such, in a short time, even by the most effective and determined reformers. But there were other problems. Not all the land was controlled by the City of Glasgow and the Forestry Commission. There were a number of private proprietors, resident and otherwise, many of whom, no doubt, sought to be excellent landlords. But conditions of location, present-day tendencies, and the profit-motive, all militated against the real people of the district, the small tenant-farmers and those who lived for and by them. They were not crofters, these people—it was not crofting country—but small sheep and cattle rearers, each tenanting perhaps twenty to fifty acres of arable in the valley-floors, and a thousand or so of rough grazing in the heather of the hillsides. But they did not, could not, pay big rents, whereas, so close to Glasgow, the proprietors could get inflated shooting and stalking rentals from wealthy city sportsmen out for a day with the gun. Inevitably, the interests of the farmer were subordinated to those of the sportsman. Indeed, it would probably have suited the landlords better if they could have got rid of the farmers altogether, for grouse and deer do not love sheep and cattle, and the coveted phrase "no crofting tenants" can always be relied upon to enhance any sporting rental considerably. So the discouragement of the hill-farmer was good policy—that was elementary, and even conscientious and tender-hearted landlords have pockets. This process, of course, had been going on for a long time.

Roddie Roy had been talking to one of the local farmers, down in Glen Corran, above Loch Ard, and he had been telling him of all that needed doing around his place of Dalnablair—buildings repaired, bogs drained, bracken cut, fences renewed, and so on. But the main trouble was the river. The Corran flowed through his forty acres of arable—or rather, more accurately, his arable was contrived out of the levels of the river haugh. Dykes were there to keep the stream in bounds, but for long the dykes had been crumbling to ruin, and the laird would not repair them—and it was, of course, a job far beyond the resources of the tenant. Each winter and spring the river in spate flooded more and more of his arable, washing away the topsoil and depositing instead a spreading wilderness of whitened stones and gravel. Without the arable he could not grow winter feed for his beasts, and he would be forced to go. Another couple of seasons, he reckoned, would finish him. And the man further down the glen, likewise.

Here then was a job for them—a task worth doing. To rebuild those dykes, and to clear the stones off the arable. It would be a big job, and hard work—but it would save one more glen from going derelict. Roddie mentioned, just as an afterthought, that the farmer's name happened to be Macgregor.

That was his scheme; the reception it got, by his colleagues, by the landlord, by the world, even perhaps by the farmer himself, didn't matter to Roderick Macgregor. That Adrian Hope supported it enthusiastically did not seem to matter much either—at least, if it did, if he recognised that the germ of the original suggestion had been his, he gave no sign. That was the programme.

They'd start tomorrow, first thing, with all hands mustered; they'd get a day's work out of the city guys, anyway. Up with the dawn ... it was a good seven miles down to Glen Corran. Supper now, and then sleep—bags of sanguinary sleep. They'd need it all.

He had the last word, of course. And it was "Shurrup!" And with reason.

So a grey dawn, only faintly barred with roseate streaks away beyond the eastern hills, saw a silent dejected company filing down through the clinging mist-wreaths of the mountain-side, their raw oatmeal and cold water heavy within them, too dispirited to be rebellious—but their chastening of the body rather than of the spirit.

Roddie leading, with Donald Lamont as whipper-in, they headed down into the high peat-pocked valley of the Abhainn Gaoithe, to leap and scramble and plowter amongst its black hags, till the firmer ground of a spur of great cloud-cowled Ben Lomond received them out of the morass. Round the long flank of this, over tall heather and outcropping stone, they proceeded, strung out now, with Macgregor, long-striding, far in front, Adrian in the breathless role of connecting-file, and Donald with his work cut out for him far-away in the rear.

Two or three little glens opened off eastwards below them, but they kept to high ground and pushed onwards to the south, on the principle, as the big fellow picturesquely put it, that it is a dirty bird that fouls its own nest; to operate too near to their sanctuary on Ben Ure would have been foolishness. The young morning lightened on the hills—but found little re-flection in the faces of the long procession of walkers. No habitation nor sign of man did they observe in all that brown desolation.

By six o'clock, with ninety minutes hard walking and nearly five very rough miles behind them, the red-head turned to follow a small stream downhill eastwards, into the trough of a long narrow glen, up which, not sunlight, but the first promise thereof, came flooding. Down there, greenwoods of birch spread themselves, and a little loch gleamed whitely, mirroring the lightening sky. Perhaps, involuntarily, the untimely travellers became just a shade less resentful. A small herd of deer, all long-legged hinds, that they put up and sent like red shadows drifting over the boundless sea of heather, was pursued by an encouraging volley of whoopees.

Once past the bog and bad going at its head, it was pleasant walking down the glen, amongst the young green and silver of the graceful birches and the rioting bracken, with the boisterous stream growing steadily on their right, and the broom-splashed slopes lifting steeply on either hand, dotted with shaggy small black cattle and shaggier black-faced sheep. At the reedy lochside they paused, and got rid of some pent-up, corporate, and understandable spleen by howling derision at Roddie Roy, who, throwing off his shirt and kilt, plunged into the peat stained waters and splashed about and swam therein with a remarkable simulation of enjoyment. After that, they all felt much better.

About half a mile beyond Loch Corran, with the glen widening a little, they came to the first of Dalnablair's sorry fields. Long and narrow, stretched along the riverside on the only level ground, they were little more than scimitars and scallops of bleached pebbles in which pathetic green patches had been scraped here and there, wherein thin oat stalks struggled gallantly. Stretches of the dyke that should have protected them were still in place—in fact, most of the grass-grown dyke still remained—but its uselessness was only the more apparent. Further down, where the river linked and coiled in serpentine abandon, the whitewashed farmhouse and steading, within its ring of rowans and alders, stood at the rim of a very plain of pebbles. No smoke curled up from its chimneys, as yet.

It was just a quarter to seven, and Roddie decided that they should start work here, at the top end—a reasonable suggestion that met with scant enthusiasm. The dyke was on the north side of the stream only, hereabouts, and started at a jutting knoll of steep rock round which the river poured narrowly, and which made an excellent anchor for the end of the earthwork. It continued undamaged for perhaps seventy yards, and then came the first breach, a gap of twenty feet. The strip of haugh behind it was a litter of stone and gravel and the jagged stumps of old trees, out of which only clumps of reeds and a few thistles grew.

When he had set all his reluctant navvies to gathering and clearing the stones from the background of haugh, and dumping them in the gap of the dyke, Macgregor came to confer with Lamont and Adrian. Undoubtedly it was no use just building the stones up into a bank again, and leaving it like that—the first spate would loosen and wash them away again. What was wanted was some sort of anchoring, something to hold them in place. Large stakes driven in, would be the thing—but where were they going to get them? Roddie answered that himself. The Forestry. There were thinnings, stacks of whole tree-trunks, all along the Loch Ard road, waiting to be sent south for pit-props. They'd need wire, too—thick wire, lots of it, to tie down and bind together their construction. The Forestry, again; didn't they put up mile after mile of fencing, to keep the deer out? And they'd want those big hammers, for driving in the posts. Once more, the Forestry fencers ought to provide. There only remained the transport . . . ?

Innocently, Donald Lamont suggested that could the Forestry Commission not complete the job? Wouldn't they have tractors and wagons, to shift their timber? Roddie seemed to consider the proposition seriously, but pointed out that this was going to be a long job, taking days to complete; while a few tree trunks and odd coils of wire, discreetly lifted, might never be noticed for long enough, taking away a tractor and trailer would be apt to attract attention. Regretfully, the tractor was dismissed, and thoughtfully Rod Macgregor turned his glance on the two long-tailed horses that grazed in a little park between the road and the steading. Still thoughtfully, he called for Jakey, and, as an afterthought, for one Dougie Chisholm, who, next to himself, was the largest man there.

"C'mon," he said to them, jerking his red head. And to Hope and Lamont, "I'll be seein' you. Keep them at it, clearin' the haughs an' heapin' the stanes. It's a mile doon tae the

91

main road, an' anither along tae the beginnin' o' the Forestry. Gi'e's a coupla 'oors. S'long."

About ten minutes later, a touch on his arm straightened up Adrian from his boulder trundling. Lamont pointed, down the glen. The steading lay some little distance back from the farmhouse, near the road-end, actually on slightly higher ground and with the stackyard between. From it, a horse and cart had issued, and was plodding off down the valley eastwards, with three people aboard.

The stone-clearance was a wearisome, back-breaking, finger-bruising, and thankless task—especially without picks, shovels, and wheelbarrows. Adrian certainly found it so, and was left in no doubt as to the feelings of his sixteen fellow-toilers. With Macgregor gone, the tempo of the work slackened progressively; Hope wisely left any urging towards fiercer activity to come from Donald Lamont. Example was probably his most useful contribution—an example in industriousness, if not in efficacy, for the truth was that he was not particularly good at this sort of thing, having neglected his opportunities for manual labour in the past.

Still, despite the general lack of urgency and ardour, seventeen able-bodied and even moderately active young men can make a notable difference to a stretch of haugh in a comparatively short space of time. Perhaps their delving did not go very deep, maybe a greater percentage of the larger stones rather than the smaller got shifted, and the gravel was left more or less undisturbed. Nevertheless, by half-past eight, when somebody noticed a blue plume of wood-smoke rising above the farmhouse, they had changed at least the superficial appearance of quite an area of that top end of the haugh, and large piles of bleached stones were heaped in and alongside the first two gaps in the long dyke.

That smoke set in motion a process of thought, and a conference rapidly developed over the question of whether any tea or other provender could be got out of the farmer, on behalf of the hungry toilers working their bleeding fingers to the bone for him. An overwhelming majority having decided that the lazy old skinflint should be given the opportunity of showing his gratitude forthwith, a representative deputation consisting of fully three-quarters of the party was about to set off, when a rumble from down the road drew all eyes. The farm-cart, precariously laden, was approaching, some proportion, anyway, of its three escorts singing lustily.

The carters were in high fettle. They had had to go no great distance, at all. Instead of having to trail away down the Loch Ard road, they had noticed a big plantation just *up* from the road-end, maybe a quarter of a mile, and here they had found not only ample stacks of seasoning thinnings, but a number of ready-trimmed and pointed fence-stobs, and also a sled-affair for hauling logs, which would do equally well behind one of these horses, for hauling stones. And in a forester's hut, they had discovered enough wire to keep them going meantime, lots of staples, half a dozen pick-axes and a couple of spades. Only the hammers were missing—and they could always use one of these stobs for that. It was all laid-on, according to the cheerful Roddie, who promptly commenced to unload modest tree-trunks as though they were matchsticks, shedding orders with equal heartiness. Nothing further was said, for the moment, about the deputation to the farmhouse.

They had got the cart cleared, and were filling it up with stones in the haugh, when a tweed-clad figure came walking unhurriedly down the riverside towards them from the direction of the farm. He was a lean-faced, grizzle-headed elderly man, tall and stooping a little, with washed-out grey eyes that were nevertheless very keen—and at present, very active—a noticeably white shirt, and no collar.

"Och, well now, indeed—a very fine morning it is, too," he greeted them, warily, in a pleasant Highland voice. "Busy you are, surely? Damn, yes—busy, indeed." That sounded entirely objective.

"Is that yoursel', man?" Roddie cried, pausing with a tree-trunk on his shoulder. "Say—could you get us yon ither horse o' yours, to haul this sledge? An' we could dae wi' a saw, an' an axe or twa. You got them?"

"I have, yes. But . . ."

"Fine. Awa' you, an' fetch them, Mister. A' your troubles are ower, noo. We're mendin' your dyke for you."

"Is that what you're after doing, then? I was wondering," the farmer said, mildly.

"Aye. I was thinkin' aboot what you were tellin' me, yesterday. If you ha'e one o' thae big hammers—for fence-posts, y'ken—an' maybe a wheelbarrow . . . ?"

The older man scratched his unshaven chin. "I'm much obliged, indeed—och, you are very good, I'm sure. . . . Are you some sort of a contractor, at all?" His glance strayed over the brawny hirsute and kilted figure before him—Roddie had dispensed with his shirt again—in perhaps understandable doubt.

"Hell—a contractor! Me?" the red-head roared. "Goad—that's a guid one!" Then he drew himself up to his full magnificent height, and tossed the larch trunk away dramatically. "Mister—I'm Roderick Roy Macgregor! That's whae I am!" and he bent a quick eye to note the effect.

"You . . . ? My goodness gracious me!" The other blinked. "Och, well, d'you tell me that! Man, man—fancy, now!" He did not look altogether overjoyed at the news.

Roddie did not fail to notice it. "You ken what that means?" he demanded. "You've heard o' me, then?"

"Och, yes—I have indeed. Surely, surely. Just ten minutes back, I was after hearing about you . . . on the wireless, whatever. About some whisky . . ."

"The wireless . . . ? Jings—is that a fact!" The big man lifted up his voice. "Boys—we're comin' on. We're on the wireless, noo! What did they say?"

"Well, now . . . they were just after saying . . . well, I'll no' can remember just all that they were saying. But . . . damn't, man, you'll get it all again on the Light Programme, at nine o'clock. . . ."

"Sure, that's right. I'll be doon." He turned, to drive away with a threatening gesture the circle of his companions who had gathered round to hear the news. "Scram!" he snarled, "we got work to dae." To the farmer he said, "I'll be doon at nine—an' I'll get the ither horse, an' the saw an' a', then."

"I'ph'mmm. Aye," the other acceded, uncertainly. "Will you, man? Och, look you . . . I'm just wondering if I can afford it, at all . . . ?"

"Afford it? Say—whae's askin' you tae afford anythin'? You're gettin' it on *us*, see—for damn-all! We're daein' this no' jist for you, man, but for the sake o' your bit glen, for the sake o' Bonnie Scotlan'. See? You jist ca' Rod Roy Macgregor your fairy goadfaither, Mister. Get it?" And with a single bark of a laugh, he clapped the other shatteringly on the shoulder.

The farmer did not actually laugh, in return. "Aye. Uh-huh. Just that," he said. "You are kind, indeed. But all this, all this material, see you . . . ? I'm not just sure that I can be paying for it. . . ."

"Whae's askin' you tae pay for it! The Government's payin' for it, see. Plenty mair where that come frae. Look, my mannie —you're gettin' your dyke repaired, whether you can pay for it or no'—whether you bluidy-well like it or no'! Get it? An' you're no' tellin' a soul, either—no' till it's done. Then you can tell the world. You got that, tae? You mind a' that, an' we'll get on fine, jist fine."

One last attempt the older man made, out of his evident pessimism. "It's the Sabbath, too, see you—not the good day to be doing a thing like this. . . ."

"Jings—what's wrang wi' it? Jist the day for it. Doesn't the Bible say somethin' aboot if you ha'e a sheep fa' into a hole on the Sabbath, you can dig it oot? Weel—your haugh's fa'en into a right coorse hole, an' we're diggin' it oot for you! Doesna' it say you're to dae guid on the Sabbath? We're daein' a guid job, an' we're daein' it for nuthin'. Anyways—this is the only day we can get a' the boys on the job. The morn, there'll only be the nine o' us. Awa' you to the Kirk, man— an' leave us to get on wi' the job."

"I think that's best, Mr. Macgregor," Adrian intervened, with a placatory smile. "You go to Church, and forget about us. Maybe it would be best if you forgot about us meantime, anyway. You pray, and we'll wrestle—with your stones! To change the chapter a bit—be like Pilate, and wash your hands of us!"

The Highlandman looked from one to the other undecidedly, and then shook his grizzled head. "As you say, then," he sighed. "I'm just hoping, though, that you'll not be getting me into any trouble, at all." He turned away, and began to walk back whence he had come, but after a few paces paused, and called back. "There'll be a pot of broth on the hob, for you—and I'll get the wife to be making a puckle scones. And tea, when you're wanting it. I'll be up-bye—the nearest kirk is ten miles!"

"Guid man!" Roddie said, grinning.

And so the good work went on. The horse and cart made the stone-clearance a lot easier—though it was a nuisance having to lift the stones up so high. The clearers made heaps and piles of them, while two men went round with the cart transferring the heaps to the dyke. Roddie went off to the farm, and came back, half an hour later, munching, and pushing a powerfully-scented wheelbarrow laden with a large fence-mallet, a wood-man's axe, and a cross-cut saw. Also, he led the second broad-backed garron by a halter.

He had been listening to the wireless, he said. It had come in between the railway strike and something about Berlin. They'd said that a valuable consignment of whisky for export had been stolen by the same astonishing organisation calling itself Rod Roy Macgregor, that had stolen the cattle a week before. They'd said a large gang must be involved, for the whisky had been handed out, free and unasked for, to many licensed premises in Glasgow. The police, who were following up certain lines of enquiry, asked all publicans and others who might have received supplies, to return same at once to the nearest police-station. It was understood that some twenty bottles had already been handed in. Twenty! Any retention of such stolen property, they'd said, would of course constitute something-or-other, and was a punishable offence. Anyone having any information which might lead to the identification and arrest of the lawbreakers, was required to communicate with the local police. All they'd missed out, apparently, was Whitehall one-two, one-two.

The Gregorach received these tidings with prolonged cheers. Jakey gave his celebrated and realistic rendering of a B.B.C. announcer giving the glad news.

With the saw to cut the logs into the required lengths, the axe to sharpen the ends of them, and the great mallet to drive them into the stony ground, progress was much speeded up. They drove the posts into the gaps in the dyke in pairs, strapped them together with the wire, linked the supports together where the gap was wide enough for more than one set, and then led the wire out to be pegged down beyond the dyke proper, using the smaller fence-posts therefor. Thereupon the stonework was filled in, with a core of pebbles and rubble, and an outer walling of large stones and boulders. Roddie declared that a few sacks of cement to pour over the whole affair, would finish the job nicely. Adrian, just a little perturbed by the implications of that, thought it probably would do fine as it was.

By mid-forenoon, corporate hunger was no longer supportable. They had brought a certain amount of stale bread and broken biscuits with them—even some of the big man's deplorable oatmeal. But the former had been nibbled away long ago, and the latter held scant attraction. With an impressive unanimity, they downed tools, and made for the farmhouse.

They got a warmer reception than might have been expected from the tone of their invitation. Perhaps the genial Mrs. Macgregor and her roving-eyed buxom daughter were less impressed by the sanctity of property and suchlike, than was the head of their house. Adequate fare for a score of men could not be produced off-hand, but the vast soup-pot, by the wholesale addition of many vegetables and a rabbit, met the occasion valiantly, a vast boiling of potatoes in their jackets supported the soup, and innumerable new-baked scones with milk to wash them down, completed their snack. The farm-kitchen could seldom have been more tightly packed in its obviously long history. Some squeezing was inevitable—of which the sonsy Jeanie Macgregor came in for her full share, amidst delighted squeals. Getting the whole party back to the haugh again, took considerable persuasion.

The work, once they got down to it, went better, after that— partly no doubt out of the satisfaction of replete stomachs, but also probably because they now had a little more personal interest in someone who ultimately was going to profit by their labours. Such is the power of woman—the power that has caused cities to be built and be destroyed, wars waged, and continents discovered. Also, of course, there was the promise of tea to be brought out to them sometime in the afternoon.

By midday, the farmer himself had so far got over his Sabbatarian and moralist scruples—possibly with some suitably practical feminine urging—as to come along and offer them, first advice, and then a hand at the job. And his was a practised hand with stones. Nothing would make the task anything but a slow one, but for all that they were now seeing something for their labours. Long stretches of the dyke were taking shape again, and the ground behind it looked at least as though it might not buckle a purposefully inserted plough.

Tea quite came up to expectations, with more scones thickly spread with just slightly rancid farm butter and last season's heather honey, sugary but strong. The young woman's skirls echoed from a dozen hills, throughout—while her father turned a long grave face in the other direction, and discussed blackface wool prices with Adrian, Donald Lamont, and a somewhat preoccupied Roddie Roy.

Five o'clock was reckoned to be as late as the city contingent could stay. It was ten miles to Aberfoyle and the nearest bus, on the east, and eight at least over the hills westwards to Rowardennan on Loch Lomondside. Three hours' walk, either way. It would be ten o'clock before any of them were home that night—and they had been up since four o'clock dawn. It was decided, for the sake of inconspicuousness, that the party should divide, five going by Rowardennan and six by Aberfoyle. And they'd all be back at Spree Cave by late afternoon, next Saturday. Strangely enough, none of them seemed in any hurry to be off, now. Despite aching backs and sore fingers, more than one began to wonder whether those who had elected to give up their workaday jobs weren't the lucky ones. Monday morning was casting its shadow. At half-past five, somebody started the thing, and inevitably it was taken up unanimously; Jeanie Macgregor kissed each of the pilgrims a grateful goodbye behind the cow shed, and the two groups set off cheerfully citywards, in opposite directions.

The nine remaining stalwarts put in another token hour at the haugh, and then knocked-off—not exactly for the night, for Roddie had another trip for timber and wire in view, an errand which all felt might best be accomplished under cover of darkness this time. But they had done an excellent day's work; much more than Adrian Hope at least had anticipated. Fully a third of the task was done.

There was no need to go back to the cave, that night. The Dalnablair barn, with its aromatic bog-hay, was at their disposal. By nine o'clock, they were all asleep therein, with Roddie Roy promising them all to wake up in due course and to go for those logs. It was sun-up, in fact, on Monday morning, before he redeemed that promise.

X

"BUT look at this," Adrian cried. "Here's the *Sentinel*, for you—MODERN ROB ROY DOES IT AGAIN. *The auda-cious transfer of some five hundred bottles of proprietary Scotch Whisky, en route for the U.S.A., to an unknown number of licensed premises in Glasgow, is the latest exploit of the amazing individual that signs himself Rod Roy Macgregor. . . . The two men on the barge that was looted, state that they were forcefully but not roughly handled. . . . Owing to the attack taking place in complete darkness, they could give no clue as to the appearance or identity of their assailants.* Hear that, Roddie—your fiver did the trick! . . . *police guards are now being placed on all barges. . . . In response to the police appeal, it is understood that so far only sixty-seven bottles of the forty-dozen have as yet been handed in. . . ."*

"Och, the *Mail* beats that!" Art M'Vey exclaimed. "They've got seventy-one. . . ."

"The *Echo* make it sixty-nine," Macgregor reported. They say, TWENTIETH-CENTURY CATERAN HOLDS COUNTRY BREATHLESS. WHERE WILL ROD ROY STRIKE NEXT? Jings— that's guid! Here—listen to this, . . . *audacious band of free-booters . . . split-second timing . . . impressive organisation . . .* That's one for you, Major. And, say, . . . *it is understood that the police are frankly pessimistic about getting any large proportion of the whisky back. It is felt that the public, rightly or wrongly, are too much tickled by their activities, perhaps too much in sympathy with them, to co-operate with the authorities to any large extent. In this connection, it is to be noted that, from all reports, so far only twenty-one of the missing bullocks, from last weekend's exploit, have been re-covered. It is unknown how many were actually slaughtered and delivered by the gang, but it is certain that a large number are still at large.* . . . Great, boys! Twenty-one, only! That means the fairmers are stickin' to them. . . ."

"Or killin' them theirsel's, maybe."

"Aye. Could be. It's a' one. . . ."

"That's fine, yes," Adrian agreed. "But what we want to see is the comments, the editorials. What the Press really makes out of it all. The reports are well enough, of course—very flattering. But after all, what we're out to do, is to try to wake up the spirit of Scotland. It's from the editorials and leaders that we'll find out how far we're doing it. . . ."

"There's a bit leader here, in the *Scots Reporter*," Donald Lamont put in. "It says . . . och, it's jist waffling, the first bit, and then it says . . . *what would appear to be the significant feature about this affair, is the fact that this whisky, like the cattle, was Government property, and was destined to leave the country. From this, it might be inferred that here is something in the nature of a campaign to counter the excessive drain on Scottish resources, both to England and overseas, imposed by the present fiscal and economic policy of the Government. While, of course, the methods taken to effect this end are to be deplored by all responsible and law-abiding people, nevertheless many thoughtful Scots are beginning to think along similar lines. Per head of population, the economic balance . . .*"

"Och, tae hell wi' the economic balance!" Roddie snorted.

"Fair enough, in a limited sense," Adrian commented. "But they've missed the real point, of course. What about the *Chronicle* . . . ?"

"Here's the *Sentinel*, wi' a bit," Alicky Shand put in. ". . . *whatever we may think of the wisdom, the propriety, or the ultimate usefulness of this amazing business—the legality, of course, is quite beyond comment—we have to recognise that the country is witnessing an attempt, whether or not misguided, at least sincere, courageous, and bold, to redress what is conceived to be a national wrong. It is not only irresponsibles, hotheads, and cranks who will agree that something is very far wrong with Scotland's situation today. These outrages, stunts, achievements—call them what you will—appear to be an attempt to alter that situation. They are innately and essentially political acts—though all the political parties have denied responsibility, some, perhaps, almost with chagrin that*

101

they had not thought of it! The man Roderick Roy Mac-gregor—if, indeed, there is such a man—is a patriot in essence, whether we call him a firebrand, a misguided fanatic, or a hero somewhat ahead of his time. Hey, Roddie—what d'you think o' that? You—a patriot!"

"Nuts!" the big man announced, succinctly. "Baloney! These journalist guys fair splash theirsel's, don't they."

"All the same," Adrian declared, "that's not so bad, you know. They're moving in the right direction, there. The *Chronicle*'s a little disappointing, though. They've given us the top of the bill—but they're not quite on the right road. They say, . . . *the question that this series of extraordinary exploits seems to pose, is—Is Scotland to remain tied to the present English (or United Kingdom) export drive and economic policy? An economic crisis is looming up, a crisis which in the opinion of many people on both sides of the Border, is being quite wrongly tackled. It is suggested that Scotland's interests demand a totally different policy. As our readers will know, this newspaper has been inundated with a flood of hundreds of letters, ninety per cent of them strongly in favour of what seems to lie behind this modern Rob Roy's campaign. The economic factor is the dominant theme. . . .*"

"Damn the economic factor!" Roddie roared, jumping to his feet. "Economics—aye blasted economics! We're no' daein' this for blasted economics. We're daein' this for auld Scotlan's spirit—it's her blasted soul, man!"

"Exactly." Hope nodded. "That's what we don't seem to be getting over, as yet. Though these editorials are valuable, you know—and so are the hundreds of letters they mention. That's the waking-up process beginning to show. But we've got to demonstrate, somehow, that this isn't just a politico-economic stunt. . . . Maybe, if we issued a statement, a sort of manifesto, explaining our real motives . . . ?"

"No' likely!" Macgregor cried. "Nae manifestos. That's nae guid. There's been ower many statements an' manifestos in the papers—shooers o' them. The folk, the real folk, dinna' gi'e a damn for them. They dinna' read them. It's actions we've got to gi'e them. We've got to *dae* things, no' *say* things. An' what are we daein', sittin' here readin' the papers! We'll no' convince the country—we'll no' build yon dyke, sittin' here. C'mon—let's get crackin'.' "

Obediently, they trooped back to their work.

It was Monday afternoon, and Adrian had been away to Aberfoyle on the farmer's old bicycle, to buy the newspapers, as well as one or two other items. The dyke-building was going well—though the stone-clearance, as the haugh widened down near the farmhouse and steading, grew the more difficult and tedious. But the dyke was the main thing—the old man could get on with clearing the stones any time, once the rot was stopped. The Gregorach concentrated on the dyke—and with Rod Roy Macgregor in it, when concentrated is the word used, concentrated is what is meant.

Jeanie Macgregor was apt to be a disappointed girl.

By Wednesday night, the task was all but finished. They had been fortunate in a number of circumstances—in the weather, especially, and in the fact that they had not been disturbed. The glen was a dead-end, of course, and only the postman came up it, to Dalnablair, many a week on end—and he came at a regular hour and so could be avoided. The farmer down in the lower holding at the mouth of the glen, Fraser by name, had been warned by Mr. Macgregor, and, without making any actual declaration to that effect, appeared to be sympathetic— as well he might, for his land benefited also quite substantially from their activities. A third horse appeared on the scene, unannounced, on the Tuesday morning—and was accepted and put into service with a comparable absence of fuss.

But despite the progress, Rod Roy was not satisfied. It was all very nice, he said; the dyke was substantial and looked well—but it needed cement to set it, concrete. They must get some concrete, to pour down into the stonework, to set it. The farmer agreed that it would be more lasting that way, but pointed out that cement was expensive stuff, and they'd need a great lot of it. He just couldn't afford it; best to leave it as it was. Adrian agreed.

But the big fellow would have none of it. Cement would finish the job, and cement they must have. Where were they to get it?

The farmer said that Mackay the builder at Aberfoyle would have some, of course—but probably not enough. They'd need hundreds of bags, to make any difference—and at about six shillings a bag. . . . And then, there was the problem of the transport. If they got it delivered, all the district would know that Angus Macgregor, Dalnablair, was having his dyke repaired, and not at the laird's expense.

Roddie nodded, and dismissed the matter—meantime. But later, amongst themselves, he had more to say about it. They were going to get that cement, somehow. The Government were bound to use the stuff, on some of their ploys, weren't they? Well, then. The Forestry—he couldn't see the Forestry leaving any large supplies lying about, unfortunately. . . . The Glasgow Water Works might have some, if they knew where to look. But the transport, again. . . .

Sandy Robb wondered about the Hydro-Electric Board.

Now they were getting some place, Roddie declared. The hydro-electric folk used tons of cement—thousands of tons. Where was the nearest scheme? Loch Sloy? Too far away. But, bide a wee—wasn't there a small scheme at Loch Finlas below Luss, there? There was a reservoir being built up one of those glens south of Luss—he'd seen the dump yon day he'd gone to Crianlarich.

Pat Kelly knew about it. He'd been camping one weekend, near Balloch. They were building a dam up there. . . .

A dam meant cement—lashings of cement, Macgregor interrupted. How did they get it up?

By lorry from Balloch Station, Pat informed. They'd been camping by yon wee tearoom at Ardgillan, and sometimes the lorry-drivers would step in for a cup of tea. . . .

Roddie's fist crashed down on his knee. That was all they needed, he cried. That solved the transport, too. Tomorrow, they'd get that cement.

To Adrian's tentative objections, that the risk was hardly worth the candle, it was pointed out that this whole dyke-building scheme, while badly needed and the right kind of propaganda for their cause, lacked public appeal, lacked the element of the spectacular. Now, it would have the chance to hit the headlines!

The following afternoon, then, two more hikers joined the throng that strolled and hung around the bridge and the tearooms and the railway-station at Balloch, at the foot of Loch Lomond. Having shaved off their beards, they were by no means noticeable—scores of their kind were apt to be in evidence at Balloch any afternoon between June and October. They had no difficulty in finding what they sought. At the goods siding, beyond the passenger station, a shed was packed full with paper bags of cement. Two men were unloading more from a truck, nearby.

They had not long to wait—twenty minutes, perhaps. Then a contractor's lorry drove up, and the men on the railway wagon left it, to come and assist the lorry-driver to load up. Satisfied, the two watchers left the station, turned right-handed in the street, and then again, proceeding up the road that follows the western side of Loch Lomond.

About half a mile up, they met Roderick Macgregor—he was rather too conspicuous a character to be having hanging around, even in Balloch. They continued up the road, briskly, eyes busy.

Their spot had to be chosen with care. A clear stretch of road on either side was essential, so that they had an un-interrupted view; also a side opening or wide entrance, for turning in. They seemed to approach some such place, perhaps a mile further along the loch-shore, when Art M'Vey shouted, and pointed back. Behind them, their lorry was coming rattling along, with two private cars fairly close behind. Glumly they drew in to the side of the road, to watch it pass, laden with bags of cement.

But before long, their faces lightened again. Another similar lorry lurched past, going the other way, empty. It seemed that there might be a service of them. Moving on, they found what seemed to be as likely a place for their attempt as any, with a good half-mile clear on either side of them, and a private estate entrance on the left, fortunately with no entrance-lodge. Here they waited.

The trouble was with the private cars. There were not a

great many—nothing like the numbers there would be at the weekends—but enough to complicate the business. If they were unlucky, they might have to wait there for long enough. It was all in the laps of the gods.

In the event, they were fairly fortunate. After almost an hour's wait, they saw their lorry rounding a bend in the road away to the south—and they cursed furiously as they perceived a large car swing round after it. But presently they stopped their vituperation to listen; the imperious hooting of the horn of the vehicle in the rear was evident, even at that distance, across the calm waters of the loch. The big car swept past the lorry, and came on at speed.

"Right, boys," Roddie cried. "As soon's it's by—get crackin'. No waitin'.."

As the limousine swept past in a rattle of gravel, Alicky Shand leapt out, bent low, and flung himself spread-eagled across the middle of the road, and there lay. Art M'Vey and the big man, with anxious eyes up and down the road, hurried over to bend over him. Apart from the oncoming lorry, the road on either side was clear.

As the lorry came up, Roddie turned, and waved his hands. The driver was already slowing down his vehicle. The red-head's gesticulations caused him to draw in to the side of the road, and switch off his engine. Climbing down from his cabin, he hurried over to the group in the roadway.

"Is he bad, d'you reckon?" Art wondered, hoarse-voiced.

The driver, a short stocky man in dungarees and an open-necked shirt, caked with cement-dust, stooped down over the recumbent Alicky. Immediately his arms were pinioned behind his back, and he was jerked upright, in a vice-like grip.

"Sorry to dae this to you, mate," Macgregor said, briefly. "But I'm needin' your cement. Nae skirlin', dae as you're tell't, an' you're a'right."

"Whit the hell . . . !" the other began, but his arms were wrenched back, painfully.

"Shurrup!" he was told. "This is Rod Roy Macgregor—an' I'm ha'ein' that cement, see? Noo—are you comin' quiet, or d'you want a ding on the head?" Roddie's glance was not on the man, at all, but up and down the road, watching for traffic.

"My Goad . . . !" the driver gasped, and gulped. "Och, here—you canna' dae this . . ."

They did not wait for him to make up his mind. M'Vey and Shand ran to the lorry and climbed up into the cabin, while Macgregor swung his prisoner round, and frog-marched him towards his vehicle.

"You're comin' wi' us, either way," the big man spoke in his ear. "Is it to be a damn spanner for you—or are you comin' quiet?"

The other swallowed. "I'll come," he decided, unsteadily.

"Guid lad. Up you get, then," and he pushed him bodily up into the cab, Art reaching down a helping hand. Roddie clambered up after him, as a couple of cars appeared around the bend.

"Traffic, Rod," Alicky said, at the wheel.

"Aye, I see it. Get crackin'."

Alicky pressed the starter. It did not work. Three pairs of eyes flashed on the prisoner. "It's jiggered," the driver said.

"The handle," Alicky muttered, and picked it up from the metal flooring.

"Wait," Roddie ordered.

The two cars flashed past, apparently without a glance thrown in their direction.

Shand, with a quick look down the road, got out, inserted the handle, cranked twice, and the engine spluttered into life. Testing the gears in their gate, for a second or two, he pressed the clutch down and clashed them into reverse. The lorry moved backwards in a series of hiccuping jerks, back into the opening of the estate drive. Then slewing the wheel hard round to the right, and changing into bottom, he sent the vehicle forward, round, and back whence it had come.

"Fine," Roddie Roy approved. "It's a hell o' a squeeze, in here. Say, you—gi'e's your cap," he said to the unfortunate driver, now half-sitting on the big man's bare knees. He took the cap off, and handed it to Alicky. "Wear that," he directed. "Make you look mair like the thing. Noo, you—get doon on the floor, there. Aye, doon oot o' sight. I'm goin' to blindfold you, laddie—but nivver you mind. You'll come oot o' this fine, see. An' jist in case you try peekin', I'm tyin' your hands, tae." He drew out two lengths of cloth for the job, and with Art's assistance trussed their captive.

"Relax, noo," he said, at length. "You're goin' a wee hurl. Hoo much cement you got back there?"

"Aboot twa hunnerd an' fifty bags," the driver mumbled.

"Jist the job. Remind us to gi'e you a receipt for it, will you?" He grinned. "Here, we're comin' doon on the floor beside you, laddie, for a wee. Doon, Arty. Losh, whatna squash! Man, man—dinna' play aboot wi' a Macgregor's kilt!"

They were rattling into Balloch again.

Just west of Drymen, they drove down a side road amongst woodland, and finding a quiet little track opening into a pine plantation, they backed therein, and switched off the engine. There they waited, releasing the driver for the time being, and offering him one of Mrs. Macgregor's scones. The Duke of Montrose was playing involuntary host to them; his ancestor had done the same for Rob Roy many a time.

It was a long tiresome wait, till nightfall, but necessary. It wasn't so very dark, either, being June, but fortunately it was a cloudy night, and at least there would be few people about on the road they were going to take.

In the dusk of ten-thirty, then, they moved on, the captive blindfolded again, hoping that a laden lorry did not seem too conspicuous in Drymen at that time of night. Thereafter, they swung north up the straight road towards Gartmore and Aberfoyle, across the benighted desolation of Flanders Moss, an unfrequented highway at any time. In one half-hour they were through the single street of Aberfoyle, unchallenged, and in another were drawing up in the steading of Dalnablair.

Eager hands helped them unload the dusty easily-torn bags. The unhappy driver was kept in the cab, his eyes still bandaged, but when his hosts had their supper, he was solicitously fed with some of it by Roddie Roy himself.

By soon after midnight, unloaded, fed, and he asserted, rested, the tireless Macgregor was ready for the road again— however his companions felt about it. This time, he was going to do the driving, and he took Adrian with him, to look after the prisoner. They could expect them back in time for breakfast.

The run back was entirely uneventful, while they rattled through the sleeping villages and the empty countryside. Adrian had given the driver his receipt for the cement, and a couple of pound-notes into the bargain, Roddie pointing out the advantages that would undoubtedly accrue to a wise man who kept his mouth shut as to identifications and descriptions of persons involved—after all, they knew his name and address from his driving-licence. Peter Dugan seemed to see the point of that. He was going to be handed his lorry back exactly where it had been taken from him. Could anything be fairer?

But a mile or so east of Drymen, the powerful headlights of a car suddenly swung in behind them, and there remained. There was room to pass, but the man in the rear seemed to prefer to stay there. Adrian, glancing through the glassless window at the back of the cab, drew a quick breath. It was not so dark as to render indistinguishable the big black car with its tall lance-like wireless aerial.

"Roddie," he said. "I'm afraid that's the police, behind us."

"Baistards!" Macgregor barked.

"They're keeping just behind—and the name of these con-tractors is painted on the back of the lorry!"

"Aye," the other said, briefly. His foot pressed harder on the accelerator.

"You can't out-run them, in a lorry, you know," Hope mentioned, unnecessarily.

"You watch me," the big man jerked. "That's Drymen ahead. So long as they dinna' get in front an' block us, before then." He edged towards the middle of the road.

"I suppose all the patrol cars will have been warned about this missing lorry, by wireless."

In a couple of minutes they were clattering through Drymen. As they came to the cross, where the main road swings away southwards towards Balloch, Roddie suddenly flung the wheel hard over, and the lorry lurched, almost on two wheels, into a side street on the right. On the corner, a white-painted notice read, TO BUCHANAN AND BALMAHA. The headlights fol-lowed them round.

The big man grinned. "They'll no' oot-run us here, easy," he remarked.

It was a narrow road, this, trending away north-westwards towards the loom of the mountains, and so long as the lorry kept on the crown of the roadway, the car behind could not pass them or draw level. Evidently the police recognised the fact, and began to blare their high-pitched Klaxon in a series of authoritative yelps, at the same time winking with their headlights. Roddie returned a continued blast on his own horn, by way of derisive answer, and hurtled on, the big lorry pitching and swaying on the rough surface. They were quickly in open country again, with the woods of Buchanan Castle policies on their left, and up-sloping fields on the right.

"There's a bit roadie on the right, some place," Macgregor announced. "A hoose at the end o' it. I've climbed the ben frae here. Aye, there it's."

Ahead, a small cottage loomed up, at a road-end. Repeating his earlier performance, Roddie slewed round the wheel, and the lorry rocked into what was little more than a cart-track, climbing due north between dry-stone dykes. Changing down into second gear on the rutted uphill road, they churned on. The car at the rear clung closely.

"As weel they dinna' airm oor polis," the red-head laughed, apparently happily. "The Yanks dae this sorta thing a sight better." Then he jerked his head. "Better untie this Dugan guy," he instructed. "He'll be gettin' his lorry back, any meenit noo."

"What's the programme, Roddie?" Adrian wondered, as casually as he could.

"Cut an' run," the other replied. "This road runs up past a bit fairm—you can jist see it, yonder—an' fizzles oot in a wood, up on the side o' the hill. Ben Bhreac, it is. When we get into the wood, this guy takes ower his lorry, an' we jump for it. Then awa' up the hill. You're no' feart that a coupla flat-footed cops'll catch you on the hill?"

"Fair enough," Hope acknowledged.

"Aye. There's the fairm, noo. Anither half-mile. You got that guy untied?"

"Yes."

"Here, you—I'm right sorry we're no' puttin' you back where we found you," Roddie apologised. "Blame the polis for that. We're goin' to jump for it, in jist a meenit. You'll take ower the wheel, as we go?"

"Aye," the captive agreed, shortly.

"Right. You'll be fine. You'll get your name in the papers. Gi'e the cops Rod Roy's love. There's the wood, Major. When I say go, then. Run like hell—an' keep by me."

"Right-o."

"Guid man. Weel—here we are. Got the door open? Jump!"

The truck lurched, and from either side of it a man leapt out into the yellow glare of the patrol-car headlights. The ground seemed to jump up and hit Adrian forcefully, and at an odd angle. He stumbled, sprawled, and fell, winded.

A lot that was incoherent happened in the next few seconds. The lorry, swaying drunkenly, careered on for another twenty yards or so, and then ground to a stop. The police-car's brakes screamed, and it came to a more sudden halt, its doors swinging open. But not before it had passed the spot where the fugitives had jumped, and they were in merciful darkness. Gasping, sick, and reeling, somehow Adrian dragged himself to his feet, and, bent nearly double with the pain in his middle, staggered across the road behind the red rear-light of the black car, and up on to the bank beyond. He could hear Macgregor plunging through the undergrowth and dead sticks of the wood, ahead.

The policemen were out now. Fortunately, only one came running back, the other hurrying forward to the lorry. But one was enough for Adrian, in his present helpless state—and the steep bank above him was just too much. Doubled over and panting as he was, he tried, tried desperately, to climb it, but only fell forward on his knees.

The constable was on him before he could rise, and the hand of the law descended in no uncertain fashion on his shoulder, first pinning him down and then jerking him up. Normally, Adrian would have put up a fair fight—he had undergone his course in unarmed combat in his Army days. But no-one who has ever been completely winded will require excuses made for him. All that he could do meantime, was to struggle feebly, endeavour to dig an elbow into his captor's middle, and gulp down great mouthfuls of air.

111

The policeman, a solid burly fellow, bawled out, "I've got one o' them, Jock. He's okay." And to his prisoner, "Come on, you. Jump to it," and wrenching him round, pushed him towards the car.

Hope attempted to twist himself free, and very promptly received a stounding buffet on one side of his head, and then another on the other, for his pains. Dazed, he would have fallen had not the constable held him up. "Cut that right out," he was ordered, fiercely, "or I'll damn-well flatten you!"

Adrian, who had seldom felt flatter, attempted to bring up his knee to the other's stomach, in the way he had been taught. But unsteady as he was, he only overbalanced, and fell again. His captor cursed, and stooping, dragged him up once more, at the same time seeking to propel him bodily to the car.

The second constable, having established that there was nothing requiring urgent attention at the lorry, came running back. "Okay—I got this mucker taped," Adrian's man shouted. "There's anither up in the wood, Jock. Get him. I'll put the bracelets on this one, an' be after you. After the one in the wood, Jock."

But Jock did not have to go after the one in the wood. The one in the wood came to him. With a roar and a trampling worthy of a charge of cavalry, Roddie Roy came crashing down on them, arms flailing. With the impetus of his rush, the steepness of the bank, and all the massive bulk of him, nothing could stop him. The policeman Jock thrust up his hands to save himself, but was overwhelmed and knocked headlong, and trampled over in that human avalanche. Adrian's man, almost at the car, turned to face the onslaught—but, foolishly perhaps, he kept one hand on his prisoner. He might as well have faced up, single-handed, to a hurricane. He was flung flat against the side of the car, Adrian too, and Roddie's great fists, like steam-hammers, beat down on him. He went down, under a hail of blows, dragging his captive with him. This time it was Macgregor's strong arm that jerked Hope rudely to his feet again.

"You a'right, Major?" he was demanded. "You're no' hurt?"

"I was winded," Adrian gasped. "Getting out . . . of the lorry. Sorry. . . ."

112

"Can you make it, noo . . . ?"

"Think so. Yes."

"Guid man. C'mon, then." He stopped to give a swinging blow to the policeman at his feet, who had grabbed at his bare legs.

"Yes. I . . ." Adrian stopped. "*Roddie*—watch out!" he yelled, and on the words hurled himself forward.

But he was just too late—as indeed was the big fellow. The first policeman had only been bowled over in the rush, by no means incapacitated. He was up now, with his truncheon drawn, and aiming a blow at the back of Macgregor's head. Adrian's leap and outflung arm, turned the blow a little, and Roddie's own sideways twist, at the warning, helped. But only a little. The baton crashed down, a glancing blow that struck the red-head's left brow and laid it open, and then came down on his shoulder. And the double crack of it had a sickening vicious sound. The big man seemed to shrink in on himself for a moment, and then he tottered, and a groan escaped from his clenched teeth. An uncertain hand went up to his head.

There was nothing uncertain about Adrian's reaction, this time. Completing his forward rush, he thrust down his head, butting the constable violently on the chest. As the man staggered back, Hope's arms reached out, grabbing him, and jerked him towards him. At the same moment, his knee came up savagely and met the oncoming victim in the belly. With a howl of anguish the man Jock folded up. Stepping back, Adrian took his time, and delivered the most telling blow he had in his power to give, to the side of the head. The policeman toppled over and fell.

He turned to Roddie. The big man knelt swaying over the other constable, holding him down by sheer weight, one hand against the car to steady himself, blood running down his face. He looked in poor shape. "Can you make it, Roddie?" Hope asked, urgently.

"Eh . . . ? Och, sure. Sure. C'mon. . . ."

"Are you sure you'll manage?" Adrian eyed the other anxiously. He reached into a pocket for his handkerchief. "Take this," he said. "Your brow's bleeding."

"Uh-huh." Roddie stood up, unsteadily. Thoughtfully, he

113

looked down at the policeman, who, the weight removed from him, started to get to his feet, hauling himself up by the car door-handle. The big man let him get nearly upright, and then, almost gently, tapped him judiciously on the diaphragm. The fellow yelped, crumpled, and slipped down whence he had risen.

"Aye, well." Macgregor sighed, dabbing at his forehead with the handkerchief. "Let's get oot o' this, Major," he mumbled, thickly.

Adrian was in entire agreement. But as they moved to the bank, they both perceived another figure, standing between the car and the lorry, a silent watchful figure, hands thrust in pockets. How long he had been standing there, they had no idea. Roddie spoke. "Aye, man—guid for you!" he commended.

The lorry-driver neither moved nor made any answer, and they left him standing motionless.

Up the bank and into the wood's welcoming fastnesses they went, the big man walking heavily and occasionally stumbling, Hope watchful at his side. Once, as Roddie tottered, Adrian's hand went out to grasp his elbow. He had it shaken off, fiercely.

"Nane o' that!" he snarled. "I'm okay, see? I'm fine. When I'm needin' your damned help, I'll ask for it. Jings—I'll walk *you* off your blasted feet, the night!"

And, lurching and frequently tripping, that he proceeded to do, leading the determined if erratic way northwards, up out of the wood on to the open heather, towards the long skyline of Ben Bhreac, black against the blue of the night.

XI

IT was long past even a lazy man's breakfast-time before two dishevelled and exhausted law-breakers lurched into the barn at Dalnablair, and collapsed into the bog-hay. Even by the most direct route, they had had over twelve immensely difficult trackless heather miles to cover—and undoubtedly they had not come by the most direct route. Indeed, neither of them could have told, then or any time, by what route they *had* come. That is the sort of journey it had been.

Roddie Roy had a broken shoulder blade, obviously, and a savage cut that had laid open his left forehead, from the eyebrow well up into the curling red hair. Adrian was merely dizzy, weary, and sick.

Sympathetic hands bathed and bound up the big man's wound, contrived, under Adrian's direction, a rough sling and pad for the shoulder, and proffered food. But neither of them were hungry—sleep, apparently, was all they craved for. But before he gave in to it, Roddie had Donald Lamont and the other six instructed in unsteady but no uncertain tones, to have the cement poured in along the stonework of the dyke. After this stramash with the police, there would be the hell of a hue and cry, undoubtedly. They might well not have much longer at Dalnablair.

All that day, Friday, they slept: Adrian like a log, Macgregor fitfully, restlessly, in a sweat of pain.

In the late afternoon, Hope awakened, hungry, stiff, but much refreshed. Not so his colleague. Rod Roy was tossing and turning, moaning in his sleep. Probably he had a touch of concussion. Adrian found the concreting of the dyke well advanced. They were merely pouring the dry cement down into the cracks of the stonework; the rain and the river would set it in due course. They had got rid of three-quarters of the stuff already. But for all that, Donald Lamont met him with a long face. The wireless was making a great fuss about the fight with the police. They knew that the fugitives were on foot somewhere in the Buchanan area, and that the leader was injured. An intensive search was being carried out, it announced, the County police being reinforced from the City of Glasgow Constabulary. The public was required to inform the police of any suspicious circumstance. Doctors were warned to report at once any strange young man approaching them for treatment of head injuries. That had been in every Scottish Home Service bulletin, that day.

Adrian, acknowledging the seriousness of the situation, at the same time saw nothing that they could usefully do about it, meantime. Roddie was too ill to be moved at the moment, he felt, otherwise he would have advised that they pack up and make for Spree Cave, to lie low for a bit. They'd be much safer, up there.

The others agreed. Donald Lamont pointed out another complication. Tomorrow, Saturday, the rest of the boys would be coming out again from Glasgow for the weekend. Unless they had the sense to stay away, they might well lead the police right to Spree Cave. If the hills were being watched, a bunch of fellows all converging on the top of Ben Ure . . .

That was true, Adrian agreed. They couldn't risk that. They'd have to get word to them. But how, in time? He glanced at his watch. Four-forty-five. A wire was the only hope. When would the Post Office at Aberfoyle shut? Six, probably. If he borrowed the farmer's bike . . .

Others offered to do the job, but Hope insisted that he went. To some extent, they knew him at the Post Office—it was there he went to get the newspapers. Then, he probably looked rather more the type that might be sending telegrams . . . and perhaps not so *much* the type that people might be on the lookout for, after the wireless announcements. This he put to them diffidently, but with his own firmness.

So, somewhat jaded and stiff, he cycled the ten miles into Aberfoyle, forthwith. He met with no challenges, had to answer no questions. Reaching the Post Office, by twenty to six, he sent off a wire to Jacob Reid, 480, Bridgate, Glasgow. AUNTIE UNWELL. DONT COME THIS WEEKEND. TELL THE FAMILY. WRITING LATER. UNCLE DONALD.

He bought a newly-arrived copy of the *Evening Gazette*, and left.

In the village street, a dozen strolling hikers and holiday-makers were a great comfort to him.

The *Gazette* obviously didn't know what to make of either Rod Roy's attack on the lorry or his battle with the police. Comment was cautious and reserved, though it did speculate on what the astonishing Macgregor might want with some tons of cement. But one item of some significance it did declare; the presumed leader of the gang was injured, the police had heard him termed The Major, and his bloodstained hand-kerchief had been found, inscribed with the initials A. C. H. It looked as though the name Roderick Roy Macgregor was just a picturesque pseudonym, after all.

Next morning, after a restless night, Roddie though obviously in much pain, professed to feel much better. A healthy creature, of course, and in a fine state of physical fitness, his recuperative powers were excellent. He agreed that Spree Cave was the place for them, straight away. He and Adrian set off thither directly after they had partaken of Mrs. Macgregor's valedic-tory offering of porridge, eggs, scones, and milk. The others would follow on later, more speedily, after they had disposed of the remainder of the cement. Adrian left the farmer instruc-tions as to what he was to say about the Gregorach and his dyke, when the time came.

After the comfort of the barn and the hay, the cave was a poor draughty place. But they felt more secure up there, on the roof of the land. From one or two viewpoints nearby, they could survey the entire area for miles around. A scout was detailed to watch them, throughout the hours of daylight.

This last fact makes it all the more peculiar that, the fol-lowing afternoon, Sunday, about five o'clock, Sandy Robb, on duty, was alarmed to perceive a young woman wandering about on the hillside not half a mile below him. How she had got there, he was at a loss to know. Perhaps Sandy still was suffering from cement dust in his eyes. Rubbing them anyway, he peered. She was looking about her, as though searching the braesides. Cursing, Sandy got up, and began to run towards the cave, where a small coil of smoke blowing away in the breeze seemed only too apparent. Glancing down at her as he ran, he saw that she had stopped, and was staring directly up at him, and something about the upward set of her bare arms revealed that she was gazing through field-glasses.

He stopped. No good going on—she would see him go right to the cave. With an oath, he made his decision, and turning, started to march long-strided downhill towards her.

She actually waited for him, an unlikely figure in trim jumper and kilted skirt there amongst the tall heather. "Are you one of these Macgregor people, by any chance?" she asked, as he came up.

"Weel, I'll be damned!" Sandy gasped.

"Are you?" she insisted.

"*You* got a nerve!" the man declared, with conviction. "Jings, aye." He reached out an authoritative hand, and grasped her elbow. "C'mon, you."

"Certainly," the girl said. "But you needn't clutch me, like that. I won't run away."

"You will no'!" Sandy Robb agreed, grimly. "Jist come on— an' hud your wheesht." At the rate he propelled her uphill, she had little option, all her breath being required.

To the entrance to the cave, where the other eight sat, feeding the tiny fire with bits of heather stems to boil their tea-pannikin, he brought her, and halted. As they stared, astonished, she cried out, "Adrian!" and wrenching her arm free, came running forward.

"Helen! Good Lord!"

But after only a few steps, she faltered and stopped. "Adrian," she said, "you're . . . you're well? Not injured . . . ?"

"No." He shook his head. "No, I'm perfectly fit."

"Oh!" she cried. And again, "Oh . . . !" And thereafter promptly burst into tears. The men gaped at each other, jaws sagging.

When Adrian attempted to lead her a little way apart, Helen Burnet would not budge. In fact, she shook his hand from her arm, much more brusquely than anything she had attempted with Sandy Robb. The man could have said several things to her, helpful, explanatory, encouraging things. What he did say, was:

"Helen! How on earth did you get here?"

She did not answer. She merely turned away from him, delving into a light haversack that she carried, first for a handkerchief to dab at her eyes, and then for a powder flapjack affair and mirror.

From where he lay a-lean against an outcrop, Roddie Roy spoke briefly. "Whae's this?" he demanded.

"A friend of mine," Hope returned, equally short.

"Hoo did she ken to find you here?"

"I've no idea. You heard me asking her!"

"Hoo much does she ken, man?"

"Nothing. No details. Only what she can have read in the papers, and pieced together. I've told nobody anything."

"She was alane?" That was flung at Sandy Robb. "Hoo did she get so close?"

"I dinna' ken, Rod—I just seen her doon the hill, a wee. But she was alane, a'right."

"You needn't worry," the girl said, in what would have been a frigid voice if she had not had to swallow in the middle of it. "I'm entirely alone."

"She could ha'e been followed—watched," Macgregor snapped. "Sandy—awa' back, an' keep your eyes skint, this time. You tae, Pat. Say—she's got what looks like a decent pair o' glesses, there. Better take them, Sandy—seems like you need them!"

The girl looked as though she was going to do battle for her binoculars, but apparently thought better of it. Instead, she looked with rather more concentration at the speaker. Roddie lay with his left arm in a very rough sling, and a bloodstained length of khaki cloth was wound round his head.

"You . . . ?" she faltered. "You it was, then, that was injured? I thought . . . I thought . . ."

"You thocht it was the boyfriend, eh? I get you, lassie. The trouble is—hoo did you get here?"

"Yes—how *did* you find us, Helen?" Adrian asked, out of his lip-biting silence.

It was the big man that she answered. "Perhaps you haven't

119

seen the papers?" She tugged a crushed copy of the *Glasgow Courier* out of her haversack. "It says here, . . . *there seems to be no doubt that the leader of this notorious and elusive company, apparently known as The Major, was more or less seriously injured. His handkerchief, soaked with blood, and marked with the initials A. C. H. within a horseshoe, was found at the scene of the struggle. . . .*" Without turning her head, she jerked it in the direction of Adrian. "I embroidered those initials," she said, levelly. She continued to read, ". . . *it is the opinion of the police that he may well be suffering from concussion, as well as head injuries, and doctors are warned . . . It is thought that the fugitives could not possibly travel far in these circumstances. They escaped on to the side of a hill directly to the south of Ben Lomond, and as the entire area is now encircled, it is thought that they must still be in that vicinity. . . .*" She shrugged. "I was aware that Adrian knew this area well. He told me about this cave once, almost a year ago—he asked me to walk here to see it, once. So I took a chance on you being here. When I read all that, I felt . . . I thought . . . I . . ." She shook her head.

"You mean, you came . . . because you thought I was injured?" Adrian cried. "After everything that's happened, you came because you thought that I needed you."

She all but stamped her foot, her voice between anger and tears. "I didn't know what sort of a state you might be in! Somebody had to do something, something sensible, in all this foolishness. I just thought . . . I . . . Oh damn! *Damn!*"

Adrian Hope smiled, mirthlessly. "Sorry I disappointed you, again!" he said.

"You . . . you are *hateful*!" she cried, furiously.

"Jings!" Alicky Shand observed. "Whatna steer! Can you beat it? Are weemin no' the deil!"

"Did you see any polis, on your way here?" Roddie asked her.

She controlled her voice with an effort. "Not on the hill, no—not today. I saw some on the low ground yesterday evening, though—round about Rowardennan."

"Yesterday! Hell—were you here yesterday, tae?"

"I stayed at the hotel at Rowardennan last night. That was

120

yesterday's *Courier*. I had a look round south of Ben Lomond, in the late afternoon."

"Guid sakes, wumman!" Macgregor cried. "You're a right menace! Rangin' aboot there, seekin' us. You'd be seen miles off . . . an' the polis jist needin' to watch you!"

Almost, she smiled. "They would have to have been very sharp-eyed, then," she mentioned. "You see, I wasn't the only one. There were hundreds. In fact, half Glasgow was out searching about the hills south of Ben Lomond, for Rod Roy Macgregor! You could hardly get up the side roads, for parked cars."

"My Gosh! Is that a fact?" The Gregorach stared at one another. "Jings—d'you hear that!"

"A' lookin' for *us*, d'you say, Miss?" Donald Lamont asked.

"Yes. Though I should say, probably a good seventy-five per cent are out to warn you." She tossed her windblown head. "Being idiots!" she ended.

"Is that so! What makes you think that?" Roddie put to her.

She shrugged again. "Judging by the talk in the hotel last night—and in the train coming out."

"Oh, yeah." He turned. "D'you hear that, Major? Looks like we're maybe gettin' some place, noo."

"Maybe," Adrian said briefly. He sounded preoccupied.

"Listen. . . ." The big man sat forward suddenly, too quickly, and groaned. "Goad!" he gasped. The sweat started out on his brick-red face.

In a moment Helen Burnet was on her knees beside him. "You are badly hurt? In pain?" she cried.

"He's got a broken collarbone, a wound on the forehead, and slight concussion," Adrian informed factually.

"And is that the best you can do for him?" She pointed at the rough sling and the dirty bandage.

"In the circumstances, and with the materials to hand—yes," he said. "I've set the bone, and strapped it up."

"He should be in bed, being properly looked after."

"I'm prepared to admit it," Adrian allowed, dryly.

The girl frowned. "Let me have a look at that cut," she said. "I brought dressings and stuff with me—I may as well use them. You look as though you could do with a little more

121

advanced attention than you've been getting from our fourth-year medical!" That was said with searing scorn.

Roddie grinned, if strainedly. "Major, man—you've got a right randy, here!"

"I agree with you," Hope nodded, mildly. "But, other things aside, I can recommend her nursing. You're quite safe."

"Lie back," Helen ordered. "On this. Yes." She unwound the khaki strip, and peered at the pad, made evidently out of a handkerchief. It came away at once, revealing a very unpleasant and open wound, fully two inches long, running right up into the damp curling hair.

"Whe-e-ew!" she said, and her frown was a thing of the merest moment. "Quite a wallop you got, didn't you! I'm afraid we'll have to get rid of some of that hair." She searched in her bag for a small pair of scissors. "Never mind, you've got plenty of it round about, haven't you!" and she glanced down at his bare chest significantly.

"Jings!" Roddie said. "You're tellin' me!"

"That is the bedside manner," Adrian explained, sourly.

"Put your head so. Yes." As she snipped away at the red curls, she asked, "Your name—What is your name?"

"Roderick Macgregor, o' course."

"Well, well. Fancy that!"

Helen Burnet made a good job of dressing and bandaging the wound, had a look at the shoulder, and provided a professional-looking sling out of her first-aid kit. While this was going on, the tea billies boiled, and she was presented with a mug of the scalding, smoked, and bitter brew. She refused the offer of a stale scone, or even a mixture of the oatmeal and hot water, producing a biscuit or two from her own bag. Thereafter, handing out her stock of bandages, ointments, surgeon's plaster, and the like—to Roddie Macgregor not to Adrian—she stood up.

"Well, I'd better be on my way, I suppose," she said. "If you take my advice, Mr. Rod Roy, you'll get yourself into a proper bed somewhere, and lie up for a bit. And under a genuine doctor's care! Or is that too sensible a suggestion to propose to any of you lunatics?"

"Jist a meenit!" Alicky Shand objected. "Whae says you'll be on your way, eh?" He turned to Roddie. "We canna' jist let her go this way, Rod. It's no' safe."

There was a rumble of agreement from the others. Macgregor said nothing.

"What d'you mean—can't let me go?" the girl demanded, hotly.

"I mean jist what I said," Alicky asserted. "You're maybe a'right, an' you're maybe no'. You dinna' sound right keen on us, at that! We canna' risk lettin' you awa', kennin' where we're hidin' oot."

"D'you think I'd stoop to giving you away?"

"Maybe you wud," Shand answered bluntly. "We dinna' ken. An' we're no' takin' the risk, see. Maybe you wudna' *mean* to gi'e us awa', but you might dae it, jist the same."

"Even if she didna', she might be seen comin' frae here, an' gi'e us awa' that way," somebody else suggested.

"Aye. Or the polis might gel a hud o' her, an' *make* her talk. They c'd dae that, fine."

"Nonsense!" she said.

"She'll jist ha'e tae bide here wi' us for a whilie," Alicky declared, still looking at Macgregor. "She'll be anither ta feed, but she'll no' eat that much."

"She'll do nothing of the sort!" Adrian exclaimed, breaking his rather noticeable silence. "The thing is absolutely absurd. She can't stay up here with us—have some sense, for Heaven's sake! It's quite impossible."

"Oh, yeah!" Art M'Vey said. "Hoo d'you make that oot? If we can bide here, she can. She came here on her ain, did she no'?"

"Rubbish!" Hope snapped. "A girl brought up like Miss Burnet can't be kept up in a cave on a mountain-side, against her wishes, with a crowd of—of toughs! I'm not standing for it. Anyway, she'd be a fearful handicap to us. . . ."

"I would, would I!" Helen Burnet said, quickly.

"Of course you would."

"Why, may I ask?"

"Good Heavens—surely *you* don't need to ask that! It's obvious. Because you *are* a girl, of course. . . ."

123

"I see. And would my menace to you arise from my being a drawback physically—or just because of the brutal passions I'd arouse!"

"Don't be a silly little fool, Helen!" Adrian told her, wrathfully.

Roddie Roy was grinning, but still saying nothing.

Footsteps interrupted the unseemly altercation. It was Sandy Robb back from his lookout. "There's some guys awa' doon in yon Glen Gaoith," he reported. "They're a guid lang way off—I wouldna' ha'e seen them wi'oot the glesses. They're no' dressed as polis, but they're snoopin' aboot. . . ."

"Right. Awa' back, an' keep an eye on them," Roddie directed. He glanced up at Helen. "That settles it, then, lassie."

"Does it?" she asked.

"Aye. You're stayin'. Och, you'll be fine an' comfortable—an' you can fecht wi' the Major as much as you like!"

"Macgregor—this is crazy!" Adrian cried. "You can't do this."

"Can we no'? Quiet, you!" He turned back to the girl. "You're stayin'," he repeated.

"Am I?" she said, meekly.

"There'll be search-parties out for her! Her father's an influential man—he'll make a fearful outcry. . . ."

"Let him."

"He won't, you know," Helen mentioned. "He rather thinks I'm away for the week—to a friend's at Helensburgh! You see, I came prepared to stay a little." She was addressing Macgregor, not Adrian at all. "I thought he might need me. I was mistaken, but . . ." She shrugged her slim shoulders.

"Well, damn it all!" Adrian Hope announced, disgustedly.

124

XII

SO Helen Burnet remained with the fugitives at Spree Cave
—and made remarkably little fuss about it, and a minimum of one sort of anticipated trouble, at least. She was
given the recess at the back of the cave to sleep in, a deep
couch of heather, and two or three sacks brought from Dalnablair as blankets, and all the privacy that she could want. She
was treated with respect by some, with wariness by others,
pointedly ignored by one or two—but suffered disrespect
from none. There was no undue familiarity—and that went
for Adrian Hope, too. He got scant encouragement, indeed—
less than any of them. Her attitude was cool, business-like,
detached, self-contained—impersonal even. He did not seek
to alter it, towards himself—far from it. But it was a little
trying, nevertheless.

Only to Roderick Macgregor was she different. Towards
him, her patient, she adopted an attitude of kindly amused
tolerance, sisterly, casual even, but with its own undercurrent
of warmth and understanding. That the big man responded to
it, in his own silent watchful way, was not to be denied. He
called her Lassie, suffered her ministrations, ignored her orders,
and accepted her scoldings, all with the same quizzical canny
geniality. She made the perfect foil and contrast to him—and
both of them knew it. So did Adrian Hope.

But Adrian, and the other less favoured Gregorach, did get
some small satisfaction out of the girl's presence with them,
for all that. Indirectly, inferentially, she was able to tell them
much that they were anxious to know, as to the public reaction
to their campaign, in Glasgow at any rate. Everyone was wondering about them, she said, discussing, arguing, comparing
notes. Rod Roy Macgregor was the common theme of the
café, the queue, and the common-room. Small boys played at
Macgreegor-and-the-Polis, in the streets. A man signing himself
American Scot, had written to the *Sunday Post* offering a

fantastic sum if Rod Roy would come on a tour of the States. Glasgow University Debating Society had held a public debate, For and Against Macgregor, at the end of which it was unanimously decided to found a Rod Roy Association. And so on. Their leaven seemed to be working its own peculiar pattern.

The weather was good, though chilly at nights, Roddie made good progress, and nobody came within a couple of miles of their hideout—Ben Ure was a dull hill, with no tracks to it, and no rocks to climb, holding little to attract either hikers or climbers. If the police were indeed making an intensive search for them, they seemed to be sparing themselves the hilltops—sensible men.

The Gregorach did not spend all their time sitting on the top of Ben Ure, of course, waiting. Their nights were busy, if their days were not. Food had to be collected, and news. Some nights only Macgregor and the girl and one companion were left at Spree Cave.

On the Tuesday night, Adrian made his way, with a foraging party, down to Dalnablair. The farmer, considering that he was rudely ravished from slumber at his good lady's side to attend to them, was remarkably helpful. He gave them oatmeal, potatoes, eggs, all the scones in the kitchen, and generally the run of his wife's larder—and even made a gesture of refusing payment for what they took. For all that, Adrian imagined that he looked considerably relieved when he was told that this would probably be the last occasion that they'd have to call on him.

No, he informed, the police had not got as far as Dalnablair yet—though he'd heard that they had been enquiring at farms in the Glen Senich and Loch Ard areas. It looked as though they were working up towards him—it likely was only a question of time.

Time—that was the point, Adrian declared. A little time was all they asked, time for Rod Roy to get well enough to travel, time for the first flush of the hue and cry to die down. If they could be left in peace, even for a week. . . . But if the police did come to the farm, there was no point in himself hiding anything, denying anything. That dyke spoke for itself. He'd have to pile it on. Say that he had had no hand in it, that he'd been terrorised, confined to the farm, that he was still scared of Rod Roy and hadn't dared to risk coming to the police on his own. Blame it all on the Gregorach—they could take it! The authorities couldn't do anything to him—and they certainly couldn't undo the good work that had been done on the dyke. The trouble was, once the police knew about Dalnablair, the search for themselves would be narrowed down enormously. They would have to try and get away immediately thereafter, if they were not to be caught. If Mr. Macgregor could fly some sort of a signal—say some colourful item of washing on a line by itself. . . . Yes, a red counterpane would do perfectly—they'd be able to see that miles away, from the hill.

Hope left three rather shaggy-looking letters with the farmer, for postage, two to be handed to the Postie the following day, the third to be retained until the police arrived, or the news of their dyke-building activities broke otherwise, when it was to be dispatched at once. Of the first two, one was to Jakey Reid, giving him more or less marking-time instructions to keep the residue of the gang together, and to hold it in readiness to act at short notice, the other to their fund-earning stalwarts in the far North, desiring that no further money-orders be sent south meantime—they might well be coming for the cash in person. The third, deferred letter, was addressed to Archibald Duncanson Esq., c/o The Press Association, and gave the full story of the Gregorach's operations at Dalnablair, with the underlying motives, and signed Rod Roy Macgregor. On how long it would be before this last document reached its destination—it must follow directly on the police discovery of the Dalnablair project—depended much.

All they asked was for a brief breathing-space. All they needed was a little time. . . .

But they did not get it, time nor breathing-space. Round about noon the next day, with Adrian and his five foragers still asleep after their strenuous night, Pat Kelly came hurrying down to the cave-mouth from his lookout, big with news.

"The polis!" he cried. "Lashin's o' them. A' ower the place. . . ."

Roddie, attempting to roast a blue hare that they had snared, on a spit over a crackly blaze of heather-stems, looked up. "Uh-huh?" he said.

"There's a right mob o' them, Rod. I jist seen twa o' them come roond a bit knowie. . . . An' then there was anither, an' then twa mair. . . ."

"Shurrup!" the big man barked. Beside him, Helen Burnet, roasting potatoes in the embers, was watching him closely, and all around men were sitting up yawning and rubbing their eyes. "Noo—take your time, laddie. Where are these polis?"

"Ower the way, Rod—across the glen. Ower on the side o' the ben—Ben Lomond. . . ."

"Then they're twa mile off, wi' bad ground to cross. Nae need to panic. What way are they goin'?"

"This way. They're comin' right for us, spread oot a' across the blasted hill. They're combin' the place, see. . . ."

"Hoo many?"

"I seen six or seevin—but there may be mair doon-brae a bit. . . ."

"Here—give me those glasses!" Adrian interrupted. "I'll have a look."

"No!" Macgregor snapped. "You bide here, Major." He smiled. "Looks like you'll maybe ha'e some organisin' to dae—in a hurry! Anither guy can ha'e the look-see. Where's Sandy Robb?"

"He's down at the burn, getting water, I think," Helen Burnet said.

"Pat—awa' doon an' fetch him up. An' keep baith o' yous oot o' sight o' thae polismen. Donald—awa' you up, an' ha'e a bit look wi' the glesses. See jist hoo many there are, what they're daein', an' if they're comin' ower here. An' dinna' be that lang awa'." He turned back to Adrian Hope. "Weel, Major—this looks like it!"

"It does," the other agreed, grimly. "If they're coming over this way, and doing the job thoroughly, we're bound to be found."

"Aye. Unless we dae a bolt for it."

"You're in no condition to do any bolting, and well you know it!"

128

"Och, I'm no' deid yet, man. I'll manage fine."

"You will be, if you start any sort of race with the police!"

"That's true, at all events," Helen confirmed.

"You couldn't run any distance, to save your life," Adrian persisted. "And the police aren't likely to let you *walk* away from them!"

"We could stay, an' fecht it oot," Art M'Vey suggested. "There's maybe nae mair o' them than us."

"That's out of the question," Hope exclaimed. "It would be the end of our campaign, whoever won. We're not risking a stand-up fight with the police."

"Weel—we've got to either run, or bide here," M'Vey pointed out.

"We'll dae baith," Roddie decided. "You run—an' I'll bide here."

"Hell, Rod—what d'you take us for . . . ?"

"Damn that for a ploy!"

"Look—nae use the hale show bein' jiggered because I canna' run," Macgregor said. "Awa' wi' you—you're better men on the hill than any dam' polismen. The lassie, here, can bide wi' me—she'll no' be for racin' the polis, either."

"No' likely. . . ."

"Och, tae hell wi' that. . . ."

"You know, Roddie's got something there, maybe," Adrian asserted, thoughtfully.

"There y'are—the Major's a sensible guy," the big man commented. "He kens what's what."

"Say—*you* rattin', noo!"

"Jings—whatna' dirty stinker, him . . . !"

Even Helen Burnet stared in surprise.

"Listen," Adrian leaned forward. "If some of us, most of us, were to slip down the side of the hill here, and then, when in full view of the police, make a dash for it, the chances are, they'd all follow us. Probably none would come up here—not at first, anyway. Likely they'd send somebody up to have a look at where we'd been, afterwards. At first, it would just be a paperchase. And Roddie, with somebody to give him a hand, could slip away quietly in the other direction."

"Say—that's an idea, Major. . . ."

"Yeah—that's right."

Rod Roy said nothing.

"I don't see any other way out," Adrian went on, eagerly. "We maybe could all get away, that way. I . . ."

Donald Lamont, running, came round the north side of the hill, towards them. "They're doon into the glen, noo," he reported. "Comin' right to us, across the peat-hags. I counted eleevin o' them, a' strung oot. They'll no' miss much, an' they look like comin' right up here."

"That settles it," Hope cried. "Roddie—you agree?"

"Yes," the red-head said, briefly. "But I dinna' like it."

"We've no choice," Adrian asserted. "See, now—we've always said that the easiest way out of this trap, was due north around the head of Loch Arklet, on to Stronachlacher, and along Loch Katrine-side to Glen Gyle. That's no more than eight miles. You could make Glen Gyle by tonight, couldn't you? Then up over the head of it by that track, and into Glen Falloch tomorrow. Say we arranged to try and meet at the head of Lochan Ardran at noon, or soon after, tomorrow?"

"Aye, maybe," Macgregor nodded. "But what aboot you ones?"

"We'll try and lead the police a dance round the head of Loch Chon, and away eastwards up the side of Ben Venue—plenty of wooded country there. Then, at night, we'll slip down to Loch Katrine, borrow somebody's boat—every house on the loch has one—and ferry ourselves across. We ought to be able to make our way over to the Braes o' Balquhidder during the night, and over Cruach Ardran in the morning, to the lochan. Right?"

"Uh-huh. An' if either o' us dosna' make it . . . ?"

"We mustn't wait. Daren't hang about for any time, in this whole area. We've got to get north, into safe country, any way we can. We want to get up into North Argyll or Inverness-shire. . . ."

"Look, Major," Alicky Shand interrupted. "If we dinna' get crackin', we'll no' get anywhere, at a'."

"Yes, I know. But we've got to get this settled. We've got to have an agreed rendezvous—somewhere to meet. Some-where we can all find our way to, but where we won't be too noticeable. . . . How about near that new youth hostel they've opened in the Mamore Forest, in Lochaber—Glen Doran? There's an old ruined castle near the head of the glen, there—Castle Doran. We wouldn't look out of place near a hostel. . . . How about that?"

"Aye—it'll dae's well's the next."

"In how long, will we say?"

"It's a fair hike, yon. Eighty—a hunnerd miles? Gi'e's a week, anyway."

"Right. If we don't meet tomorrow at Lochan Ardran, then a week from today at Castle Doran. All got that? Whoever's there first, just waits for the others. No doubt, if any of us are caught, the rest will hear about it through the papers."

"And if any o' us *are* caught . . . ?" Art M'Vey wondered.

"Then the rest just carry on with our efforts, as best we can. Eh, Roddie?"

"Sure."

"Well—who's staying with you?"

Macgregor looked round. "Better Donal', I reckon. He's the auldest."

But Adrian wanted Lamont with him, to help control his difficult team. "He's a good runner," he objected, "I think Donald should be with me. How about Kelly—he's got a bad ankle?"

"Uh-huh. Okay."

"Suits me," Pat Kelly shrugged.

Almost reluctantly, Adrian looked over to where the girl knelt. "You'll be all right, Helen?" he asked. "If you just wait here till both parties have gone, and then make back on your own to Rowardennan, you'll be all right. You can do that?"

"I could, yes," she answered slowly. "But I'll see my patient safely down on to a decent road, first."

"That's quite unnecessary, of course. . . ."

"Och, lassie—dinna' heed me."

The young woman said nothing.

"Right. Time we were off, then." The others had been gathering together their scanty gear, while the discussion had been going on. "Leave everything bulky and weighty in the cave," Hope directed. "If we don't travel light, we won't travel at all! Shand—can you see them now?"

"No," Alicky called back. "They must be under the hill, now."

"We'd better move, then. Down the side of this shoulder—in the burn-channel, there. Then, when we're about half-way down, we'll up on to the shoulder and let them see us. Then—scram."

"Uh-huh."

"Okay then. . . ."

Hope looked at Macgregor. "Well—good luck, Roddie."

"Aye," the big man said. He shook his red head a little. "Mind—I dinna' like it. It's . . . och, to hell! Awa' wi' you—get crackin'."

Adrian's eyes lifted to the girl, and met hers. For a moment they held, there. "Well . . ." he said.

She nodded, still-faced, unsmiling. "Take a—a certain amount of care of yourself, Adrian," she told him, levelly.

"Yes. I'm sorry . . . about all this, Helen."

"Yes. Well—I think you'd better go."

"Perhaps. Well . . . goodbye."

"Goodbye."

Hope shook his head, and then abruptly lifted up his voice. "Here we go, then! All ready? Come on." And without a backward glance, he led the way downhill.

Soon they were into the trough of a burn-channel, and down this they filed, with a small shoulder of hill between them and the advancing police. Perhaps half a mile down, they halted, while Adrian crept up on to the little skyline, and peered over. A thousand yards away, a long line of dark-clad figures came methodically towards them, strung out across the heather, each something like seventy yards apart. He could count eight of them, but the configuration of the land obviously hid others. In their present position, he reckoned that they were near the centre of the line.

Back down to the others he wriggled, and they moved on down the deepening groove of the stream. After about five minutes more of it, with their protective ridge beginning to flatten out amongst the peat-hags of the lower ground, they stopped again. A peep over revealed the nearmost end of the police line no more than five hundred yards off, and, owing to the shape of the hill, swinging in towards them.

"This is it, then, boys," Adrian announced. "Up on to the higher ground in front, show ourselves, a shout or two, and when we see we're observed, off down towards the head of Loch Chon there, at the double. It should be easy—we're fresh, and they can't be. If I seem to hang back a little, at first, it'll just be that I'm making sure they're all following us. No questions? Good. Here goes, then."

Up on to the short heather of the spine they ran. Plain before them the police were striding. They did not need to shout— the opposition did the shouting. Whistles shrilled, and continued right up the line and away over the contour of the hill. The constabulary came to a ragged halt, staring.

"Right!" Adrian yelled. "Scram!" and swinging about, began to run whence they had just come. Making a great fuss about it, his companions followed suit.

Once over the ridge, Hope let the others pass him, and turned to gaze back through the heather-stems. The police were running now, too. But it was up the hill that he looked, where unseen, whistle-blowing was still going on. One by one, black figures appeared over the skyline. Three . . . four . . . he counted. Added to how many lower down? Four . . . five —that was nine. Incidentally these lower ones were getting rather too close. . . . There was another. That was ten. Hadn't Lamont said eleven, altogether? Need he wait—dare he wait? Thank Heaven—that was the other. . . . Confound it—another still! That made twelve. Lamont had counted wrong. Anyway, they were all after them—that was all that mattered. . . .

Jumping up, Adrian Hope began to run in earnest.

XIII

THAT was a good chase, as chases go—at least, to start with. They did not have to run too fast, and though the peat-hags made rough going for them, they were probably much harder on the police, who no doubt were tired, and were unlikely to be in such good training for this sort of thing either. Also, for the first mile or so, at any rate, their route lay downhill.

In loose order they ran on, past the Loch Katrine aqueduct, and into the alder-dotted haughlands at the head of Loch Chon, keeping the pursuit a comfortable quarter of a mile behind them. In good style, they splashed through the little river that drains into the loch, and then, pounding on beyond, at a shout from Donald Lamont, stopped short. There was a small road to be crossed, ahead, the road from Loch Ard to Stronach-lacher, and patrolling slowly along it were two motorcyclists, ominously dressed in blue-black.

Only for a moment, they stared, and then Adrian called out. "There's only the two of them, boys. Bunch together, and rush it!"

That they did, drawing together into a compact group, and plunging forward across the haugh for the road. Behind them, some deep-chested constable had enough wind left to blow his whistle. The two policemen in front waited for them, astride their vehicles—though it was possible to detect some hint of uncertainty in their attitude.

As the Gregorach came panting up, the patrol seemed to decide that a gesture was all that could be expected of them, in the circumstances. Starting up their machines, they drove them up the road a little way, and then turning, came roaring down on the party just as it was going to cross. But it was obvious that they were not going to run them down, any more than they were going to commit *felo de se*. As they came up, Adrian led a rush towards them, and promptly both bicycles

134

swerved away. The Gregorach howled their derision as the drivers thundered off, to turn again at a safe distance in a repeat of the performance. And from behind, in the haugh, a whistle piped disgustedly.

They wasted no more time over the motorcyclists, but hastened straight on up the long, long lift of Druim nan Càrn, itself only a sprawling spur of the great massif of Ben Venue. Mile upon rolling mile the heather climbed upwards, a daunting spectacle to panting runners—but almost certainly more daunting still to panting policemen further back.

Druim nan Càrn was a sore test undoubtedly, for thudding hearts, bursting lungs, and aching muscles, especially in the lower reaches, waterlogged and peat-pocked. Soon they were only walking, often forward-bent with hands on knees—though even then, a glance behind them revealed them as steadily gaining on the pursuit. But Adrian Hope's mind was neither preoccupied with the murderous ascent, nor elated at their outdistancing of the constabulary. It was the longer-term geographical problem that was worrying him. He had observed those two motorcyclists, after contact with the foot police, to go roaring off, one north, one south, along that narrow road. Their object was all too clear.

The fact was, that however well they were going, they were islanded now, isolated on this land mass of Ben Venue and its satellites. To the south of them were the strung lochs, Chon, Dhu, Ard, and Dundhu, and worse, the Stronachlacher-Loch Ard-Aberfoyle road, and to the north, the long barrier of Loch Katrine. It was a big island, certainly, but with enough police warned and drafted in, they were bound to be cornered eventually. And if the police enlisted others—Forestry workers, keepers, and so on. . . . It was only one o'clock now; they had ten hours to fill in before it would be dark enough to risk crossing Loch Katrine. Ten hours of dodging.

They made the hog's-back ridge of Druim nan Càrn at long last, gasping. The police were almost a mile behind, and in a very ragged line indeed—but still they came on. They looked down now into a dark lochan at the head of a deep corrie, almost a glen indeed, down which a fair-sized stream poured, to empty itself eventually into Loch Katrine. Across the gut of

135

the corrie, Venue itself rose ruggedly. To their right, south-eastwards, was another great lumpish hill of two summits, blocking out the view in that direction.

They held a brief, breathless conference. The general consensus of opinion was that they'd be safer on the northern, Loch Katrine, side, where there were no good roads. On the other hand, this corrie and glen below them could be a positive deathtrap. If they moved round the head of it, and so on to Venue itself, keeping to the north side. . . . That was accepted.

They were half-way round, and going fairly strongly in the short heather, when Alicky cursed, and pointed. Coming into view within the V of the opening glen, were a couple of boats down on the loch—from their speed and the directness of their course, obviously not fishing, and propelled by outboard motors. Even as they watched, another hove in sight. Adrian, who still carried Helen Burnet's binoculars, focused them on the loch.

"Yes," he nodded, grimly. "Police in each of them."

"Jings—a blasted regatta!" Shand complained. "The fleet's in, boys!"

"If they've got binoculars with *them*, then they've seen us," Hope pointed out. "And if they've one of these walkie-talkie sets. . . ."

"Hell—will they ha'e yon . . . ?"

Adrian shrugged. "Many of the police are being equipped with them, worse luck. We'd better get over the hill, out of sight of the loch. It gives them too good a view."

So, using what cover they could, they swung southwards again, and in a hurry. Any minute now, the police at their backs would be appearing over the skyline. If they could get over this high ridge, before the pursuit topped Druim nan Càrn. . . .

They did not. While still that seemingly unending slope curved away up in front of them, the first of the constabulary —in shirt-sleeves now—came into view behind them. And promptly a whistle blew, high and clear.

On they hurried, over the bare gravelly summit, plain for all the world to see. And just beyond the top, they halted. Away below them, a couple of miles nearly, but noticeable indeed, a long line of black dots was strung out and moving upwards.

"Damnation!" Adrian swore. That was nothing to what his companions said.

Art M'Vey proposed that they carry on, due east, on high ground—they could outflank this lot down below, maybe, and outdistance the crew behind. Hope pointed out that it was what was in front that would matter; it was unlikely that they would leave any side open, once they started. Alicky Shand said they ought to split up into ones and twos, and scatter— some would be sure to get through. Adrian was against that, too. Some would, as inevitably, be caught, and that was relative defeat; also, while they stuck together, they were strong, safe enough against arrest by any but a large body of police. They had seen what had happened back at the road, with the motor-cyclists. They had got the name of desperate characters, to be handled with discretion. Seven of them in a bunch would be apt to daunt anything less than their own number of police. Donald Lamont agreed; they should stick together.

What else, then? Adrian saw nothing for it but back across to the north flank of Venue, and down to Loch Katrine-side. They would be observed from the boats, of course, but there were thick woods there, all along the loch-shore, that would take a lot of beating-out. They would have to try and go to ground, down there, till darkness. It was a policy of despera-tion, but he saw nothing else for it. Even as he argued it out, they were heading that way, back north-eastwards, over the ridge again.

They were in sight of the first batch of weary police all the way round the rough-hewn side of Ben Venue, and for most of it in sight of the water-borne forces also. It was a trying progress, physically and psychologically. They felt as exposed and unprotected as flies on a window-pane, and tired, tired. Just before they turned away round a thrusting north-westerly spur, three-quarters of an exhausting hour later, they perceived the first of the beaters from the bottom of the hill appearing over the ridge behind them. There would be a lot of hot policemen in Rob Roy's country, that day.

Whenever they were well out of sight of the pursuit—though not of the beaters, unfortunately—they turned downhill, and started on a hectic dash towards the cover of the trees, a good mile below. It was a jarring, frame-jolting, breath-bludgeoning charge, slithering, floundering, falling. When they were not tripping in long heather or leaping from tussock to tussock, they were skimming light-footed over quaking moss or stumbling amongst hidden outcrops or scrambling through black peat-hags. Sprained ankles seemed the least that they could expect, especially with so many back-flung glances. The trees seemed to be possessed of an infuriating and devilish capacity for keeping their distance.

But at last the heather gave place to heightening bracken, and out of its green fronds stunted birches began to thrust. Then they were amongst the outliers of the trees, and into the blessed green cover they plunged. Though, when last seen, the two nearest boats had been turning in towards them, there was as yet no sign of the line of police on the high ground that they had so precipitously left.

After a short breathing-space, they turned sharply left-handed, doubling back parallel with the loch-shore. Down here, the slanting woodland proved to be by no means so thick as it had appeared from above, open birch-woods dotted with clumps of junipers and black Scots pines. But it provided fair cover, both from the loch below and the hill above. Unfortunately, though it seemed to continue lengthwise mile upon mile, it averaged no more than four or five hundred yards in depth. Obviously they could be very easily cut off in it.

Taking their time, going cautiously, they had moved back, westwards, perhaps a mile, when a pair of roe deer, bounding gracefully, fleetly, came across a ferny clearing in front of them, directly towards them, only swerving away uphill in wide-eyed alarm when fifty yards or so from them.

"Those brutes were scared," Adrian pointed out. "They were in a hurry. Something in front there had disturbed them."

"Aye," Sandy Robb confirmed. "They dinna' run that fast, unless they're scare't."

"The polis, frae one o' thae boats, maybe?" Donald suggested.

"Perhaps—though they might have other people out, beating the woods."

"Say—if one o' us was to go on ahead, for a look-see . . . ?"

"No. Better back a bit. Remember, we passed a sort of open ride, about quarter of a mile back? And a little further still was a rocky knoll? We'd get a view from that, and if anybody is advancing across here, we'd see them cross that ride. . . ."

"Guid enough. Back then."

They turned on their tracks once more. Their open space, somewhat overgrown with scrub-birch, proved to have the remains of a roadway running up it—no doubt a relic of the days when these hills and valleys supported a population of sorts. Two or three hundred yards beyond it, rose a tall bluff of dripping rock, mantled with a few stripling rowans. Climbing to the top of this, they could observe the ride reasonably clearly, only an odd tree or two intervening. Unfortunately the rock-summit was bare, providing no cover. Only one man dare remain up there. Leaving Alicky with the glasses, the others climbed down and hid themselves in the bracken below.

They had barely stretched themselves, glad of the chance of a rest, when Shand was back down to them.

"They're comin'," he reported. "I didna' wait till they got to yon space. I seen them back before yon. I seen twa polismen, an' twa guys in plus-fowers, wi' dugs!"

"Dogs!" Adrian cried. "Lord of that! Keepers, they'll be?"

Around him, the Gregorach had jumped up at the news. Dogs painted a different colour to the picture, altogether. They couldn't lie low in woods and thickets, with dogs after them.

"Aye. Likely. I seen three dugs, an' fower men . . . but there could be mair. . . ."

"Time we werena' here, then," Lamont declared, and started off eastwards, at a run. All followed him.

They had not run far, when, crossing a glade, somebody pointed upwards. From here they could see a wide segment of the hill above. And filing down towards them, not in a line any more, but one after another, came their persistent escort.

"What noo?" M'Vey demanded.

Adrian shrugged. "Nothing for it but to carry on. We'll get

139

a bit lower down, so that these people above don't see us. There's just the possibility that the way east *may* be clear." That was said cheerfully, but with a minimum of conviction.

It was similarly received.

Their trending downhill, and an unexpected indentation of the loch-shore, precipitated a crisis. Suddenly they broke to the edge of open ground, and below them was a little sand-fringed bay, lined with alders and Junipers. And in the middle of it, a couple of hundred yards out, rocking gently on the wavelets, was a boat in which sat three policemen, watching the shore, binoculars in their hands.

Crouching down urgently, the fugitives stared, confounded.

"Jings—we'll no' get by yon, easy," Shand panted. "Goad damn them a'!"

"Losh—we've had it, chums," Robb said. "They're a' roond us. . . ."

"We can still fecht it oot!" Art M'Vey reminded truculently.

"Aye, we'll fight it oot—but we'll dae it oor ain way." Donald Lamont answered, strongly. "Look—yon boat's oor answer . . . if we can get it."

Adrian drew a quick breath. "How could we?" he asked.

"If maybe jist twa o' us creeped roond an' showed oorsel's at the ither side o' the bay, kiddin' on we were right pecht, they'd likely come in. If we started runnin' awa', ay trippin' an' fallin', they'd likely follow—a bittie, anyway. The ithers could cut them off frae their boat . . ."

"Damn it—it's worth trying! Could you handle a boat like that . . . with one of these motors?"

"Guid sakes, man—I've been handlin' boats a' my days!"

"Fine! Shand—you and me'll be the decoys. The rest of you—if it comes to blows, don't be too rough with the police. We've enough on our plates already." So, reeling drunkenly, tripping and stumbling, the two emerged from their hiding and went lurching down the hill towards the water's edge. They were observed immediately, but they pretended that they themselves did not see the boat, even when, presently, the engine started up with a stuttering throb.

They were almost down to the sand and pebbles of the little beach before they elected to perceive the boat, now only fifty or so yards from the shore. Then Adrian pointed, and shouted, shouted wildly. Alicky answered in corresponding panic. They both began to run, shamblingly, in opposite directions. Adrian bawled for Shand to come back and follow him, which the other apparently did only with reluctance. By which time the boat was in the shallows. As though absolutely all-in, they started to stagger away along the shore eastwards, constantly tottering and even falling. Possibly they overacted their parts, but these policemen were new to them, and evidently accepted it all. As they turned, reeling, into the bushes and trees at last, they had the satisfaction of seeing the three men from the boat coming long-strided after them.

Increasing their pace only gradually, to entice the pursuit on, they climbed a little way up again, till, from an eminence, they could see their friends streaming down to the water's edge and the unattended boat. Nodding to Alicky, Adrian gave the thumbs-up sign, and discarding their lame-duck antics, they set off at their fastest, at a tangent, downhill again for the shore.

It was a near thing, for the constables, no great distance behind, were able to cut across. Also they were fresh men, and long-legged. For a minute or two it was touch and go, as they made up on their quarry hand over fist. And then, the noise of their own engine starting up came to them, and they faltered, halted, and looked back, alarmed. Irresolute, they stood for a moment, and then, turning, they hurried whence they had come.

Donald and M'Vey were in the boat, the others standing in the water alongside. They were gazing in the direction of the chase. Seeing the policemen returning, they recognised the position, and Lamont ordered the other three to pile in, the last man to push off. Even as the constables came splashing hugely into the water, their boat chugged round and headed out into the loch. While the Gregorach shouted gleeful advice to the law, Donald at the tiller stood up and waved to their two stranded companions, now out on the shore again, further along. He gestured towards a little wooded point, the easternmost horn of the bay. Hope nodded and waved, and began to run thither.

The police saw, and ran too, but they had no chance. Boat and runners had the advantage of them. Before they reached the point, Adrian and Alicky were wading out fifty yards offshore, on the pebbly bottom, with the boat coming along to them. Willing hands hauled them aboard.

Heavily-laden and low in the water, the little craft swung round in a semicircle, to head for the other side.

Though fifteen miles long, Loch Katrine is nowhere much more than a mile in width. Donald reckoned that five or six minutes should see them across it—if they were not interfered with. And there seemed every chance that they would not be. There had been a number of boats scattered about the loch, but most of them had moved in to the south shore. The stolen craft would be half-way across before any of them were likely to notice it. Only two boats remained more or less in mid-loch, and one of them was too far away to the west to be of any danger. The other, apparently containing two policemen and a civilian, was half a mile off, to the east, evidently placed to watch the north-east face of Ben Venue. Its occupants took a little time to decide just what they should do, when they saw the errant and heavily-laden craft—as who would blame them? When, eventually, they started up the engine and began to circle round towards the fugitives, it was in a very wide arc indeed. If they kept that up, they ought not to be a great deal of trouble.

It was a strange sensation, after all their hectic activity, to be sitting there idly chug-chugging across the placid waters— and knowing that innumerable enemies were watching them and cursing them. They even found two packages of sand-wiches in the boat—also helpful to the morale. This was a much more suitable way of making their exit, than all the undignified running. The only problem was—what might be waiting for them on the other side?

The northern shore was wooded, but less densely than was the southern. Somewhere through there, a road ran. Adrian swept it with his glasses, but could make out nothing, neither road nor any reception-committee—only a house or two em-bowered in trees, each with its own little jetty at the lochside.

And then, as he was lowering the binoculars, something caught his eye, away to the east—movement. There it was again—a car speeding along the road, visible intermittently through gaps in the trees. A large black car.

They were two-thirds of the way across and more—in a minute or so they'd be in. The car had perhaps a mile and a half to cover, to reach their landfall. A hasty council decided that they had no option but to carry on.

The road ran only a couple of hundred yards up from the shore. Avoiding any of the little piers, they grounded the boat on a pebbly beach, and leapt ashore. The wary craft trailing them still kept its distance astern. Round a bend, quarter of a mile away, they glimpsed the black car come speeding. Obviously it was a powerful police vehicle.

"We've just time to get across the road an' inta the bushes," Lamont shouted.

"An' then mair damned runnin'!" Alicky groaned.

Adrian nodded, incisively. "That's it—that's the trouble. We can't go on running much longer. We'll soon be foundered. And these are fresh police, this side. Look—are you game for another of these lame-duck efforts, with a car as the prize?"

"Hell—aye!"

"Sure. Jings . . . !"

"Good. Maybe it'll work twice. Well—no time for planning. Shand and I will do the decoy again. Get down in this bracken—and jump on the cops when you get the chance. Come on, Shand—let me lean on you. I'm a casualty. . . ."

They limped out into the middle of the road, and began to stagger along it, westwards, Adrian stumbling and falling repeatedly, Alicky trying to support him but reeling realistically himself. Hope had just managed to tie a handkerchief round his head, when they heard the car come tearing round a turn of that twisting road behind them. There was the scream of hastily-applied brakes. Alicky turned, panic-stricken, and Adrian collapsed groaning on the sandy roadway. It wasn't a bad show.

As the car doors swung open, Shand turned back to tug and drag desperately at his fallen companion. Adrian got as far as his knees, and slumped forward again. The men came running from the car, an inspector and two constables. Hope waved his colleague away, gallantly. Shand waited till the policemen were almost upon him, and then plunged on.

For the second time in his life, Adrian felt a policeman's hand fall heavily on his shoulder, and promptly flattened himself prone on the road. His captor tried to drag him up, but he resisted with all his strength.

"Here, I'll give you a hand, man," the inspector said. The other constable had run on after Alicky.

As a situation, it was just a gift for the other five Gregorach. They leapt up out of the bracken, and while Robb took charge of the empty car, the remaining four hurled themselves on the stooping police. The latter had no chance, especially when Adrian, underneath, turned to the attack and pulled his constable flat on top of him. The inspector, an elderly man and tending to portliness, managed to produce a yell, before he collapsed under Art M'Vey's knowledgeable fists. The second constable, still a yard or so behind the suddenly invigorated Shand, heard, and turning, came hotfoot back. So also did Alicky, throwing himself at the policeman's legs in a creditable rugby tackle. In less time than it takes to tell, the three upholders of law and order were flat on the road, being sat upon, and Sandy Robb had drawn up alongside in the big car.

"Quick," Adrian gasped. "Those others from the boat'll be up in no time. Bind their wrists with their belts. And we want their jackets . . . and their caps."

"Jings—what for?"

"Never mind—get on with it." Adrian had already donned the inspector's braided cap, and was struggling to get off his tunic. The others did as he directed, grinning.

"Robb—get on this cap and jacket. Donald—you too. And come in the front of the car, with me. The rest of you, pile in the back—and try to keep down out of sight if we pass anybody. Can you turn her, Robb?"

"Aye. But I'll ha'e to back a wee. . . ."

"Turn?" Lamont demanded, struggling into a police tunic. "We want to go west, do we no'?"

"This road peters out in a few miles. You can't get through Glen Gyle. Anyway, that's the side they'll look for us. We want to lead the chase away from Roddie. . . ."

"Okay. Whativver you say."

Leaving the cursing constabulary in the middle of the road, wrists bound, coatless, and with their trousers dragged down over their ankles to keep them immobile, they ran after the reversing car, and tumbled aboard. Zigzagging backwards at a crazy speed, Sandy Robb took them an erratic three hundred yards before he found the roadside flat enough to turn on. Then, lurching round, and slightly up the opposite bank, they were off, the throttle wide.

"Try and look like a confounded policeman!" Adrian admonished the driver. "Button up your tunic, man—and don't break all our necks!"

"Where we goin'?" Sandy enquired, inserting silver buttons in quite the wrong holes.

"Straight on, eastwards. Right along the Trossachs road." He smiled a little. "Where twines the path . . . !"

"Eh . . . ?"

"Skip it. We've no option. There isn't a road turning off to the north till the Pass of Leny, up to Strathyre. That's almost twenty miles—through Brig o' Turk, nearly to Callander."

"Jings! An' if we meet anybody—any mair polis . . . ?"

"Drive slap through them. You're driving one of the fastest cars in Scotland—and you've got an inspector sitting beside you!"

"Whoopee!" Sandy cried.

"You're for Strathyre, then, Major?" Donald Lamont queried.

"Yes. And further north than that—if we can. May as well be hanged for a sheep as a lamb. We'll take this car up through Glen Ogle into Glen Dochart, and dump it somewhere in the middle of Perthshire. . . ."

"What about Roddie, then? We'll no' meet him at yon lochan tomorrow, that way."

"No. It would be madness to go back into that hornets' nest, now. No good turn to Roddie, either—bringing them all about his ears. No, it's Castle Doran for us . . . if we survive

Sandy Robb! Man—go canny, won't you! Remember this car's Government property."

"Damn't—so it is!" cried the driver, joyfully, stamping on the accelerator.

XIV

IT had been about three-thirty when they purloined that car,
and it was barely six o'clock when they parked it in scattered
woodland along a little side road in lonely Glen Lyon, eighty-
odd miles away, north-eastwards. Which, considering the
serpentine and difficult nature of those miles, the narrowness
of the roads and the gradients involved, indicated that Sandy
Robb had not neglected his opportunities.

Of course, he had had it all more or less his own way. They
had suffered no real hold-ups. While undoubtedly the ether
was throbbing with short-wave agitation about a stolen patrol-
car, there were ample excuses for the local police forces failing
to intercept it. For one thing, the whole area had been mani-
festly drained of its constabulary to provide the beaters in the
Lochs Lomond-Ard-Katrine triangle. For another, the entire
countryside was largely depopulated, empty; in all those long
mountain-cradled miles, they had passed through no larger
villages than Lochearnhead and Killin—neither of them notable
seats of population despite their attractions. And lastly, and
perhaps most to the point, it would have taken a bold village
bobby indeed to stand out and hold up a furiously-driven
patrol-car, with a smudged number-plate, with either a noted
desperado or a Police Inspector sitting beside the driver. Of
the only two policemen that they had seen, standing at road-
ends, one had saluted smartly, and the other had scratched his
head. Their only delay had been caused by a flock of sheep;
the few other road-users encountered, had hastened to give
them passage. Leaving their borrowed plumes in the vehicle,
with just a little regret—and a brief note of appreciation pinned
to the inspector's tunic, and signed Rod Roy—they set off
westwards, walking a little stiffly, back on their tracks. They
had deliberately driven quite a lot further east than they had
desired to go, even in Glen Lyon itself, in an effort to suggest
to the authorities, when the car was found, that they were

heading for the other side of Scotland. They rejoined the main road, if such it could be called, at Bridge of Balgie, and plodded on into the westering sun, secure in the knowledge that there was nothing more than an isolated house or two in front of them for fifty miles, that the road itself came to a dead stop in twenty, with not a side road to the length of it, and that the open heather was ready to receive them on either hand.

With no hurry on them in the world any more, they strolled all that evening along lovely Glen Lyon, with the foaming river below them on their left, and the great hills marching above them on either side. About nine o'clock, with the lilac shadows filling every gap and gully and glen, and only the bald brows of the high tops retaining the smile of the sinking sun, they made for a lonely shepherd's cottage, deciding to ignore its wireless aerial, and sought to purchase provender. They were able to buy milk, eggs, a few of the inevitable staleish scones— and if the shepherd and his wife suspected that they were anything other than just a group of hikers, they were much too mannerly to say so. Wishing them a very good night, they wandered on another mile or so, into the boundless lifting moorland, ate their meal with scant attempt at preparation, and let the mountains enfold them, the soft breeze hush them, and the heather receive them. Before the last flush of rose had faded from the remote head of Stuchd an Lochain, they all were sleeping the sleep of the just.

Next morning, with the mists still brooding heavily on all the hillsides only a hundred feet or two above them, they moved along the road again for a few miles, and then struck off northwards into the welter of the hills. From now on, for many a league, the only way that they could be found would be by aeroplane—and Adrian, from his Balkan days, knew just how difficult it was to spot men, individual wary men, in open road-less country, from the air; unless it is too high to be of any use, the aero-engine gives infinitely too much warning of approach. They went up the narrow glen of the Allt Phubil, between the towering cloud-capped masses of Stuchd an Lochain and Meall Buidhe, and into the watershed that cradled lonely Loch Damh. They were in utterly empty country now, with neither house nor road nor any works of man as far as eye could see, and incalculably farther. But remote and deserted as this area was, it was as nothing to the vista that met them, about noon, when reaching the long ridge of Meall Cruinn, they looked out north and west over the vast and frightening wastes that was the Moor of Rannoch, stretching in far-flung boundless loch sprinkled desolation to all infinity. Look as they would, they could see no end to its daunting rolling expanse, a lost sombre world of brown heather and black peat and grey stone, lightened only by the glitter of water, water everywhere, running, seeping, falling, standing water. A hundred, a thousand lochs lay lapped in hundreds of thousands of acres, literally hundreds of square miles, of utter wilderness, in the maw of which even the hurrying cloud-shadows were lost and swallowed.

The Gregorach, appreciative as they were of its enveloping anonymity, were just a little abashed as they filed down into its yawning trackless immensity.

It took them almost two whole days to cross and vanquish Rannoch Moor, two fatiguing hungry active days of trudging and tacking, of striding and circling, of plunging and plowtering. They saw many deer but no men, no sheep even, nothing to remind them that this was a populous land, certainly nothing to indicate that men were looking for them, were in any way interested in them. Twice they saw an aeroplane, but each time it was miles away and appeared to be flying on a fixed route, and they took it to be one of the regular services to the Hebrides. Otherwise, they might have been on the moon. And they were hungry, hungrier than any of them had ever been before in their lives. They snared and roasted one or two rabbits, guddled a few trout, and that was all. Rannoch Moor was a jealous as well as an extensive wilderness.

They made a limp, weary, and haggard company, when, late on the Friday evening, in drizzling rain, they dragged themselves to the door of the first house that they had seen since Glen Lyon, another shepherd's cottage, above little Loch Chiarain, six or seven miles south of Loch Treig, on the eastern fringe of Mamore.

The shepherd accepted them kindly, welcomed them indeed,

for he was a lonely man, a widower, with his nearest neighbour six miles away. He gave them all that they required—food, lodging, news. As to food, his very remoteness was an advantage for it necessitated his keeping a great stock of essential victuals in hand; also, in certain items he was self-supporting, having his own little fields of potatoes, vegetables, and oats, his hives of bees, his cow, and his hens. For lodging, there was the spare stall in the stable-cum-byre, and the hayloft. And as for news, though his wireless-set was unfortunately out of action owing to a run-down battery, the post-van came twice a week to the road-end four miles away, on Tuesdays and Fridays, and today he had collected his three current copies of the *Scotsman*.

The Gregorach found that they had no reason to complain of neglect. Though the *Scotsman* hailed from Edinburgh and the East of Scotland, their Wednesday's activities were featured to the extent of a full column in the Thursday's edition, and still more amply in Friday's, as fuller details and eye-witnesses' accounts became available. In dry, factual, poker-faced prose their crazy cantrips were catalogued, inevitably rather from the police point-of-view—though there was no attempt to gloss over the fact that the constabulary had been somewhat noticeably checked at every point. Eye-witnesses' stories were extremely inaccurate and fatuous, as usual, and tended to cancel each other out. The missing police-car, it seemed, had been discovered on the Thursday evening, by a gamekeeper, and some little play was made on the note found pinned to the inspector's tunic. It was only down at the foot of Friday's columns that a separately-headed paragraph informed briefly that, according to the Press Association, Rod Roy and his organisation, as well as playing at hares-and-hounds around Ben Lomond, had put in a considerable amount of hard work repairing the flood-dykes on the farm of Dalnablair near Aberfoyle, apparently without the invitation or the consent of either proprietor or tenant. No comment was offered on this astonishing proceeding.

The Friday paper contained a leaderette, on the theme of the resurgence of the brigand-spirit in present-day life, relating it to the wartime training of commandos and paratroops, and pointing out that despite modern methods of interception by radio and air, it seemingly still was possible for determined and audacious men to defy such measures with apparent impunity and alarming success. Without actually saying so, it gave the impression of wondering whether perhaps the police were burning with enthusiasm for this chase.

Curiously enough, it was left to the writer of the *Scotsman's Log*, a daily column of discursive commentary, mild-seeming, witty, frequently shrewd and sometimes devastating, to recognise and remark on the significance of the dyke-building report. Here was something new from Rod Roy, he suggested, a constructive effort apparently quite at variance with the sort of freebootery they had come to expect from the Roys, both Rob and Rod. This, in the writer's humble estimation, was quite the most spectacular thing that their caterans had done yet. Dykes were for preventing arable land, so precious in the Highlands, from being flooded by winter spates. That dyke at Dalnablair, undoubtedly, had been falling into decay—like the Highland economy all round—for many a long year. Now, somebody, unasked, even unwanted, had stepped in and repaired it, free gratis and for nothing—unless you were such a hair-splitter as to drag in the small matter of a lorry-load of the Hydro Board's cement—thereby restoring the essential arable to a farm otherwise doomed. This seemed to be a unique happening—actually a forward step being taken in the Highlands. The other exploits had pinpointed two glaring examples of current discontent in Scotland, that many Scots rightly or wrongly counted amongst the unwise and unfair fruits of bad government—imposed on the country from without. But this latest demonstration was an indictment of Scotsmen's own folly and neglect—and also an example of what they could do about it. Could it be that a prophet—a militant, two-fisted, thoroughly Old Testament prophet—had arisen in Israel?

"That fellow," Adrian cried, his mouth full of potato, "knows his onions! He ought to be elected to honorary membership of the Gregorach!"

He obtained only a chorus of yawns and sleepy assent.

The hay beckoned.

* * *

151

Since John Campbell, the shepherd, obviously guessed who they were—though with Highland politeness he forbore to ask—and being presumably sympathetic, or at least non-hostile, in that he remained entirely hospitable, Adrian confessed their identity first thing in the morning, and enquired whether he wanted them to vacate his premises forthwith. The Highland-man disclaiming any such sentiment, Hope followed up with the information that they had one or two days on their hands, and if Mr. Campbell had no objections, they would like to spend them there. They were somewhat leg-weary, and could do with a rest from heather-hopping, and incidentally, it would do no harm for them to lie low for a day or so. But they would pay their way; they couldn't just hang about in idleness, for more than a few hours at a time. If Mr. Campbell had any tasks that needed doing about the place, man-size tasks, now was his chance. Was there anything shouting to be put right around Loch Chiarain?

John Campbell scratched a bristling chin, hummed and hawed for a bit, protested that there was no need at all for them to be doing a hand's-turn, and admitted eventually that if there was one thing that was ruining the place for his sheep, it was the bracken, the creeping damnation bracken. The braes were getting fair covered with it, destroying the pasture and making a breeding ground for the fly. Nothing could be done about it far out, of course, but round about the infields and the loch-shore, where he needed handy sheltered grazing in rough weather. . . . He did what he could, of course, but he had plenty on his hands, and one man was not much use against the bracken, whatever.

So, for the next three days, the Gregorach laboured, with varying intensity, at cutting and raking the spreading, smothering, ubiquitous bracken that clothed all the lower hillsides around the loch. The shepherd, fortunately, had recently bought a new scythe, and with the old one that it replaced, two of them were able to lead the attack on the ferny foe. Art M'Vey knew how to wield the thing, and the others tried their prentice hands in rotation, with unequal degrees of success. An old sickle, a couple of large knives, and

152

two pairs of superannuated wool-shears, had to serve the rest for weapons. And a back-breaking, hand-tearing, wearisome business it was, with the hot sun and the midges and the flies—though the sparkling loch was always there for a dip, and the heaped bracken-fronds made an enticing couch, flies or none. The Sabbath problem cropped up again, but they compromised with John Campbell, continental fashion, by conceding the forenoon, and assuring that the bracken-cutting was sheer recreation thereafter. The shepherd's devotions, with the nearest church at Kinlochleven, sixteen miles away, apparently consisted of leaning over a gate and contemplating the everlasting hills by the hour on end—and perhaps no inadequate worship, at that.

By the Monday night, the seven of them had cleared quite a considerable acreage of bracken-grown pasture, nevertheless. It would grow again, of course, next season, but in a mildly discouraged fashion, from bled and bruised roots. The only way was to keep on cutting and cutting, Campbell said, till the damned plants gave up the struggle—and that wouldn't be tomorrow.

They parted, in the morning, with mutual esteem.

Their route now lay due westwards, into the jagged savage mountains of Mamore, that lay north of the long scimitar of Loch Leven and south of Glen Nevis, difficult country to cross, empty and wild as the Moor of Rannoch behind them, but vastly steeper and more confined, if neither so waterlogged nor extensive. They considered that they had done reasonably well when, that night, they camped in a corrie under the frowning peak of Binnein More, and perhaps seventeen crooked miles from their starting-point. Another eight, in the morning, ought to see them at their rendezvous.

Glen Doran was a pleasant green place, opening northwards off the wider if harsher valley of Glen na Lairig that split the high deer-forest of Mamore into two. It had been a populous place once, judging by the mounds of green rabbit-cropped turf and crumbling stonework scattered here and there over its sheltered verdant length. There remained only the grey-stone farmhouse amongst its guardian trees, now converted into a youth hostel—an unlikely situation for such an establishment, at first sight, but actually well-placed as a half-way house for climbers tramping between their meccas of Glencoe and Ben Nevis. The Gregorach, who had passed with suitable comment three rather top-heavy looking girl hikers on the way up, received a cheery wave from a few more of their enterprising kind, sitting on the hostel doorstep, as they passed below. Hereabouts, at any rate, they were unlikely to attract much attention—though they were perhaps suspiciously lightly-burdened. A little regretfully, they trudged on.

A mile or so further, where the glen was beginning to narrow and tail off into a high and beetling pass, they came to Castle Doran. Round a birch-clad knoll, they sighted it, standing proudly on an eminence, a square tower, riven and roofless but tolerably complete to the wall-head, amid the tumbled masonry of its less substantial outbuildings. And almost as one man, they pointed to the drift of blue wood-smoke that coiled from its single remaining chimney-stack, pointed and halted.

"Folk there," Lamont jerked, warningly. "Bide a wee."

"Roddie, maybe. . . ."

"Aye, maybe. But maybe no' . . ."

"There's somebody movin' aboot in the front o' it, see. Twa o' them. . . ."

Adrian had his glasses out, now, and was focusing them. They heard him draw a quick breath. "Yes—it's Roddie, all right," he said, after a moment. "Two of them, as you said. *Only* two." And as sharp as the click of the metal as he snapped the binoculars shut, "And the other is Miss Burnet!"

XV

RODDIE ROY'S great shout of welcome echoed from a dozen hillsides as they neared the ruin, and he came down the slope towards them long-strided. Evidently the convalescent's condition was much improved. Behind him, Helen Burnet remained standing on the green knoll.

"Weel, boys—you made it!" came the authentic roar. "The hale bang-jing o' yous! Wheer's a' your polisman's uniforms?"

They all answered him at once—all except Adrian Hope, that is—and great was the uproar.

Into the laughter and the profanity and the incoherences, Adrian's voice penetrated at length, level but tense. "Where is Pat Kelly?" he asked.

"Eh . . . ? Och, Pat. Pat's ankle wasna' tae guid—hirplin' he was. So I sent him back, frae Crianlarich, wi' a bit message to Jakey an' the boys. Me an' the lassie came on on oor lane—aye, an' we managed fine. Did we no', Hel'n?"

Hope drew a hand over his so tell-tale features. "Indeed!" he said.

They climbed up the turf of the castle knoll towards the watching girl, and the boisterous bonhomie died on them all. She it was, indeed, who spoke first.

"Hullo," she greeted, smiling. "Had a good trip?" Her regard included them all. She made a pretty picture of fresh young and assured loveliness against the grim ancient stonework of Castle Doran.

"This is a surprise, Helen," Adrian observed, obviously in entire control of that pleasantly-modulated voice. "I . . . we hardly expected to see *you* here. I thought you were going to see—er—our friend down to the nearest road, only?"

"Well, you see, the nearest road *was* at Crianlarich—after you didn't turn up at that Lochan Ardran." She spoke brightly, with an easy confidence, only slightly offset by a hint of heightened colour—and that did her looks no harm, either.

"When Pat Kelly left us, there, it was obvious I couldn't just let my patient carry on on his own. So I tagged along, and saw that he looked after himself." She arched an eyebrow at the big fellow. "I've made a good job of him, haven't I? Goodness knows in what sort of state your Rod Roy would have been in, by now, if I'd left him to his own resources! You should be grateful to me, Adrian!" And just for a moment, her lustrous eyes rested on Hope, and were perhaps neither easy nor assured.

"Aye—she's been a right wee brick," Roddie commended, generously. "Looked efter me like a hen wi' one chick! Jings—I've been fair hudden doon, I'm tellin' you. Dressin's, an' foamentations, an' wee rests—dinna' dae this, dinna' dae that . . . !"

"Yes—and look at him now!" Helen Burnet said.

Certainly that week had made a difference in Roderick Macgregor, though his sling was still there, and the adhesive-taped dressing on his brow was not so very much less notice-able than was the former bandage. It was in his whole bearing and carriage that the change was so apparent. Any slight concussion was quite gone, evidently, and any drain on his strength resulting from his injuries, well-nigh dissipated. It might be that Rod Roy had benefited from that week in more ways than one.

"And the two of you have been together since then—alone?" Adrian demanded. "The whole week?"

"More or less," the girl agreed. "We were very lucky, I suppose. . . ."

"Och, it was deid easy," Roddie assured. "Jist a dawdle. Once we were past Loch Lomond, we didna' see a polisman. At Crianlarich the lassie gangs into the Bookin' Office, bold's you like, an' buys twa return tickets to Oban—returns, mind you! We got in a carriage wi' an auld wife that gi'en me sweeties for my sair heid! Jings—British Railways are the boys for me, every time!"

"In Oban that night we stayed in a hotel," Helen went on, perhaps a little hurriedly. "The Clachan Temperance Hotel, a most respectable place, with beds like iron. And we read all about the disgraceful ongoings of Rod Roy Macgregor the day before, stealing boats and cars, even people's clothing. . . ."

"Aye, hell—the name you're gi'ein' me! An' the next day we got a wee bus to a bit ca'd Benderloch—that was a' we had the dibs for, efter the hotel an' the return tickets, an' some chuck. . . ."

"And a visit to the chemist's, Roddie!"

"Aye—fine that. An' then we started walkin'. Roond a Loch Creran, an' up its glen, then ower a bit pass, an' doon to Ballachulish. Then we crossed the wee ferry, an' wandered along yon muckle Loch Leven, an' ower the hill, here. Three days it took us. . . ."

"Did it!" Adrian sounded as though he thought they had indeed been dawdling. "Then you've been here two days, waiting?"

"Jist that, aye. I've been teachin' Hel'n hoo to guddle for troots—it's no' easy wi' one hand. We've been makin' pals wi' the hostellers, doon-bye. . . ."

"But you've slept up here?"

"Sure—you've got to be a member o' yon hostels racket," Roddie said, innocently. "But, och, the auld castle's no' that bad, wi' a pickle heather, an' a sack ower the windy . . ."

"Very cosy, I'm sure. It seems to have been quite an idyll! Almost a pity to break it up . . . !"

"Adrian . . . I think you must be hungry!" the girl exclaimed. "You betray all the signs. Come away inside, all of you—we've got quite a little store of eatables, of one sort or another. It's food you need."

"Guid for you, lassie. Lead us to it!"

"Jings—you're right there . . ."

"Aye," Roddie cried. "Come awa' ben. An' let's hear a' aboot what *you've* been up to. You canna' believe a' you read in the papers, mind!"

Adrian Hope was the last to file in at the gaping doorway of Castle Doran, and notably the least voluble of the seven raconteurs thereafter.

As Donald Lamont remarked, some considerable time later, it looked as though the Major had something on his mind.

*　　　*　　　*

That Adrian had indeed something on his mind had to be recognised, in due course, by even the least intuitive and perceptive amongst his companions—even though he obviously made some sort of an effort to achieve at least an appearance of normalcy. His moodiness, silences, and brevity of temper, came to be an accepted feature of life. In any other, less vehement and boisterous company, it probably would have produced a greater degree of remark and resentment. It was not without its effect, on certain personalities, for all that.

The rest of that day, Wednesday, was spent resting at Castle Doran, deciding on their immediate future, and reading and discussing the reports in the newspapers that Roddie and Helen had brought. These, being from Saturday's and Monday's press, had had time to deal with and consider the news of the Dalnablair activities, and whether following the lead of the perspicacious writer of the *Scotsman's Log*, or out of a spontaneous general assessment of the situation, there was a recognisable and satisfactory appreciation that this demanded a new line of thought on the matter of Rod Roy Macgregor, a deeper and more searching analysis. Acknowledgement that this campaign evidently meant more than had at first seemed likely, was fairly widespread. The difference between destructive and constructive criticism was underlined everywhere. Few newspapers indeed were at all critical of the dyke-building gesture, and all that it implied, even to the extent of condoning the theft of the cement. Many, in fact, looked forward quite frankly to what might happen next.

And if the journalists reacted thus, their readers, as typified by the Letters-to-The-Editor writers, were still more impressed —or at any rate, more outspoken. Two other papers besides the *Glasgow Chronicle* had started to devote whole pages to readers' views on the Macgregor affair, one of them a London-owned daily. And few organs' correspondence columns contained a reference to any other subject. Of all the letters, a negligible percentage were critical, save of details, and of the failure of the Gregorach, so far, to blow up sundry Government buildings, kidnap the Secretary of State, or otherwise do something really useful. Even entire associations wrote, in the names of their secretaries, for information as to whether it was possible to affiliate with the Rod Roy organisation, others offering, under secret pseudonyms, their readiness to take an immediate part in the campaign, and awaiting instructions.

The *Herald* announced that the Members for Dumbarton East and West Perthshire had given notice of questions on the subject to the Secretary of State, in the House.

It was all very heartening. They seemed to be on the way to wakening that slumbrous spirit of Scotland, indeed.

The problem of where they went from here, physically at any rate, produced no great argument. They had scant choice. Little or no money was left, and their coffers had to be replenished before any further activities could be contemplated. Which meant that they must contact the money-earners up at the Findart hydro scheme. Also, Roddie had had a letter from Jakey Reid, addressed to Eric Gregory, c/o the Post Office, Ballachulish, quoting Danny Sinclair at Findart to the effect that there was plenty for the gang to turn their hands to up in that remote area. Why muck about with tuppeny ha'penny ploys around Loch Lomond, he asked, in effect, when there were real man-size jobs waiting to be done in Findart? So the decision was made, and the die cast. They would move north in the morning.

This decision brought about the surprising assertion that Helen Burnet intended to move north with them, meantime, at any rate. Apparently she considered her patient in no fit state to be left, as yet—an opinion which the said patient, strangely enough, did not contest. Her father would now be away on a lecture-tour in England, and she was quite enjoying her holiday, thank you! They had forcibly restrained her, a while back, hadn't they? Well, they could take the consequences, now! Also, by her presence, she indicated pointedly, she might be able to restrain *them* from some of the more deplorable and idiotic of their excesses—she might even lend them a certain valuable air of respectability! She certainly gave no hint that she was coming along because she had become a convert to freebootery. But neither did she seem to consider as valid any suggestions that she would be infinitely wiser to go away home—especially Adrian Hope's clipped assertions to that effect. Perhaps the fact that Roddie Roy himself made no sort of objections, carried most weight with her. They might well have discussed it all beforehand; they certainly had had ample opportunity.

So it seemed to one of their number, at all events.

That night, the men slept on the heather in the vaulted basement of the tower, while Helen had the entirety of the upper floors to her maidenly self. The old Cameron who built the place, would undoubtedly have groaned in despair.

On the morrow, then, they resumed their travels. Findart lay north by west of them some seventy miles, on the west coast of Inverness-shire, due north of Knoydart and east of the Sound of Sleat. To reach it, they had to cross the Great Glen, somewhere north of Fort William, make their devious way through the mountains of Locheil, Morar, and East Knoydart, to salt water at Loch Hourn. It was no daunder. If they made it in much less than a week, they would be doing well, with such country to cover, and with all the places it would be wise to avoid.

They began, after climbing up through their pass and down into Glen Nevis, by avoiding Fort William, turning off, when two-thirds of the way down the glen, and taking the pony-track that led up below the soaring west face of Ben Nevis, and that eventually brought them down to Lochy Bridge, a mile or so north of the town. This was fairly populous country, and feeling themselves to be a somewhat kenspeckle company, they decided to get out of it just as soon as possible—especially after a policeman on a bicycle had given them rather a searching stare as they were crossing the bridge. They abandoned their plan of following the road west along Loch Eil, and struck off instead straight into the great lumpish hills above Banavie, little as they relished the interminable climb. Nightfall saw them camped in a high empty valley that Adrian's map called Glen Laragain, a good fifteen miles from Castle Doran. It was further than they had intended, with Macgregor only convalescent—and it must not happen again, according to Helen Burnet.

An easy ten miles the next day, walking over short heather

all the way, and a slightly rougher one the next, brought them to the western end of long Loch Arkaig, and their half-way mark. The weather broke, here, and they were fortunate to have an inadequately closed-up school to sleep in that night, and a fairish road down Glen Dessarry to walk along in the following morning's rain. With the clouds low on the sombre hills, they were glad to stick to sandy gravelly tracks for the next two days, risking encounters; it was empty depopulated country, anyway, like nine-tenths of the Highlands, and three houses a day was a fair average. By Monday night they were over the watershed between Glen Carnoch and Glen Barrisdale, with the salt waters of Loch Hourn gleaming redly before them in a vividly colourful sunset. Beyond the loch, the blackly scowling mountain masses must enclose Findart, and journey's end.

Tomorrow, they would get across there, and reconnoitre. No, the young woman said, tomorrow they would rest at Barrisdale Bay, wash clothes, darn socks, and generally make-and-mend and recuperate. And her tame giant mildly agreed. Adrian named Roddie that only to himself, of course.

XVI

FINDART was really a peninsula, between Loch Aror, an arm of Loch Hourn, in the south, and long Loch Elg in the north, jutting out into the upper Sound of Sleat, perhaps twelve miles long from its roots in the mountains of Glen Shiel, to its most westerly point in the towering headland of Rudha More, and averaging approximately eight miles in width, between the sea lochs. Dividing it into two very separate compartments, was a long and almost unbroken spine of high ground, running from the lofty three-thousand-foot Ben Gair on the east, to the aforementioned cape of Rudha More in the restless waters of the Sound. South Findart, the slightly larger segment, had been a single deer-forest, and was now the scene of hydro-electric development. North Findart, as far as the Gregorach were concerned, was an unknown quantity. The name Macdonald of Findart, if Adrian recollected aright, had meant something in Highland history.

After their day's resting at Barrisdale—where they read, with mixed feelings, that an association was being formed, calling itself The Sons of Rob Roy, with branches in Edinburgh, Glasgow, Aberdeen, and even London, determined, as it said, to follow with vigour the lead so ably given by Roderick Roy Macgregor—they had themselves ferried across Loch Hourn, rounded the head of Loch Aror, and climbed into a secluded valley under Ben Gair, which had wood and water as well as a tremendous view to commend it, and there they bivouacked. Art M'Vey was deputed to go on ahead and locate the hydro-electric contractors' camp, and to contact their four members therein. They had seen signs of development on their way hither—widespread drainage, an excellent road not yet finished, and sundry dumps of materials—but no men.

M'Vey arrived back in the evening, with Danny Sinclair, as representative of his hard-working colleagues. The main camp was in a glen about three miles away, where a great dam was being constructed. Sinclair was much excited to see them, his reaction strangely compounded of satisfaction at their arrival, and something almost like perturbation. It fairly soon transpired that he and his companions were rather enjoying life on the power-scheme workings, and were in no hurry at all to see it upset.

He was able to give them a fairly clear picture of local conditions. The southern part of the peninsula was entirely depopulated, had been for long enough, and had recently been sold outright to the Hydro Board. Major Macdonald of Findart however, still owned the northern half, which contained, besides an extensive sheep-farm in the proprietor's hands, quite a large crofting township. These crofts, down at the coast, supported a fair population—though perhaps, in Sinclair's estimation, supported was not just the right word. They had a certain amount of arable on the low ground near the shore, a vast amount of useless bog called pasture, and the right to run a given number of sheep on the high ground. The fishing it was that saved them, and the fishing had been bad for three seasons. Apart from two or three working seasonally for the Hydro Board, there was not a man under fifty living in North Findart.

If they wanted somewhere to improve, North Findart was waiting for them; only, Danny Sinclair seemed to infer a little diffidently, it would be a pity to upset *South* Findart too much, in the doing of it.

It is to be feared that he got no such reassurance from Roddie Roy, despite the warmth of thanks with which the big man pocketed £40 in Treasury notes. Two last items of information their benefactor gave them before he set off in the darkening, to tramp down to his hutted camp, perhaps a little less light-footed than he had come—there was an empty stalkers' bothy, that would make an ideal headquarters for them, in a little glen about three miles up from the township of Alisary; and there wasn't a policeman in the whole peninsula.

In the morning, keeping to the high ground around the great flanks and buttresses of Ben Gair, they moved north. This was part of the catchment area for the hydro scheme, and all around were the black scars of drainage ditches cut in the peat and heather, symmetrically patterning the hillsides. And below them the rolling moorland sank brownly to the sparkling Sound, while beyond, behind the serrated peaks of Skye, the isle-dotted western ocean spread, illimitable.

Beyond the watershed, though still hilly, the land was kindlier, greener, sloping down almost in a series of terraces, through sheep-strewn heather and bracken and woodland, to a patchwork of strips of cultivation, brilliant in their several greens against the yellow sands of the machair and the lace-edged blue of the sea, with dotted amongst them a scattering of whitewashed croft-houses. This looked more like the thing that they had come seventy miles to see.

They found their little glen and the stalkers' bothy without difficulty. It was a pleasant place, a cottage of three apartments and a large loft, set beside a little lochan, guarded by a crescent of trees from the overhanging hillside, and looking out down a widening wedge of green valley over a spread of machair and a blue bay, far into the rimless plain of the western sea. It was a darling place, Helen Burnet cried at sight of it, and no man, even Adrian, gainsaid her. And though the door did not stand open for them, one window did.

They moved in forthwith, and inside, as of right, the girl took charge. There was little in the way of furnishings—a worm-eaten deal table, a broken chair or two, some shelves, and a few rusty pots and pans beside a choked and rustier grate. But to that company, such was luxury. And the cottage was clean, at least from all the grosser forms of dirt that empty houses tend to attract in the south. Helen, in a matter of minutes, had them all at work sweeping out with heather wisps, scouring rusty iron with wet grit from the lochan-shore, and even washing the windows in some sort of fashion. She herself cleaned out the grate in the kitchen, and soon had a cheerful fire of aromatic birchwood blazing therein. In less than an hour, porridge was bubbling, tea was infused, and life looked considerably brighter. For the first time since they had rejoined forces, Helen heard Adrian Hope whistling.

The young woman allocated the accommodation. The

kitchen would be the common-room, the little chamber off it she reserved for herself, the apartment at the other side of the front and only door would serve Roddie and Adrian and Donald, while the boys could have all the loft upstairs to themselves. Roddie it was who, winking genially, pointed out that there was a skylight in the roof up there, from which any reasonably active guy could jump on to the slope at the back without creating any disturbance around the front door. The convenience of this was appreciated and acknowledged by the majority of his hearers.

Helen Burnet's only qualms, perhaps not unnaturally, related to the legality and security of their tenancy; in other words, what would the owner say? Despite her sojourning with them, she had not yet reached the stage of seeing such matters entirely from the Gregorach angle. Roddie Roy cheerfully told her not to fash herself; the owner, whoever he might be, would accept his terms all right, one way or another—if he ever got to hear about them. And he patted the comfortable wad of banknotes in his pocket, and then clenched a vast fist significantly, and grinned. With such assurances, the girl had to be content. Her education, as well as his, was proceeding.

In the evening, after sufficient heather-bedding had been cut, Roddie, Donald, and one or two others, set off down their little glen, on an exploratory visit to the crofting township of Alisary, about three miles distant. Sinclair had told them that there was a place there, not exactly a shop nor a pub, but just a house, one of the crofts, that sold a variety of goods—including astonishingly good liquor—to select customers, and where the men of the district were apt to congregate of an evening for a crack and a dram. This was obviously the place for them.

Adrian excused himself. He had started to construct and weave a sort of mattress out of sapling birches and heather, and he wanted to finish it. No need for them all to descend on this Alisary place, anyway. But would they see if they could buy him some hooks down there, small ones that he could use with worms, or tie a fly to—he'd seen decent-sized trout jumping in their lochan. He had some line, and could contrive a rod. . . .

When they were gone, he repaired to the edge of the little wood at the back, where the materials were to hand, and worked at his mattress, amongst the hopping rabbits and the busy ants. After a while, Sandy Robb and two of his companions came and watched him for a little, offering contradictory and frequently lewd advice, and then continued on uphill, snare-wires in their hands. Hope wrought on. It was intricate, finicky work, but pleasant and satisfying after so much mere trudging. He hummed as he wove the heather-stems in and out of the sapling framework.

Presently, Helen Burnet's voice behind him came quietly. "It's a change to hear you singing, Adrian," she mentioned.

He glanced up and round. "Sorry," he jerked. "Didn't know you were around. I won't let it happen again." And then, as something of the petty sound of this statement struck his own ears, he attempted an amendment. "I'm not much of a singer, I know."

"You don't give yourself much practice," the girl observed, evenly.

"No," he said.

For a little while there was silence, save for the soft murmur of a pair of wood pigeons in the birches above them. Then Helen spoke again.

"You are getting on quite well with this thing, aren't you. An army accomplishment, I take it? One of the many!"

"Yes."

"It looks quite effective."

"Not bad."

In a little, she sighed. "Well, I suppose I'd better be getting back. I'm trying to bake some oatcakes in that oven."

"M'mmm. Difficult, I expect."

"Yes." She paused. "It's *all* rather difficult . . . !"

"Quite," he said.

Shrugging, at his back, she turned and went down to the cottage.

He worked on industriously, but he did not resume his humming.

In time, he got his mattress finished, and carried it down to the bothy door. Then, searching about, he found four flat stones, approximately of a size, took them indoors and erected the mattress an top of them. He lay on it, to test it, and it seemed good, comfortable. He heard the girl upstairs in the loft, no doubt cleaning. The smell of new-baked oatcakes was appetising.

Lifting his eyes, in the doorway, the glory of the sunset struck him almost like a blow. Flooding levelly up the glen, reflected in dazzling splendour from sound and sea, the day was dying in savage fantastic conflagration out there in the emptiness beyond the Hebrides, its death throes staining land and water and sky in a flaming riot of colour, scarlet, crimson, purple, gold, lemon, and palest green, against which the isles were etched in ebony, and Skye was only the jetty jagged teeth of a giant saw. Even their own little lochan blazoned the magnificence of it in its humble mirror.

Much affected, Adrian moved down the few yards to the water's edge, and sitting on a stone, stared unwinking into the florid west.

It was thus, in due course, that the girl found him. This time, he perceived her coming.

"Spectacular, isn't it," he mentioned, with a quite unsuitable casualness. "Putting on quite a show for us."

"It's wonderful," Helen Burnet said. "Breathtaking. I'd heard of these Hebridean sunsets. . . ." She kept her eyes on its flaunting challenge, as was not difficult. "Adrian—you've put that mattress in my room. I'd no idea you were making it for me. It is very kind of you. . . ."

"Nonsense," he returned, too forcefully. "Nothing of the sort. Just an experiment. If you find you can sleep on it, I might make one for myself!"

"I see. I'm to be the guinea-pig, am I! Still, I suppose even that is better than being entirely ignored!"

"Ignored! Ignored, my dear Helen, is the last thing you've been. Ever since you attached yourself to us, this whole outfit has revolved round you and your wishes and your opinions. . . ."

"Adrian—what rubbish!"

"Unfortunately not. Your influence, direct and indirect, is all-pervasive, I'm afraid."

"But not with *you*, at any rate!"

"My position is not the important one—that must be apparent. Macgregor is the kingpin. He's the man the others will obey—not me. This whole campaign of ours stands or falls by him. He's the big noise," Adrian laughed briefly and without amusement as he said it. "Definitely, the big noise!"

"And what of it?"

"Surely *you* needn't ask that! You've seen to it that your influence with him is—is paramount. You've made your kill, and . . ."

"What do you mean—I've *seen* to it?"

He shrugged, and sighed. "Need we go into all the grim details? *How* you've seen to it, you know better than I do. Why, is another matter. I can see only two reasons, myself; either out of sheer scalp-hunting, out of your feminine need to make a conquest of this outsize piece of masculinity . . . or because you aim to wreck this whole attempt of ours!"

She drew a quick breath, opened her lips to speak, and then closed them again.

Her silence caused the man to turn and look at her, and for a moment or two they considered each other in the gaudy flush of the sunset.

"I see," she said, at length, quietly. "And which of these alternatives do *you* think is responsible, Adrian?"

"I'm not quite sure. Possibly both."

"Oh."

"Yes. And if it is the first, I'm sorry about it . . . for Roddie's sake! But if it is the other, I'll have to do something more about it than just be sorry!"

"Do?" she questioned. "Do? What will you do?" There might have been just a hint of mockery there.

He spoke levelly, carefully. "If it comes to a showdown, Helen, there are always things that a man can do, a determined, shall we say ruthless, man. I don't think I need say more. . . ."

"*You* wouldn't though. You wouldn't dare . . . !"

"I've dared a lot on account of this campaign," he reminded her. "And because of that—and because of what the others too have dared and risked, I'm not going to let the attempt be wrecked by a slip of a girl. . . ."

168

"Wrecked!" she exclaimed. "Who's talking about wrecking anything?"

"I am. Purposely or otherwise, your presence here is tending to wreck our efforts. Already you've created disharmony, you've softened Macgregor. . . ."

"What utter nonsense! Any disharmony has been created by yourself—the rest of us have been the best of friends. And has it never occurred to you that if it hadn't been for me, you probably wouldn't have had Roddie with you at all, now? I saved him for you and your crazy campaign! Injured and helpless and, and obvious, as he was, he would never have got through the police cordon, got here at all, if I hadn't been there to camouflage him, and get him through—apart altogether from nursing him. . . ."

"And why did you do all that, Helen, may I ask? Not out of love for our cause, obviously!" The girl, after her outburst, was silent.

Her companion nodded. "That would be telling, wouldn't it! Anyway, whatever your reason, the fact remains that today Roddie Macgregor is largely influenced by you. And since you disapprove of our attempt, and the success of it hinges on him, that influence becomes vital. So, I want you to leave us. To go home."

"Do you! I'm surprised. I would have thought that you wouldn't have dared to let me go, in case I went and revealed your identity and your whereabouts to the police!"

"We must take that risk," he said, evenly. "After all, we don't need to stay here. And my identity must be known to the police, anyway, by now."

"Must it?" Quickly she looked up.

"Well—certain members of the University staff know that I'm involved, don't they? And I'm bound to have been missed from my classes. . . ."

"Missed, yes. But you're rather thought to be ill . . . with dysentery!"

"Ill! Dysentery . . . ?"

"Yes. At least, that's what I led Dr. Kennedy to believe. And your friend Stirling. And your landlady. And I believe Daddy indicated much the same thing to his colleagues. You're

169

thought by most, I imagine, to be up with that aunt of yours, somewhere in Moray. . . ."

"Good Lord!" He blinked, striving to assess this new evidence.

Defensively, the young woman spoke. "Naturally, we wanted to keep your folly as dark as possible—for our own sakes! Quite a number of people were aware of our—our former association, you know—and not all of them, probably, knew that it had ended."

"Ah," the man said. "Ummm. I see." He was thinking hard, scarcely listening to her. This put rather a fresh complexion on things. "So, you don't think the police are actually hunting for me, after all?"

"Not as Adrian Hope, I imagine—unless you've given them some other clues to your identity. There were the initials on your handkerchief . . . but I hardly think that would pin-point you. . . ."

"Perhaps not. Well, at any rate, I've to thank you for providing me with a convenient recurrence of dysentery. . . ."

"No thanks are required, I assure you. I tell you, it was for our own benefit. . . ."

"M'mm. Perhaps. . . ." He was looking at her frankly enough, now, searchingly, speculatively—for all that the ruddy light from that sunset was fading. "Perhaps, after all, you came to change your mind a little bit, about the enormity—the folly, I think it was you said?—of my idea?"

"No. . . ."

"Perhaps, when you read that we were being reasonably successful, when you saw the Press reaction was not so un-favourable, you came to the conclusion that there might be something in the attempt, after all . . . ?"

"No—you are quite wrong!" She was very vehement. "Entirely wrong. I thought then, and still think, that the whole thing is crazy, doomed to failure. It can only end in disaster. . . ."

"But you are not actually working against it? Not trying to break the party up?"

"Of course I'm not! Why on earth you should have imagined such a thing . . . !"

"Then," he said, and his voice changed, steadied, and became almost deliberate, "there is only one thing, that I can conceive, that could have made you act as you have done. I think you must be in love with Roddie Macgregor, Helen!"

He heard her gasp, heard the quivering intake of air thereafter. For a little, it seemed as though she did not trust herself to speak. She got no help from him. "That, of course, is quite ridiculous!" she said, at last.

"Is it?" He shrugged, scoring lines with the toe of his boot on the gravel of the lochan-shore. "At first glance, I would have said so, myself. But, thinking about it, I'm not so sure. He's a fine physical specimen, fearless, tough, all of a he-man . . . and probably very attractive to women. And class distinctions aren't the barriers they used to be. And, of course, he's soft, quite literally soft, about you. . . ."

"Adrian—you're being absurd and objectionable. . . ."

"No—only objective. I want to get at the truth. It's important for me, you see. . . ."

"Is it?"

"Yes—for me, and for all of us. Situated as we are, here, any emotional upset in the party is important, could be dangerous. Especially where the leader is concerned. Fugitives as we are, the affairs of one become the affair of all. . . ."

"My affairs don't, at any rate!" the young woman cried. "What's more, I'm not going to stand here and have them objectively dissected by you, Adrian Hope! I've had enough of this. You are . . . insufferable!" And swinging around, with a swirl of her kilted skirt, she started off up towards the bothy.

He remained seated on his stone, but he called after her. "I'm sorry, Helen. I didn't want to be offensive. But it's as well that we should know where we stand. . . ."

He got no answer, except, presently, the slam of the cottage door. Sighing, he returned to face the sunset. But now its brilliance had faded, and the shadowless half-light lay upon land and sea. Not that Adrian noted it, or even the frequent plop, the gleam of silver, and the widening circles on the leaden surface of the lochan, as the trout leapt at their evening rise. His thoughts were otherwhere, and, judging by his expression, bitter. And after a while voices and laughter, rough and unrestrained but strangely softened and muted by the grey cloak of the night, sounded from the hillside above the little wood. Sandy Robb, in that remote glen, was singing something that belonged more properly to still remoter jungle. Adrian got to his feet, and moved slowly up to the house.

Later, considerably later, Sandy Robb's crooning was surpassed, outclassed, quite cast into the shades of night, by the great singing that came up the glen to them. Lying on his couch of heather, Adrian heard it, groaned, and muttered. From above, in the loft, came pointed and knowledgeable comment. Roderick Macgregor, aided and abetted by the lesser chanting of his companions, was still intoning,

> "While there's leaves in the forest,
> And foam on the river,
> Macgregor, despite them,
> Shall flourish for ever!"

as he crossed the threshold of the bothy. The entire building vibrated to the sheer thunder and resonance of his vast lung-power.

"Shut up!" Hope yelled. "Other people are trying to sleep. Miss Burnet's been turned-in for a couple of hours. . . ."

He might as well have saved his breath. He barely heard his own voice above the heartfelt agonies of Clan Alpine.

Roddie Roy was not actually drunk, merely drink-taken, and strongly sensible of much that was apt to escape him at other times. He was also convinced that life was on the whole very good, that they were the boys, and that a new and finer Scotland was well on the way to being born. Also, that the old fellow down-bye, name of MacIver, had an unrivalled supply of excellent liquor—made it in his own still, probably. Och, he had a lot to tell the Major—lashings. But first he'd got this blanket to give to Hel'n. He'd had the hell of a job, getting this blanket for Hel'n. . . .

No arguments of Adrian's, obviously, were going to prevent his gift's immediate presentation.

Roddie's mingled grief, disappointment, and rage, when he

found the door of the girl's little chamber off the kitchen apparently locked, were titanic. It seemed, in a flood of reproach, entreaties, and declamation, that he was about to tear the said door down with his bare hands, and Adrian was grimly preparing to sacrifice himself in the hopeless but requisite attempt at prevention, when the offending door opened, and Helen Burnet apparently said something apposite, soothing, and at the same time authoritative enough to be beyond argument, accepted the gift of the blanket graciously, kissed its donor lightly on the point of his red-stubbled chin, and wished him, wished them all, a very good night.

Quite mollified, perfectly happy indeed, Roddie came back to the room he was sharing with Hope and Lamont. She was a grand lassie, Hel'n, he averred. And this old MacIver was a grand guy too, and his whisky grander still. Indeed, this Alisary dump, Findart itself, was a grand place—though it had everything wrong with it. Jings, it had—the land wrong, the laird wrong, bracken, bogs, fences, deer—all wrong. And no road, no pier—nothing. But they'd sort all that, in the morning. He'd got it all fixed. Jings, aye—just a cake-walk it was, apparently.

On this confident note, the dissertation slid off naturally and of its own volition into the noble and sonorous rotundity of *Macgregor's Gathering* once more, which, eddying and echoing and reverberating impressively between the heather-couch on the floor and the low wooden ceiling and the four fairly tightly-enclosing walls, suddenly ceased entirely, and was succeeded by a mild and contented puffing, that only the uncharitable would have called a snore.

What Adrian Hope called it, as he lay awake far into that Highland night, is neither here nor there.

173

XVII

IN the morning, it transpired that of all the plethora of troubles that afflicted the crofting community of Alisary, lack of drainage and of a proper road constituted the most serious and urgent. The one invalidated a large and increasing proportion of their precious usable land, and the other cut them off from assistance, from their kind, from the rest of the world, and ensured the departure of their young folk just as soon as they could escape; a steamer calling two days a week, weather permitting, dropping the mails and the wrapped bread half a mile offshore, to be picked up by a fishing-boat, lacked something to youth as sufficient contact with the great world outside. Though the Gregorach could not do much about a road, in a hurry at any rate, they *could* do something about the drainage. Or so Roddie Roy declared. He was away off to see Danny Sinclair at the camp about it, right now.

Adrian did not attempt to dissuade him, but announced that he was going for a walk in the other direction. Last night's envoys, under the pressure of greater events, had forgotten to try and buy him his fish-hooks.

Helen Burnet, very quiet this morning, but most annoyingly self-possessed—or so felt certain of her companions—indicated that they could all do as they pleased. *She* had work to do about the house—and would Adrian, if he was going down to this village-place, bring back some more oatmeal, salt, matches, and sundry other necessities, if his mind was not above such matters?

Alone then, he walked down the glen in the forenoon sunlight, and however gloomy and distracted his thoughts, they were not entirely proof against the young beauty and fresh urgency of the morning. Everywhere the larks were shouting and the bees humming, the rabbits were scampering and on the hillside above deer waved white flags at him as they bounded for the skyline. And all before him the plain of the sea was a sparkling dazzling challenge.

174

The glen opened on to a shelving moor, boggy, reed-grown, and dotted with outcropping stone, more than a mile of it, sloping down to the little sandy plain around the coast. Down there the croft-houses were scattered, whitewashed, thatched with reeds, hump-backed and seeming to dig their shoulders into the breast of the braeside. And, as scattered, the narrow pathetic strips of cultivation made fantastic patterns on the smiling face of the land.

Adrian found Murdo MacIver's croft without much difficulty, and discussed the weather, the crops, the disappearance of the grouse, and the little that money would buy these days, with an old lady there, who, when at length they had got the conversation round to trout and fish-hooks, sent him off to the peat-bog up-bye, where himself was to be found. There, digging peats, he found four or five elderly men, all of whom remarked on the grand weather it was for the peats and the holidaymakers, and one of whom admitted to being Murdo MacIver. Thereupon, Adrian had a similar though somewhat deeper and still more catholic conversation with the gaunt grey-bearded husband of the lady, touching on religion, emigration, the colorado-beetle, and the Council of Europe, before working round to fish and the means of catching them, while his colleagues leaned on their spades and considered various aspects of the Creator's handiwork, much too polite to go on working in the stranger's presence. Eventually, Mr. MacIver consented to walk back towards his cottage, discussing the curious life-cycle of the sea-trout. Fish-hooks were only mentioned in a general, almost philosophical, fashion.

Shopping, conducted in this style, was a somewhat protracted proceeding—though infinitely more rewarding, of course, in a spiritual sense, than the usual sordid take-it-or-leave-it business. Adrian felt that a good morning had been put in when, loaded with a borrowed basket of oatmeal, cocoa, matches, and other necessities, which had been indicated rather than purchased during their discourse, and with an order placed for wrapped bread, he edged towards the cottage door. He recollected the fish-hooks only as he was bidding the MacIvers a detailed farewell, and thereafter necessarily spent a pleasant half-hour dealing suitably with the matter. After

175

which, Murdo MacIver triumphantly pointing to the old wag-at-the-wa' clock, announced that it must be round about time for the legal dispensing of excisable liquors, and would the gentleman honour him by joining him in a dram? The visitor felt himself in no position to refuse, and the old man's companions from the peat-cutting, apparently gifted with a similar instinct for the appropriate celebration of the passage of time, arrived in a body, and joined in the hospitality. Thereafter, some unnoticed and quite unimportant time thereafter, Adrian departed amid the esteem and well-wishing of a substantial proportion of the male population of Alisary. Murdo MacIver, escorting him to the top of the knoll behind his croft, remarked, just by way of valediction, that they all were very much in favour of this gentleman Roderick Ruadh Macgregor that the papers did be full of—a right brollach indeed. He could be reading all the latest about him in yonder Monday's newspaper covering the bit basket, there.

Back in the mouth of his glen, Adrian seated himself on an outcrop, feeling just the slightest bit dizzy, and conned the newspaper. It was Monday's *Chronicle*, and amongst other matters of interest, contained two items, marked curiously enough with pencilled crosses, of especial significance to the Gregorach. The first was an article by a well-known agriculturalist M.P., setting forth the urgent need for a national voluntary bracken-cutting campaign, on the lines of the harvest-help scheme, following the example so admirably shown to the country by the extraordinary Roderick Macgregor at Loch Chiarain in Argyllshire, and which the writer himself was prepared to lead and organise during the summer holiday months; apparently John Campbell, their shepherd, had been engaged in more than mere shepherding since they left him. The second item was a report of the proceedings of the annual conference of the Scottish Wholesale Meat Traders' Association, at Ayr, where a demand had been passed unanimously that the policy of sending prime Scottish beef out of the country in return for minute quantities of frozen meat from the Argentine, should be altered forthwith by the Ministry of Food. An amendment, which evoked considerably more discussion and frequent reference to Rod Roy Macgregor, to the effect that the Scots meat trade should not indeed petition the Minister thus, but take the matter into their own hands and only send south their exportable surplus, was eventually withdrawn on the Chairman's plea that it would be sufficient to consider such action when the Government had indeed refused their demand.

Adrian Hope, as he proceeded up that glen, felt like doing a little singing himself—even if it was a comparatively sober song, with a suitable theme of romantic melancholy at the back of it.

Roddie Roy arrived back from the neighbourhood of the power-scheme camp in great fettle. He'd got it all taped. They'd have the crofters' land drained in next to no time. All they needed now was a few horses, garrons. They'd be able to borrow them down at Alisary, sure. . . .

Hope was irritatingly slow at seeing just how it was going to be done. And what were the horses for?

Patiently, the big man explained. There were hundreds of acres of hillside and bog to be drained, to have any real effect on the situation. They couldn't do that with picks and spades— they'd be the rest of their lives at it. The hydro people, now, knew how to go about this drainage business—hadn't they drained thousands of acres of their catchment areas? Well, then—they'd take a leaf out of the Board's book. They did it with machines, special deep-cutting ploughs, designed for the job. He'd been seeing Danny Sinclair about it. They had three of these ploughs on this scheme. They weren't doing any draining at the moment, and these ploughs were lying rusting on a hillside only a few miles away, waiting till the next time they were needed. Well, they were needed right now. They'd borrow them. . . .

That was all very well, Adrian conceded, as far as it went. But what about the important point, the motive power? He wasn't going to suggest that they pull these ploughs by horses, surely?

Roddie disclaimed any such futile suggestion. A tractor was what was required. Danny had been on the draining job for a week, earlier on, and they had used tractors. A tractor was the thing.

177

Hope didn't doubt it. But where were they going to find a tractor? They wouldn't get one at Alisary, that much was certain.

Macgregor knew that, too. The hydro people, if they were not using the ploughs, might not be using their tractors either. . . . But Danny Sinclair didn't seem to think.

You bet he didn't, Adrian agreed, grimly. Nor did he! Any idea of filching the Board's tractors could be ruled out, right from the start. They'd never get away with that. Look at the manpower they were up against—Sinclair had said that there were nearly two hundred men employed on the scheme. Even if they got the tractors away from the place, they wouldn't get a day's work out of them before their owners were over for them, in force. . . .

Grumpily, regretfully, Roddie admitted that it would be difficult. . . . But, brightening, he reminded that there was always the guy they'd talked to at Barrisdale, the crofter-guy that ran the Department of Agriculture tractor on contract. If they could get that, hire it if need be—there was no ploughing or harvesting going on just now, and it likely wouldn't be much used. They'd have to bring it round by sea, of course, there being no road.

And if this fellow refused?

He wouldn't refuse, Macgregor assured, grinning—he'd see to that. Anyway, wasn't that what the sanguinary tractor was for—helping the crofters? They'd get one of the Alisary fishing-cobles—that would be big enough to ferry a tractor, surely—and go to Barrisdale that very night. And the rest of the outfit could get the horses, and away and collect a couple of these ploughs. And tomorrow they'd get cracking on that bog.

Obviously, there was nothing more to argue about.

But it would all take a bit of doing.

It did. They had a busy night of it; all save Helen Burnet, who was left alone in the bothy by the lochan—though undoubtedly she would have gone with either party, had she received any encouragement. *En masse*, they went off down the glen to Alisary, where they found the crofters helpful enough, if scarcely so urgent about their help as the visitors could have wished, and from whence, in due course, Roddie and three others rowed out in a big blunt-prowed black coble south-westwards into the dark waters of the Sound of Sleat, and Adrian with the other three, plus Sinclair and one of his companions, led four shaggy long-tailed broad-backed horses south-eastwards into the night-bound hills.

The suggestion was put forward that this landward party's task was the easier. It seems improbable, though indubitably it was the more humdrum. They had to find certain rusty pieces of iron on an unfamiliar hillside above an only approximately indicated glen in the dark of night, and when they did at long last find them, they had to harness two of them to a pair of garrons and somehow drag, push, trundle, roll, even carry, the wretched perverse devil-possessed implements over miles, leagues, of impossible country, bad enough for walking, in the dark, but quite fiendish for plough-pulling, where every yard contained a pitfall and every foot a snag. It was nearly sunrise before they got the accursed machines down to the rendezvous—there to find a spike-wheeled tractor under a canvas cover, a few jerry-cans of fuel, and nothing else. They ran Roddie's party to earth, at length, comfortably asleep in the bothy, amidst the mixed fumes of crude oil and whisky. They did not sleep long undisturbed, needless to say.

The tractor-party's trip had been straightforward and un-eventful. It had taken an hour to row round the headland of Rudha More, but not much more to run up Loch Hourn beyond, with the wind behind them and the sail up. At Barrisdale, they had found their man doubtful at first, but amenable after a little persuasion, financial especially. He hadn't wanted to hear any details as to what the tractor was wanted for, other than that it was for croft-improvement. Unfortunately, he had pointed out, owing to being incapacitated by a bout of toothache—or was it earache?—he would be unable to come and drive the thing himself, as was normally the custom. He had, however, with the skilful use of a couple of planks, helped them to manoeuvre his tractor aboard the coble, where it stood amid-ships on its planks like a howdah on a whale, and thereupon, after a certain amount of appropriate refreshment, they had parted with entire good-will. It had been a tough row back, but Donald Lamont had worked wonders at making that boat sail into the wind, tacking about the loch like a Clyde regatta—and thanking his Maker that there was nothing of a sea running. It had all been just a piece of cake, it seemed.

Disgruntled, the plough-draggers retired to lick their wounds.

It was almost midday before Roddie's cracking process really got going. On the open slopes above the crofting township they planned their assault, and fully half of the population of Alisary turned out to see them do it, men, women, and one or two children. And they had plenty of scope for their efforts. The land formation has been described as a peninsula divided longitudinally by a great spine of high ground, which, however, was considerably more than one single ridge, and acted as a watershed from which streams had to flow north and south. While the great majority of such undoubtedly trended southwards, and were now being collected and harnessed by the hydro schemers, quite a proportion spilled over towards the north. This northern portion of Findart was indeed little more than a vast apron of land shelving down from the high watershed to the coast. Though it was furrowed and pierced by a number of little glens, like the one in which the Gregorach's bothy was situated, the general character of the territory was that of a long sweeping slope. But a shelving terraced slope, of comparatively gentle gradients, save in its upper reaches. And on these shelves and terraces the water which spilled over from the plateau above was apt to collect and lie, before eventually it was pushed over down to the next level. The entire slantwise terrain, in fact, was waterlogged. But it had not always been so, evidently, and from above faint traces of former drainage-ditches could still be made out, here and there.

After a rather prolonged conference with Murdo MacIver and his fellows, the Gregorach decided that the drainage plan must be something like the veining of a leaf, a branched pattern of innumerable ditches leading successively to larger, or at least, more important channels, following the lie of the land, making full use of any and all existing burns, and culminating in two or three main outflows, which, naturally, lay down the little

180

glens aforementioned. It was an ambitious project, and they could have done with another tractor, definitely.

With Adrian tracing out the direction in front, following approximately the lines of a rough plan they had sketched, Donald Lamont driving the tractor, and Roddie Roy mounted on the seat of the plough-affair, they started off. Danny Sinclair had explained just how the thing was worked. Wisely, they chose a fairly firm and levelish stretch of short heather for a beginning, and after a few false starts had the satisfaction of leaving behind them a quite impressive ditch, perhaps something over a foot deep and of similar width, rather tortuous and uneven admittedly, but not bad for a beginning. And though it was slow work, with the tractor coughing and spluttering and bucking, it was infinitely faster than hand digging.

But very quickly they ran into difficulties. The plough was apt to skip over declivities in the ground, to dig its nose in every now and then and almost overturn, and either come to a dead stop or slither crazily over the larger stones; outcrops of course had to be circumnavigated—and there were a lot of outcrops. The unsuspected semi-fossilised roots of ancient trees—relic of a forest long disappeared—were even worse than the stones. The tractor bogged itself down in soft ground, and tended to side-slip on hummocks. Hidden snags in bracken and long heather frequently stalled, confounded, and almost upset it, so that a man had to go immediately in front of it, sounding the way with a stick. And while they eschewed all knolls and hillocks equally with hollows and dips—since it was water that they were seeking to lead—there were frequent unavoidable gradients which were too much for both tractor and plough. Plentiful argument, vituperation, not to say impiety, was expended, as well as energy, fuel oil, and sheer muscle-power.

After a few hours of it, a certain system of reacting to problems was forced upon them, and accepted of necessity. The boggier patches, when unavoidable, were skipped, circumnavigated, and left for hand-diggers to link up. So were large stones, or clusters thereof. Whole areas were left severely alone, and their sketch-plan drastically curtailed. A root-drawing process was perfected, using the tractor and a chain, and a de-bogging party stood by the spiked wheels continuously, ready to lever out the heavy machine with crowbars and to tuck solids under the floundering birling wheels. No man of the Gregorach was inactive, and many of the crofters found themselves working harder than they had done for many a long year. Helen Burnet, even, took on the job of preceding the tractor with a probing stick. Every spade, pick, and shovel in Alisary was pressed into use.

It was a weary begrimed company that knocked off with the darkening that night—too weary even to accept Murdo MacIver's offer of hospitality. And looking back, into the dusk, only a pitifully small proportion of the task was done—and that on the best and firmest ground. Undoubtedly, Rod Roy was up against it, this time.

For a whole week they laboured intensively, persistently, almost without a break, in good weather and bad—and their labours included two night trips in the boat to Barrisdale, for more fuel oil. Their dourly angry perseverance undoubtedly stemmed from Roderick Macgregor, who was determined not to be beaten by anything under the sun, and saw to it that others acted accordingly. They became, by experience, considerably more expert, but to counter that, the crofters' supporting effort fell off rather noticeably—and not un-naturally, for they were elderly men, with their own crofts and fishing to attend to, and a sense of urgency was not in them. Also, the ground, as they worked lower, grew steadily worse, less stony but more boggy. Fortunately, the Hydro Board's contractors presumably did not notice the loss of their ploughs—or even of a few spades that found their way over the hills—for they made no complaint, betrayed no awareness of what was going on to the north of them, indeed. And there was no further talk of Helen going home or leaving them; she was kept more than busy feeding the enhanced appetites of her eight companions, as well as taking spells of tracing the route for the tractor. Toil and sweat alone counted during those long days of early July.

But though progress was substantial, and the upper slopes were beginning to be scarred professionally, if a little patchily, with satisfactory black scores, it became increasingly evident to them all that they were not going to be able to finish the job, thus. And if they did not finish it, on the lower ground, they might as well not have started it, for the crofters certainly would never be able to tackle it on their own. Daily, Macgregor and Adrian and Lamont became more preoccupied, concerned, and gloomy.

Which was a pity, for the pattern of their life in that bothy in the little glen was a pleasant one, with a sort of idyllic flavour about it of peaceable essential continuity, sweet even to the most determined of fugitives. And since his talk with Helen that night by the lochan, Adrian had made a very apparent and not entirely unsuccessful effort to be more cordial, in a noble and long-suffering fashion, to both the poor deluded Roddie and the deluding and erring young woman—who was, after all, *only* a woman. A pity it was, altogether.

It was in such a situation that Jakey Reid and Jimmie Maxwell found them, one night, as they trudged sore-footedly up from Alisary, heavily-laden with packs and impediments. They just hadn't been able to stick it in Glasgow any longer, Jakey said. The town was like a bees' bike, he declared, fair buzzing with talk of Rod Roy and his doings, with the papers full of it, associations being formed, demonstrations held, a march to Bannockburn being planned, students going off in parties to cut bracken and build dykes, gangs of kids playing Rod Roy and the polis, kids following folk in the streets demanding if they were in favour of Rod Roy and if they said no dinging them over the head with a paper ball on a length of string. It had been too much for Jakey, and him out of it all. So he and Jimmie had packed up their jobs, got their cards, and come away. Likely others would be following. Jings—if they just advertised where they were hiding out, and asked for volunteers, they'd have half Glasgow packing up and joining them! That was a fact. Talk about waking up Scotland . . . !

The rousers of the nation nodded sleepily, stretched and yawned hugely, and went to bed.

XVIII

IT was two evenings after Jakey's arrival that the ditch-diggers, coming mud-spattered and weary over the hill to their sanctuary in the glen, found it spoiled, invaded. As they clumped heavily in at the door, Helen Burnet's voice sang out melodiously, but in warning for all that.

"Gentlemen, mind your manners, we have company!"

A man was sitting on the edge of the kitchen table, swinging one leg, a man of about fifty, iron-grey, keen-faced, and dressed in a reddish kilt, a Lovat jacket, and all the appurtenances proper thereto. He eyed the newcomers searchingly as they crowded in at the doorway, and he did not rise to his feet.

"Good evening," he said, and his voice was deep, authoritative, and entirely confident. "My name is Macdonald."

"*Major* Macdonald . . . of Findart!" Helen amplified significantly.

"Oh, yeah!" Roddie Roy commented, briefly.

"Yes. I only arrived back from the South, last night—otherwise I would have been over to see you before this!" He said that meaningfully.

Macgregor shrugged his uninjured shoulder. "We've managed along," he said.

The other's jaw became a little more prominent, but otherwise his expression did not alter, and his leg continued to swing. Adrian Hope noted the boniness of the knee with a kind of fascination. "So I notice," he nodded, and his glance flickered round the room. "This house belongs to me, you know."

"Blasted capitalist!" Jakey shrilled, from the back.

"Shurrup!" Roddie mentioned, without turning his head. At the visitor, he merely stared. "Uh-huh?" he said.

"Yes. And I hadn't thought of letting it!"

The big fellow grinned. "Fine," he announced. "An' you dinna' need to, either, noo. It's let!"

"Roddie—I think you'd better let me handle this," Adrian interposed. "My name, sir, is . . ."

"Shurrup! This guy isna' needin' to ken your name, Major. Anyway, I'm handlin' this mysel', see."

"Major . . . ?" Macdonald questioned, from the table.

"Only the I. Corps," Hope assured. "Merely a nickname—nothing genuine."

"Ah," the other said. But he considered him speculatively, for all that. "Well, as I was saying, this house is mine, and . . ."

"Look, Mister," Roddie broke in. "You own this wee hoose. Okay. You own the hale bang-jing aroond here—the crofts an' the land an' the hills, eh? Includin' the hillsides we're sweatin' oor guts oot to drain an' improve—the job *you* should be daein'. Maybe you'll no' be sae keen on talkin' aboot ownin' *them*, wi' the bonny-like mess you've made o' it!"

"Touché!" Major Macdonald actually smiled, if thinly. "I was coming to that. But first, if you please, we'll deal with this cottage."

"Deal, my foot!" Roddie roared, with his sudden upsurge of fury. "Nae dealin' in it. We're *in* this hoose. It was empty, an' we need it—need it to dae what *you* should ha'e done long ago. Here we're bidin'. If you want a rent for it, I'll gi'e you it. . . ."

"No, I don't want a rent. A rent would give you certain rights, tenant's rights. I might not be able to have you evicted when I wanted—and it looks as though I'll require to have you evicted pretty soon!"

"You will, will you! Goad, then—you try it, Mister! Evict awa'. We'll be ready, see! Noo—get to hell oot o' here, before I throw you oot!"

"Roddie! Don't be a fool. . . ."

"This is ridiculous, utterly crazy!" That was Helen Burnet. "Roddie—do have a little sense. . . ."

The visitor was on his feet now, facing Macgregor. And a striking pair they made, both kilted, the older man tall and thin, stooping a little, hawk-like, quietly authoritative, Roddie Roy huge, splendid, assured, naked save for his kilt as was his habit nowadays, stained and splattered with peat-mud. Like a greyhound and a mastiff they eyed and measured each other.

185

"So you would throw me out of my own house!" the Macdonald said.

"Aye, I would! An' quick, tae. I'm hungry, see. I've been slavin' a' day on your damned waterlogged hill, an' I'm wantin' my supper—we a' want oor suppers."

"Rod Roy Macgregor!" the other commented. "So this is the grim reality! Instead of the romantic hero—just a great ill-mannered boor!"

"No!" That, strangely, was Helen Burnet again, and sharply. "That's not true, Major Macdonald. It's . . . well, you don't understand. But he's not that, I assure you. . . ."

Their caller turned to glance at her, curiously. Adrian turned, too; they all looked, and with varying expressions—except Roddie Roy.

Meeting their glances firmly, almost defiantly, she seemed to accept them as a challenge to continue. "Roddie—every man here, in fact—is doing something pretty big, something precious few Scots have had the wit or the courage to do, for a long time. If he's a bit, a bit forceful and impatient about it, he has plenty of cause. Years, centuries, of neglect and, and spinelessness, aren't going to be cleared up by pretty speeches!"

Varied but very definite were the reactions to this unexpected outburst—surprise, approval, speculation. Adrian Hope pinched his lower lip between thumb and forefinger—a sure sign that he was much affected. A confused rumble of attaboys and fair enoughs and requests to give it big licks came from the tight-bunched Gregorach about the doorway, and Findart himself inclined his falcon head gravely, in some sort of acceptance.

"Perhaps you are right," he acknowledged, courteously. "As one of the most notably spineless, I am suitably rebuked. Still, even pretty speeches can be a help, don't you agree . . . ?"

"They can be a damned waste o' time—an' there's been ower much o' them, right noo!" Macgregor barked. "Are you goin'—or am I puttin' you?" and standing back, he sheared a way behind him, with his sound arm, through the press. It was a significant gesture.

Major Macdonald apparently recognised its authenticity. Half-shrugging, he nodded. "I am getting a little past fisticuffs," he said. "I hardly came prepared for this sort of thing." He moved down the line of them to the door, unhurriedly. "Next time, I'll have to see that I come better equipped!"

"You dae that," Rod Roy told him, following him out. "Bring a' your keepers an' your gillies wi' you—aye, an' your polis tae—an' I'll throw you oot, jist the same! Till this job's done, I will. Efter that, you can ha'e your damn bothy, an' welcome! Noo—will you get crackin'? I'm hungry."

"Look, Major Macdonald," Adrian Hope said, from the doorway. "You've caught us rather on the wrong foot today, I'm afraid. I think, perhaps, if we could see you some other time . . ."

"You will, never fear, young man," their visitor assured, a trifle grimly.

"Yes. But, I suggest . . ."

"You're suggestin' naethin'!" Macgregor interposed, with his abrupt bellow. "There's been plentys o' that, a'ready. Awa' hame wi' you, my mannie. The rest o' yous—inside. Hel'n—sees that supper!"

"Aye—doon wi' the capitalist exploiters!" Jakey got in as a parting shot.

"Och, can it, Jakey. . . ."

Major Macdonald of Findart stood, pursed his lips, shrugged again, and then turning on his heel, set off along the path down the glen.

"Good night, sir. I'm sorry about this," Adrian called after him.

"No doubt," came back from the walker, over his stooping shoulder. And that sounded pregnant with meaning.

"That," declared Helen Burnet, with emphasis, "was extremely foolish, and quite uncalled-for."

"I entirely agree." Adrian nodded, as he peeled his hot potato.

Roddie, chewing steadily, looked from one to the other, and said nothing.

"You've antagonised a man that can be dangerous, for no reason," the girl went on. "He might even have been helpful—I had quite a talk with him before you arrived, and he sounded reasonably sympathetic."

187

"He can keep his sympathy!" Alicky Shand announced loyally, with his mouth full. "We dinna' need anythin' frae yon kind."

"Jings, no! His kind it is, that's caused a' the trouble . . ." Jakey Reid began.

"Don't be silly!" Helen interrupted, warmly. "Major Macdonald hasn't caused any trouble—yet! And we, *you* anyway, certainly need something from him. You need this house, for one thing. You need his non-interference, for another. I'd have thought you'd want his good-will, at least. He might even have been able to help you, in some way. . . ."

"How?" That was Macgregor.

"Well, I can't say, off-hand, of course. But he's bound to be an influential man up here—the Macdonalds have owned this place for centuries. . . ."

"That's jist it," Roddie said. "They've owned the place for centuries—an' look at the state it's in! Ruination, that's a' they've been to the Hielants, your Laird Macdonald an' a' his kind. Jakey's got the rights o' it, this time. It's them an' their work that we're fightin' against."

"I don't agree," Adrian contended. "While the landlords are not blameless, by any means, neither are any of us. They're hard-up, to a man—the old proprietors, at any rate. Economics are against them, and Government policy—plus the apathy of the whole people of Scotland. . . ."

"Och, aye. Economics again! It's ay economics. If these lairds had had any guts, if they'd been any damned use at a', they'd no' jist ha'e sat snug in London or some ither like place, an' watched their Hielants dyin'. They're nae use to us—nae use to anybody any mair. Let the word get roond that we're workin' in wi' the likes o' yon, an' we lose half the support o' the folk o' Scotlan'."

Keenly Hope looked at him. "So that was the reason behind your display!"

The big man grinned. "Och, I didna' like the colour o' his tartan, either!"

"And for that you were prepared to offend him, to make an enemy of the man, and more or less ask him to bring the police down on you!" Helen exclaimed.

188

Lazily the red-head smiled, leaning back against the wall. "He'll no' dae that, Hel'n—no' him. No' for a bit, leastways—no' till we've finished this job. He's no' a' that foolish, your lairdie. This drainage is goin' to increase the value of his property—an' he's gettin' it done for naethin'. Yon one's no' goin' to bring the polis doon a-top o' us, offence or nane, while we're makin' shekels for him!"

"You think that? I wouldn't be too sure. Injure a man in his pride, and he may forego material gain, to get even. . . ."

Adrian, who reasoned in the same way, whose mental processes worked along similar lines, and who felt that he ought to be supporting the young woman's contentions, found in himself a strange reluctance to do so. He felt that she in all probability was right, and yet . . . Perhaps it was some purely masculine reaction, an inherent loyalty to the bold devil-may-care and essentially male tradition, against his reason and his judgement. Perhaps it was more personal, more elemental, even—the paying-her-out motive, after her shameful treatment of him. Perhaps it was that he suspected, even resented a little, the girl's sudden apparent conversion to their cause, as indicated by her surprising outburst to Macdonald—a conversion which could only have its roots in her infatuation for the self-same Roddie Macgregor whom she now was challenging. Women were the devil. . . .

"M'mmm," he said, consideringly. "I think probably Roddie is right . . . for the time being. The laird will likely postpone his revenge—till he sees an end to our draining his hill. Then, I imagine, he won't waste any more time!"

"That's aboot the size o' it, I reckon," Donald Lamont spoke up. "An' it looks like he'll no' ha'e that long to wait! The way things are, we're jist aboot stuck, an' that's a fact. Yon low groond's a scunner. We'll never dae yon by hand in a month o' Sundays—an' the tractor's jist aboot had it."

"By hand, jings!" Art M'Vey exclaimed. "Nae fears. . . ."

"Hell, no!"

Roddie Roy's right hand crashed palm down on the table, setting the crude furnishings dancing. "There y'are!" he cried. "There you bluidy-well are! This fixes it. There's nae guid beatin' aboot the bush, any mair. I said we'd got to finish the

189

job, whativver the cost. Weel, noo we've got to finish it in a hurry. There's only one way to dae it—the way the Board does it. We've got to get a caterpillar-tractor. We're *gettin'* one, see!"

There was a moment's silence. This was an old controversy, a well-discussed subject. It was at Adrian that they all looked.

That man refused to be drawn. He merely raised his eyebrows. "You all know my views," he said, evenly.

"Aye—fi we ken them," Macgregor growled. "But you'll admit that we'll no' finish that drainin' *wi'oot* a caterpillar-tractor—no' this year, anyway?"

"I'm not denying it," Hope returned. "But . . ."

"But naethin'!" Roddie snapped. "There's nae twa ways aboot it. We've got to finish that job, or we've failed—an' that's worse than if we'd never begun. Can you no' see your newspaper heidlines, if we make a splurge o' it? An' the only way we can finish it, is wi' a caterpillar—naethin' else can cover the soft groond. An' the only caterpillar-tractors in this hale damned countryside are jist twa-three mile awa', at the hydro dump. We've got to get them."

The murmur of agreement was just a shade slow in coming, and dutiful rather than enthusiastic.

"We could try an' hire one frae them, maybe?" Donald Lamont suggested, but not hopefully.

"I'ph'mmm. We could *try*—but they wouldna' gi'e us them. Thae tractors belong to the contractors, no' the Board. They're hired to the Board a'ready, see. The contractors—that's the guys on the spot, here—couldna' hire them to us, forbye. That's what Danny Sinclair says, an' I reckon he's right." He pushed forward his pannikin. "Gi'e's some mair spuds, Hel'n. Aye— if we want one o' yon tractors, we'll jist ha'e to take it."

"The taking, I imagine, will be the least of it," Adrian mentioned grimly. "The point is, you'll not keep it. And if you get it taken back from you, especially by force—as you would—that would be apt to gain worse publicity than if you just packed up here quietly."

"Then we'd damn-well ha'e to see that they didna' get them back," Macgregor asserted. "No' till we'd finished wi' them."

"That would mean fightin', maybe," Lamont pointed out.

190

"Weel, fight then."

"A dozen against two hundred!" That was Adrian, pointedly.

"Aye—if need be."

But if such odds did not daunt Rod Roy Macgregor, his companions' attitude seemed to indicate that they had a better grasp of elementary arithmetic. Into the silence, Alicky Shand suggested, doubtfully, "Maybe these crofter guys'd back us up?"

"No' them," Donald declared. "Anyway, they'd be nae use. They're ower auld."

Roddie, who seemed to have said his last word on the subject, munched steadily. The rest considered each other, moodily uncertain. After a pause, Adrian Hope got up, and walking over to the fireplace, turned, his shoulder propped under the mantel.

"Look," he said, slowly, almost reluctantly. "I'm not keen on this tractor-stealing business, at all—though I recognise that we'll not finish the drainage job without one. But if it's settled that we *are* going to finish it, then I'd say, don't let's do our stealing on our own doorstep. On Roddie's principle that it's a dirty bird that fouls its own nest. Murdo MacIver tells me that there is another small hydro scheme over in Skye—just across in Sleat, there."

"Eh . . . ?" Macgregor looked up. "You mean . . . ?"

"I mean that you've already shown that it's possible to ferry a tractor on a fishing-coble. I suggest that we repeat the performance—across the Sound. If the thing was to disappear quietly at night, it might not occur to the hydro people to look for it over here, for long enough. Is it feasible, Donald?"

"Goad, I guess you've got somethin' there, Major!" Roddie said.

"Jings, aye. Yon's mair like it. . . ."

"Bide a wee, bide a wee," Donald Lamont answered, cautiously. "It's no' jist sae easy as a' that. There's four mile o' the Sound to cross, wi' likely a bad tide race. An' your coble'll no' carry one o' thae caterpillar-tractors. They're big muckle heavy things."

"Will it no'?"

191

"Are you sure, Donald?"

"Aye, I'm sure. Yon are near twice as heavy as an ordinary tractor, an' bigger every way. You'd jist aboot need a ferry-boat for yon."

Roddie Roy's crestfallen features suddenly lit up, with a radiance of pure bliss. "Fine!" he cried. "Grand! Jist the job. A ferry-boat it is! We'll take a lend o' the Glenelg Ferry, up-bye! We'll take it for the night, an' dae the thing in style!"

With an admiration that had something of awe in it, the others stared at the big fellow. Even Adrian looked impressed.

"The public ferry?" he said.

"Sure. Jist that. They'll no' use it at night, an' we'll ha'e it back to them in the morn. Donal'—you can drive the thing?"

"Och, likely. But . . ."

"Right. Then the morn, one o' us'll awa' ower to Sleat, an' see if we can find a tractor wi' tracks, an' we'll get crackin'." His good humour entirely restored, Roddie Roy beamed round on them all. "Aye—an' to hell wi' the Macdonalds!" he said. "They were ay jist baistards!"

XIX

O N the morrow, then, Adrian and Donald Lamont left
the drain-diggers, and set off northwards for Glenelg.
They had a walk of about eight miles, with the head of Loch
Elg to circumnavigate. There, they found that the ferry was a
couple of miles further north still, opposite Kylerea on the
other side of the Sound, which there narrowed considerably.
They had, however, a copy of the day before's *Sentinel* which
they had obtained at Glenelg Post Office, to enliven this last
lap. Two items of personal interest they gleaned therefrom.
Firstly, that there was still sufficient general interest in their
doings to warrant a leaderette entitled WHERE IS ROD ROY?,
which speculated on that elusive individual's next activity and
ultimate aim, as well as on his current whereabouts. Second,
that the Secretary of State was to be asked in Parliament if, in
view of the widespread concern in the country, he would
promote and convene a round-table conference broadly
representative of Scottish interests, to thrash out a solution to
the nation's ills, of which the Macgregor campaign was only
a sign and symptom; and it was suggested to the Scottish
Office, that if and when such a conference was held, Rod Roy
Macgregor himself could well be asked to attend, as a patriot
with ideas and initiative, however unorthodox.

It was nice to know that they were not forgotten.

They found the ferry-boat tied up at a small jetty near a
house that was marked Inn on their map, but was now a youth-
hostel. It was a squat stocky shallow-draught craft, motor-
driven, wide enough to carry a couple of cars, and it had the
appearance of fair seaworthiness in Donald's eyes.

They had an hour to wait till the ferryman and a youth
appeared, and they were transported across the Sound of Sleat
in company with half a dozen mailbags, a party of hikers, and
an old man attached to a curly-horned ram. They noted how
the boat was headed sharply up-Sound for a good way, out of

deference to the tide-race, before going about on the other tack, to fetch the Skye shore directly opposite. Lamont nodded significantly, and kept a knowledgeable eye on the ferryman's handling of the ungainly craft.

At Kylerea a ramshackle little bus was waiting, and together with the old man, the ram, and certain of the mailbags, Adrian and Donald piled aboard. The hydro scheme was somewhere down in the Ostaig area, a good part of the way to the Aird of Sleat. Thitherwards, after a round-about trip across the peninsula to Broadford, they rattled and lurched, at a quite incredible speed, over a narrow twisting road that doubled back through the hills and then hugged the shore.

There was no need to have the whereabouts of the power-scheme pointed out to them by their pleasantly informative driver—its dumps and hutments and its fine new broad road striking up off the old narrow one, shouted aloud. Since the bus was carrying one of the mailbags up to the camp, by merely sitting still its passengers got an excellent and unchallengeable view of the vital area. A short way up the new road, they passed a large dump of concrete and steel pipes, a little higher, another of bricks, girders, cement, steel-reinforcing and other building materials. It was still further up, beyond a pine plantation, with the hutments of the camp in sight ahead, that Lamont nudged Adrian with his elbow. Here was a third dump, or rather, a vehicle park. In it a great variety of wheeled and tracked vehicles were drawn up—trucks, lorries, mechanical grabs, concrete-mixers, even a steamroller and a bulldozer. And beside a row of tractors of all types and sizes, towered no less than three monsters, wholly tracked, with little cabins a-top, resembling miniature tanks. The watchers exchanged congratulatory glances.

A hundred yards or so on, Adrian got up, and tapped the driver on the shoulder, saying that if he was just going on to the camp and then coming back, they'd stretch their legs for a little walking down again, and he could pick them up on the return journey. This brought forth no objections, and presently they were sauntering back past the vehicle park. A quick look-round assured them that it was at present unattended, that it was entirely open without gate or fence, and that there was no sign of a hut or shelter for a nightwatchman. Two black tanker-wagons, near the road, presumably were the source of petrol and oil fuel. They risked no closer inspection. For their purpose they had learned sufficient.

They were half-way down to the coast-road again, when the bus drew up for them. Adrian sent it on. They had decided just to wander along the shore for a bit, he declared. How long would the bus be before it returned from the Aird? A couple of hours? That would suit them beautifully. They'd be waiting for it along the coast-road somewhere, on its way back. Agreeably, the driver rattled on his way.

So they strolled down past the last of the dumps, nodded to a couple of foreign-looking individuals loading pipes on to a tractor and trailer, examined through its cobwebby windows a locked hut that stood near the road-end but which proved to be empty, and so reached the shore of the Sound. There, amongst the rocks and the multi-coloured seaweed, it was not long before they discovered a small strand of sand and pebbles, with suitable access to the road—suitable for a caterpillar-tractor, at any rate. Satisfied, they established their landmarks, found a convenient hollow amongst the brackens, and went to sleep in the smile of the sun.

A very approximate two hours later, their bus retrieved them, and hurtled them headlong back to Kylerea and the ferry. The sun was setting as they watched the boat tied up for the night, and set out on their long walk home through the gloaming hills.

Exactly twenty-seven hours later, they were back at Glenelg Ferry. This time, however, they were much reinforced. To cover all eventualities, it had been thought wise to bring a force of eight men, two-thirds of their company. They might well be needed.

They reconnoitred the ferry area cautiously. The youth-hostel and the two cottages nearby—one of them the ferryman's house—were dark. To approach the tied-up boat at the pier silently, to board her and unslip the two hawsers, was easy. To pole her off into deeper water, with a boat-hook, shallow-draught as she was, called for no effort. The act of piracy was all too simple. The difficulty was, to make away with their prize—for they dare not start up the engine till they were out of earshot of the houses. They had reckoned on the tide-race carrying them off southwards down the Sound—as no doubt it would, once they got out a bit. But meantime, the unwieldy craft just lay sluggishly on the water—indeed, tended to drift shorewards again on the south-westerly breeze. And there were no oars or other means of propulsion. Eventually, they dealt with the situation by three of their number doffing their scant clothing and slipping overboard with ropes tied round their middles, to tow the wretched thing in the most elementary fashion, while their colleagues assisted by dipping a board or two, and even hands, over the side, as paddles. Very gradually, listlessly, crab-wise, the lumbering vessel moved out into the Sound.

Three or four hundred yards out, as the pull of the current began to tell, they hauled the gasping swimmers aboard. The boat was drifting now, slowly but steadily, southwards with the tide, and already the land was only a dark looming mass, featureless, though the water gave off a wan luminosity of its own, that was only the cold memory of light. Soon it was agreed that they were far enough out and down-Sound to risk the engine, and Donald Lamont, who had been fretting at the starting handle, tickled the carburettor, gave the crank a couple of turns, and the motor spluttered into life. It sounded shockingly loud in the ears of the temporary crew, but they heaved a sigh of relief nevertheless. They were impatient young men, all of them, and a lazy drifting was to none of their tastes—especially Roddie Macgregor's; he had been growling about getting cracking ever since they cast off.

Heading south by west, Donald kept the craft almost in mid-Sound, and on a steady course they chug-chugged comfortably through the night, the small waves slapping rhythmically against the blunt bows. Above them a few pale stars were winking in a sky of deepest blue, against which the serrated outlines of Ben Gair and the Sleat hills were etched sheerly.

It was not so simple placing their position even by well-established landmarks in that half-light, with only the actual

196

ridges of the hills standing out of the flat blackness. Even the entrances to the sea-lochs, opening off the Sound on either hand, made no break in the level walls that flanked them—and they were relying on one, in especial, to guide them.

With Adrian's half-inch Bartholomew's map lit by a shaded electric torch, Lamont held to some sort of a course. With the tide to aid them, they were making perhaps six knots. An hour of this, and he reckoned that they must be somewhere between the opening mouth of Loch Hourn on the east, and that of Loch na Dal on the west. Isle Oronsay should lie close to the land on their starboard bow, but no hint of it showed against the loom of the land. Another half-hour or so ought to bring them approximately to the level of the Bay of the Mill, for which they were heading. But how to pick it out . . . ?

It was the jutting headland of An Fhaochag, The Forehead, most westerly point of Knoydart, thrusting out into the Sound on their left, that eventually provided them with the certainty of their whereabouts. There could be no doubt about the identity of that pointing finger of land. That meant that they were almost due east of Armadale Bay on the other side of the Sound, and just over two miles south of their objective. Swinging the squat craft's prow round a few degrees north of west, Donald headed straight across to the Skye side.

Half a mile offshore, he throttled down the motor, and they crept in quietly, the engine just ticking over. In the end, their landfall was an excellent one, the jagged gables of a ruined croft-house—possibly the mill—rising on a small cliff against the sky, pin-pointing their bay. Just a little feeling along the shore, brought them to their sandy beach, and on to its gently-shelving strand Donald steered his craft. With a soft crunch of pebbles, the prow grounded, and the Gregorach leapt over into the shallows. It was exactly half-past one.

Lamont was left with the boat; it was essential that she should lie a little way offshore, both to avoid possible attention through being lit up by a car's headlights on the road round the bay, and to ensure that she did not ground on the ebbing tide. The rest of the party followed Adrian and Roddie up on to the road.

They moved northwards for a few hundred yards, and then

the new road opening off, they turned up it in single file, past the empty hut, clinging close to the upper verge and ready to drop for cover at a sign.

At the first dump, that of the pipes, Adrian left his companions and crept ahead to scout. He was back in a couple of minutes, with the word that all was clear; there was no sign of any watchman. The next, the builders' dump, was similarly deserted. In front lay the black mass of the pine plantation, and beyond it the vehicle park.

In the cover of the trees they waited once more for Hope's report. This time he was away for quite a period, so that the watchers were becoming restive before he got back, with the explanation that he had been peering into the cab of every truck and lorry in case a watchman might be using such as shelter. But there was nobody there. The coast was clear.

He led them down through the jumble of assorted vehicles to the caterpillar-tractors. All three were still there—which seemed to suggest that there was no drainage going on at this scheme, either, meantime. Jakey and Alicky, their mechanics, promptly set about an inspection, with the aid of the shaded torch. It did not take them long to make a pronouncement, and a choice. One of the tractors was definitely in better condition than the others, a newer machine; also, its tank was three parts full of fuel. It looked as though it had been in use recently. Its ignition and priming system seemed to be the same as that of their own tractor back at Alisary. What more could they want?

Not a dam' thing, Roddie Roy agreed—except maybe a bit honest shoving from a set of bone-idle so-and-so's. Shoulders to the wheel was all that was wanted, now. Shove, you blagyurds—shove!

And shove they did, push and strain and heave, with might and main—but all to none effect, or precious little. Labour and sweat as they would, they could move the massive thing only by inches. At first, they thought it must still be in gear, or with some auxiliary brake still on. It was only when these theories were disproved that they began to realise the difference in frictional resistance between tracks and wheels. It was a painful and salutary lesson. Save under its own power, they would not move that tractor more than a dozen yards.

Once the situation was clear, and the first blast of his profanity exploded, Rod Roy wasted no time on repining. "Look, noo," he said, tensely. "This thing'll make one hell o' a racket to start. The camp's nae mair'n half a mile up-bye. We've got to ha'e a racket up there that'll droon the racket doon here. See? Art—you an' Sandy an' Fachy, come wi' me. We'll awa' up there an' start somethin'. The fower o' us'll start a fight, kid-on we're tight, or somethin'. We'll bang on the hut doors, break a windy or twa maybe, kid-on we're a wheen furrin navvies, shout an' start a rammy anyway we can. But we'll ha'e to make it snappy—an' make it loud. We'll make it so's you guys can hear it, doon here. Then you can start this baistard up. Got it?"

"Yes—but what about you?" Adrian demanded. "How will you get away from whatever you start?"

"Och, we'll dae fine. We'll get awa', never you fear. Gi'e's quarter o' an 'oor to get the rammy started, jist. See you doon at the boatie. Okay?"

Somewhat doubtfully Adrian, Jakey, and Alicky nodded. With a cheerful wave, Roddie Roy led his three companions to the slaughter.

Half a dozen times Jakey Reid turned over the starting handle, primed up the carburettor, and checked the ignition—anything for a quick start. Half a dozen times Alicky Shand made sure that there was a clear route through the press of vehicles to the road, and that nothing should hold them up. Half a dozen times Adrian Hope hurried out on to the road and stood staring up towards the darkness that was the camp, listening, listening. And the curlews called wearily from the lifting moors, and the night wind sighed sadly through the surrounding heather, and no other sound at all broke the stillness of the night.

"Och, to hell—they've gotten catched!" Jakey burst out, at length. "They've been awa' half an 'oor, anyway. . . ."

"Mair," Alicky contended.

"Oh, I wouldn't say that," Adrian demurred. "Not more, anyway." It had occurred to none of them to note the time when the party had split up. "All the same . . ."

"They've gotten catched," Jakey reiterated, gloomily.

"But Roddie would have made some sort of noise, even if they had been collared, surely. . . ."

"Listen!" cried Alicky.

But there was no need to strain their ears. A great gong, possibly a fire-alarm, was clanging and booming from up the road, and through and above its reverberations a fusillade of eldritch shrieks rang out, faint and thin at that distance, but no doubt potent enough at close quarters. A steady thumping noise also could be made out, and snatches of bellowed song— from the timbre and volume, indubitably part of Rod Roy's contribution.

"I hope to Heaven he watches his shoulder . . ." Adrian began, when his own words were drowned in a whirr and then a shattering roar, as Jakey tried the self-starter and the tractor burst into mighty clamour. Throttling back hastily, Reid choked the engine, and it expired in a series of explosive belches. Cursing, he tried the starter again, but with only the whirring as a result. Alicky grabbed the starting-handle, and birled furiously, but without effect.

"The priming!" Jakey yelled, and Shand leapt round to the carburettor, fiddled with it, and then back to the handle. A couple of turns, and the engine coughed and spluttered into activity once more. Jakey was more careful with the throttle, this time, and in a few moments had the machine throbbing deeply, powerfully, loudly it is true, but not deafeningly. They could hear nothing now, from up the road; whether the reverse applied, was another matter.

"Okay," Jakey shouted. "Let's go," and putting the gear-lever into bottom, promptly stalled the engine again. Those tracks were hard to set in motion.

But Alicky had the thing roaring again in half a minute, and Reid, revving up the engine warily, coaxed the monster into reluctant movement. With Adrian leading the way, and Shand walking alongside ready to administer immediate first-aid, Jakey drove through the parked vehicles to the road, their tractor rolling forward with commendable smoothness once it was started.

Out on the metals of the road, a glance upwards showed

them lights winking all over the camp. That might be satisfactory, or the reverse. Setting the tractor into second and then third gear, Jakey drove off downhill in fine style, Adrian and Alicky running rather foolishly behind, with many a glance over their shoulders.

Their trip to the shore was entirely uneventful, neither internal nor external sources giving the tractor occasion to pause. They suffered no challenge, saw no sign of life, and covered the mile or so in under ten minutes. They ran down over the bracken and the greensward to the shingle without a falter, and Donald, who had heard them coming, brought the ferry-boat in gently to meet them. While they were getting out the gangplanks that were part of the craft's necessary equipment, Donald was informed of the situation. He was, curiously enough, relieved to hear it. He had heard a faint echo of the hullaballoo up at the camp even down here, seen the lights go on, and feared that it was the starting-up of the tractor that had caused the alarm—though he had not heard the latter till it must have been half-way down the road. That, in its turn, was a relief to them all.

Getting the tractor aboard was a much simpler process than Adrian, at least, had anticipated. A detachable section of the boat's freeboard was run to one side. Donald saw to the placing of the gangplanks both on the little deck and ashore, and thereafter Jakey just drove aboard, the machine taking it in its reptilian stride, without so much as a hiccup. Lamont was very particular as to just where the thing was to be placed—he was risking no cargo trouble in mid-sound.

Once this activity was over, and they had nothing to do but wait, their mutual relief began to ebb. And as time went on, and there was no sign nor sound of Macgregor and his party, they grew anxious, steadily more anxious. It is an ill business, idly waiting for colleagues to emerge from a lion's den, especially at nearly three o'clock of a morning. Reassure themselves as they would as to Roddie's ability to look after himself, by three-thirty, though the lights appeared to have all gone out again, up at the camp, they could stand it no longer. Leaving Donald once more to his ship, the three of them jumped ashore, and set off again towards the new road.

They had not gone far when Adrian thought that he heard a halloo. But the others had not noticed anything, and listen as they would, could hear nothing more. They decided to carry on up towards the camp—though what they would do when they got there, they had little idea. Scout around a bit, of course. . . . But hardly had they started walking again before another call sounded, faint but clear. This time there was no dubiety about it—they all heard it. And it was behind them, somewhere—they all agreed on that. Turning, they made back for the boat at the double.

Donald Lamont, when they reached him, was still alone. But he had heard the cries too—they came from further down the coast, southwards. Thither the three of them hurried.

Another halloo came to them before long. It was not far ahead now, obviously on the coast. That fact decided them that they could risk answering it. Alicky lifted up his voice, and immediately there came a reply. Pressing on, they presently met up with Sandy Robb, clambering over the rocks towards them.

"Whaur the hell ha'e *yous* been?" he demanded, wrathfully. "We been waitin' on yous for 'oors. An' whaur's the blasted tractor?"

After an exchange of incoherencies, it transpired that Roddie Roy and his party were waiting at a little cove perhaps half a mile further south, which they took to be the one in which they had left the ferry-boat. They had come back across the hill from the camp, not down the road. . . . When Adrian pointed out that they had a perfectly good landmark in the ruined house on the little cliff, to keep them right, Sandy asserted vehemently that that was just what had guided them. The cottage was there, all right. . . .

And so it was—at least, a ruined cottage crowning a headland stood guard over a little bay and strand, which if by no means identical with the original was like enough to be mistaken for it by people who had only seen both in the dark. And there sat Roddie Macgregor and Art M'Vey. Fachy was away searching for them on the farther, southern, side. Sandy was sent to fetch him in, while the explanations were exchanged anew.

202

Donald was a thankful man when he saw them all back. The wind was beginning to rise, and he wanted no complications with a strange and unwieldy craft in a choppy sea. Also, the dawn would be breaking in just over an hour. It was high time that they were on their way. He cut short all explanations, and even accounts of prowess up at the camp, with the curt commands of a preoccupied ship-master.

With at least one other member of the company, he heaved a grateful sigh as the vessel swung slowly away from Skye into open water.

Having the freshening breeze largely astern, and with only ten sea miles to go, in a little over the hour they were across at Alisary. The tide had ebbed nearly to its limit, and the semi-ruinous jetty was useless. Donald nosed the craft in to the shingle, the gangplanks were run out, the tractor started up and Jakey ran the thing ashore with no more fuss than if he had been taking his own lorry out of its garage in the Dumbarton Road. Thereafter, as it rumbled away off up the gravelly track across the machair, the ferry-boat chugged northwards up the Sound once more. And not a lamp lit up amongst the scattered croft-houses, not a door opened. In the dead hour before the dawn, Alisary either slumbrously or discreetly turned its face to the wall.

The grey shadowless pallor of daybreak was creeping over all the mist-bound mountains as Lamont and Adrian and Alicky reached the Glenelg Ferry. Donald had discovered just how low he could run the engine without it dying on him, and ticking over gently they eased their way towards the pier. Some three hundred yards offshore, however, he switched off the motor. The small way they had, the making tide, and the breeze behind them, carried them forward slowly, slowly. With half the distance covered, and progress almost ceased, Donald had his two companions take up an old tarpaulin that lay in the well, and hold it up open between them in the bows, as an extemporary sail. At first it seemed useless, futile, but very gradually movement forward became perceptible. That last lap took them a long time—with the light ever waxing about them. Also, with no steerage-way they were drifting in too far to the south of the pier. At fifty-odd yards from land, and the sandy bottom showing clear, Donald ordered his crew overboard, where, up to their chests, they waded not so much ashore as pier-wards, dragging the heavy ferry-boat by its hawsers. The water was icy cold—so much colder than it had been at the swimming five hours previously. They were shivering but thankful when at last they slipped the hawsers over the bollards on the pier, folded up the tarpaulin, sought to clear away any other traces of their piracy, and stole silently off, southwards, along the beach. The cocks in the ferryman's garden were crowing lustily.

It was sunrise by the time that they reached Loch Elg, and most assuredly breakfast-time before they wearily entered the mouth of their little Gleann na Lochan. But over to their right a deep and persistent throbbing came and went and came again, on the young morning air. Roddie Roy the indefatigable, the untireable, the impossible, was getting cracking already.

XX

THE caterpillar-tractor was a great success. For such a massive and heavy machine, it was astonishing how well it was able to cope with the soft and waterlogged ground. Only actual bogs and peat-hags held it back. Roddie Macgregor, who insisted on driving it himself, was like a triumphant charioteer, challenging all obstacles. The stirring if not very tuneful strains of *Macgregor's Gathering* became, with the rising and falling growl of the tractor, more or less chronic over the lower slopes of North Findart.

The patchwork of drains now began to assume a recognisable pattern, as bits and pieces were linked up and new leading channels appeared. Like the veining of a great sycamore leaf the black scores showed up, pools and sumps and hollows began to empty themselves, and everywhere water was flowing and gurgling instead of lying and seeping. So long as these drains were kept reasonably clear, a couple of thousand acres of hill grazing would be reclaimed, a quarter of that area of permanent pasture would be rescued from frequent flooding, and something like seventy precious acres of possible arable made available. For Alisary, it meant a new lease of life. If only they had a road, so as to take full advantage of it all. . . .

Whatever stir the Gregorach's purloining of the caterpillar-tractor had created over in Sleat—if indeed its loss had been noted, at all—no repercussions thereof reached remote and inaccessible Alisary. On the second afternoon they ran out of Diesel oil, and a trip was made that night in the fishing-coble to Barrisdale, for more. The opportunity was taken, at the same time, to return the original tractor to its custodian, who, possibly out of thankfulness at seeing it safely back—aided no doubt by both the dimensions of the financial incentive and the dimensions of its offerer—let them away, in return, with his two last drums of fuel oil. Roddie reckoned that that would

205

just about do them. Another couple of days ought to see the job finished.

The next evening, as Adrian, spade in hand, was thinking about knocking-off, Murdo MacIver came up to him amongst the fragrant bog-myrtle where he was working, with a strangely conspiratorial air. After much nodding and winking, glancing over his stooping old shoulders, and jerking his grey head at Jamie Maxwell who was digging nearby, he confided to Adrian that the Laird was down-bye, and would be liking a word with him. Just himself, it was to be—none other, at all. The Laird had been dead-set on that—just the one that they do be calling the Major. He was down at his own bit house, there, was the Laird. If the gentleman would be coming, and quiet-like, so that the others would not be after seeing him. . . . Yes, yes—the Laird was just alone by himself.

A little mystified, Adrian shouldered his spade, called over to Jamie, despite the old man's shushes, to tell the others that he would bring up the bread with him later, and followed on.

He found Major Macdonald leaning on the only leanable-on portion of Murdo MacIver's garden-fence—part of an iron bedstead still resplendent with two out of three brass knobs. Politely, warily, they greeted each other. MacIver, as politely, effaced himself.

" 'Evening," Findart said. "Fine night, again. You have had a remarkable spell . . . but I fear it is going to break." That last seemed to be enunciated with a certain significance.

In recognition of it, Adrian inclined his head. "Yes," he said. "Perhaps. I imagine you are probably better acquainted with local conditions than we are."

"Quite," the other nodded. "It is often profitable to pay some heed to the man on the spot, in weather as well as in other matters!"

Hope had nothing to say to that.

Macdonald eyed him from under bushy brows. "You seem to be as busy as ever—most industrious in attending to other people's business, aren't you?"

"And you," Adrian retorted, quickly, "*you* haven't called the police yet, have you?"

The older man shrugged. "We are not overloaded with

police, here in Findart. But that doesn't mean that we have no respect for the law—nor that we are powerless to keep it!"

"No?" Hope raised his brows. "You wanted to see me about something, I gathered, sir?" he mentioned evenly.

"Yes. I have some information that it occurred to me might affect you—and I imagined that you might be the most reasonable and, er, civilised of your extraordinary gang."

"You honour me."

"No. I'm not so sure about that. Possibly the reverse. *You* ought to know better!"

"That is arguable," Adrian suggested. "But your information . . . ?"

"It is just that a friend of mine over in Glenelg tells me that he had a visit from a gentleman from the Hydro-Electric Board this morning, looking, it seems, for a caterpillar-tractor! It's lost, apparently—an extraordinary thing! He was asking the best way of getting to Alisary—evidently he is not an enthusiastic walker; it seems that he had been glancing across the Sound from Sleat with his field-glasses, the day before, for some reason or other, and his eye happened to light on a caterpillar-tractor working on ground considerably north of where his colleagues at South Findart usually operate. So he came across in his car, but came up against the road trouble. My friend couldn't give him any information . . . about a tractor, of course, but was able to tell him that the best, the only, way to get here was by boat, either to Alisary direct or to my landing-stage at Findart House. And at the hydro gentleman's request, he agreed to hire a motorboat for him . . . for tomorrow."

"I see. Tomorrow."

"Yes. And my friend said that this engineer-fellow mentioned that a large boat would be best, as it might be wise to bring a good number of men with him . . . to remove the tractor, I imagine!"

Adrian was looking at the man searchingly. "I understand," he said. "But why are you telling me all this, Major Macdonald? I hardly would have expected it. . . ."

"Because I thought it might interest you, that's all."

"Yes, but . . . well, you don't owe us any civility."

"No, that's true. But I'm not entirely dead to the sporting proposition, getting on though I am! Also, though unfortunately I had to sell them a lot of land, I'm not so much in love with the Hydro people that I want to see boatloads of them descending on North Findart, as well as South. Again, I rather like that young woman you have up at my cottage—despite the somewhat peculiar circumstances in which she seems to have placed herself!"

"What do you mean, sir—peculiar circumstances?" That was stiffly said.

The other raised one eyebrow. "Well . . . the circumstances of one young woman, an attractive young woman and apparently unmarried, living in a very small house alone with a group of rather noticeably tough customers. . . ."

"Major Macdonald, if you are suggesting that Miss Burnet is in any way loose, immodest, or, or remiss, in being with us . . . !"

"Dear me, no. Nothing of the sort. And if I did think so, most evidently *you* would be the last person to suggest it to. That would seem to be obvious. . . ."

"I imagine the same reaction would be aroused in any or all of us, sir!"

"Indeed? Interesting. Most refreshing, in fact. And what about the big fellow—the great Rod Roy himself?"

"I should think that, if you said anything derogatory about Miss Burnet to him, Macgregor would fell you where you stood!" Adrian told him grimly.

"So?" Findart stroked his chin, his glance very keen. "And then *you* would have a go at felling the big fellow, eh? Most intriguing. . . ."

"Just what d'you mean by that?" Hope snapped.

"Nothing—nothing at all. You have almost finished your digging activities up there, Murdo tells me?"

"Yes. Which is just as well, apparently."

"Just what I was thinking. You have put in quite a deal of hard work, by all accounts?"

"The accounts are correct," Adrian nodded, formally. "And your land will have gained quite a deal in value, because of it."

"The fact has not escaped me," the other admitted. "You might even say that I am grateful—not so much on account of the gain to the estate, as to my tenants the crofters. For, despite your friend Macgregor's assumptions, you see, I am not entirely blind to the tragedy that has stricken the Highlands."

"M'mmm. Yes. I see. . . ."

"I merely mention the fact," Macdonald shrugged. "You will just be moving on, I presume, to continue your activities somewhere else?"

"I suppose so, yes."

"A pity, rather."

"What . . . ?"

"I just mean that it seems a pity that all these spectacular efforts should be so widely dispersed, such a scratching of the surface of the problem, in each district—though I will admit that you've scratched the surface of this hillside to some effect! But . . ."

"Our task is not to solve the problems of individual areas, but to awaken public opinion," Adrian explained. "We are only making a series of gestures."

"Quite. Gestures is the word! But . . ."

A stentorian hail from up above them, caused them both to look up. There could be no mistake about whose bellow that was. Roddie was wanting to know if the Major was coming along with that bread?

Findart coughed. "Lord, I'm off!" he said. "I couldn't face another session with your Macgregor, just yet. He scares me to death . . . especially as you say he's liable to fell me at any moment—as I can well believe! Well . . . no use telling you not to do anything foolish, but . . . be discreet in your folly!"

Adrian smiled his first smile in that interview. "That is my constant endeavour," he assured. "Goodbye . . . and thank you, sir."

"Don't mention it," the other said, turning away. "Especially to your large friend up there! Good night."

Adrian did just that, of course; in fact, it was the first thing that he did, when he caught up with his colleagues, panting a little, burdened with his sack of wrapped bread.

"That was the Laird, down there," he told them. "He says one of the Hydro Board engineers is coming here tomorrow, with a big squad of his navvies, to collect his tractor!"

"Hell!" Roddie Roy jerked. "Hoo does he ken that?"

"A friend of his at Glenelg told him. The hydro fellow had been questioning the friend today about how to get here. They're hiring a boat tomorrow—a large boat!"

"The baistard! An' us near finished!"

"Jings, aye."

"I know. But there it is. Anyway, it was mighty decent of Macdonald to tip us off."

"Oh, yeah?" Macgregor doubted. "I'm no' sae sure aboot that. I'd no' trust yon one beyont what I could throw him."

"Maybe he's jist tryin' to scare us—to get rid o' us," M'Vey suggested.

"Nonsense," Adrian contended. "Having waited so long, he'd surely let us finish the job of draining his land before he did that. Anyway, he spoke fairly appreciatively of what we were doing. He's not such a bad fellow. . . ."

"He's a bad landlord!" Rod Roy asserted. "An' that's plentys for me."

"He's a hard-up one, anyway. . . . But no use arguing over all that, again. We've got to decide what we're going to do."

Donald Lamont spoke. "I'd say, get the tractor back to Sleat the night. If they find it back there the morn, they'll no' likely bother comin' ower here."

"What I was going to suggest myself," Adrian agreed.

"That means leavin' the job unfinished, when a' we need's anither day at it," the big man objected.

"We could finish it by hand, now—there's not so very much to do. Better that than having a burst-up, and having to get out of here in a hurry afterwards."

"Aye—an' we could get anither twa-three 'oors oot o' it the night, first," Donald pointed out. "We'd ha'e to go for the ferry-boat—that'd take fower or five 'oors . . ."

"Och, to hell wi' that!" Art M'Vey cried. "We're no' goin' to let oorsel's be run oot o' this, like yon. Let the geyser come, an' his navvies tae, an' see if they can *take* their damned tractor. . . ."

"Don't be a fool, M'Vey!" Adrian snapped—though it was at Roderick Macgregor that he looked, apprehensively. "That sort of talk's no use. For one thing, even if you drove off the first crowd, they'd be back with unlimited forces in no time—they'd collect any number from this hydro scheme here, if need be. You don't realise the manpower you're up against—and pretty tough customers too, lots of them. Anyway, that would bring the police down on us, right away. We'd have to get out of Findart at the double. We'd be all on the run, again—all for one day's use of a tractor. . . ."

"But we'd be finished here, anyway, would we no'?"

"Not necessarily. I . . ."

"The Major's right!" Roddie declared abruptly, with his inimitable finality. "Nae use ha'ein' a rammy here, an' then needin' to scram oot o' it. I'm a' for a bit fight, but it's no' worth it. The tractor'll ha'e to go back the night. Gi'e's a loaf o' that bread, Major—I'll awa' back an' get anither few 'oors oot o' it. You an' Donal' an' a coupla the boys, awa' for that ferry-boat. Okay?"

"I suppose so, yes. We'll have to have some supper first—it's a long walk, you know, a damned long walk."

"Och, take a piece in your fist, an' chew as you walk, man," the giant recommended cheerfully. "It's eight, noo. It'll be dark before you get there. We'll need a' oor time."

Donald Lamont looked up and around at the sky. "Aye," he said. "I doubt we're goin' to need mair than jist time, tae!"

So, nearly three weary hours later, the four men once more circumspectly approached the Glenelg Ferry. Once again, the place was in darkness—darker than that previous night, indeed, though the hour was earlier. Heavy clouds saw to that. But Donald, at least, was not suitably grateful for the extra cover provided, and the blanketing sound effect of a fitful wind that came and went and eddied amongst the night-bound hills. At frequent intervals he glanced up a the sky, consideringly.

The weather, however, proved to be only one of the circumstances that did not match those of their former visit. The ferry-boat, tied at the pier, provided the second instance. When they climbed down, quietly, on to its deck, it was to find the starting-handle gone, and the sparking-plugs removed from the cylinder-head. Also, from the pier, Alicky whispered down that the hawser was not just looped over the bollard—it was padlocked tightly to it. The boat would not sail that night.

Crestfallen, the would-be privateers considered each other. Apparently their last piracy had not gone undiscovered. The ferryman, once bitten, was shying. What to do now?

There seemed to be surprisingly little choice. Presently, glumly and in a hurry, they turned about and went back whence they had come.

XXI

IT was almost two o'clock before, footsore and morose, the walkers arrived back at Alisary. There, at the tumbledown jetty they found Macgregor and a couple of companions waiting with the tractor—and not in the most amiable frame of mind, either. They had been waiting there for some considerable time, it appeared.

Rod Roy's reaction to their news was the violent one that they ought to have gone straight to the ferryman's house, routed him out with his starting-handle and sparking-plugs, and forced him to sail them down here under threat of dire reprisal. Having got that off his chest, he did not wait while they countered with excellent arguments against such a course, but promptly declared that since they *had* made such a mess of it, the only thing that remained was for them to ferry the damnation tractor across on a fishing-coble. It was the only course left to them.

While that might be true, Donald Lamont found ample arguments against it. A coble was too small, it would take too long, and he didn't like the look of the weather. To which Roddie retorted that the caterpillar-tractor wasn't so greatly larger than the other tractor which they had transhipped twice without any trouble; that four miles directly across the Sound was all they had to cover in the boat—the tractor would just have to be landed wherever they reached the shore, and sent on thereafter under its own power; as long as they got rid of it before daylight, it wouldn't matter if they were seen sub-sequently—a fishing-coble, unlike a ferry-boat, would attract no attention in the Sound of Sleat; and the sea was calm, calmer than usual.

That last was true, certainly. The fitful wind had died away, and the surface of the sea, as far as could be seen from the jetty on a dark night, was almost glassy though there must be a swell running, judging by the long regular rollers that curled and broke in rhythmic succession on the beaches right and left.

Adrian was in two minds about the business. He was inclined to trust Lamont's judgment in a matter of this sort, rather than Macgregor's; but he felt that it was essential to get the tractor off their hands that night, somehow, and he failed to see how else it was going to be done. They could run it north or south along the coast somewhere, of course, and then abandon the thing—but that was a thoroughly unsatisfactory solution, out of keeping with all he was campaigning for, and besides, on a dark night, it would be no easy matter to drive a tractor any distance in a roadless country. And if the machine wasn't back at its dump in the morning, they'd have the hydro people over in force, asking questions, and with the new drainage system gaping open in front of them, wherever they hid the tractor. If it was possible, at all, to get it across in the coble, then he felt that they must attempt it.

"Are you sure the weather's going to break, Donald?" he demanded. "Soon, I mean?"

"You canna' be a' that sure aboot the weather," that man pointed out, reasonably. "But it looks that way to me. I didna' like the sound o' yon bit wind we had. It'll break, I reckon—but I canna' say when."

"D'you think it'll break before dawn, or what?"

"I canna' say, I tell you. It might, an' it might no'."

"But even if it did, it would take the sea a while to rise, wouldn't it, to be difficult, that is? After all, it's calm enough now, and we've only four or five miles to go—with the tractor aboard, that is."

"Och, to hell wi' a' that!" Roddie burst out. "Cut the cackle. We're goin', see. Whae's scare't for a bit wind or a shooer o' rain, anyway? C'mon—get crackin'."

And, needless to say, they did.

They were getting fairly expert at running tractors on and off boats, now, and it did not take them long to push one of the cobles down to the water, row it round to the jetty, improvise a gangway out of miscellaneous planking, and drive the machine aboard on to a platform of more planks built on the thwarts, the tracks assisting enormously. Their only difficulty was the rise and fall of the boat at the jetty-side caused by the swell, but careful timing overcame that. Once safely on board, they used some of the roping from the nets to tie their cargo securely in place. This tractor, certainly, was considerably more of a handful than had been the other, both as regards burden and bulk, weighing the boat noticeably low in the water and taking up practically all the space abeam. But the coble seemed buoyant enough under it, and Donald grudgingly reckoned that it would probably take them across so long as they had no seas to contend with.

Roderick Macgregor assured them that it would take them, anyway.

In that spirit, then, or the other, they cast off—leaving three of their number on the jetty to wave them farewell. The bulkiness of their freight left no room for more than four of a crew—which indeed was the minimum required to handle the boat—and even that was a tight squeeze. The fishing-coble of the north-west seaboard is a sturdy adequate craft, but not designed as a cargo-carrier.

The mast-socket was set well forward, and with it erected, Donald took one of the bow oars, so as to be able to run up and lower the sail as occasion demanded. Alicky Shand partnered his thwart with him. Rather too close to them for comfort and efficiency, Roddie and Adrian rowed amidships, the former, with his damaged left shoulder, taking the starboard oar. The tractor occupied the whole of the afterpart of the boat, forcing the bows, already high-set in construction, higher still out of the water, so that the two rowers perched up there had to manipulate their oars at a very steep angle. There would be some aching arms in the morning.

Pulling away from the shore, a little raggedly at first, they felt the craft heavy on their oars. But gradually, getting into the swing of it, and their muscles loosening, they realised that they were making good progress. The incessant south-west wind of those parts, that would have been almost head-on, had gone, strangely, completely, the ebbing tide was in their favour, and there were no waves to buffet them or spoil the steady timing of their oarsmanship. Only a great smooth swell that lifted them slowly up and up, poised them, and then let them sink down and down, as slowly. It was a bows-on swell, coming up the Sound from the wide Atlantic, and Lamont kept the coble's prow directly into it, on a course which, if it added to their passage an extra mile or two, suited them very well as regards direction. Rising and falling, rising and falling, pulling with long strokes back and forth, back and forth, they fell into a curiously soothing hypnotic rhythm, trance-like, silent save for the creak of the rowlocks, the steady splash of the oars, and the even sigh of their deep breathing. Time became unimportant, forgotten; only timing mattered, the constant unhurried flexion of muscles. It was the sort of effort that eats up the miles, even sea-miles, almost unnoticed. It was around three o'clock in the morning, and the men's minds sank away into a waking sleep.

They were, Donald calculated, fully two-thirds of the way across, and approximately off the mouth of Loch na Dal, when the breeze struck them, an uneasy shuddering sigh that came moaning across the water. The sound and feel of it, and more especially the airt from which it came, effectively wakened Lamont out of his dovering. "Hell!" he cried. "Due south! She's goin' to blow frae the south. We're like to ha'e oor work cut oot, the night."

Rousing himself, Adrian looked over his shoulder. "Better than south-west, surely—or even west?" he suggested. "It's not right in our faces, now, and it will help us on our way home."

"Damn that," Donald snorted. "It's the sea I'm thinkin' on. A south wind'll blow up this Sound like a funnel. An' it'll blow with the swell an' against the tide. Forbye, it's an unnatural wind—an I dinna' like unnatural winds. An' it's goin' to freshen, quick."

"Och, nivver heed," Roddie advised, yawning. "We're daein' fine. We'll be there in a wee, so what the hell!"

The wind freshened, as Lamont forecast, not steadily but in bursts and surges, varying in strength but in the aggregate becoming ever more vehement. It was useless to them, as regards their sail; the gusts were striking them abeam, and would be more apt to overturn their top-heavy cargo than to

216

help them on their way—anyway, they didn't want to be forced north; the reverse indeed. And the speed of the wind's effect on the sea was quite extraordinary. The underlying swell very quickly became ridged and furrowed with short steep waves, and its crests curled over in white-tipped combers. The standard of their oarsmanship suffered accordingly.

Donald had turned their bows more and more into the south, but now, reluctantly, he was forced to change his tactics. "We'll ha'e to pull straight inshore," he declared, "or we'll be gettin' pooped, maybe cowped. Wi' the tractor, she'll no' take these seas—the dam' thing's workin' loose a'ready. Yon'll be Isle Oronsay lighthoose—that means we're a mile or so south o' it, and maybe a mile offshore, tae. We'll try an' pull in, an' then work doon the coast, under the lee o' the land."

"Okay—you're skipper," Roddie acceded. "Pull her roond."

Rowing broadside on to those jabbly waves was an unpleasant progress, with the light high prow tending to swing away round northwards, the heavily-loaded stern wallowing sluggishly, and every timber creaking with the strain. But fortunately the long Sleat peninsula was now shielding them from the worst of the swell, if not the waves. Crab-wise they crept shorewards—and thanked Heaven that the tractor was fairly securely tied on.

Quarter of an hour's difficult pulling, and they were inshore, as near as Lamont dared go along a rock-bound coast. Turning the coble's bows south again, they started to row into the wind once more. Macgregor had suggested that they should run in and land the tractor at the nearest available beach, but just thereabouts the wide and boggy promontory of Baravaig thrust out into the Sound, behind which the road skirted, and over which the tractor would have to plough its uncharted way to reach good going. Since a number of lochans dotted this promontory, a landing further south was indicated.

But it was an unprofitable and alarming business, pulling into what was rapidly blowing up into a half-gale. And strain as they would, they were not making much of it, either. Steadily they were being forced nearer and nearer to the shore. Donald's eyes turned more and more frequently to the ominous line of white that glimmered out of the darkness on their right. The thunder of the breakers could be heard plainly between the gusts of the wind. If they could only make Knock Bay, round the headland. . . .

They made it, but only just—and not without a price being paid. Rowing their strongest, they kept offshore just far enough to scrape round the blunt southern point of the promontory. But in the very act of turning in westwards, towards calmer water, they slid down in the trough of the swell right on top of a thrusting line of semi-submerged skerries. Donald saw the foaming white of it, pierced with vicious black, below them, shouted a warning that set them pulling madly. But it was too late to clear it, though they were saved from complete disaster. They struck the rock a glancing blow that shook and shivered the coble horribly, grated over what must have been a reasonably flat shelf, and then slid into deep water again. Sighing thankfully, they moved on into the comparatively sheltered bay.

Obviously they dare risk no more land-hugging, and Donald headed them due west and ran straight to the shore at the head of the bay. There they found ample shingly beach, and without any casting about, rowed in. There were small waves breaking even here, but the high prow and flat-bellied stern had been designed for just such landfalls, and they grounded without any undue friction. Jumping out, Donald and Alicky dragged a rope ashore, and they were safe.

It was five-past four on Adrian's watch.

Getting the tractor ashore, in these circumstances, with no jetty or pier and from a high-sided coble, was less easy, but the still-ebbing tide helped, and with the machine moving on to the planking gangway, the boat heeled over and lessened the steep angle of descent. A wheeled vehicle might well have come to grief, but the caterpillar-tracks gripped and clung, Alicky, driving, kept his head, and the massive contrivance rolled safely down on to the shingle.

The road ran just above them, only a few yards off. They were near Knock Castle and about two and a half miles north of the new road up to the power-scheme camp. Leaving Donald with his boat again, Alicky driving and Roddie and Adrian hanging on behind, the tractor rumbled up the bank on to the metalled highway, and turned south.

Twenty minutes or so's uneventful if noisy driving, brought them, past the scattered township of Kilmore, to their road-end. They had decided that since it was quite likely that the vehicle-park would now be guarded, it was unnecessary to drive the tractor right back to its former stance. The first dump would do. But as they were running up to the road-end, a light suddenly went on in the formerly empty hut thereat, only twenty or thirty yards from them.

Very promptly they reacted. Alicky slewed the tractor in to the side of the road, and braked. They all jumped off, and Shand was about to switch-off the roaring engine, when Macgregor stopped him.

"Let it be," he cried. "It'll dae fine. Let them think we're still there. C'mon—let's go!"

Starting to run, they dashed back along the road that they had come.

They did not run all the two and a half miles back to the boat. Prepared for pursuit, and ready to leave the road for the heather at sign of it, when none materialised they presently slowed to a walk. But a brisk walk. For the wind was wild at their backs, and the sooner they were safely back over the Sound of Sleat, the happier they would be. The trio completed the return journey to Knock Bay in just under half an hour, which speaks for itself.

But even the fifty minutes during which they had been away was too much for Donald Lamont. Preoccupied with wind and sea, he was both urgent to be gone, and chary about going. If there had been any other means of getting back to Findart without sailing, he would have advised leaving the coble, and coming back for it on a more auspicious occasion. But Skye was an island—and an island that might well be too hot for them in the morning.

Though it was five o'clock, and dawn, there was no lightening in the sky. They pushed the boat down to the receding water's-edge again, and into the waves, and clambered wetly abroad. Even here in the bay, the sea had risen noticeably. But as noticeable was the buoyancy and easy handling of the

219

unladen coble, which more than counterbalanced their absorption with the elements. Pulling strongly, they headed eastwards.

Donald intended to turn north up the Sound and run before the wind, just as soon as they got out beyond the point of the guardian promontory. But the great combers coming up from the south and meeting them broadside on forced them round further and further into the north before ever they were out of the bay. These were no seas for an open boat to take abeam. Anxiously the rowers' eyes turned leftwards, in the direction of the headland. They could see nothing of it in the inky dark, but the gleam of phosphorescent white around it was plain enough. And with the tide still dropping, those projecting skerries would be further uncovered still. Donald kept them rowing a course as far east of north as he dared. But it was going to be touch and go.

By how wide a margin they cleared the point they never knew. It is difficult to judge, in the dark, just how far away one is from white water. All they could say was that they were too near for the comfort of any of them. And just when they were at the worst of it, a distraction occurred.

Adrian, now rowing with Roddie on the thwart astern of the one they had used on the outward journey, suddenly realised that his feet, even raised on a stretcher, were over the ankles in water. And, so far, he had not noticed them shipping any seas.

"Donald!" he shouted, "the boat's half-full of water!"

"Eh?" Lamont cried. "Man, it's no', is it?" Owing to the upwards-raking construction of the coble, there was little or no water about his own feet.

"It's right enough," Roddie confirmed. "It's fair sloshin' aboot."

For a moment there was silence in that boat, and then Donald spoke, grimly. "We've shipped nae water," he said. "Sae there's only the one thing to it. We sprung some o' the timberin' when we hit yon skerry."

Alicky whistled. "But it would ha'e showed before this, would it no'?"

"No' necessarily. It's thae cross-seas will ha'e strained it. Jist a strained seam it'll be, an' each sea openin' it a wee."

"Jings!"

"Keep your hair on, boys!" Roddie Roy cried. "We're no' drooned yet. We've got a tinnie to bail wi', have we no'? Sae lang as we've a tinnie, we'll dae fine." And he laughed, with his own heartiness.

"Will I start bailing now, Donald?" Adrian asked.

"No. Keep you at your oarin'. We've got to get by these damned skerries. Time enough for the bailin'. Wi' this followin' sea, she'll no leak that much. . . ."

"We're aboot by your skerries, noo, anyway," Macgregor interrupted. "There's nae mair white, efter yon bit, there."

And that was true. They seemed to have cleared the outriders of the promontory. Only tossing open black water lay before them. With a mixture of relief and apprehension, they surged on into it.

The Sound of Sleat runs approximately on a north-north-east-south-south-west axis, and though the wind was almost due south, the swell, which had now turned into great rollers, ran up it from the open sea in the same direction as its axis. By keeping these seas behind them, then, and turning a point or two more into the east—in fact, running due north-east—Donald aimed to cross the Sound slantwise, aided by the fact that it narrowed considerably in its upper reaches. By this means, he hoped to avoid having to turn broadside on, at all—at least until they had to make their landfall at Findart, when they ought to be sheltered somewhat by the jutting cape of Rudha More to the south. But it meant a long voyage, of all of ten miles, ten extremely unpleasant miles.

Fortunately, they did not have to wear themselves out with strenuous pulling. The following wind and seas carried them forward, with only moderate rowing to assist and guide. Indeed, as far as speed went, they seemed to be making excellent progress. But concerned as they were for a quick crossing, it was the increasing size of the seas that took up most of their attention. Steadily growing as they drew out into mid-Sound, the vast black monsters came hissing menacingly down on them in unending succession, their crests swept off in front of them in angry spray. Each looked as though it must engulf the small craft, but to each one the coble's blunt stern rose, and it slid away beneath her. Lifting, climbing, lurching forward crazily on curling crests, and sinking, plunging sickeningly down into inky foam-veined troughs, they drove. Fascinated, the rowers watched each bear down on them, and saw in each possibly their last. But still they pulled, regularly, monotonously, almost involuntarily.

The first wave-crest to come aboard, decided Donald Lamont. That meant that their stern was rising too sluggishly, which indicated that the water in the well had reached danger-point. Taking Alicky's oar, he sent him aft to bail. The coble was too wide for the effective handling of two oars by one man, but he could be ready with either to correct any slewing.

The tops of two more combers came in before Alicky had squeezed past Macgregor and Adrian, and found the bailer. Hurriedly he dipped and emptied, dipped and emptied, and seemed to make no headway as crest after crest poured in. Desperately he worked. One of the others would have joined him, but there was nothing else wherewith to bail. They could only watch agonisedly, and pull, pull.

At length, Roddie could bear it no longer. Yelling to Adrian to hold his oar, he flung himself forward, wrenched the bailer out of Shand's hand, and pushed that panting man back towards his thwart. And hugely, savagely, kneeling on the bottom, he scooped that water out, one-armed as he was, in what was little short of a constant cascade.

And his fury, matching the storm's, matched and for the moment, won. After the third crest, no more came inboard. But he went on bailing, as fiercely, and presently they were able to see something for it. The coble was riding the seas more lightly, and they began to hear the metallic clang of the bailer on the floorboards. At length, he flung it down.

"That'll dae, the noo," he gasped. "Gi'e's my oar, Alicky."

This private battle seemed to have effected a change in Roderick Macgregor, liberated some wild defiant spirit within him, that essential challenge that was the man himself. He began to sing, bawling enormously, he roared with laughter at every foaming breaker that came bearing down on them, and hurled triumphant profanity at them as they slid snarling onwards. He railed at and cursed his companions for snivelling faint hearts and weak-kneed swabs, and dug in his oar to such effect as almost to swing the coble off its course. And he sang and sang—if singing it could be described. Adrian, sharing his thwart, from glancing askance at him, felt the sheer power and magnificent strength and dynamic force of the man, and came to be strangely comforted. Beside his potency, that of the elements appeared less daunting.

For how long they proceeded thus, none of them could have told. They were concerned with other things than minutes and hours. How far they had got, and how much farther they had to go, went unheeded before how to get over this wave and how to climb out of that trough. They guessed that they were making good progress, with that gale behind them. How good, they did not realise.

Abruptly, they were informed. A boiling of white water only a yard or two out from Adrian's oar, jerked his head round. Beyond, no great distance beyond, was endless foaming surf. And farther still, as he peered, he thought that he could make out the black loom of land.

"We're across!" he yelled, above Roddie's singing. "Look out—we're across! There's land!"

Lamont glanced over his shoulder, and cursed. Not only was there land to their left, there was land dead in front of them, close in front, land ringed with foam. And over to the right, too. There could be only the one explanation. They had crossed the Sound, and were driving down on the little island at the point of Rudha More. He could just distinguish the soaring cliff of the great headland in the lessening dark. There was a narrow channel between cape and island. . . .

"Back water!" he shouted, desperately. "Back, Roddie—back, Alicky! Row, Major!"

They dug in their oars. But Adrian, who had heard the command to back water, began to do just that before the order to row reached him. And striving in mid-stroke to change, he met disaster. A large wave surging the wrong way, backwash from off the skerries, struck the blade of his wavering oar, swept it violently sternwards, and its shaft, inevitably, the other way. With a stounding crash it smashed up against the rower, full on his chest, and tossed him backwards off his seat.

Gasping in agony, Adrian fell doubled-up on the floorboards, and the oar swinging on in its circuit, slipped out of its rowlock, and overboard.

Groaning, the man lay where he had fallen.

Hope's companions would have attended to him, but they dare not. For dear life they were battling, with three oars, amongst a shoal of jagged skerries, to force the coble into the narrow channel between cliff and island. Like men possessed they struggled, the screaming windblown swell aiding them, but the angry backwashes from the skerries tossing them hither and thither. Half a dozen times they slithered over weed-grown rock, shipping water, before they were swirled into the boiling passage beneath the cliff. Their managing it at all could be attributed to the force of the swift-running seas, funnelling into the narrow bottleneck.

With Macgregor and Shand pulling a desperate oar each, Donald crouched in the bows, peering ahead and trying to guide them through. Pitching and tossing alarmingly in the onrush of confined waters, rising and falling awesomely beneath the beetling cliff, they lurched forward. If the tide had not recently turned, it would have been quite impassable. The islet lay perhaps a hundred yards out from the cliff, but out-reaching rocks narrowed the clearance considerably. Sweeping along it on the tide-race, they could do little more than hope and pray. Roddie Roy shouted his own brand of petition.

But it was a very small island, and in almost less time than it takes to tell, they were through. Ahead of them, beyond the point, the Findart coast receded north-eastwards. Along it the seas and two oars would take them. Donald staggered aft to attend to Adrian Hope.

That man was still huddled where he had collapsed, and was in imminent danger of drowning—for there was a lot of water in the boat again. He was conscious, but dazed with pain. He had struggled to rise, but the agony in his chest had forced him back. He could scarcely breathe—winded, undoubtedly, but more than winded. Lamont tried to raise him, but at the yell of anguish, desisted. The crest of a wave breaking inboard, left him in no doubt as to his most immediate duty. Kneeling, and resting Adrian's head against his side, he started to bail.

But work as he would, soon it was apparent that the water was gaining on him. It was not coming in over the top so much now, for the waves were a little less fierce here, Rudha More and the island shielding them to some extent. It was the coble that was leaking fast, her sprung timbers further damaged by the recent scraping and bumping.

Donald shouted his news to the rowers. They couldn't carry on. The boat would founder under them. They'd have to get to land. But it was a wicked rock-fanged coast. . . . It improved as they went north, though—they could be only a couple of miles from Alisary. He'd go on bailing as long as he dared, and they'd go on rowing, rowing like hell. . . . Then, at the last, they'd turn in and run for the shore. And God have mercy on them!

So they rowed and bailed, counting every stroke a gain, every yard, every minute. And the stern sank lower and lower, and the water rose up to Adrian's chest, and Lamont's middle. And the tops of the waves began to come in, regularly. Still keeping their stern to the seas, they were rowing inshore at as acute an angle as they dared. But between them and land a long seemingly unbroken line of snarling surf betrayed the skerries.

A curling comber, larger than the recent ones, hurled itself down on them. Sluggishly, inertly, the weighted stern lifted to it. Too inertly. Hissing menace, the wave crashed in on them. Hope and Lamont, in the well, were lost in a chill foaming flood. It seemed to be the end.

But, as the breaker rolled on, the coble heaved, seemed to shake itself feebly, and somehow survived. The broad well was almost full, but the upward-raking forepart retained some buoyancy. Clutching the floundering gasping Adrian, Donald shouted.

"Turn her roond, Roddie! Turn her half to the shore. She'll no' take anither." And desperately, he slopped the water out with his bailer.

Macgregor dug in his oar and heaved mightily, dragging the heavy boat's prow round through thirty degrees in one vast wrench, even with Shand still rowing his hardest. The shore was no more than five hundred yards off, the skerries half that distance.

Yelling his defiance again, Roddie seemed to lift that waterlogged hulk onward, by sheer will-power, wind and tide and Alicky together counterbalancing his crazy effort on the port side. They shipped some of each of the succeeding waves, half-astern now. A series of them were smaller than the giant that had pooped them, but it could be only a question of time till another such came. Wasn't there a theory about every seventh wave . . . ?

What they feared, hurled itself down on them while the coble was still a hundred yards from the skerries. Macgregor seeing it come, backed water fiercely, pulling himself to his feet in his effort, hauling the wallowing stern round to meet it end-on. This time, they all were overborne in the swirling flood.

For all that, astonishingly, the boat remained afloat—or, at least, not totally submerged. Like a half-sunken log, yawning. And almost before it was apparent that they still survived, Rod Roy was on his feet again, heaving the labouring bows round once more, shorewards. Spitting the salt water out of his mouth, he raved and swore and bellowed, at the sea, the storm, the boat, and his colleagues, damning them all. And the fury of his oar-work—rowing was no name for it— was almost frightening in its intensity. Dazedly, next to involuntarily, Shand went on hopelessly pulling, and Donald hopelessly bailing. Adrian was supporting himself by clutching a thwart now, only his head out of water.

A new penetrating sibilant sound came to them now, through the cacophony of wind and storm and shouting man— the continuous hiss of water seething boiling and foaming over rock. They were almost on to the skerries. Straight for the cauldron of them, Roddie urged the lifeless coble. Roused by the sight and sound, Lamont raised his voice.

"We'll no' dae it, Roddie," he gasped. "We'll no' get by yon!"

"Goad damn it, we will!" Macgregor cried. "Ower yon, an' we can swim for it."

They were in white water now. Ahead, close ahead, they

could see the evil teeth of the skerries. In another few seconds they would be on to them.

"Back water!" Roddie cried. "Blast you—back water!" and he dug in his own oar and pushed, pushed. On the very verge of destruction they hung, as the rowers sought wildly to stem forward movement. For a ghastly eternity, as it seemed, they hung there, lurching on, pushed back, wallowing nearer. Twice the boat checked and shuddered beneath them, and slid clear. Then, the big man yelled, like a bugle-note.

"Noo! Here it's. Row, you baistards—row!"

The great comber for which he had been waiting swept down. On it, with it, in it, they were hurled forward, on, on, in a welter of foam and spray. There was a series of jolts, ripping, tearing, and then a jarring smash, and the doomed boat lifted up stern over prow, poised for a moment thus, and then crashed down, overturned, her voyaging over.

Adrian, flung clear and swirled hither and thither, found himself sinking, sinking. Despite the agonising pain at his ribs, he struck out as best he could. But the press of the water forcing him down was overwhelming, intolerable. Every movement of his arms was a searing hurt. Great weights seemed to be dragging him down into a black pit, black shot with bars and arrows of fire. His head was splitting open, there was a clanging beat in his ears, and his lungs were bursting. If he could get but a breath, a single breath. . . . But there was no strength to him, no energy . . . only a helpless limpness and a comprehensive pain. . . .

And then, suddenly, he found that he could breathe. Caught in some uprush of that boiling sea, he was tossed upwards, hurled like driftwood. Gasping, he drew in gulps of air, that were exquisite relief and exquisite torture in one. He flailed about, but feebly, with what little power was in him. And he sought to shout, shout his need—but whether he did or no, he knew not; all the dreadful clangour of hell was about him, and in his ears, in his head. He slid, struggling frantically, back into the smothering depths.

Some time, some incalculable time later, he came up again. This time he did not struggle and he did not try to shout—the

227

horror had too firm a hold of him, and all his little strength was gone. But somewhere, far away perhaps, or in another dimension altogether, he thought that he heard a shout, nevertheless. Impersonally almost, he noted it, a strong vigorous confident shouting, even if remote, and so foolishly futile against the horror that held them in thrall. Almost in sorrow he heard it, sorrow for the shouter, not for himself, before he sank again.

Down there, sinking deep into blackness, the sorrow remained with him. That was all the emotion that he knew, a poignant impersonal regret, profound, all-embracing, but undetailed. For and of himself he cared and knew nothing now, nothing but the memory of a great pain and the awareness of utter weakness, awareness and acceptance.

And then, to his weakness came strength, abruptly, an urgent alien strength, dominant, forcing itself on his quiescent will, forcing him, drawing him up, back into the hellish state of pain and struggle once more. A great hand clutched him, dragged at him, and would by no means let him go.

On the surface again, above the fury of the storm, a huge voice came to him, now a roar, now a whisper, from near, from far. What it said he knew not, nor cared greatly. But there was an insistence to it, that wearied and flailed his failing spirit. The folly of it, the senseless insistent folly.

"Let be," it said. "Let be, noo. You're daein' fine . . . you're daein' fine. . . ."

A great arm wrapped round him, round his burning chest, round his crushed ribs, and the unspeakable agony of it surged in a crescendo that was beyond all bearing. Blackness, complete, irremediable, blessed, closed over Adrian Hope.

XXII

IT was a strange and far journey on which Adrian was embarked, an interminable journey through uncertain places, blurred and unreal. Fleeting impressions he gained here and there, throughout its unchancy course, but they were elusive, and none of them he retained. Or none save an indefinite pattern of kindness, oft-recurring, mild, vague but comforting. And, deep within him, he knew enough to recognise that he was in need of comforting.

When comparative clarity at last returned to him, briefly, momentarily, clarity of vision and coherence of mind, it was to find himself in a pleasant sun-filled room, with a tall tree outside the window whereon birds flitted and sang. He gained no other impression of that place then, and desired none. He had neither the strength nor the inclination to turn his head. But it was a pleasing vista, after those that had surrounded him for so long, peaceable, serene, and undemanding. With a little sigh of near-content, his eyes closed, and he dropped away again into a less malevolent darkness.

When next he opened his eyes, it was to look into others, large, compassionate, bent near to his own. It took him a little while to focus them, but they remained there for him, steady, reliable. And after a time, he recognised them. They were Helen Burnet's eyes, and very kind. He sought to smile, to speak, but she laid a finger on his lips, and shook her head, gently. He was glad enough to obey. That was all that he asked of life— to be able to obey, and lie still. She hung above him, there, until he slept again.

The girl was not there when he awoke again, and he knew a new emotion—disappointment, hurt. He had not the strength to be angry, but he knew that if he could have been, he would. He spoke her name, he called for her—at least, he thought that he did. And she did not come. He was aware of a deep sorrow for himself, a sorrow that he cherished for as long as he could. But sleep overcame him and his sorrow again. He could not struggle all the time.

Next time that he knew consciousness it was dark, save for a tiny light that burned near his head. He thought that he heard someone stirring nearby, but he could not remain interested for long enough to investigate. He returned to his own darkness, familiar now, and on the whole beneficent.

So, waking and sleeping, and lying in a state that was neither one nor the other, time passed, unspecified, unimportant time. Often Helen was there in person, often just some aura of her presence, sometimes she was not, and then he knew variously hurt, desolation, hopelessness. And sometimes there were others there, men whom he recognised vaguely, and did not recognise, as vaguely. One of them was apt to be a nuisance, poking and prying and touching. But he was really indifferent to them all, so long as they did not disturb him and come too close—for he was very hot, and cramped, and badly needing air. He had difficulty enough in drawing breath, without great staring men crowding him and poking things into his mouth. Helen, though she pushed things at him to swallow, too, was different, of course . . . only, he could not be sure of her being there. It was hard, hard. . . .

Then, one time, he awakened to the noise of a door opening, and turned his head quite simply, naturally, casually, to see who came. It was the first time that he had done so, and Helen Burnet, in the doorway, did not fail to note it. She came forward smiling, with something like a skip. "Well, well, well!" she exclaimed. "Look who's sitting up and taking notice!"

He opened his mouth to say something, found no speech, licked his dry lips, and shook his head a little, only a little. "Hullo," he said, huskily. "Helen."

She nodded. "None other. The inescapable Miss Burnet!" Stooping, she felt his brow with a cool and expert hand. "Better," she asserted. "Definitely. Temperature down a bit. I've brought you your M. and B."

He frowned, and formed his difficult lips into a circle. "What?" he asked.

"M. and B.," she told him. "You get it every four hours.

230

You know all about M. and B.—a medical student! To bring down your fever."

"Fever . . . ?"

"Just that. You've been running a disgraceful temperature, m'lad. Congestion of the lungs—that's you."

The man stared at her, with some concentration. "Oh," he said, at length.

"Yes. Now, I hope you'll get these over with less of a battle than usual. Will you?"

He opened his mouth obediently, and she placed the tablets on his dry tongue. Then she brought him a glass of water. As he saw it coming, he made the beginnings of a movement to sit up, to receive it.

"No, no!" she cried, her hand to his shoulder. "You mustn't move. Lie still." That was a peremptory command. Not that it was necessary. Even that faint genesis of motion had brought the sweat out to bead his brow, as his head sank back. He was grinning with pain, gasping; his chest felt as though it was crushed within iron bands.

"Silly," she chided him, but gently. "You have two broken ribs, as well as congestion, you know. You're all strapped up."

When he could achieve it, he spoke again. "Oh," he said.

Helen held the water to his lips, and somehow he managed to get it over. She smoothed his bedclothes, his pillow.

"Wh . . . where . . . are we?" he wondered.

"We're in Findart House—Major Macdonald's house. We've been here ever since the storm—three days ago. He's been kindness itself."

"Storm," he repeated. "Three days." One or two words at a time was as much as his tongue could cope with, at the moment—and his brain not so much more. Suddenly his eyes widened. "Roddie . . . ?" he whispered, urgently. "Where's Roddie?"

"Ssshhh, now," she told him. "No flap, no excitement. Absolutely forbidden. Roddie's just next door—in the next room. He's almost as big a crock as you are. I spend my time running between the two of you."

"Is he . . . is he all right? He . . . he . . ."

"Yes, he brought you in. He's not so bad—except that his

shoulder is all smashed up again, and he's broken three of his toes. Also, he's torn a lump out of his thigh. You're a terrible pair!"

He considered that, while she busied herself, woman-like, about the room. "He did that . . . bringing me in?" he suggested, at length.

"I don't know how—he just did it," the girl said. "Now, that's all for now, Adrian. Too much, probably. You're to go back to sleep again. At once."

"And Donald . . . and Shand?"

"They're well enough—no broken bones, anyway. But you mustn't talk. . . ."

"But . . . Findart House?" he muttered. "How did we get here . . . ?"

"Quiet, you. Not a word. Shut your eyes, Ian. I'm not answering another question."

He was glad enough to shut his eyes—he could hardly keep them open, anyway. He could think with his eyes shut . . . and he had a lot to think about. He would, too—he would think about them all. But some other time. Just now, he was a little tired. And it was a long time since Helen Burnet had called him Ian.

Major Macdonald looked in to see him that evening. Also Art M'Vey and Sandy Robb. But the girl would not let them stay longer than a brief minute, nor say more than half a dozen words. She was essaying the role of sick-room martinet with considerable success.

On the morrow, the doctor arrived all the way from Shiel Bridge, to tell Adrian that he was much better and his fever gone—which he knew already; that he would have to stay in bed for a week or two and then take things very quietly for several weeks more—which of course was absurd; that he wasn't to excite himself or get overtired—the which, how could he, in bed? and that he was a very lucky man not to have punctured his lungs—which conception of luck, the patient considered, depended almost entirely on the point of view. He must have given some such encouraging news to Roderick Macgregor next door, for Hope heard and applauded, albeit feebly, a succession of highly-reassuring bull-like roars from through the wall.

All the same, it seemed that Helen Burnet and Major Macdonald took the doctor's old-maidish instructions seriously. After they had seen him off—probably in the pony-and-trap which the creature no doubt affected—they came back to gloat over the helpless sufferer, the burden of their refrain that the patient was there for a nice long time, and fortunate to be so. The inference was, of course, that he deserved infinitely more than he had got.

Protesting, Adrian started to cough again, and when he coughed it was an agony excruciating. The struggle left him limp. But determined, still. "All that is absurd, of course," he contended, in a husky whisper; "I'm not going to lie here for weeks. Anyway, the campaign must go on."

"Fiddlesticks!" said Helen, flippantly.

"The campaign must go on," the patient repeated, frowning his reproof. "Can't just leave things in mid-air, like this."

"More like in mid-water, m'lad."

He turned to Macdonald; such heartless levity was best ignored. "This Macgregor business is serious. The thing's vital . . . we're all risking a lot over it. We're not going to let it all tail off, unfinished . . . after all we've done."

Findart glanced over at the girl. "I quite understand," he said. "But perhaps it *is* finished—this phase of it, at any rate. Your job may well be done—at least, the spectacular side of it."

"It is." Helen Burnet nodded, quite definitely. "You've had your freebootery, Ian. From now on, you're returning to the role of respectable citizen. And don't pretend that you aren't glad, really—you know that, at heart, you are!"

"I know nothing of the sort," the invalid asserted. "And what makes you think, even if I'm crocked up, and Roddie too, for a week or two, that the Gregorach won't carry on?"

"They won't, for two reasons, Adrian. First, because they're leaderless. Second, because . . ."—her eyes flickered over towards Macdonald, as though for help and support—"because the campaign is officially closed." She drew a hurried little breath. "I closed it."

"You . . . ? You *what?*"

"I closed it. A couple of days ago, I wrote to the Press—to your friend Archie Duncanson at the Press Association. I told him just what had happened here, all you had done, the drainage, the tractors, and everything. *And* the boat and the wreck—and the state you are in now. . . ."

"Good Lord!" Adrian's splutter started him coughing, once more. "What in the name of all that's wonderful . . . did you do that for?"

"I did it because it had to be done," she said, simply. "I've wanted all this brought to an end for a while, as you know. But now it has become imperative. The doctor left me in no doubts as to that. You don't realise how close a shave you've had—apart from drowning! Pneumonia might have been the least of it; your lungs were as near pierced as no matter—and they still could be. And you've been taking too much out of yourself for a long time. The doctor says you must go very carefully, for quite a bit. I wasn't having any more heather-hopping, or nonsense of that sort."

"So, having got us safely bed-bound and under your hand, you promptly inform the Press, and therefore the police, as to just where to find us!"

"Put it that way, if you like. But in the account I sent, I did full justice to all you had done here, the size of the effort you made. And I made your present state sufficiently dramatic—the romantic sacrifice of the leaders of the Gregorach, made in the interests of an ideal, the returning of borrowed property! I imagine you will get all the adulatory publicity you could want out of it, for your campaign."

"That will be a great comfort for us—in jail!" Adrian acknowledged.

Patiently she shook her nut-brown head. "No," she said, "I don't think you need worry about the police, or going to jail, any more, Adrian. Look." And from over at the dressing-table, she brought a folded newspaper. "Read that."

It was the *Scotsman* of four days ago, the very day of their disaster, and the item marked was a report of proceedings in the House of Commons the previous day, when, in answer to two Members' tabled questions, the Secretary of State for

Scotland declared that he was indeed conversant with the latest known activities of the so-called Rod Roy Macgregor, that he had studied the Press and police reports on the subject, and that His Majesty's Government had reached certain conclusions on the matter. Hon. Members, he felt sure, would not wish him at this stage to do more than indicate that Ministers were fully aware of the significance of the campaign being carried on, and could be relied upon to take all appropriate steps. Pressed for an answer to a specific question, the Scottish Secretary agreed that the acts set forth, while illegal and in some instances deplorable, were admittedly of a political rather than a criminal nature, and self-interest and gain obviously were not the motives. While to wink at such floutings of the law was to postulate a state of anarchy, he was prepared to concede that punitive measures might well not achieve the best results, and might further arouse public feeling. More discerning and suitable methods must be devised to bring to an end an intolerable situation. In reply to the Member for Dumbarton East, he said that, while he could not guarantee to call off police intervention entirely, in view of the state of opinion in Scotland, and the danger of martyring these youthful offenders carried away by an excess of misplaced patriotic zeal, he was advising a policy of leniency to the authorities involved, in the hope that there would be no further outbreaks of violence. He could assure the Hon. Member that there would certainly be no sort of victimisation. When another Member asked if this was not tantamount to a free pardon, and if it was not true that the police forces involved had already been instructed to discontinue this unseemly manhunt, no further reply was given. Nor was there any reply when one or two Members asked if this whole incident did not indeed underline the urgent necessity for Scottish affairs to be dealt with by Scotsmen in Scotland, instead of at five-hundred miles distance. After the Secretary of State had left the House, however, the Under-Secretary announced that the Scottish Office was prepared to convene such a conference as had been proposed by the panel of Highland Members, to discuss the overall situation in Scotland. There would be no official objection to the presence at such a conference of the so-called Rod Roy Macgregor or his representatives.

"You see," Helen said, eagerly. "You're obviously quite safe from the police—in fact, it's been evident for a while that they weren't looking for you very earnestly, or they'd have found you before this. And you've impressed the Government sufficiently for them to have to convene this conference—at least, you've impressed public opinion so much that the Government *has* to act. What more could you want? I'd have thought that you'd be mighty pleased with yourselves, and glad to lie back for a bit."

"M'mmm." Adrian tried to sound unimpressed and as resentful as before. "That's all very well, but . . ."

"But, what?"

"Well . . . what's Roddie got to say about all this?"

"Roddie, I'm glad to say, is amenable to reason."

The patient produced as nearly a snort as his state would allow. "That's new, anyway!" he said. "Your influence with him must be quite . . . phenomenal!" That was sour.

The girl said nothing.

"Miss Burnet seems to me to be talking good sense, Hope, just the same," Macdonald suggested. "You may as well face the situation. What she did strikes me as being admirable, from your point of view."

"From my point of view, what she did was interfering, uncalled-for, and, and presumptuous!" Adrian asserted dogmatically. "But, of course . . . I'm not Roderick Macgregor!"

Helen moved over to the window, and looked out. "I'm sorry, Adrian," she said quietly. And then, turning, walked quickly to the door, and out.

"You are not very fair to that young woman, you know, Hope!" Major Macdonald mentioned. "She deserves better of you, I'd say, on the face of things."

"On the face of things, sir, you might be right!"

Findart smiled the smile of a man who is not going to be offended. "She strikes me as having your best interests very much at heart. What she did, she did only after much deliberation—I know, for she sought my advice."

"Indeed!" Adrian was hardly helpful.

"Yes. And I advised her to go ahead."

"Why shouldn't you?"

"Why shouldn't I, indeed. I agreed with her that this stage of your campaign had gone on long enough—in fact, that to prolong it much further would be a retrograde step, as far as you were concerned. You are at the crest of the wave, the peak of public acclaim, the summit of popularity. So far, everything you have done has been a success—and though this last effort was touch-and-go, the spectacular ending will only add to the triumph. But you can't repeat that. Anything else will be apt to be anticlimax. You can't even guarantee continued success—and failures now would only injure your cause. I'd say it is a wise man who knows when to stop."

"You seem very concerned for our little efforts, Major Macdonald?"

"I am, admittedly. As I hinted to you once before, I'm not unaffected by the Highland tragedy—and in more than my pocket. I am in entire sympathy with the objects of your campaign . . . if not necessarily with all your methods! In that, I imagine, I'm like the great majority of Scotsmen, possibly the majority of Britons generally. But even accepting your methods, I'd say it was time you changed them. Time you changed your tactics."

"Changed tactics . . . ?" Adrian began to cough. "What . . . d'you mean?"

The other waited till the paroxysm was over. "Perhaps I ought to leave you to rest? Am I tiring you? I'll go, in a minute. But first, I want to leave you something to think about. This question of changed tactics. So far, you've been concerning yourselves with waking-up the country, and only incidentally showing the way, blazing the trail for what you hope will be the big battalions to follow. Right?"

"More or less, yes. Though all our Highland efforts have been constructive."

"Agreed. But the emphasis has been on the spectacular. But that, after all, is only a flash in the pan. Having been so successful in that, in riveting the attention of the public on your doings, what you want to do now is to indicate the Highlands' real basic need—population. Resettlement. I suggest that you make that your objective, now—and lead the way. In fact, I suggest that you stop being picturesque freebooters flitting over the face of the land, and become good honest hard-working settlers. With the influence you've gained, think what the effect might be on the land-hungry, the city-weary, the frustrated. . . ."

The invalid was eyeing him keenly now. "Yes?" he said.

Macdonald nodded, examining his fingernails. "I have a proposition to make to you—and to your friends, or at least, some of them. I have a home-farm here, if you could call it that. Fifty-odd acres of arable, and five thousand hill pasture. It is shockingly neglected—a liability rather than an asset. My manager is seventy-six, and failing. He knows his stuff fairly well, though he's old-fashioned, of course—but he has lost his energy and interest. He has one elderly shepherd and a halfwit to help him. I can't give it personal attention, for I have to spend a lot of my time in the South, unavoidably. Also, there is a bunch of derelict crofts at Minsary, and one or two back at Alisary, as you will have seen. Now, suppose you took on the job of manager of the farm, on a profit-sharing basis, with old John Macleod to advise you for a year or so. And if such of your company as would care for the job, took over the crofts, rent-free, and worked them in connection with the farm, on a sort of communal basis, I think you might make something worthwhile out of that—don't you?"

Adrian Hope was staring. "You're . . . you're suggesting . . . that, that . . ." His voice tailed away.

"That here is an opportunity to demonstrate that the Gregorach can do more than make spectacular gestures. I understand that you had thought of taking up some sort of crofting activities, before all this—that you had lost interest in your medical studies? Here's your chance, then—and mine! For you needn't think I'm so damned magnanimous, with this suggestion. I've been needing a new manager to try out new methods for a long time—and couldn't get one under seventy, up here. And my whole place has been dying for want of occasional labour—like most other Highland properties—and an infusion of youthful and energetic crofters would be a godsend. Also, I imagine that a bunch of crusading specimens like you would be apt to do more for the district than just work their crofts! I can see your Rod Roy becoming quite a force to be reckoned with, hereabouts. No—I wouldn't be the loser, I think. Of course, I'm taking a chance—you might be a complete failure as a farm-manager, and your friends might all pack up and return to Glasgow in six months. It's a chance I've got to take, though we might make the arrangement on a year's trial for a start, as far as you are concerned. That should be fair enough?"

"Yes. Oh, yes. Very. I . . . well, I don't know what to say, at the moment."

"Nothing," Macdonald advised. "Don't say anything. Just think it over. You've plenty of time to think about it. I'm off, now—before Miss Burnet comes and turfs me out. I hope I haven't wearied you, or upset you. . . ."

"You may have upset me, in a manner of speaking, sir— but you certainly haven't wearied me!" Adrian assured. And as the other opened the door, "And thank you for your hospitality—taking a collection of malefactors under your roof, like this."

"Malefactors, maybe—but potential tenants!" Findart smiled. "All part of a deep-laid scheme to snare some youthful labour, and improve my land. Good night to you."

XXIII

IT was an elderly maid, not Helen Burnet, who brought Adrian his breakfast next morning, and though the girl did come in later, it was only to utter a brief and impersonal good morning, push a thermometer into his mouth, stare purposefully out of the window, read his temperature without comment, and then leave the room again, just as though he were a mere article of furniture. Not that he expected or wanted anything from her, especially any annoying fussing, but he was a very sick man, after all, and had had a restless night, wherein nobody had come near him, as far as he recollected—that he was feeling much better this morning was entirely to his own credit and no thanks to the nursing. And now he could hear her, next door, talking and laughing with Roddie Macgregor—which was only to be expected, of course. Adrian coughed—but only a little, for such oral evidence of his suffering hurt his ribs devilishly.

Major Macdonald did not look near him either, all forenoon. When, around eleven, the aged maid brought him a glass of milk and a footering biscuit, she informed him that the Laird was away at Invershiel, and wouldn't be home till night. The patient's humph was eloquent, even though it nearly choked him.

Shunned and deserted, thus, he was almost asleep, somewhere about noon, when a faint sound from the doorway turned his head thitherwards. The door was opening, very gradually, cautiously. Surprised, he watched, between half-closed eyes. A tangle of red hair, a segment of forehead, and a single eyebrow appeared in the gap. A moment later came a penetrating whisper.

"Say—Is she aboot?"

"No, she's not," Adrian assured, distinctly.

Obviously relieved, Roderick Macgregor inserted himself within and closed the door carefully behind him. "Goad, Major," he said. "She'd fair skin me if she catched me!"

240

He made an astonishing figure. Bandaged voluminously about the shoulder and chest, the thigh and foot, with his left arm in its sling, he was dressed only in his old khaki shirt, faded and torn though undoubtedly recently washed—none of the Laird's pyjamas, in which Adrian was decked, could have been stretched to even sketchily enclose his vast person. Hopping on one long and very hairy leg, he came urgently across to the bed.

"Weel, Major," he greeted, in a sort of modulated bellow. "Hoo goes it? Hoo're you daein'?"

"I'm not so bad, Roddie. Nothing far wrong with me that a spot of rest won't put right—thanks to you! But you shouldn't be out of your bed?"

"Hell—dinna' you start that, noo!" the big man cried. "I get plentys o' that, I'm tellin' you. She must be oot, some place—I was feart she might be in here, maybe, an' you sleepin'."

Adrian shook a pained head. "Hardly," he said briefly.

"Fine." The red-head sat down on the bed. "So they couldna' droon us, eh? We're the boys, are we no'! It was a right caper, yon."

"Caper, maybe. But it was pretty near curtains for some of us, just the same. For me, certainly, if it hadn't been for your efforts. You were tremendous—especially with a burst shoulder. How you did it . . ."

"Och, skip it, will you," the other growled.

"No, I won't. Look, Roddie—it's not an easy thing to thank somebody for your life. . . ."

"Shurrup!" That was the authentic and authoritative bark. "I didna' come hirplin' oot o' my bed to haver aboot yon ploy—we've mair important things to discuss." He leaned closer. "Was this Macdonald guy gi'ein' you the dope?"

Adrian nodded.

"An' what d'you think o' it?"

"I'm not very sure," Hope said, carefully.

"Eh?" The other looked at him, incredulously. "D'you think he's no' on the level, or what?"

"No, it's not that . . ."

"But, man—it's jist the job. Couldna' be better. He's offered

241

us crofts, as many o' us as'll take them, an' work forbye on the farm, where you're to be the manager."

"Quite."

"Jings, then—d'you no' see it? What mair d'you want? For a whilie I've been wonderin' where we were goin' frae here—we couldna' cairry on oor campaign jist indefinite, mind. An' jist lettin' it fizzle oot wouldna dae, at a'. But here's the answer. We'll make a right do o' this place—make it a proper show-place o' what can be done. We'll get yon road built, an' a decent pier. We'll try oot some o' Jakey's ideas on communal croftin', poolin' labour an' implements an' marketin'. Och, man—it's a cinch. This is jist the next step, frae what we've been daein'—an' damn't, we'll be gettin' paid for it!"

"Yes. No doubt. I agree with all you say, but . . . well, I take it, you'll be accepting this offer? Staying on up here?"

"Sure, boy-o—what d'you take me for? Better than awa' back to Glesgy, this—or Australia, either!"

"M'mmm. I daresay."

"Weel—what's wrang wi' it, man? Oot wi' it—what's your objection?"

"My objections are purely personal," Adrian said. "They needn't affect you in the least. You carry on, by all means."

"But, Major—b'damn, it's you that's needed. You're the kingpin. It's you he wants, as farm-manager."

"You can be the manager, Roddie. Better than myself, probably. . . ."

"Och, to hell, man—dinna' be daft. It's a man wi' education he wants, to run the farm on the new scientific lines—a' the latest methods, experimentin' wi' thae new high-protein grasses, new crosses o' cattle for the hill, peat-soil treatment, an' a' that. I couldna' read up a' yon—it's you he needs."

"A pity," the other said, shortly. "But no doubt he'll be able to find somebody else."

Even Roddie Roy recognised the futility of arguing with this man when he used that tone of voice; it was necessary to overpower him entirely, or change the subject. Probably Macgregor was wise in choosing the latter alternative—or perhaps, he was even wiser than that.

"Aye, then," he said. "Uh-huh. I wonder where that lassie is?"

"She'll turn up, undoubtedly."

"Aye, maybe. But I wouldna' like yon one to be catchin' me oot o' my bed. She's a right wee terror, is she no'?"

"Something of the sort," Adrian conceded.

"Aye. Though, mind you, I'm gettin' right fond o' her, tae, in a sort o' a way."

"Yes. I know you are."

The big man looked away towards the window. "I'ph'mmm. I'll be right sorry to lose her."

"You . . . ?" That, jerked out of Adrian Hope, set him coughing. The spasm over, he spoke weakly. "Are you thinking of losing her?"

"We a' are. She says she's leavin'."

"Leaving?"

"Aye. She was talkin' aboot bein' awa' hame to Glesgy, the morn."

"But . . . but . . ." Adrian's mind sank away into unplumbed depths. Presently, his eyes met Roddie's. "Hell!" he said, emphatically.

The other nodded entire agreement. "Jist that."

For a little, Adrian was silent. Implications and emotions were crowding in on him in fine disarray—resentment, disbelief, wonder, remorse, sorrow, and away beyond all, at the back of them all, an unspecified, nebulous, but quite unmistakable reflection of what could be happiness, bliss. As not infrequently occurs, it was out of the least worthy, least authentic, that he spoke.

"She can't do that," he declared. "She can't just leave two sick men to nurse themselves, like that!"

"Och, she said we'd manage fine wi' the District Nurse."

"District Nurse, indeed! This is ridiculous. Did . . . did she tell you what was behind this sudden decision?" It was Hope's turn to stare out of the window.

"Jist that she reckoned we'd dae fine wantin' her. An' she said we couldna' object to her goin', noo, when by today's papers the hale country'll ken where we are." He sighed, gustily. "I guess there's naethin' for it—one o' us'll ha'e to set aboot marryin' her!"

"Good Lord!" Adrian gulped, and began to cough.

"Och, she'd make a good wee wife, her," Roddie contended. "She's bonny, she's handy aboot the hoose, an' she's no' jist as refined as she sounds. . . ."

The other almost choked.

"Mind, she's no' perfect—but what wumman is?" That was accompanied by a philosophic sigh. "An' she can ay cook. . . ."

"I wonder you haven't asked her, then, already!" Adrian interrupted. "You seem to have all the pros and cons of the situation well summed up!"

"It didna' jist occur to me," the big man admitted. "But noo we've a' got the offer o' guid jobs. . . ."

His companion produced something between a snort and a sigh. "If you're thinking of making a crofter's wife out of Helen Burnet, you'll have to think again!" he said. "She wouldn't touch it with a barge-pole. She told me so, herself. She's not burying herself up in the Highlands." He paused, and shrugged. "At least, not for me!"

"Is that a fact? That'll be why you're no' for takin' this manager's job, then?"

"No. No—quite the reverse, in fact."

"Eh . . . ?"

"I mean . . . Oh, skip it!"

Macgregor scratched his shaggy head. "You said you were browned-off wi' the doctorin', that you were thinkin' o' takin' a croft . . . ?"

"There are other places than Findart for crofts. I've all Scotland before me. . . ." Hope smiled twistedly. "Even Australia!"

"Goad! You, noo! Efter a' you said to me, yon time! Look, man—if . . ." He stopped, his mouth open. Light quick footsteps sounded in the passage outside.

"Jings!" Roddie declared with conviction. "That's torn it!" The door opened.

She stood looking at the big man, one scimitar eyebrow raised, a bundle of newspapers in her hand. "Roddie Macgregor," she said ominously. "What are you doing here?"

"Naethin'—naethin' at a', Hel'n." He had got to his feet— or to one of them, at any rate—and now stood on one leg,

244

making a quite ludicrous figure, his tattered shirt inadequate costume even for a sick-room. "I was jist ha'ein' a bit crack wi' the Major. . . ."

"Indeed!"

"Aye. I thought he might be needin' somethin', you see—an' there was naebody aboot. Jist deserted, we were." He shook an eagerly censorious head. "The Major's no' jist in a state to be left by his lane for that long. . . ."

"Be quiet, you idiot!" the girl commanded. "*You're* not fit to be left, at all, evidently. If you've disturbed that shoulder again . . ."

"No' me. I'm fine." Hurriedly he changed direction. "You been oot, Hel'n—ha'ein' a bit walk?"

"I've been over to Glenelg Post Office on a bicycle, to try and get some papers for the pair of you. Major Macdonald's *Scotsman* doesn't come till evening, with the mail." She tossed the papers in her hand down on to the bed. "There you are—read all about the wonderful Gregorach. You're all heroes, magnificent! Scotland's yours, and the Government's ready to eat out of your hands. I expect the Press will be up here *en masse*, just as soon as they can discover how to get here. All you have to do is to lie back and take it!"

"Ummm," Rod Roy said, doubtfully. "Oh, yeah."

Adrian, at whom she had not directed even one glance, cleared his throat, but said nothing.

Their silence did not seem to soothe the young woman. She all but stamped her foot. "Don't stand there gawking, like a, a stork, or something!" she cried. "Come on—I'll get you back to your own room."

"Sure, sure. But we're no' jist finished oor crack, Hel'n. We were talkin' aboot gettin' married, me an' the Major. Were we no', Major?"

"Look here . . ." Adrian began, hoarsely.

"Married!" Helen Burnet gasped.

"Aye. It was you sayin' you were awa' hame, started it. We reckoned we couldna' well dae wi'oot you, an' maybe it would be the best way o' keepin' you, for one o' us to marry you. The Major's no' jist that keen, so I . . ."

"Shut up, you fool!" Hope shouted.

"Roddie—are you clean crazy!" the girl cried.

"Me? No' likely. Listen, you—I'm talkin' guid sense. I like you fine, lassie—an' I'm no' that bad a match. I'd make you a fair enough husband. I'm a famous man, these days—you've jist been sayin' so—Rod Roy Macgregor, wi' the country at his feet an' the Government eatin' oot o' his hand! Half the lassies o' the land'd jump at the chance! Damn't—I'm a fair catch, come to think o' it. Forbye, the Major's awa' to Australia. . . ."

"Adrian!" Half-strangled, the cry was wrung out of her, as she turned to him at last.

"Pay no heed to him, Helen," he began, and then the coughing surged up to shake and rack him. Hunching forward he sought to save his damaged ribs, sought to hold in the intolerable convulsions, sought to speak. "He's . . . talking nonsense," he panted.

She was standing over him now, biting her lip, her hand hovering above his heaving shoulders. Eyeing them both sardonically, Roddie smoothed a hand over his mouth.

"Nonsense, is it! An' him sayin' jist five minutes back that if you wouldna' be a crofter's wife, he'd ha'e to be off to Australia!"

Adrian could do no more than raise a hand, and point a wavering but accusing finger at the man.

Helen's hand descended on the bent shoulder. Almost, she shook it, shaking as it was already. "Did you say that?" she demanded. "Did you, Adrian?"

"Dinna' worry the laddie, Hel'n," Macgregor advised judiciously. "You'll ha'e him fair flummoxed. He'll no' ken what he said an' what he didna' say. He's scatty aboot you, anyway. You'll jist ha'e to take my word for it. An' I ken fine the way o' it. He wants to marry you, but he'll no' thole askin' you to be a farmer's wife. No' me—I'd marry you, an' *make* you into a crofter's wife. Damn, yes. But our Major's ower muckle o' the gent—sae he's awa' to Australia. Me, I'm awa' to my bed—my hurdies are gettin' cauld. When you twa ha'e warstled it oot whae's goin' where, an' wi' who, you can come ben an' tuck me in. But, jings, I'll no' be expectin' you for a whilie yet! Here—gi'e's those papers." And, the longest speech of his life delivered, Roderick Macgregor hopped absurdly to the door. There, he paused for a moment, turning. "An' if you canna get him to the bit o' proposin' marriage, Hel'n Burnet, come you right through, an' *I'll* make an honest wumman o' you!"

And the door slammed.

Adrian, lying back exhausted on his pillow, opened his eyes. "He's gone?" he asked, weakly. "I'm sorry, Helen—terribly sorry. Believe me, I am."

She was looking at him, thoughtfully, her brow puckered. "I'm afraid I don't know what to believe," she said, and her voice quivered a little. "What does it all mean, Adrian?"

"Nothing. Nothing, at all," the man answered her, flatly. "It is just that great blundering oaf playing at being the tin god, as usual. Nothing more than that." And then, as he saw the corners of her mouth droop and tremble a little, he sat up suddenly as though galvanised.

"No!" he almost shouted, and by a next to superhuman effort forced back the resultant cough. "That's not true. Lord, it's not!" His hand reached out to grip her wrist. "Listen, Helen—you want to know what to believe, what it all means. I'll tell you, then. It's that I've tried not to love you, tried and tried—and failed. It's hopeless, chronic. I'm your's, always will be, whether you want me or not! I won't be any trouble to you, I won't pester you. But wherever you are, wherever you go, wherever *I* am, I'll be loving you. D'you understand? Just loving you. No—cut out the just. I'll be adoring you, worshipping you!"

Wordlessly, she shook her head. Her eyes were swimming, those large and lustrous eyes. But her fingers were grasping his, tightly.

He went on, as if in a tremendous hurry, as though it was a race that had to be won possibly with his ebbing strength. "I was jealous of Roddie, wickedly jealous. Still am. But I can't make that stop me loving you. He was making a fool of himself there, for my sake. Don't misjudge him, Helen. If you're fond of him, don't let this spoil anything. Don't be unfair to him. . . ."

247

"Adrian," she said, almost whispered. "It's too late. I think I've been unfair to him all along. From the very first I've used him, just used him—or misused him. I like him, of course, admire him—almost love him in a way, since he saved your life. But I've only used him as an excuse to keep near you. And he knows it. He's told me so. I . . . I . . ."

"Helen! D'you realise what you're saying? D'you mean that . . . ?"

"Yes," she nodded. "I do, Adrian. I'm saying it very badly, I know, but I mean that I love you too, my dear, more than ever I did, and always will. I tried not to, as well, you know. But it was no use. We are an awful pair, aren't we!"

When he tried to speak, she laid a finger on his burning lips. "Hush, you," she said. "Let me finish, this once. I love you, and I'm terribly proud of you, of all you've done, but more, of all you are. And I'll be proud to be a farmer's wife or a crofter's wife, or any other sort of wife to you, Adrian— so long as I'm one quickly. Oh, quickly. For I can't bear living next to you and not *being* your wife, any more. You see, I'm quite shameless, Adrian. Marry me, my love, and put me out of my misery! Won't you?"

"Yes. Yes. My dearest, my heart. But . . ."

"Oh, no buts, Ian. You can, you know—you must. Haven't you a manager's job, and a fine house in your pyjama-pocket? And didn't I work so very hard to put them there? You've no excuses left, Adrian Hope—not a one!"

"Well, I'm damned!" that man said, sincerely. "And *I* started out to waken up Scotland!"

THE STONE

Plundered from Scotland by Edward I in 1296, the Stone of Destiny lay beneath the Coronation Chair in Westminster Abbey for 700 years—but for centuries rumour and speculation have surrounded the origins of this legendary symbol of Royal Power. Was this the *real* Stone, or merely a 13th century fake, a lump of sandstone hastily quarried at Scone to deceive the English invaders?

The Stone is Nigel Tranter's extraordinary tale of the quest for the true Stone of Destiny, and with it the possible solution to a mystery that has endured for more than 700 years.

'If you have not read Tranter, this is a good one to
start with; if you have, you will find it one of his best'
YORKSHIRE EVENING POST

HARSH HERITAGE

The story opens in the western Highlands of Scotland in 1817. The Highland Clearances have begun, and everywhere land-owners are brutally evicting their tenants, condemning them to a grim future of starvation and despair. One particularly terrible act of cruelty leads to a dreadful curse being placed on the family, lands and descendants of the man responsible—Edward Macarthy Neill. From that moment on, Neill's family will never be out of danger, as the curse pursues them relentlessly down through the generations. . . .

THE QUEEN'S GRACE

Set in the north-east of Scotland during Mary, Queen of Scots' visit in 1562, as two powerful nobles struggle for control of the Kingdom, *The Queen's Grace* is a superb evocation of the intrigue and drama that characterised the life and violent times of Scotland's most celebrated monarch.

'Nobody does it better'
DAILY TELEGRAPH

KETTLE OF FISH

The Tweed Fisheries Act made it illegal to fish for salmon off the mouth of the River Tweed. The ban infuriated local fishermen, and poaching was rife on dark nights, until local schoolmaster Adam Horsburgh decides that the Act should be challenged openly. When poaching gangs from the cities and even the Royal Navy join in, Adam begins to feel out of his depth—but by then things have gone too far. . . .

'He is a magnificent teller of tales'
GLASGOW HERALD

BALEFIRE

Balefire is a gripping story of courage, honour and divided loyalties set during the Border warfare that raged at the start of the 16th century. In the chaos following the massacre of the Scottish army at Flodden in 1513, the life of Simon Armstrong, a young Scottish Laird, is spared only upon his promise of a huge ransom. Yet this is only the beginning of Armstrong's fight for survival. . . .

'A tale of border warriors, blazing homes,
heroism, vengeance, and a lust for ransom'
MANCHESTER EVENING NEWS

BRIDAL PATH

Bridal Path charts the adventures of Ewan MacEwan, a young crofter living on the remote isle of Eorsa, who leaves his native island and journeys to the mainland looking for a wife. But his arrival in Oban is swiftly followed by a catalogue of misunderstandings and misadventures which land him in deep trouble—with the police, poachers, dynamite and numerous young women.

One of the finest novels of Scottish island life in the 1940s, *Bridal Path* was made into a highly successful film in 1959, starring Bill Travers, George Cole, Annette Crosbie and Gordon Jackson.

ISLAND TWILIGHT

Set in the Inner Hebrides in Napoleonic times, *Island Twilight* tells the story of Surgeon Major Aeneas Graham's return from the wars. Wounded at Waterloo he comes home to convalesce, but is soon involved in the desperate struggle to save his native Island of Erismore from a legacy of ancient evil.

*'He has a burning respect for the spirit of history
and deploys his characters with mastery'*
THE OBSERVER

THE GILDED FLEECE

Set in the Western Highlands in 1809, this novel tells the story of Adam Metcalfe, a young Englishman who travels north to become deputy factor of a large Highland estate and is soon involved in the tragedy and drama of the infamous Highland Clearances.

'This is a strong and stirring story, beautifully written'
MANCHESTER EVENING NEWS

---

*Available from all good bookshops,
or direct from the publishers:*

 *B&W Publishing,
233 Cowgate, Edinburgh,
EH1 1NQ.*

Tel: 0131 220 5551